The 1000 Year Reich
And Other Stories

Also by Ian Watson and published by NewCon Press

Beloved of My Beloved (*with Roberto Quaglia*) (2009)
Orgasmachine (2010)
Saving for a Sunny Day (2012)

For Sue!

The 1000 Year Reich
And Other Stories

Ian Watson

Introduction by
Justina Robson

*Ian Watson
26th March 2016*

NewCon Press
England

at Mancunicon

First edition, published in the UK April 2016
by NewCon Press

NCP 048 (hardback)
NCP 049 (softback)

10 9 8 7 6 5 4 3 2 1

This collection copyright © 2016 by Ian Whates
Introduction copyright © 2016 by Justina Robson
Cover art © 2016 by Juan Miguel Aguilera
"Beloved Pig-Brother of the Daughter of the Pregnant Baby: a Transgenic Story of Genius" copyright © Ian Watson and Roberto Quaglia
All other stories copyright © Ian Watson

"The 1000 Year Reich" copyright © 2014 first appeared in *Squirrel, Reich, & Lavender* (PS Publishing).
"How We Came Back From Mars: A Story That Cannot Be Told" copyright © 2011 first appeared in *Solaris Rising* (Solaris).
"Blair's War" © 2013 first appeared in *Asimov's Science Fiction*.
"The Name of the Lavender" copyright © 2014 first appeared in *Squirrel, Reich, & Lavender* (PS Publishing).
"Forever Blowing Bubbles" copyright © 2011 first appeared in *Fables from the Fountain* (NewCon Press).
"The Tale of Trurl and the Great TanGent" copyright © 2011 first appeared in *Lemistry* (Comma Press).
"The Wild Pig's Collar" copyright © 2010 first appeared in *Aberrant Dreams: The Awakening*.
"Red Squirrel" copyright © 2014 first appeared in *Squirrel, Reich, & Lavender* (PS Publishing).
"An Inspector Calls" copyright © 2015 first appeared in *Postscripts* (PS Publishing).
"Me and My Flying Saucer" copyright © 2014 first appeared in *Nature*.
"Faith Without Teeth" copyright © 2014 first appeared in *Solaris Rising* 3 (Solaris).
"The Travelling Raven Problem" copyright © 2013 first appeared in *Daily Science Fiction*.
"Spanish Fly" copyright © 2014 first appeared in *The Mammoth Book of Erotic Romance & Domination* (Constable and Robinson).
"Having the Time of His Life" copyright © 2008 first appeared in *Celebration* (NewCon Press).
"Breakfast in Bed" copyright © 2015 first appeared in *Analog Science Fiction & Fact*.
"In Golden Armour", "Beloved Pig-Brother of the Daughter of the Pregnant Baby: a Transgenic Story of Genius", and "The Arc de Triomphe Code" all copyright © 2016 and original to this collection.

All rights reserved.

ISBN: 978-1-907069-38-3 (hardback)
978-1-907069-39-0 (softback)

Cover art by Juan Miguel Aguilera
Cover layout by Andy Bigwood

Invaluable editorial assistance from Ian Watson
Interior layout by Storm Constantine

For Roberto Quaglia,
whose words are here too.

Contents

1. Introduction by Justina Robson — 9
2. The 1000 Year Reich — 13
3. In Golden Armour — 33
4. How We Came Back From Mars: A Story That Cannot Be Told — 45
5. Blair's War — 65
6. The Name of the Lavender — 70
7. Forever Blowing Bubbles — 99
8. The Tale of Trurl and the Great TanGent — 107
9. The Wild Pig's Collar — 121
10. Beloved Pig-Brother of the Daughter of the Pregnant Baby: a Transgenic Story of Genius (with Roberto Quaglia) — 135
11. Red Squirrel — 155
12. An Inspector Calls — 171
13. Me and My Flying Saucer — 183
14. Faith Without Teeth — 187
15. The Travelling Raven Problem — 199
16. The Arc de Triomphe Code — 202
17. Spanish Fly — 211
18. Having the Time of His Life — 219
19. Breakfast in Bed — 239

THE 1000 YEAR REICH: AN INTRODUCTION

Justina Robson

This introduction starts to read like it's all about me but, in the immortal words of Tilly, from the TV show, *Miranda,* "Bear with..." – I'm building up to something.

The first time I read an Ian Watson book is one of those moments I remember with strange clarity of detail, as you do when something momentous happens. I was sitting on the floor of my study surrounded by the heaps of books that I'd been sent to read for that year's Arthur C Clarke Award (2005). There were over seventy of them and I was a few days in to what would be more than two months spent reading a novel a day. I wasn't to realise until afterwards that until then I hadn't really understood what reading was. This will sound odd, since I'd already spent most of my life reading, but it was illuminated most of all by the moment, five pages in from the start of *Mockymen,* when I stopped reading, turned the book over, looked at the cover closely, read the back and then scoured the front and rear for clues, thinking all the while with a sense of baffled incomprehension – "What IS this?"

The thing is that most books in the genre of SF are penned (typed, whatever) within an intentional storytelling format which is so straight you could use it to rule lines. You lay out your world, intro your characters, set up the arenas of their conflicts and kick off the struggles in a serious and straightforward frame of mind for serious and straightforward readers who know that what they are finding is what they are getting. It's straight. It's not always linear or uncomplicated but it is not fancy, it's not talking about itself or making remarks to camera or nudging and winking at you from the story's strange back seating area where all the author's crazy thought-fishsticks are stored in their ice locker. This kind of SF is down-home honest-to-goodness SF like Mom and Pop made. Actually it's more of a North American canonical assumption that has become the de facto method of SF, but at the time of reading Ian's book I had never had this thought and it wasn't going to go through my head for a good while yet.

Why, it was as if I'd never read a book by an English eccentric or any postmodernist! Although I had, and had often run from them as from a Spring-woken bear, so I may as well not have. I was allergic. They were mind-messing monstrosities that engaged you with sincerity one minute and then ripped out the rug from under you with their crabby little meta-claws: it's similar to being asked if you love fairy tales and enthusiastically agreeing, thinking you're talking to a fellow devotee, only to have them smash you in the nose and say, "Well they don't even EXIST, you stupid noob. And nor do you. And nor does anything. Except in your thoughts. And they're rubbish, as I've just pointed out. OMG you actually think anything matters, or happens! Happy Existential Day!" –

I did Linguistics and Philosophy at University and the horrors of unfettered Saussure were still fresh in the memory on Clarke Reading Day, as was my love of the theory of grammar and the study of the relationships between language, thought, identity and reality. These things were the stuff of intoxicating, hyperventilating excitement to me, in the same way that I imagine that the calculus affected Ada Lovelace (I like to pretend we're in some kind of strange geek sisterhood out of vanity) but in my own work I barely dared touch on them. They're the actual stuff that magic is made out of. Working on them puts me into a kind of white-out where my mind goes so fast it turns into random particles. As a result, no sense emerges and I do tend towards mystic blither, for which there's no excuse, and because I was scared of putting this on paper I wrote my own books without them. But here IN MY HANDS Ian Watson did manage to do it all – the story, the characters, the thinking, the information, the fun, the nod to the reader, the knowledge – without breaking stride and without coming over as anything other than a friendly, happy narrator, and when I found this on that gloomy day in the study surrounded by towers of novels I realised that there were more possibilities here, Horatio... It was a game-changing moment.

My second nerve-wracking encounter with his work was when I read *Orgasmachine* in order to review it for the BSFA. I knew by now that Ian was smarter, better educated and more well-read than I was, had written schmackdoodles of good books, and that he didn't run away at the first sign of the mighty Meta-phron (Angel of Things That Are Pointers To Other Things But Indirectly Via A Much More Illuminating Route, With Footnotes). I feared that I wasn't really up to the job of reading that book, and the one you have in your hands, let alone saying anything 'proper' about it. In fact I missed entirely that *Orgasmachine* was a satire. Straight, you see. Rule lines with me. But in reflecting on that book's excellent analysis-and-critique-of-the-world-via-a-tale and in reading the stories for this collection I've had another bang-up insight (which is hardly original in the world but it was new to me) that Science Fiction itself (and Fantasy, all the literatures of the unreal) is an inherently satirical form and I don't think anyone excels at exploiting this more than Ian Watson. You don't just write about any old Nazis, you write about future Nazis on the moon being blasted by orgone energies directed spiritually via a sense of poetic justice. You write a fake history of Hitler that is so acutely telling of human nature that it OUGHT to be true and I really wish it was! Because if life won't give you lemonade you take the damn lemons and make it yourself, retrospectively. Ta dah! Such *fun*.

Yes, that is my excuse for having missed the blindingly obvious. Anyway, there is more satire here, and more delightful anecdote, fascinating history, more insightful connection and lucid metaphor and deeply entertaining cultural critique than you can shake a stick at: all done with a ringmaster's flourish and expertise. Reading this collection is hugely enjoyable, like sitting at a bar with an old friend who's a great raconteur come to tell you all the weird and wonderful things he's seen before he sets off on his worldly travels again. In fact that is exactly what meeting Ian in real life is like, too. Whatever he's writing about there is a warmth, a wit and an effortless ease about his stories so that however clever they are (and they are) they are an easy pleasure to unpack.

I know that at least one story here (because he says so) is written in the tradition of Lem's *Cyberiad* but there is an engine of the absurdist philosopher zooming everywhere in Watson's stories, not to mention puns and pratfalls and more obvious humour. To see the mighty conceits of physics and semiotics alike wafted around like the perfumes in an exotic boudoir is such fun, but oh, *the calendar* in "The Name of the Lavender" – that's whimsical genius at work, that is. And the CIA special investigators who seem too ludicrous to be true and end up revealed as not being Watson's invention but REAL... You couldn't make this stuff up, apparently.

It would be unwise to make too much of the quicksilver wit and humour at the expense of the very intelligent, ruthless tour of the nature of perception and consciousness which has been Watson's forte in his novels and which shine out here in many stories. His style, which bursts that 2D envelope, can be startling, but because he's able to tell a story and remark on it at the same time – I've never really come across anyone else so good at this who doesn't burst their own bubble of suspended disbelief – he is able to sketch out ideas of complexity and subtlety with incisive power in record time. He can see many angles on an idea, at once explaining and questioning it, all without losing track of his human characters for a beat. What a presticomputational feat! I think what he shows best are the aggrandizing notions and vanities of human beings and the tragicomic results of these ideas being believed in and becoming hellish (and very occasionally heavenish) realities. Others among us might say it, but Watson shows it in action from every angle.

As in many times when people are mostly taking things, and themselves, very seriously indeed Ian Watson is one of those writers who has fallen into the gap of a collectively po-faced self-regard, at least he had fallen into the gap of mine until I paid more attention and started to understand that you can often be more successful with the massive cloud of alien laughing gas than with the post-apocalyptic survival tragi-drama. Watson's work in this collection is part of a larger broad-brush flourish which includes Pratchett, Miéville, Willis and Adams in its Venn diagram cloud, and not a small amount of comic book and superhero writers whose names, alas, I haven't got on the tip of my tongue. Oh, and of course we mustn't forget, Dan Brown. Now that I know of the existence of a Watson expert-riff on the inimical *Da Vinci Code* I have to go buy a copy right now! Meanwhile you get yourself comfortable, dear reader, you're in for a treat.

exit with credit card

Justina Robson
Yorkshire
January 2016

THE 1000 YEAR REICH

From **Orgopedia**, the encyclopedia of freedom
Wilhelm Reich (24 March 1883 – eternity)

As the whole world knows, Wilhelm Reich graduated in medicine from the University of Vienna in 1907 and within a couple of years became the deputy director of the Vienna Ambulatorium. Anglophone readers might visualise the **VA** as being the **van** which Reich and his colleagues drove around the suburbs of Vienna to bring erotic enlightenment to the working classes – a sort of ambulance for sexual first aid – but in fact the VA was **Sigismund Freud**'s walk-in clinic for psychiatric outpatients, of which the van was a roving offshoot.

Freud's discovery that the majority of people suffer from **repressions** was transcended by Reich's realisation that repressions result in the formation of **character armour** which good orgasms dissolve. What's more, the theories of **Hans Surén**, the apostle of German nudism, expounded in his book **Man and Sunlight**, inspired Reich to the realisation that orgone radiation pervades the cosmos, leading to Reich's invention of **orgone boxes** which concentrate this radiation upon a naked subject seated within. Thus, too, Surén was able to reconcile naturism plus group nudity with orgiastic sexuality.

In Reich's view sexuality and politics interpenetrated one another intimately. Additionally, Reich was a potent and spell-binding public speaker, hence the foundation of his **SexPol Party** which campaigned successfully for practical sex education in private schools and in selected public nudist schools, not without some opposition in still mainly Catholic Austria.

Towards the end of 1911, **Adolf Hitler** became Reich's chief lay apostle and, according to slurs, 'Reich's Enforcer'. Lay, in the sense that Hitler was unqualified in medicine and psychiatry, nursing thwarted ambitions instead as a fine artist. Hitler had twice been rejected by the Vienna Academy of Arts. To support himself, he was selling upon the more prosperous city streets such as Ringstrasse architectural watercolours and postcards while living in comparative poverty in a hostel for the homeless – in Meldemannstrasse in a suburb of north Vienna, where he famously encountered the VA van, now equipped with an orgone box. Accounts vary of the first encounter between Reich, who still often accompanied the vehicle, and Hitler. It is reliably rumoured that Hitler, as a schoolboy at the Realschule in Linz, had been sexually used by an older boy from a rich Viennese Jewish family, **Ludwig Wittgenstein**, who wore a truss and who was to become a minor philosopher. This experience caused Hitler to form character armour like a protective crust and prejudiced him against Jews – amongst whom were Reich, Freud, and most members of the VA. This prejudice may have been somewhat tempered (or inflamed?) by the fact that the hostel for the homeless, where Hitler stayed, was a revolutionary social project financed by other rich Jews including the Rothschilds. Most likely is that Hitler was swayed by Reich's hypnotic street oratory and, after experiencing a spontaneous orgasm within the orgone box, Hitler underwent a process of **transference** so that he linked his own frustrated creative ambitions to the aims of SexPol.

Meanwhile, the juggernaut of macrohistory was rolling towards the folly of a war in Europe. Thinking that this might be a new kind of war, which could be fought without wholesale slaughter and suffering, Reich developed the **orgone gun**. Hans Surén, who had formerly been an officer in the German Army and who was the son of an officer, brought the orgone gun to the attention of then-recently-retired General **Paul von Hindenburg**, and it was successfully field-tested. Hitler, blossoming within the SexPol Party and increasingly vocal after the manner of Reich himself, likewise persuaded the Austrian military to pay attention.

And this is where our story begins...

"You can't possibly call your guy *Reich!*" Norris Harper protested to Zooza once he'd finished eyeing her presentation on the main clingscreen upon the curving wall of their largish workcubicle in Liberty Luna. Windowless – no distracting outlook upon the bay off of the Ocean of Storms, north of Kepler, nearing the rugged Carpathian Mountains.

Her name was actually Zsusza, which was Hungarian, but Zooza was simpler and sounded the same as Zsuzsa. As for her family name, Szekeres, pronounced Sekeresh, forget it; that meant a cart-maker, so in the United States of Free America, USFA, she was Zooza Carter.

"Big fucking *coincidence* this sexpot or whatever having the same name as the Nazi Third Reich itself, unless you're aiming for slapstick! Come off it, Zooza. Otherwise, it's pretty inventive destabilising stuff, but you got to change his name to, oh I dunno, Wilhelm Schmidt, Wilhelm Schneider, anything else."

USFA consisted of Canada, the west half of the former USA, most of the Caribbean and Central America including the all-important Panama Canal, the client Andes States, and the part of the Moon where they were.

"Norris, he's *authentic* – Reich was gassed in 1943, along with the rest of his largely Jewish orgone-isation. Their books and docs and orgone boxes went on a big bonfire."

Billy Fever joined in, tall and scrawny as a scarecrow; he was a moon-babe, whose bones Earth would fracture unless he wore an exo.

"*Un-believ-able!*"

"See," said Norris, "nobody can take the name seriously, even if the guy existed."

"No!" said Billy. "I mean *out-of-this-world-fucking-amazing-discovery.*"

"Out of this world..." Norris repeated quietly. Billy was gay, consequently he would be snuffed were he ever to land on the wrong parts of Earth to be identified pdq as a pervert in view of the Tom of Finland tattoos on his sinewy slim lunar arms and legs. Two of the tattoos exposed by Billy's tight black shorts and black tee-shirt were of iron-buttocked and brazen-biceped machos jauntily sporting Waffen SS caps — but the way those mighty physiques needed to wrap around Billy's lunar limbs shrank them from superhuman, making them satiric. Otherwise, some of the 2K other residents of Liberty might perhaps have lynched Billy.

In the rival Nazi settlement, Festung Speer, twelve hundred miles away to the east, its own blond moonborns reportedly exercised like hell in the effort to become powerful giants. The Nipponese base in the Sea of Fertility — Hoshimachi, Sky Town — was proposing a Lunar Olympics; basic co-operation protocols just *had* to apply between the three relatively vulnerable lunar settlements, more so than in Antarctica where at least there was plenty of air and water.

But anyway, Billy was never likely to set foot on Earth, even in an exo with reinforced feet and all else, a situation which made him deeply melancholic at times. Truth to tell, Billy was bipolar, but currently on a high.

"*Absolutely ace, Zooza!*" Billy applauded. "The late great Adolf was a love-idol to all Teutonic women. To have him creaming inside a box built by a Jew, *phew*. You did say your Reich's a Jew, didn't you?" Billy was beginning to rhyme like a rapper, a sign of euphoria with him.

"Ethnically partly, according to Gates2Info. Almost all of Reich's colleagues were full Jewish."

"You got all this background from Gates2Info?" asked Norris. "This went *unnoticed* till now?"

"Gates2Info's Suckerman vacuums up everything that gets *near* an electron," said Zooza. "Which includes via our wormholes into 3Reich and DaiNip. But a lot of DaiNip never gets eyeballed by a person, unless a threat is flagged —"

"Yeah yeah yeah," said Norris. Hungarians such as Zooza didn't normally labour the obvious, but were usually at least one step ahead, as befitted brainboxes who could learn Hungarian in the first place; Zooza must be really attached to her scenario to hammer in so many pegs to secure it.

"So you hit a hint in G2Info —"

"— and I sent a SearchJobs hunting refs to Wilhelm Reich. Found a small bonanza of docs in DaiNip, must have reached Japan in the 1930s, scanned in 80 years later by a Nip Prof who died of fugu."

"Murdered by SD agents, or by Kempeitai?"

"No, Prof Nakashima was into the erotic potential of fugu poisoning — tetrodotoxin toxin stiffens muscles and makes them tingle like funlube — so he wondered *what if* you snack on fugu while you're inside an orgone box. Might minimise the negative and maximise the positive. This seemed to work on rats. Nakashima's research died with him but no one deleted it. I guess the Nip Kempeitai never noticed, still less any Sicherheitsdienst Germans in Tokyo."

"Fugu being that freaky fish with spikes all over like some poisonous swimming cactus, right?" said Norris. Nor would Norris from Oregon ever return to Earth, him pushing 100 kilos when he emigrated to the Moon, and more like 200 kilos by now, though that was only 40 kilos on Luna.

"Always puzzled me," piped up Billy, "how the Nips first found you can eat fugu so long as you dissect it right. Me, I imagine a shipwreck on an atoll, not that I ever saw an atoll, lagoon's crowded with fugu blowfish, zilch else to eat. Captain sends Sailor One to catch and cut up a fugu and eat a piece; bye-bye Sailor One, then Two, then Three... till only the Captain remains alive but by now he knows the dissection secret to take back home with him when he's rescued, makes him a fortune. Me, I heard you can survive the poison *if*, the instant you feel numb, you're buried up to the neck in a pit of hot sand, which a tropical atoll has aplenty but never a fugu restaurant." Billy had stopped rhyming but by now he was almost free-associating.

"Forget fugu!" said Zooza. "Think Reich. Thousand Year, but starring Wilhelm."

Hungarian people divide into two categories, apart from the obvious male and female. The greatgreatgrandkids of those in Hungary who had allied with Hitler's Reich historically, to be rewarded after WW2 by the return of Romania, Slovakia, and Transcarpathia to their control, and those whose greatgreatgrans and greatgreatgrandads decamped to the west of the once-USA, where their ingenuity brought about the Alamagordo Project, deterring further Nazi expansion across North America. While Werner von Braun delivered Nazis to the Moon, Hungarian refugee Ferenc Pavlics did likewise for the USFA.

Together with Norris and Billy, Zooza's speciality was subversion games. Homeland USFA employed thousands of coders back on Earth, since cybergames obsessed most of the non-slaved population of the planet. Reich3 promoted games where, for instance, valiant Aryans civilised the jungly chaos of Africa from a starting point in Italian Ethiopia, or from German Egypt. The Babelsberg film industry of 3Reich and the Hollywood of the USFA were quite minor players in the entertainment industry compared with much better-funded cybergames. Which competed globally. No political oppression dared stifle the addiction of a billion players in the world's three main power-zones, downloading at superspeed from Earthsats to the homecomps without which a multination would provenly stagnate. (Er, excluding the Chinese peasant protectorate within the Co-Prosperity Sphere.) Gaming's the Opium of the People, sort-of said someone who might be remembered by a few ancient bearded descendants of Communist fanatics lurking in the Russian wastelands.

This was surrogate war, known in 3Reich as Ersatzkrieg. The best cybergames competed, many of the Deutsch and Nipponese games being powerfully seductive to a whole swathe of USFA residents due to sexy Waffen Valkyries and Geisha Samurai.

"Cut to some action, then," invited Norris.

"Okay," said Zooza. "World War One: the Allies are using heavy tanks as well as faster and more manoeuvrable Whippet tanks to trash the Germans. But a tank is like 'character armour', and an orgone gun *disrupts* character armour. So the armour falls off the tanks, like a tortoise suddenly losing its shell. The big guns of the Allies, like prosthetic phalluses, go floppy and droopy. Lee-Enfield rifle barrels too, and howitzers and trench mortars and machine guns and all those things because the war is now of inanimate machines *versus* vital orgone radiations."

"Will uniforms fall off too?" asked Billy eagerly. "Uniforms must be a sort of character armour, uniformising individuals. The brawny, tanned German forces advance naked 'cept for thongs and sandals, and grapple and wrestle, and *do stuff*... though I guess we also need some

Brynhilde brigades for gender balance."

"Hang on," said Norris. "Do these orgone guns simply spray rays, or must they target accurately? If the latter, for how long must they fire till armour falls off a tank? And how about recharging? What on Moon is an orgone gun *like?*"

Zooza told him, "In the real mid-1930s Reich built a prototype for busting clouds, to alter the weather. Prof Nakashima scanned a blueprint. And a photo. Here." She fingered her pad's remote.

They saw two long tubes resembling gun barrels, mounted on a strong frame, accumulator in the boxy base presumably; eight thick segmented metal connective cables; two big steering wheels, front and side, to rotate and elevate the equipment, quite like an old anti-aircraft gun.

"Want to see the technical details?"

"Clouds are a lot flimsier than tank armour," observed Norris.

"Not at all," Billy said. "Storm clouds store *tons* of water and energy, *not* that I'm any expert on *weather*. Why, a cloud is like five thousand elephants floating in the sky, not that I *personally* saw an elephant nor a sky *neither*." Oh dear, don't let him become downcast, or overcast. "That's a hell of a lot more mass than an armoured tank," he concluded. "If you can bust a cloud that's all spread out, you should easily bust a tank concentrated in just one place," he continued concluding.

So what was *orgone energy*, anyway, eh Zooza?

Why, OE was primordial and everywhere. OE filled space, possessed no mass, penetrated matter and pulsated. It accumulated in living bodies. And it was powerful when concentrated. According to Reich.

"Reminds me," said Billy, "of like that good ole *dark energy*. The result of having *space*. Very dilute due to all the space, but still two-thirds of everything. Supposedly."

"I guess," said Norris, "you can *condense* what's diluted, unless," and he snorted derisively, "it was homeopathetically diluted... a drop in an ocean."

"I've never stood beside an ocean," said Billy. "Of water, I mean."

"Oceans of water are overrated," Zooza hastened to say. "Oceans of dust are fine. Let's forget about that ole dark energy. Orgone energy is much sexier."

"And that's precisely what I like about this," said Norris. "The future First Führer sidetracked by the Kaiser's Germans making love not war. We can have an Adolf avatar heroically embracing a denuded Gallic infantryman as the climax, ha, to a battle; maybe to a tear-jerking humming of *The Faithful Hussar*. That'll mess with the psyches of 3Reichers. They'll wish they were Wilhelm Reichers themselves. Hey, how about a beer to celebrate?"

So the three subversive games designers left their workplace and moonambled along corridor 17 until they came to Bar-With-A-View windowing an expanse of churned trampled dust, mining machines, and much of blue and white Earth in its permanent position. A cargo ferry was landing, bringing volatiles from sheltered north polar craters, pluming up dust to fall back slowly.

Tables, about a third of them occupied by chatterers or by the meditative, were arranged around a few broad curving tiers, upstairs-cinema-style.

"Three double Smalls," ordered Norris as the trio presented their allcards.

"Pushing the boat out, eh Norry?" The Canadian bartender was also an emergency rescue worker who was also completing a doctorate in lunar geology. He registered their alcohol order, a normal Small being 2% abv, a double 3.5%, max for any 24 hours since you shouldn't get more than slightly tipsy in a moon colony.

"Maybe we got us a neat idea."

They took their flavoursome brews to the least frequented tier, and supped.

"So," said Zooza, "Germany gets at least a draw in WW1, the Treaty of Versailles isn't hammering, consequently no embittered Nazis, but Adolf still has a big and ridiculous role to play. Wonder if we should rename postwar Germany *Orgonia*? Berlin, *Orgonopolis*? Why-ho, instead of peace, Orgonia could try to liberate North America from sexual repression by sending in sex troops armed with orgone rifles."

"I like Orgonopolis," said Norris. "Full of giant phallic and bosomy Speer buildings."

In honour of the bygone Hitler's mega-architect and chum, Festung Speer on the moon had used blocks of toughly resistant lunar basalt, precision-cut by laser, to rear its massive stronghold. A bit like Machu Picchu, its polished earthquake-proof dry-stone walls precisionmasoned by differently-abled indigenes lacking even wheels, except on toys.

Billy, who was sitting somewhat like a half-collapsed giraffe he had never seen in the flesh, or the skin plus coat, took a big sup of the double-Small. "Hey, do you think orgone guns might actually work? Build us an orgone *gun*, for *fun?*" he rhymed briefly. "Never before tested in vacuum. Can't do no harm. Just to see."

"See *what?*" asked Norris. "This Ocean of Storms doesn't have weather."

"Don't I know it." Billy gestured Earthwards. "Look at all that cotton candy."

"So aim the gun at some of the cotton on Earth. Nothing's going to happen – on account of Willy Reich is *freak* science. That's why we're using him."

"We'll need engineering assistance," said Zooza eagerly. "Who else do I see over there but Giant George Wysocki sinking a Small?"

The Polish-descended engineer was XXL size because of being inherently big, not due to being born and reared on the Moon, nor to alleged pineal gland obesity, or maybe overeating, as in the case of Norris. People possessing bodily peculiarities were welcome at Liberty so long as they also had special skills.

George Wysocki deeply resented what 3Reich had done to his slav-slave country of origin. The mocking cybergame should appeal to him.

Soon the trio were deep in conversation with Giant George.

Mounted on the back of the moon buggy, the completed orgone equipment looked like some specialised, twin-tube telescope – it could hardly be any sort of double-barrel anti-aircraft gun due to the total absence of ammunition, likewise of aircraft. Clipped to the rear of one tube indeed were telescopic sights, but any curious onlooker would most likely think: experimental detector of some sort.

Not that George had encountered any bureaucratic problem about building the machine in his spare time over the course of three weeks, or about borrowing the buggy; after all, he was deputy head of Engineering. Turned out that George's grandad on his dad's side had been a pataphysicist, who built machines for imaginary purposes as an artist in Paris before France became Frankenreich run by a Gauleiter. Here was a way for George to honour his grandad for escaping from

Europe, giving George an existence, certainly more noble than weeding cabbages to be turned into sauerkraut, if he was lucky. So, while the trio developed game details – which might take two months more before they transmitted an encrypted package to California for further development by a throng prior to coding by a horde – George proudly built a purposeless pataphysical machine. It may as well have been for astrology, an astrological telescope.

The reason for driving beyond the nearby horizon was to get away from the dust, 'soft and queasy' in the immortal words of an early astronaut. Any incoming ferry or passing mining machine might kick up clouds which could drift through the non-air for several hundred metres before settling. Just over the horizon was an outcrop of flat basalt magma the size of a baseball field, maintained for sports and some science experiments. The orgone gun deserved its due.

So presently they stood around the gun in their spacesuits, XXL for George, lanky for Billy, rotund for Norris, standard for Zooza. In sight were only blank basalt, unblinking stars, and a fairly full Earth, all of Europe and North Africa currently clear of cotton wool.

"Which reminds me," Giant George said over the little group's waveband, "Earth's magnetosphere deflects most charged particles if particles charge at it."

"Aren't particles also waves?" said Billy. "I've never seen waves breaking on a shore. Never seen surf."

"Over-rated," Zooza reassured him. "Surf 'n' turf? Give me turf any day."

"What you gassing about?"

"Steak with lobster," said Norris. "Omigod... lashings of cayenne mayo."

The eight segmented metal cables snaked down to the base-box accumulator made of alternating layers of metal and di-electric non-metal. Presumably the orgone gun had been powering itself up ever since the device was completed, although no gauge existed to report full, half-full, or empty. A simple trigger could be pulled by a spaceglove.

Spacesuited Giant George rotated his handiwork, working the two wheels till the twin barrels pointed approximately Earthwards.

"So what are we trying to aim at?"

"How about Berlin?"

"Let's be satisfied with Europe in general."

Zooza peered through the telescopic sight, up against her faceplate, while George finessed.

Up, up, left, down, right a bit, down a bit.

"I think 3Reich's about there, *stop...*"

A clamour from Billy: "Let me pull the trigger!"

"No, me," said George. "I'm the engineer."

"Did you see?" called out Zooza a moment later.

"See what?" from George.

"A blink of blue light from the barrels."

"*I* must have blinked."

Billy admitted, "Shut my eyes for a moment in case of flash."

"I swear I saw some blue, thin as thread," Norris said. "Vanished immediately. Everyone stare at those muzzles now; that means you too, Billy. Pull that trigger again, George."

Nothing visible happened.

After a while they returned to Liberty, George driving, the others moonambling alongside. He parked by Engineering Storage but then accompanied the trio through Airlock 4, where they dusted off then helped each other unsuit. By now almost an hour had passed since the test.

Within, a corridor clingscreen showed breaking news. Behind the black bobbly-haired anchorwoman: backdrop of an enormous avenue ending with a mighty dome upon a vast podium.

"*...reports coming out of 3Reich say that Berlin's Great Hall of Glory at the northern end of the Avenue of Magnificence has disintegrated. The Great Hall, built to house 180,000 people, is constructed of granite and marble. Maybe we ought to say was constructed. Witnesses claim that the Great Hall suddenly dissolved like sand, which now blocks the River Spree, which coincidentally is an anagram of Speer, the architect of Nazi Berlin including the Great Hall...*"

Giant George pounded his hands together in joy.

"Hot shit," said Billy.

"Oops," said Norris.

"Yes indeed," from Zooza, "but we mustn't let this abort the game! Nobody knows we built an orgone gun, or that it works!"

"*Assuming* a connection," said Norris. "Think of the sheer *coincidence*. George aims from quarter of a million miles distance, and scores a bull's eye — how likely is that? But we shouldn't talk where someone might hear us."

With Giant George inside too, their work cubicle seemed a bit crowded. By now a satellite image was up on their main clingscreen. Berlin's river was obstructed at a bend, silvery water spreading out behind a shapeless heap.

"I rang the bell," said George. "Resonant frequency."

"Bell?"

"The dome acted as a *bell* — biggest bell in the world, biggest possible complex resonance. The orgone beam *sought* that potential. Shook the granite and marble to dust."

"I'd say," suggested Billy, "your thoughts played a big part, George — your aversion to Nazis. When you pulled the trigger, what exactly were you thinking?"

"I cleared my mind, so as not to jerk."

"Letting your subconcious arise?"

Zooza said, "That's a Zen thing. Putting an arrow into the middle of a target in a darkened space."

"So," said Norris, "either orgone has an *anti*-Empire-of-Evil mind of its own, or Gorgone I mean George vibed with the beam, or else it's a total coincidence that the Great Hall of Glory collapses soon after he fired."

Enthusiastically the engineer said, "Assuming the gun recharges, give it twelve hours say, shall we shoot again? To confirm or refute?"

"Meaning that you'll 'unthink' another big Nazi building?"

"Norry, if I'm *un*thinking..."

"You know what I mean."

"*...red alert across 3Reich. All air traffic is grounded or turned back, and there's a state of emergency in Berlin. Gestapo are reportedly rounding up hundreds of workers and witnesses from the vicinity of the collapsed Great Hall, while the River Spree continues overflowing its banks. 3Reich estimates that forty staff and guards were suffocated or crushed in the collapse; so far ten have been dug out alive. As yet there is no explanation of how a building designed to stand for a thousand years could disintegrate into sand...*"

"We've killed people," said Zooza.

"Whatever," said George. "Who else but *Nazis* would work there?"

"Cleaners? Maybe Polish slave-workers?"

"I don't care if they were French polishers."

"There might have been a school visit."

"3Reich would be sure to emphasise *that* – but only if they suspect sabotage by an enemy. Otherwise it's some fault in construction. Inferior granite, inferior marble, a veneer over sandstone, for instance. The Great Hall was too heavy. Anyway, a school visit – by Junior Hitler Youth? 'I want young men and women who can suffer pain,' quoth the Führer. 'The weak must be chiselled away.' Okay, wish granted. Not that there seems to have been any school visit!"

"180,000 people could have been inside."

"How many million Slav underpeople have been exterminated, and Jews and gypsies and blacks and disabled and," with a nod at Billy, "the differently sexed?"

"Yeah," said Billy.

"Let's not argue about casualties," suggested Zooza, "especially while we don't know where the news is going. This could still be a coincidence."

"*...we have live from UCLA a specialist in atomic instability...*"

"Which is why we need another test," said Giant George.

"I'm with you there," agreed Norris. "A game that puts the concept of orgone weapons into people's heads mightn't be a bright idea if the fucking things work. Sorry, Zooza, but we must take this into account. Our game could inspire 3Reich to start experimenting."

"Maybe only good positive guys can use orgone energy," she said feebly.

"So suppose the USFA develops orgone weapons, 3Reich reacts *how exactly*? With nukes?"

It was 40 years since 3Reich had caught up and tested atomic then hydrogen bombs inside what long ago had been the Soviet Union. Fortunately the First Führer himself was dead by then, consequently Reichnukes had only been used a few times since, in rebellious India.

"*...as I understand it, the hall decayed into molecules of sand, constituents of rock. This has nothing whatsoever to do with nuclear decay. Some entirely different force or phenomenon must be the reason.*

Maybe something presently unknown to science."

"Professor Gomez, *do you mean a miracle worked by God?*"

"*The concept of a God is a delusion.*"

"*Shared by many good souls. We shan't take up more of your time, Professor.*"

"Let's hope Gomez already has tenure," said Norris.

By the following day the final reported death toll of the Great Hall collapse was 46, including two holidaying SS swimming-ace twin brother frogmen who had burrowed into the giant sandcastle in search of survivors, becoming known posthumously as The Molemen – a state funeral was scheduled for those heroes. By now a channel had been dredged for the Spree to resume flowing, draining floodwater.

Nevertheless, our team took the moon buggy bearing its orgone gun out to the field of basalt again. The gun was already traversed and elevated, and Earth remained in the same place in the non-sky, so it was only necessary to park just so and make the most minor adjustment.

"Are we sure?" asked Zooza quietly, as if to exonerate herself. "Are we quite quite sure?"

"Sure we are sure," said Giant George, and promptly pulled the trigger.

A blueness occured, seen this time by all four of them.

"That seemed more intense," Norris said. "I don't mean brighter. I mean..."

Zooza tried: "As if there were different blues simultaneously. Summing them darkened the look against the black of space, yet also deepened the, um, impact, on the eye. I'm thinking indigo."

"If only I'd seen last time," said George.

"Take your word for it," said Billy. "I'm no great expert on blues, such as skies..."

"Though you get them sometimes, the blues," murmured Zooza.

"Back to *base*, at a leisurely *pace*," rapped the lanky Lunatic, stress on the second syllable. The inhabitants of Liberty Luna could scarcely call themselves Libertarians, otherwise Homeland USFA would have become upset; and as for Lunarians, that was too much like Aryans, enough of those already at Festung Speer.

The anchorwoman on the main clingscreen was saying:

"*...Hitler's birthplace, Linz in former Austria, which the First Führer adorned with the colossal complex of the Führermuseum designed by Albert Speer. Early reports speak of two major structures, the Great Theatre and the Opera House, simply 'turning to dust'. As a result a great cloud of dust currently masks the city, blocking the view from satellites. Apparently the vast Adolf Hitler Hotel* *still stands, as does the Great Art Gallery housing priceless paintings, porcelain, tapestries, and sculptures plundered long ago..."*

"I guess those'll all need dusting," said Zooza, "but at least they didn't get crushed by tons of sand. And hundreds of volk could have been staying at the Adolf Hilton, but they're spared. There's selectivity."

"No Hiltons in 3Reich," commented Norris.

"You know what I mean. And just dust, this time. Finer than sand. Two megalobuildings instead of one. Targeted, yes. Of course there'll be casualties, but all in all... selectivity. So George, did you think Linz?"

"Well I don't know. I mean, after Berlin where's the next biggest Hitler heritage site? One biggy the first time, two this time – so will it be three next, or *four*? That would lead to large numbers pretty soon... Next time will it be atoms instead of molecules? After that, atoms splitting, *voomph*... Oh but granite doesn't contain enough uranium..." The engineer muttered to himself about quartz and feldspar and silicon and oxygen, aluminum and sodium, till Norris said:

"Shut it, please, George. Did you think about the Führermuseum at all?"

"I may have done. Don't know now. It seems as if I should have done, but did I? Maybe for our next test tomorrow I should deliberately concentrate on the Evil Eiffel."

"Remind me?" said Billy. "I don't get to Earth too much."

"The Führertower spanning the Rhine at Mannheim, at the confluence with the smaller river – the Nicker? the Nacker? But that tower's steel, not stone."

"So we'll get instant *rust*, 'stead of *dust*?"

"I think," said Norris, "we should delay further outings for a week or so, all things considered, especially since we haven't considered them all. How 3Reich will react this second time, for instance."

"Just wondering," Giant George said idly, "what if we aim the gun in the direction of Festung Speer? Okay, Speer's way below the horizon, even if there weren't mountains in the way, but maybe Moon's gravity might guide the beam. Specially as Sea of Serenity's a mascon –" Speer was on the western edge of Serenity, which was indeed an area of anomalously high gravitational pull. All three gaped at George in horror, for he had spoken abomination.

"You'll be out of the nearest airlock in your birthday suit," snapped

Zooza. "And 3Reich could take Liberty out any time with a nuke missile, then bye-bye to most of the Earth as habitable pretty soon after."

"Retaliation after retaliation," rhymed Billy.

It simply never occured to the trio that Giant George might take the gun-buggy out solo at moon-midnight according to Liberty clocks. Such was George's hatred of Huns, his rancour at Rhinelanders, his hostility to Hamburgers which he would never eat despite his and their USFAmericanisation, even if the burgers at Liberty were made of flavoured soya hydroponically grown.

The first that Norris and Zooza and Billy, each in their separate snoozies, knew was when an alert *whoop-whoop-whoop-wheee-wheee-wheee*ed. Almost immediately audio invaded the snoozies, the familiar part-silky, part-guttural voice being that of Chief Safety Officer Carmen Jones, herself sounding roused from sleep.

*"...Liberty itself is **not** endangered. Repeat, there is **no** perceived **problem** for Liberty at present. However, Festung Speer has suffered a **major breach of integrity**. Folks, it seems Speer's basalt walls have suddenly **dissolved**. That's according to a Save-Our-Souls in plain English as well as Nip and Deutsch gated."* Short for Gates-translated.

*"...Speer's interior wall has **ruptured** at several points, soon **sealed** by quote **heroes** unquote, so we guess they're dead by now. Rupturing may worsen. The exact composition of the interior wall is a 3Reich state secret, but it's presumed to be part anorthite-derived fibreglass, part pure aluminum. Nothing wrong with that, provided the inner wall stayed sheathed by basalt. Trouble is, aluminum expands and contracts more than most metals. Exposed to extreme temperature variations between lunar day and lunar night, aluminium can be **vulnerable**."*

How ironic that at Yuletide the Speermenschen would reportedly sing *Ein feste Burg ist unser Speer*, A Stronghold is our Speer. No longer so.

"We should get ready right off to receive possible refugees, including evac them from Speer. Obviously Star Town will take as many Speermenschen as the Nips can cram into their giant Zen garden" – which was where the Nips suggested staging a lunar Olympics *–"before 3Reich will resort to Liberty..."*

What? Have hundreds of blond-beast Übermenschen und Überfrauen stomping around Liberty, sneering at supposed inferiors?

Ah but they mightn't look so proud now they were scrounging their next meal (and air), vacuum outside, no vector home..."

"...which would be some kind of perilous situation! *Anschluss und Blitzkreig!* The refugees would have to be locked in Hydroponics, tending cabbages and bean sprouts, guards outside the airlocks with incapacitating puff-guns. Or inside Engineering storage with basic amenities laid on, *Scheisse*. A big part of Liberty could become a crapulous Konzentrationslager.

"*As to the **cause** of the outer basalt dissolving, we are **rejecting** the idea of a tenuous cloud of **antimatter** atoms from cosmic space impacting Speer. Mutual annihilation causes a significant flare of energy release — which our Sats would have spotted...*"

Norris, Zooza, and Billy rendezvoused very soon at their workcubicle.

Billy demanded, "Is Giant George still out there? He's done an abomination, like he threatened!"

"He didn't actually *threaten* as such," Norris pointed out. "He just voiced the idea. I've tried to voice him too, but no responses. I don't think he's inside Liberty. Hmm, that buggy must have a transponder beacon – so I guess we ought to discuss this pdq with CSO Carmen. Who *won't* be well pleased."

"Something else is more important first," Zooza said firmly. "We gotta come clean with Homeland USFA Earth right away, doubleplus encrypted. Lay this mess in their lap – they have mega-experts on how to clean up messes. In fact I have an inspiration or two to put to HUSFA."

One step ahead again, eh, Zooza? Maybe even two?

"Carmen works for Homesec," said Norris. "Shouldn't she –?"

"Carmen mightn't like my idea. Tell you what: you both go see her while I report to Homeland – I mean home in a *loose* sense, Billy, respect to you."

The buggy's transponder beacon proved to be switched off. However, if Giant George was obsessed with getting close to Speer in a buggy, he would need to avoid mountains by first heading north around the Carpathians. Sats located the little vehicle within an hour, heading just so. There it was, circled on a screen under zoom in suddenly busy Security, bit over twenty miles away, moving at nine-per.

What was George thinking of? Solar power would serve for part of his trip, and presumably he had taken extra fuel cells, but he would need to cover more than sixteen hundred miles before he could feast his eyes on his handiwork in person. At top safe speed, which couldn't be safe all the time, that meant a hundred and sixty hours, going on for seven days ignoring sleep. Realistically more like ten to twelve days travel – in a moonsuit which simply couldn't contain enough food and water, nor store enough waste.

"Conclusion," said Carmen Jones, "he wants us to think he's gone off his head. Really, he's putting a bit of distance between himself and Liberty. Probably hoping to hide the buggy in deep shadow up against some big rock, which he ain't found yet. While we're all hyperbusy giving refuge to Nazis he'll sneak back, starting sniping your crazy orgone beam at them. That's my bet for his plan – which doesn't mean he *hasn't* gone off his head."

Stocky Carmen Jones wore her thick glossy black hair in a plaited whip that pedulum-ed in the low gravity when she swung her head.

"Many Speermenschen will be in emergency transfer suits." Right, like walking jelly beans. Pretty vulnerable even to a puffgun. "We can't have that. An act of moonwar."

"*CSO! Couple of Speerferries just lifted off, heading towards Hoshimachi.*"

"Maybe," said Norris, "George thinks we won't take any Nazis into our home while he's out there with a big gun?"

"Maybe," conceded Carmen. "Meanwhile, we'll send a geology launch to his location. Do our best to net Mr Wysocki, throw a camouflage sheet over the buggy as a temporary measure, bring Wysocki back."

Net George...? Carmen had a trick up her sleeve? Which wasn't a sleeve, since she was wearing a sleeveless day-glo yellow vest with many velcro pockets over an orange tee-shirt, displaying prominent golden biceps; she gymed and she sunned. "What's *netting*?" asked Norris.

"Well, we can't hypo him –"

"Ah, suit integrity, I see, of course..."

"No, we could slap on a patch afterwards. I was *going* to say that the needle might snap off, 'specially if he resists. Suits are made *tough*. A contracting stickynet is best for incapacitating a guy in a moonsuit. Only been used once before, on a Mexican who mooned out, but it worked fine. Talk about some fat fly fastwrapped by a spider."

"I never seen a fly," said Billy, "nor a spider."

"*CSO! Three Nipferries lifting off too, on course for Speer.*"

"Okay, better advance couple of our own ferries to the Sea of Vapours. Make that *three* ferries – we can't seem to lag, supposing we're needed."

"*Two more craft departing Speer, direction Nips. Nazis must fear Speer's going to fail big.*"

Someone said, "Nasties don't fear."

"Look, I won't have snarky comments. Remember this: we house a few hundred Nazi refugees, then 3Reich won't likely put a nuke down our chimney, just *supposing* there's escalation for any reason."

Such as outsiders finding out about George and his Orgone Gun...

Tension was high. By now, three terrestrial days later, three hundred and fifty mostly blond Speermenschen, Speerfrauen, and Speerkids were benefitting from the hospitality of Liberty Luna; *enjoying* wouldn't be accurate. Food and water rationing had been introduced temporarily while production and ice-ferrying stepped up. Air rationing just wasn't rational, so everywhere within Liberty there was a faint fetor of armpits. Two youngish Speerfrauen had defected – one a foodtech, the other a nurse. Those women couldn't be trusted to roam freely. Secretly they might be Sicherheitsdienst and could go poking. Necessarily they were confined to snoozies. The UnterKommandant of Speer, Siegfried Stubenrecht, who had accompanied the refugees, was making demands of the Head of Liberty, Neil Attwater, for the return of the two defectors, although this might only be to deflate suspicions about the women.

Apparently about a third of Speer had sprung open to moonvacuum, unpatchably, though without further loss of life by heroes. Fairly major repairs needed there, including recladding. Bound to take months.

On Earth, 3Reich was on black alert.

"Carmen allowed me see George in the clinic for ten secs through the peekaboo in his door," Norris told Zooza and Billy. "Strapped and middling sedated."

"*...interrupting with breaking news: USFA government has just announced that the south face of heritage national monument Mount Rushmore, bearing the monumental sculpted heads of Presidents Washington, Jefferson, Lincoln, Teddy Roosevelt, and Truman, has disintegrated...*"

"Oh wow, oh wow!" as Zooza clapped her hands.

"*The site in South Dakota is just one hundred miles from the USFA border with 3Reich –*"

"No, don't go down that route..."

"**More** *breaking news: the Statue of Liberty has apparently melted into San Francisco Bay –*"

"*Witnesses speak of a shining 'flying dish' moving away at huge speed –*"

"Oh yes, oh yes! Ace!"

After 3Reich subdued Adolfstadt, oops NY NY, they raised a Führerstatue on the remains of Liberty. Liberty's replacement on Alcatraz Island was twice the size of the original, but not three or four times, so as not to snub one's nose too obviously at triumphalist 3Reich structures.

"Thermite, plus a hologram projected from a high-flyer?" queried Billy.

Zooza smiled a Mona Lisa.

"And Mount Rushmore, how?"

"Remember how I did a Lakota Sioux versus German colonists game years ago? There's a big vault – *was* a big vault – behind the heads of the presidents. Meant to become a hall of historical records, but money ran out, so the vault was sealed up. *Controlled demolition* is a phrase that comes to mind, though I leave precise details to others."

Norris said, "We'll need to leave a lot of things to others – no hope now for our Thousand Year Reich game..."

"My fellow Free Americans, we cannot as yet be certain, but available evidence strongly suggests that the destruction of two of our national shrines may have been due to extraterrestrial activity – and that similar activity destroyed two of the Third Reich's heritage sites on Earth, as well as seriously damaging the Speer base on the Moon.

"By extraterrestial," continued the honeyed voice and fuchsia lips of USFA President Gabriela Cruz, *"I mean beings from beyond our own solar system, in other words aliens, possessing a technology in advance of our own. Just before the 'flying dish' was seen above Alcatraz Island, radars at both San Francisco International Airport and Oakland International Airport blacked out.*

"The intentions of these alien beings are not necessarily hostile. I must emphasise this: a human being walking through a meadow does not intend to destroy spiders' webs, for instance. However, we must be very wary. The USFA government

is urgently setting up an investigatory committee of military and civilian experts to be known as Majestic – this name chosen because majestic structures were destroyed, whatever one's personal opinion of the purposes of those edifices..."

"It's good that no Nip shrines or monuments were smashed," observed Norris. "That should confuse 3Reich."

"I suppose," said Billy, "after a while George and the gun will get transferred to the wilds of Nevada or somewhere for study..."

"Lightbulb!" exclaimed Zooza, "how about us doing *Nazis versus Flying Dishes*? Extraterrestrial aliens with tentacles invading 3Reich, in the 1950s?"

Norris considered. "I like that. I think it'll fly."

In this story I altered history a little by having Wilhelm Reich born fourteen years before he actually was, though since warfare persists between sceptics and disciples of Reich who denounce his Wikipedia page as hopelessly corrupted by hostile attacks, who knows? Personally I've never been in an orgone box, only in a sensory deprivation tank in San Francisco in about 1988 – which did have a big, silent, time-altering effect – so I can't say if unverifiable life-energy pervades the universe. The real Reich only developed the orgone gun after he fled from the book-burning Nazis to the USA, where his books were also bonfired by the Food and Drug Administration; and the gun's main use was against clouds, to try to massage the weather, as well as to weaken perceived UFOs.

Sigmund Freud was authentically born Sigismund. The gigantic Nazi buildings destined for a new-look Berlin, brainchild of Albert Speer and the Führer, already existed in model form, awaiting a Nazi victory in World War Two which would usher in the Thousand Year Reich, not Wilhelm's. Yet surely Wilhelm Reich's name is a hint at how events might have spun otherwise?

"The Faithful Hussar" is the song that Stanley Kubrick's future wife, actress Christiane Harlan, sings movingly at the end of Paths of Glory.

By the way, to give a sense of proportion, the United States minus Alaska fits almost exactly on to the surface of the Moon visible from Earth – and on to the invisible side equally, but we don't want to go into Nazi lunar bases... or do we?

In Golden Armour

Consciousness returned to Jax with the urgency of a needle-point stiletto bursting the balloon of oblivion that cocooned him. He jerked, and was a marine again.

His suit had stabbed him with adrenaline directly into the marrow of the long bone of his right arm to restore his function – restricted though that function might be.

The terrible flaying and charring by ovenlike heat had washed away. He glanced down to see the flexible brassy hoops of his armoured right leg still attached to him, although he could feel no sensation. His left leg was drifting away from him many metres below. At least his suit hadn't amputated both legs at the groin, leaving a torso with arms to carry on fighting when revived. His left leg must have shaded his right leg sufficiently from the roaster beam, and for now his right leg was anaesthetised and balmed.

No movement – other than that of his diminishing left leg – was visible in the depths which went on forever, speckled with stars. Beside him, the black cliffside of the asteroid was maybe ten metres away. Elevating his gaze, overhead he saw a vast overhang like a jutting ceiling. Despite that stony canopy and the lack of any sunlight in this lee he felt exposed, no cleft or crater in sight to take cover, supposing his attitude thrusters still functioned – his suit was apeing defunct, and the Worm that beamed him must have detargeted him rather than waste energy.

His detached left leg could almost be mistaken for one of the Worm warriors. Maybe the Worm's image recognition had overridden a final chest-become-oven kill-shot directed at Jax.

Where was that warrior now?

Where was it – that segmented golden tube, its snout bristling with sensors and its preferred weapon, the roaster?

Jax dared not swing round yet to try to spot the Worm.

Think. How long had he been unconscious before his suit stabbed him awake and alert? Just a couple of minutes, while his suit's medpack adjusted his metabolism after the shock of snap-amputation while it balmed his remaining leg?

More time than that? Enough time for the battle to have moved onward out of sight? Or was fighting continuing silently and unseen behind him? If only he were rotating, he would know. Yet he was almost still with respect to the asteroid.

In defunct mode, Jax's suit neither transmitted nor received; he heard nothing, felt nothing, although his right gauntlet still gripped his long ripper railgun almost at right angles to himself. Suppose he fired one single depleted uranium flechette, that might give him enough momentum to spin very slowly, maybe undetected...

The so-called "Sondar" flexible space armour of the marines contained a two-centimetre-deep smartfoam cushion between a human's flesh and the brassy hoops. Impregnating that smartfoam was the ultimate in compressed oxygen – metallic oxygen, its supermolecules locked by nanotech for slow release; a suited marine could breathe for twelve Earth-hours before recharge of the zeta-oxy. Amplifying the body's muscular signals, servomotors compensated for relative inner stiffness, which of course diminished as the zeta-oxy was used up and the wearer's exhaled CO_2 vented into space symmetrically and almost invisibly.

Jax's regiment was the Armadillos, and to begin with they patrolled a quadrant of the asteroid belt, tasked for police actions mainly against the Chinese, whose spaceguards were known as the Terracottas.

The asteroid belt was vast in volume, like a giant tyre around the Sun between the orbits of Mars and Jupiter. That fat tyre was two hundred and fifty million kilometres wide from its inner rim to its outer rim – and it was mostly empty space. From any asteroid – biggish, smaller, little, or tiny – you were unlikely to see another asteroid anywhere in sight in any direction, only far-away stars. The total mass of all asteroids was only 4 per cent of Earth's Moon. And yet that 4 per cent amounted in total to a lot of resources worth exploiting. Three quintillion metric tonnes. 1,000,000,000 Mount Everest's of material.

The other role of the marine regiments had been to become effective star soldiers for when interstellar travel was developed. Just in case hostile intelligences lurked out among the stars. No colonists should head out there unprotected.

Three years earlier this secondary role had become the primary role – not because humanity had developed interstellar travel but because the Worms arrived from the stars.

Eighteen months before, First Sergeant Rolly Piper had addressed the Armadillos thus, back on Luna:
"It might seem bizarro that the Enemy looks like one of our own armoured legs about ten times larger, suited in flexy golden rings. Our scientists say this may be a copycat camouflage thing..."

Well, if so, that might have saved Jax's life for the moment.
Fire one single DU flechette, then maybe one more, to set him turning slowly?
The flechette railgun was a mercy weapon, really. Its depleted uranium rounds pierced armour then sharded apart once inside and tore the soft contents to shreds almost instantly. A far cry from the roasters used by the Worms which turned your limb armour into a non-instant inescapable oven. Like being burned at the stake. Like a steak on the griddle.

Jax was a marine, and an Armadillo, which meant the best. He had lost a leg – roast leg of Jax – but what of it? Legs were mostly unnecessary in space. He still had two fighting arms. And those arms were *not* doing any fighting right now, while maybe his comrades were burning up just out of sight.
"Gun online!" he commanded. An orange light blinked high in his visor.
Something else to be done... Jax was still a bit woozy.
Yes, to undamp the gun. So that he recoiled equal and opposite to the discharge of ammo. Given the way the gun was pointing, well away from his personal centre of mass, this should push him into a slow spin.
If your attitude thrusters failed, you might push yourself out of harm's way by undamping and releasing a stream of flechettes – not the idea this time.
"Non-damp," he told the processor in the neck of his suit. "Single shot."
Motionless but for the slight squeeze of one finger of his gauntlet,

he fired a flechette.

Now he was moving ever so slightly relative to the asteroid. But not enough. At this rate he'd take fifteen Earth-mins to turn.

Highly unlikely that the Enemy would notice a tiny supervelocity flechette strike the side of the asteroid. Puff of dust maybe, no obvious direct relationship to himself. His railgun magnets betrayed nothing, nor the muzzle. Not unless you were really searching, spot on, with sensors.

He fired another flechette, then a third. The magazine still held over a thousand of the little depleted uranium devils, depleted in the sense of being much less radioactivite but dense as could be. The power-pack on his back was at fifty-five per cent. Slowly but surely he began to rotate away from the cliffside.

One of those disorienting flips of perception that were common in space occurred, and he was *above* the surface as if falling fatally towards it. But he dismissed this illusion by flicking his gaze at his visor tell-tales then quickly back again at the scene.

For a moment Jax thought he was seeing Worms in their suitships. But what was coming into view were two amputated gold-ringed legs of marines and what must be an armoured arm in slow ballet near to one another. No sign of the former owners.

Was the Enemy taking prisoners? Amputated prisoners?

The horror of being a powerless torso and head – after the roasting of limbs and the snipping off! – taken for experimentation by Worms! Kept alive with force-feed tubes of nutri-sludge and water passing through the oxymask stuck tight over your maybe broken nose and ruined mouth. Electrodes sliding through the sides of the eyes directly into the brain. Only able to roll or rock slightly in protest or in agony, tethered in a cradle, while your memories cavorted crazily in a viewtank. Transparent caps over your rolling, watering eyes to exclude most of the chilly acidic greeny chlorine gas mixture that Worms like to breathe.

This was a marine's nightmare. The corps had never yet found or liberated any such prisoners, but they must exist.

First Sergeant Rolly Piper had said, "The Scorpions captured an intact Worm that failed to self-destruct its suitship and itself..."

A screen behind Rolly Piper lit up with snips from a vid.

Of armoured marines sporting the Scorpion regiment crest

manoeuvring the battered segmented alien vessel into a chamber.

Of the trial drilling for an atmosphere sample. Soon, a chlorine gas mix provided, to match.

Of the slicing open. Of the extraction by hooks of the giant slithery black maggot-thing, its three frontal tentacles not meaning that it was some sort of squid, no no, nothing so Earthlike – those proved to be snakish suckery organisms in symbiosis with the Worm; one was kept alive separated from the host for several days while the other two were being dissected...

Snips from the days of experiments and then of the full vivisection, never knowing if regular anaesthetics might be lethal therefore using none to be on the safe side...

A couple of Armadillos had vomited their rations. Others looked as green as chlorine. No shame.

"We need to know as much as possible," insisted the First Sergeant. "The Worms came sneaking from out of nowhere. Based statistically on contact-actions since then, there may be upward of a coupla hundred thousand Worms in our asteroid belt. The Chinese Terracotta Command concur. Yes, I said the Terracottas! Effectively we're in this together. Worm contacts are moving closer to Mars orbit. We suspect the Worms' nest-ship is out by Saturn, maybe hiding in its rings. That's because the Chinese base on Titan fell silent, as the Chinese reluctantly admitted, and all recent high-speed probes at Sat have failed – those were robo-probes which would have gee-flattened a human pilot. We need that nest-ship because it has to be interstellar. Its tech might break us out from Sol space. Marine recruitment is way up now that the good folks of Earth are aware of the Worms."

This was followed by some snips of the alien suitship yielding up some of its tech. As yet, no one knew why Worms favoured writhing through empty space in their flexi suitships, which wasted energy. Why not go in straight lines? It wasn't as if the asteroid belt was full of hazards little and larger, otherwise no probe nor ship would ever have got through it to Big Jupe or Saturn intact! Space was full of lots of space. How they had laughed at a pop-science vid showing a probe forever ducking up and down and side to side to avoid collisions with a multitude of rocks.

As for evading capture, a marine's armour didn't include a self-destruct option because a marine should fight and fight until the end. Also, the plutonium power-pack that fed the railgun through its tether and drove suit functions had been designed with fail safes in mind, not catastrophe.

Into Jax's field of vision now slid: action. What had been a great overhang was now a cliff, its craggy top littered with dusty boulders. Dozens of those boulders had been dislodged and were drifting loose. Some of the marines carried explosives and had used them. The very feeble gravity of the asteroid might take several days to reattach those giant chunks of rubble.

Meanwhile, hide and seek was happening within this three-dimensional maze between surviving Armadillos and surviving Worms in their suitships. Jax was reminded crazily of that old pop-sci vid – supposing you disregarded the vast irregular bulk of the asteroid itself.

As he gazed, a beleaguered marine forced his way underneath a slab the size of a school bus and strained with his power armour to shift the slab as a shield. That was a lot of inertia to overcome. Might the Armadillo overload his power-pack? Yet the slab was slowly on the move. That marine was some kind of superhero. The Armadillo slid further beneath the shield while a Worm writhed closer between drifting boulder and drifting boulder. Gas and dust boiled off the rock close to the Armadillo. And a second Worm was in the offing.

"Full activation reboot!" Jax commanded his suit.

For a few seconds he thought nothing might happen; feared that the Sondar suit might be confused by 'full' when in fact it was missing one limb. But tell-tales blinked. The Mark Five version did not make such logic errors. As Jax resumed control, radio traffic recommenced:

– *Martinez at verty 13, zonty 81, westy 29. Heating up.*

A grid overlayed Jax's field of view; his smarthelmet was prioritising nearby activity on the basis of urgency – but the remainder of the call from Martinez was a rising scream, almost immediately cut off by the system.

– *Edwards. Defensive at verty 11, zonty 83, westy 31. Two Worms incoming.*

A new grid appeared, corresponding to what Jaz was seeing currently.

Quick as could be, more and more radio reports came in, until...

– *Armadillos, Sove Key Purr!*

That was on the command channel, the venerable instruction of

Sauve Qui Peut, every man for himself – rush to escape!

The Armadillos were to break off the action, flee to their frigate which was floating ten klicks off, fast and well-armed and reasonably manoeuvrable but vulnerable to mass attack by enemy suitships according to current assessments. Let the frigate retreat with escapers from the action, and the alien enemy would have wormed its way even closer to the orbit of Mars.

"Hold for two minutes!" broadcast Jax. "Emergency override Alpha Omega Kappa. Jax back on line, and *engaging*."

This was preposterous vaunting egotism. How could one marine make a difference? He was just a lance corporal, not yet even a junior officer. A lance had a right to cry AOK in exceptional circumstances – say, if the balance of combat had suddenly shifted in a favourable way unknowable to the commander in the frigate who was monitoring transponders showing suit locations as well as the radar profiles of rocks and semi-stealthed enemy suitships. A lance only had one such call at his disposal during any one extended mission and was well advised to use this wisely only *in extremis*. Post-mission analysis of bad calls resulted in disgraceful discharge, punishable by discharge naked through an airlock into vacuum.

Jax believed that the balance had indeed shifted enough. Fighting had passed him by while he and his amputated leg floated inert. More Worms were coming into view, concentrating on the surviving marines who were using jagged rock cover as best they could. Of course by now Jax was no longer inert, far from it, but these thoughts only took moments.

Aiming his now damped railgun, Jax fired a stream of flechettes at one then the other Worm menacing Edwards. The lateral hits on the enemy suitships didn't ricochet. Flechettes punctured through then erupted within. One suitship buckled and sprayed rapidly expanding greeny chlorine gas mixed with orange blood and other juices. A moment later, the other suitship curled around upon itself, as a person might if stabbed in the belly. By writhing through space, the enemy usually tried to remain frontal to their human foe. Supervelocity flechettes from side on were the most effective, although the most difficult positioning to achieve. By sheer accident of his temporary immobilisation, Jax had the positioning.

Two Worms destroyed. Damped recoil pushed Jax back gently, but he took that into account as he aimed at another exposed Worm and fired. Visible hits: gases plumed into the void, almost looking like some sea creature gusting out ghastly-coloured ink to camouflage its position, but no cigar for the writhing Worm.

A suitship was sneaking up on him out of the void!

Glance, *no*, that was another amputated golden leg, its true size deceitful in the middle distance. *Ignore.*

Again he targeted a Worm as it exposed itself unawares, first the bristling snout and then the forebody. Enough flechettes impaled the neck of the suitship behind the rounded snout to crack its rings, releasing chlorinous atmosphere. Bizarrely, the headsnout opened up like the jaws of a crocodile; Jax even glimpsed the writhing blackness dying within. Dozens of other flechettes must have overshot or undershot, or glanced onwards – for another Worm maybe three hundred metres further onward lost the frontal bristles of its sensors, and its roaster began to glow. Jax ramped up his faceplate visuals; yes, the blocked-vent roaster was going to 'plode. Let the Worm experience some of the agony it dealt to marines before a too merciful, too sudden release: of energy that haloed the front of the suitship, then snaked along the sides – glaring clinging jagged blue lightning. After which, the husk of the suitship was inert.

"Jax. Four Worms knockout."

Now Armadillos were arising from defensive positions – and not to carry out *Sove Key Purr* but to attack. Streams of depleted uranium flechettes flew. Many flechettes would continue onward at the same supervelocity, mostly out of the plane of the solar system. Incidents of postdate friendly fire were extremely rare, since space was so vast. Fifty thousand years hence, or a million years hence, tiny potent flechettes might reach another star system and still strike nothing, or be captured and orbit inward eventually to fall into a star.

Momentarily, immensity haunted Jax's imagination – infinity and eternity – but *capturing* was an immediate concern, stickynetting and stabilising any disabled suitship that still carried a living Worm, injured or otherwise.

For the enemy must be understood. It was still unclear exactly how their tentacles manipulated suitship controls mostly unseen by their beady eyes, or how this symbiotic alien species could have arrived at starflight in the first place.

If the cubic kilometres of the field of battle was cleared of active Worms, the frigate would move in, perhaps even settle on to the asteroid itself, while its scavenger drones set out to harvest the aftermath of conflict: cooked corpses of Armadillos, severed suit limbs, above all the remains of enemy suitships.

Now enemy suitships were writhing away from the jagged cliffy asteroid, rotund tails flaring irregularly as they accelerated, jinking up, jinking down, to left, to right – five Worms, six, seven. Those banded golden suitships were speedier than a marine's space armour. Jax sent supervelocity flechettes streaming after them. Other Armadillos did likewise, for sure. One fleeing suitship broke open, disgorging within a green cloud the black and red mince of a wormbody.

And then something happened, never before seen by Jax. The half dozen surviving suitships came together, like fuel tanks clustered around a rocket at launch. Of a sudden the multisuitship was out of sight except for a fast-shrinking tail of fire.

The field of battle had been thoroughly scavenged. Injured Armadillos were tethered in the medbay, almost all of them amputees. Worms seemed to delight in roasting arms and legs to incapacitate, putting a burden on resources. Like malevolent boys burning off the legs of spiders until only one leg remained, still striving like some bent pole to propel the body away from total annihilation.

A punishment detail had buried cooked human meat underneath a slab lasered loose from the asteroid by the frigate, then stickied back after the ceremony, after which the same laser burned upon the upper face of the slab the service numbers of those who died.

Discipline must be strict, thus minor infractions of rules were inevitable – Marines were persons, not programmed robots. Unpleasant duties as a punishment weren't resented because someone must carry out dirty duties. Marines must depend on each other utterly.

Who knew if anyone would visit that slab ever again? At least the location was logged, along with the current orbit of the asteroid. The service numbers would also go on the wall of honour on the Moon.

"A well-deserved field promotion," Captain Harker said to Jax as he lay in the medbay, his stump anointed with sproutlimb which tingled though not too irritatingly – biochem inspired by the biochem of salamanders.

Within three months, including strenuous physio, Jax should be fully functional again. Other injured marines were plugged in to virtual realities, but Jax refused the pastime; he wanted to relive the combat in his brain over and over, including that glimpse out of the corner of his eye of his own amputated leg, and to *think*.

"Congratulations, *Corporal* Jax. We turned the Worms."

"Permission to speak freely, Sir."

"Permission granted."

"Sir, the eggheads say that the Worms' suitships resemble our own armour superficially as a sort of mimicry camouflage – so we might mistake them for marines just long enough to give them an advantage over us."

"Yes, Corporal. Evidently."

"Sir, but what if they originally intended to look like us – superficially – as a way of *identifying* with us?"

"What do you mean, Corporal? Identify? A soldier identifies a target and destroys it."

"Sir, I mean identify in the sense of... I dunno, seeming compatible, alike in some way? And they roast our armoured limbs to incapacitate us, not mince us as we do to them? They mightn't understand the pain we feel."

"Tell that, Corporal, to those whose heads have been roasted!"

"Sir, might it be that the Worms originally came to, well, encounter us, wearing something they thought might look at least semi-familiar? Our Sondar suits!"

"Corporal, do you think the scientists you refer to so contemptuously as *eggheads* mightn't have thought of this?"

"Sir, and mightn't the Worms be like, well, emissaries from something even stranger than the Worms are? Something which has difficulties conceiving how to begin to communicate with us?"

"Be silent! You have euphoria drugs in your system, Corporal. Any such fevered fantasies have obviously been discarded in the face of evidence."

"Sir, an alien something which now thinks that combat is our preferred way of interacting, and communicating?"

"This is mischievous nonsense! – which will only undermine morale! Corporal, I regret to say that I am now obliged to place you on punishment. Your limb regeneration will cease. Special new Mark Six Sondar suits are currently being beta-tested, designed for various classes of amputees. I'm advised that we are failing to process new recruits quickly enough, and that the Corps cannot wait three months for disabled marines to resume service with regrown limbs. Our casualties are rising. Indeed our losses could have been much worse in this present action, but for your initiative, *Corporal*, thus your field promotion stands. Soon after we call in at our base on asteroid Vesta, you will begin to test one-leg amputee armour in combat conditions. A possible jump-promotion to Sergeant awaits you in a newly established Amputee Squadron. We'll show those Worms what Homo sap can do! Rejoice that you will resume action sooner rather than later!"

So saying, Captain Harker pushed himself away from Jax's hammock. Thinking had not been such a good idea, Jax concluded. He had been stupid; the Corps knew best.

Presently, Jax raised a hand to summon a medic, to ask for virtual reality goggles. He wanted to be on a more ancient simulated Earth where there were no incomprehensible alien threats, only human ones.

In the early 1990s I wrote the first ever Warhammer 40K novels for Games Workshop, including my Space Marine, *which quite a few enthusiasts have called the best 40K novel ever written, I modestly add. Basically I invented how to write Warhammer 40K fiction, and I was happy with what I did, so I put my own name on the books instead of using pseudonyms as did other authors who wrote Warhammer Fantasy. 40K gave me the way to write the space opera which I'd loved reading, but never thought I'd be able to write myself, by making the space opera dark and lurid and Gothic and psychotic.*

For bizarre reasons mostly connected with their games designers, Games Workshop then banned Space Marine *for many years, even though dog-eared paperbacks were changing hands on eBay for $100 or so. Eventually GW allowed* Space Marine *to appear again, though only as print-on-demand from their website, but the novel seems to have been suppressed once more. Heigh-ho, as regards what were once my most popular books, judging by fan-mail and sales – strangled by the publisher for being successful!*

Twenty-five years after my invention of 40K fiction, Ian Whates felt it would be interesting to see what sort of 'marines in space' story I might write nowadays specially for this NewCon Press collection – without using any of the 40K background or names or weaponry which are all trademarked and registered and verboten. So I have invented different space marines and a different alien menace.

HOW WE CAME BACK FROM MARS: STORY THAT CANNOT BE TOLD

Our ascent engine had failed, marooning the five of us on Mars. In ten years' time the Chinese might land on the red planet near our Birdie and diagnose what went wrong.

Neither our own efforts nor suggestions from Earth made any difference. We were stuck. Enough air, food and water with us for ten more days, our safety margin in case something unexpected such as a dust storm delayed our departure. Up in orbit were the bulk of the consumables we'd need for the long journey home.

At no point did we panic. Us Mars astronauts were chosen for our equanimity. Three married men and two married women confined in close proximity for a total mission profile of almost two years needed to have mild personalities. In actuality, for assorted reasons, all five of us were planning to leave our spouses some time after we returned to Earth, but for public relations reasons it was important that us five spacefarers should all be seen as contentedly wedded to spouses back home. A requirement for the mission. Likewise, that we had no children yet, which had narrowed the field of hopefuls. We'd all gone through the ritual of storing sperm or ova.

We could have spun out the food and water, but not the air. So our final day came. We sent our last messages to supposedly loved ones, then the 'heroic statement' for public release. This was *not* scripted by NASA – we really worked on that, together.

Then static disrupted our radio contact. Consequently we couldn't report that a craft, several times the size of our own lander, floated down beside us. I refuse to use the term 'flying saucer' even though that's appropriate for a fat grey disc without any visible windows or nozzle exits.

Distorted and unnatural sounding, an English-speaking voice broke through the static. I couldn't say if we were hearing the synthesized speech of a machine intelligence, a program translating the language of some alien, or a human voice disguised electronically.

We were invited on board. We'd be returned to Earth alive. This was being done to honour our bravery. A hatch opened from the lower part of the disc, becoming a ribbed ramp. We should board right now, or else our window of opportunity would close. So we had no time to record any message for delayed transmission when the disruption cleared.

In our Mars suits we transferred, our cameras and datapads zipped in the pockets. The suits bore a close resemblance to those in Kubrick's *2001* because that was such a good design. A NASA specialist had advised on those.

After mounting the ramp, we found ourselves in an oval chamber, softly lit and windowless, which swiftly pressurised. We took off our helmets and breathed clean warm air.

Five padded couches were around the walls. Evidently belts or harnesses were unnecessary. A toilet opened up, then a shower cubicle, and finally a cupboard containing plastic bottles of water and sandwiches wrapped in clingfilm. *Sandwiches!* I opened one and devoured most of it: cheese and ham in a Kaiser roll with some sauerkraut and German-tasting mustard. A bit of the roll I kept, to wrap in the clingfilm and put in a pocket for, well, later analysis by NASA. Where on Earth did ET go shopping for sandwiches?

"We have left Mars," the voice told us very soon, though we'd felt nothing unusual. "We shall land on Earth in three hours."

Not even weeks, but *hours*! How this mocked our seven-month journey to the Red Planet. The technology involved couldn't be human.

"Who are you?" Juno asked.

"*What* are you?" asked Chuck.

"That is not for you to know," was the answer. And it *never* was for us to know; it never was.

We gladly used the facilities. No sense of motion accompanied our journey, yet after a while I began to feel heavier. So did we all. Our weight was increasing from martian towards terrestrial, to adapt us somewhat. From time to time we tried to engage our invisible rescuer in conversation.

That is not for you to know.

Finally the voice said, "Put on your helmets again to contain any contamination."

I'd almost forgotten about the ten days of mandatory isolation scheduled for us after our return to Earth. We rose, feeling heavy. Obediently we refitted our helmets. Why did the voice remind us about the quarantine aspect? Ah, this implied we'd be landing somewhere close to a NASA facility; and also ensured that we'd look fully like proper astronauts, newly returned...

Presently the ramp opened in the wall and sunlight flooded in brightly. For a few dazzled moments the scenery looked like Mars, except that hereabouts sparse vegetation was growing in the dirty-looking desert. And the sun was bigger. Were we in Arizona? Nevada? New Mexico? Texas?

"You will leave now."

"Thank you so much for saving us," said Juno. "God bless you." The rest of us chorused our gratitude.

Rutted hills of dirt. The height of the sun suggested early to mid morning – unless the time was mid to late afternoon, but an instinct said morning. We all had about two hours of EVA air left in our suits.

I completely understood that a 'flying saucer' mightn't wish to land in full view at Houston or Vandenberg. So: choose a deserted area nearby. From which presumably we could now walk to a nearby highway where someone must drive by soon enough even if no one was paying attention to our suit radio frequency. I presumed the flying saucer had used some sort of stealth.

How would most people react to our heroic last words on Mars being followed a few hours later by us 'miraculously' turning up in New Mexico or Arizona? "We were brought back by a flying saucer." "Oh *really*?" I was very conscious of this.

We climbed a shallow rise. Some way downhill in the distance were wooden buildings exactly like those of a town in the old Wild West.

Over the suit radio I said, "So we've been brought home alive – but *to the past?* We've been saved, yet everybody in our own time will still believe we died on Mars?"

"The past?" echoed Juno doubtfully.

"If that's so," said Jim, "maybe we ought to bury our cameras and datapads deep, so we don't disturb history. Heck, our suits too."

"Using what to dig?" asked Chuck. "Our helmets?"

"Then we walk into town out of the blue in our underwear?" queried Juno. "*Hey guys, Indians robbed us. Buddy, can you spare us some blankets?* We can't start a new life that way. I'm not dancing in a saloon. Black Beauty, the Belle of Bonanza, Nevada. What'll you do for a living, Jim? Shovel horseshit?" The situation was making Juno a bit outspoken, but I saw her point. And to prevent what kind of contamination were we still wearing our helmets, when obviously we would need to take them off fairly soon?

Evidently we'd been spotted, because a cowboy on horseback was heading our way, galloping up the slope.

Boots, white trousers, baggy white shirt, leather vest unbuttoned, red neckerchief. Hanging from his belt, a six-gun in a holster. A pocked moon of a face, long greasy-looking black hair. He reined in, gaping at us. Then he addressed us in throaty Spanish, which I understood -ish. Immediately I snapped back from the Wild West to the present day, and opened my visor. Quarantine could go hang. Hot air wafted in.

I told the others: "He just asked *Who we with?* He doesn't know of a *Sci-Fi commercial* shooting. Do you speak English?" I asked the presumed Mexican.

"I speak, Señor. Classes. Yeah."

"To become a citizen?"

He looked blank, then said, "I am Pablo."

"Where are we, Pablo?"

"Lost in desierto? Hey, you seem how those guys on Mars! Great costume!"

"We *are* those guys," said Jim. "We've been brought back."

"Where are we *exactly*?" I asked again.

"Here is Texas Hollywood."

"Hollywood isn't in Texas," protested Juno.

"Texas Hollywood *Spain*," said Pablo to our black co-astronaut. "Is near Almería."

That rang a bell. "Where they made the spaghetti westerns?"

"Many commercials now. Here and Mini Hollywood and Fort Bravo. Amigos, you need drink. You tell," with a boisterous laugh, "why you look Mars!"

This was all bad news. The spacecraft had put us down right by a movie set. *Capricorn One*, anyone? This could not be a coincidence.

In that movie, instead of blasting off for Mars three astronauts are suddenly whisked away to a desert base where their journey and their explorations will be simulated. That's because at the last moment the life-support system on their ship is found to be faulty. For reasons of national prestige, the mission must still be seen to go ahead. Two years later, the returning empty re-entry module – supposedly with the astronauts on board – burns up in Earth's atmosphere, posing a big problem. What's to be done with the astronauts who are actually alive in that desert base?

We weren't in America, where our return could perhaps be hushed up – along with new identities for us similar to the witness protection program, so that we could disappear to avoid major national embarrassment. *But also where we couldn't be snuffed out and buried in unmarked graves.* Had our alien rescuer been aware of that aspect? Did his 'people' watch Sci-Fi movies? Maybe, if they bought German deli-style sandwiches.

As Pablo led us down the gritty slope, I said quietly, "Guys, we'd better be careful what we tell people."

We entered the wild west town by way of its picket-fenced cemetery, low wooden crosses askew. Nearby on a raised platform stood a gallows, a stool waiting underneath a dangling noose. Several Hispanic cowboys who were feeding horses stared as Pablo led us along the sandy main street. We passed a bank built of adobe, then the red brick and barred windows of a Sheriff's Office. Opposite, a clapboard-sided barber's and an undertaker's, so said the weathered signs.

Just then the undertaker's door opened and out stepped a tubby man sporting a Stetson and sunglasses, camera slung round his neck, accompanied by a tubby woman in a long pink-striped dress and baseball cap. The man promptly began taking photos of us while the woman called back inside, "May, will you come and see this!" A moment later May appeared, cameraphone in hand, visibly the woman's sister.

The undertaker's must be a mini-hotel where tourists could stay Western-style, authentically as it were. Other buildings along the street might be likewise.

Led by Pablo, we tramped through batwing doors into a big saloon in our Kubricky spacesuits. What looked like an unkempt outlaw in a long duster coat lounged against the bar, cradling a rifle, his blond hair long and tangled. Beside a stage a quartet of young women dressed as cancan dancers were chatting and giggling. The outlaw glared at us menacingly, acting in character I supposed. The cancan girls advanced on us, as though they were the local talent bent on relieving Jim, Chuck and me of our hard-earned silver dollars. Stairs led up to a balcony running around three sides of the saloon. Could it be, when the saloon got into full swing, that a cancan girl might take a guest up to a private room? No: two kids kitted out as junior cowboys came romping downstairs, firing blanks at each other, before gawping at us. Family entertainment here.

We took off our helmets and placed those in a row on the bar as if we were bikers, almost.

"You want drinks?" asked the thin-faced barman in English, an unlit cheroot in his mouth, silver armbands on his shirt sleeves like a croupier.

"I'm sorry," said Juno, "but we don't have any money."

Pablo laughed. "They not take dollars to Mars. Drinks for them obsequio de la casa. On the house."

"We'd better have Coca Colas," Juno said.

"Me, I'm for a beer," Chuck said.

"Count me in," agreed Jim.

"But it's only morning," I pointed out, as mission commander. "And it'll be your first alcohol in over a year. Surely it's wiser to stick to Coke or juice."

"We just escaped *death*," said Chuck. "Champagne might be the order of the day."

"I got good cold champán," said the barman.

Compared with the likely effects of champagne, beer seemed safer if Chuck and Jim insisted, so I pointed at the beer tap. "Two of those. Coke for me."

"Yeah," said Juno.

"Me too," from Barbara.

"Hey mister, hey mister," clamoured one of the kids, unmistakably American, "are you actors in a space movie?"

"No, we are *not* actors," Barbara said.

"You look actors," piped up a cancan girl.

At that point up bustled a plump, tanned, beaming middle-aged woman in jeans and a billowy yellow blouse.

"Boys, go and play in the street," she instructed. "Chicas," to the cancan dancers, "help with the drinks, las bebidas okay? Pablo ¿que pasa?"

Pablo spoke rather quickly in Spanish, the woman nodding and saying *Si* from time to time.

"I have to sit down." Juno headed for a big round empty table, us four others following gladly.

Joining us at the table, the woman told us in a British accent, "I'm the wardrobe mistress of Texas Hollywood. My name's Rachel. Where *did* you get those spacesuits? They're so authentic looking. Is there a commercial I don't know about?"

"It's pretty hot in these," complained Juno.

"They from planet Mars," Pablo told her. "Hace muy frio… makes very cold on Mars."

A couple of the cancan girls brought our drinks, then Rachel shooed them away.

"Look now," Rachel said in a motherly way, "if you'll just step over the street I can fit you all out in something much more comfortable. Your spacesuits will be perfectly safe over there. May as well take your helmets with you too."

Chuck drained his chilled beer in one go. "I guess we oughta borrow someone's mobile… You know, phone the US embassy. That'll be in Lisbon, I guess. No, Madrid."

"Why would you want to do that?" asked Rachel. "Phone your director, your producer."

"We don't have those," said Chuck. Was his voice slurring already? "We have Mission Control."

"They say they brought back from Mars, not say how."

"Oh God, it's so awful," said Rachel quickly. "I watched on TV. I'm so sorry for your countrymen, those brave astronauts."

"We *are* those astronauts," said Chuck. "This is real. A flying saucer."

"No," I hissed.

"— a flying saucer brought us back in – *three hours*, can you believe it?"

"I think he has heatstroke," I said. "In these suits. Or maybe it's the beer."

Rachel rose. "Come on, all of you. Over the street." She herded us.

Within twenty minutes we were arrayed for the Wild West, the gals in ankle-length sleeveless striped dresses, me as a corporal in the US Cavalry in blue uniform, yellow neckerchief and chevrons. Chuck was a Marshall with pointy silver badge, Jim an ordinary cowpoke. Necessarily we'd abandoned our thermal long-johns cum long-sleeved vest combos, so we lacked underwear, which the wardrobe room didn't stock. On impulse I transferred the clingfilm with its bit of evidence to my new uniform.

Back to the table we went with Rachel, Chuck taking his Mars camera along as though he too had become a tourist. More beers and Cokes appeared,

Juno aired herself, and smiled at Rachel. "Sure feels a lot better."

"So, hombre," our cowboy said to Chuck, "not spaceman now, feel different?"

Chuck drank then yawned. "We still gotta phone."

"Phone American embassy, they believe you? Send black helicopters?"

I shook my head. "They'll be unlikely to believe us at first."

"So we phone Houston," said Chuck. "They know our voices."

"You have the number on you?"

Chuck looked frustrated. "Look, we don't have money, passports, anything of the sort. Just our suits. And cameras, datapads. I can show you us on Mars," he said to Rachel. So that's why he'd brought the camera. "Look, look," presenting images on the camera's screen, of us in a stony reddish desert, the big landing module standing there, a metal cabin on legs that looked like a model.

Without our noticing, more tourists had arrived in the saloon, mostly distinguishable from authentic pretend cowboys by cameras and pallid or lobster-red faces. One silvery-bearded crewcut fellow, who'd been here already, was shifting his chair ever closer to our table.

"Excuse me for butting in," he said. "You seen that conspiracy movie about how the Apollo 11 Moon landing was simulated? The White House was worried there mightn't be live TV from Apollo 11 on account of technical problems, so to be on the safe side they got Stanley Kubrick to simulate the video secretly on the set of *2001*. Flew over to England with moon suits and a spare lunar exploration module that Armstong and Aldrin had practised with. Allegedly."

"There's footage of Kissinger and other White House big-wigs authorising the plan – *except* if you pay close attention they're merely talking about *a* plan, unspecified. It's the voiceover that says this is about Apollo 11. And there's an interview with Kubrick's widow Cristiana, and her brother, what's his name, Harlan, Jan Harlan, that's it, talking about how impressed Kissinger was – Christiana mentions Kissinger by name, but again it's the voiceover that says this is about Kubrick shooting a simulated Apollo-on-the-Moon in England. England, of course, because Kubrick lived near London and wouldn't fly. Clever bit of editing, that film! I'm a connoisseur of conspiracy theories. And *do* I seem to be in on the ground floor here and now!"

"But *look.*" Chuck displayed more images for him. "These are *real* photos."

"They're real electronic photos, there's no denying. Kubrick's genius was in making *2001* look real with the technology of the late Sixties. Boy, have we moved on from there!"

Chuck put the camera on the table and slumped.

Our busybody went on: "I couldn't help overhearing you saying about having no documents or money, only those spacesuits and, before you went off to get changed, I'm sure I heard *flying saucer*. That's a beautiful touch, if I'm reading this correctly. So who's your director?"

"There ain't no director," I told him.

"You mean it's an amateur production like *Indiana Jones* reshot in a garage? Just you five guys on your own?"

"Mister, it's *real*. What kind of movie has no cameraman?"

The bearded fellow winked. "Who needs a cameraman? Soon as you came into town, folks would be uploading vids of those spacesuits to YouTube. Those vids will go viral, so you don't even *need* to make a movie yourselves – very astute. Tell you what – I'm Mike Appleton, by the way – those suits looked worth three grand apiece."

"More like a hundred K each," Juno said hotly. NASA hadn't stinted on our Mars environment gear.

Appleton stroked his chin. "That sounds a bit greedy, but I'd go to twenty-five K for the complete set. Me being, as I say, keen on conspiracy theory movies and associated paraphernalia, and you do keep insisting you need money. Unless," and he darted a wary glance at Rachel, "there's a higher offer on the table."

Rachel was indignant. "Five supposed astronauts walk into a bar and tell a tall tale to a naïve wardrobe mistress. Then a total stranger, who happens to be conveniently present, pipes up, 'Wow, what great sci-fi costumes! I'll pay you tens of thousands of euros.' I wasn't born yesterday!"

"That was dollars," corrected Mike Appleton.

"So the silly wardrobe mistress promptly says, 'I'll raise you five thousand,' and she empties her bank account. Away walk five happy actors with their accomplice."

"Rachel," I said gently, "we are *not* acquaintances of this gentleman. *Mister Appleton*, you are spoiling our hitherto cordial relationship with this good lady who has been kind enough to help us out."

"And isn't it a bit of a coincidence," persisted Rachel, "your Mr Appleton being so knowledgeable about that hoax film by Kubrick?"

"Alleged hoax," said Appleton. "That's the beauty of it. My offer stands."

Chuck seemed to have gone to sleep, and Jim was looking half-canned. The beer, and the fact that about five hours ago we'd been destined to die on Mars.

"Mister," said Barbara, "if we sell you our suits, at a ridiculous garage sale price, what do we do next? Use our five thousand dollars each — that would have to be cash, by the way, in the circumstances — to fund a new life in Spain with no ID? Fuck!" she cried. "I'm forgetting all about our families, who must be going through hell at this moment believing that we're gonna die!"

"That," I pointed out, "is because our spouses aren't exactly in the forefront of our minds."

Appleton seemed like an accomplice of whatever had returned us to Earth so near to this film-set theme-park where he happened to be staying, his intervention pushing us towards a route and a way of thinking that not long before I'd have regarded as absurd. Appleton was the mechanism by which a major part of our physical proof might be removed from us while we were in a disoriented state of mind!

"Five K each could get us back to America," went on Barbara, "but we can't board any plane without ID. We'd have to smuggle ourselves by boat to Mexico, sneak over the border like illegals, catch a Greyhound and turn up on our own doorsteps at midnight..."

Appleton clapped his hands. "I assume you watched *Capricorn One* a lot."

I could have groaned. Ten years on, if the Chinese land on Mars, since the USA mightn't risk another failure, it would become clear that our bodies had vanished. But meanwhile…

"We have a clear and urgent duty," announced Jim of a sudden, reviving, "not just to our grief-stricken spouses but to NASA and to our government and to the people. Yet here we are, cooling our heels in a bar."

"Hey, did you forget about you and Becky separating?" asked Barbara.

A commotion and gunfire somewhere in the street drew most of the tourists outside. A buckboard clattered by, bearing a coffin, and the bartender called to the few remaining tourists, "Gentlemen and ladies, outlaw will hang soon for murder!"

Chuck was snoring noticeably. Astronaut selection procedures had eliminated noisy snorers, although purring was acceptable, as NASA used to joke. Juno had been quite a purrer. Spanish air and the beer had started Chuck rumbling.

"A duty," said Appleton, "to alert everyone about *UFOs*? After all the previous official denials? Is that what this is all about, then – UFO revelations? That could be seen as bad taste, capitalising upon the deaths on Mars, even if you *do* resemble those brave guys quite closely. In fact it can't be coincidence that you're spitting images of the Marsonauts. So this must have been cooked up months ago – as if knowing *in advance* that the lander wouldn't be able to take off. That's as good as saying that NASA is a party to this, and – yes! – they set this up ahead of time in case of any tragedy in order to minimise that. Maybe NASA never completely trusted the lander's engines. I guess your spouses will be able to tell the difference, so they need to be sworn to secrecy. Hey, but you guys need to be available for a media tour around the world! So you need to know astronaut talk and be wise about Mars, same as the real crew. Unless the UFO revelation distracts everybody…"

Appleton's brain was working overtime. Me, I was starting to feel unreal, as if I'd merely been hypnotised to imagine I'd been on Mars.

"So they'd set all this up in case of a national tragedy," Appleton continued, "at the cost of endorsing flying saucers and aliens! Wow, that's one giant step for the space agency, you might say. If you must tell a lie, tell it big."

"We never saw any aliens. We only heard a voice."

"In your heads?"

"On our radio."

"We oughta phone," repeated Jim.

"I'm serious about buying the suits. I'll go to thirty-five K – K for Kubrick, hey? – for the set including your cameras. That's cash. Euros'll be more use to you, so let's say 40K euros. You come along to Almería with me so I can visit a bank. I'll throw in overnight at a decent hotel. My hire car'll hold three of you. Ma'am," he addressed Rachel, "may I hire one of your vehicles and someone to drive it? For the other two guys and the suits."

"I drive," said Pablo, doubtless in expectation of money.

"I really don't know," said Rachel.

"Two hundred euros for vehicle and driver, how's that? Better than a taxi fare."

"We don't have authority to sell our suits," Juno said, as though selling them was even a plausible proposition. The trouble was, we weren't highly assertive, any of us. That's how we got to Mars in harmony.

"Supposing," said Appleton, "you'd come down in Amazonia or the Gobi Desert, you'd need to improvise to survive. Might have meant bartering your suits to Jivaros or Mongolians... Hey, see how I'm talking as if you really are astronauts! For this prank to work properly, those suits ought to disappear, leaving only the photos and video clips taken here uploaded and viral. The suits will vanish into a private collection."

"You're planning to sell them on!" Rachel accused Appleton. "You could easily ask a million each from rich obsessives. Or Russian billionaires."

"Ma'am, you have the option any time soon to make a bid of your own. Except that you think this is a hustle and that I'm in cahoots with these good gentlemen and ladies."

"You did choose a convenient time to visit Texas Hollywood."

"Look, lady, the supposed flying saucer dumps them here because movies made here *pretend* to be made in America. Part of Spain pretending to be the Wild West. Me, I'm fascinated by movies about pretences, or which are pretences themselves. 9/11 conspiracy stuff, or those allegedly faked Moon landings. So of course this is a place I always wanted to visit – but I might just as easily have come here last week or last month and missed all this. My presence is pure luck! What's going on here with these actor-astronauts is what you might call a meta-pretence because the genius is that *no movie even needs to be made.* The internet will make the movie spontaneously."

Hadn't it occurred to Appleton that Rachel and Pablo might be in cahoots with the five of us? That Rachel *the wardrobe mistress* might have kitted us out in our Kubrick suits, knowing that Mike Appleton was booked for a couple of days, and having cleverly hacked into his finances beforehand? Which would mean that they routinely did likewise with other tourists too, awaiting their chance... and now Rachel had upped the ante considerably with her accusation about Russian billionaire collectors...

"I've been trying," said Juno, "to remember my home phone number. It's in my mobile's memory. But not in my brain."

Nor could I remember mine clearly! Digits danced in my mind's eye like on some slot machine in Vegas, with a very wide window, but no jackpot lined up. This wasn't too amazing. Since when had I needed to recite my own phone number?

"So what's it to be?" said Appleton. "Sell the suits, or is there a Plan B?" He chuckled. "You must have a Plan B from outer space. B for back-up. I mean, some colleague's vehicle had to bring you here all suited up." He still wasn't suspecting Rachel!

"It was a *space* vehicle of unknown design," I insisted.

"Sure, sure, piloted by aliens fond of movie sets. *How* would they know where this place is?"

"By googling?" I suggested. "Obviously they're familiar with Earth. They laid on German-style deli sandwiches for us."

"Aha!" exclaimed Appleton. "Here's the Nazi version! Hitler's scientists go to Antarctica by submarine and build a base underground, or under the ice, to make flying saucers designed in the Reich. Decades later the base is still operating, the source of every UFO sighting since 1947. Plus there's a big Aryan breeding programme. By now the Swastika flies inside the caverns of Phobos, which explains how rescue was close at hand for you. Maybe the Nazi ufonauts are in cahoots with rightwing billionaires allied to the Illuminati or whoever, since why should NASA build big chemical rockets if antigravity is available to the US government? Look, you can't have both versions at the same time –

aliens *and* Nazis."

"I never said *anything* about Nazis!" I protested.

"You mentioned sandwiches made in Deutschland."

"I'm just telling you what happened."

"Hmm, a Nazi sandwich... Symbolic none the less. Did your aliens buy sandwiches in Germany as disinformation? To throw people off the scent of aliens? This is more devious than I thought. Are there any other surprise details you'd like to add?"

"Yes! Why aren't you wondering if Rachel and the management of Texas Hollywood set this up, *in league with us* supposing we're actors, in order to con you out of forty K euros? And whether *that's* why Rachel accused *you* of setting this up to con *her*, so as to inoculate you against suspicion of a money sting!"

How could I have been drawn into such a weird way of thinking?

Appleton shrugged. "I know illegal things happen here all the time. Gypsies, drugs, property swindles. And this country's awash with illegal immigrants. But that's a bit imaginative."

Rachel burst out laughing. "I ought to resent what you just said, Jack," she told me. "But I can see where you're coming from. I still think Mr Appleton plans to sell your suits on at a huge profit."

Appleton looked momentarily disconcerted, but he rallied with the vigour of someone whose favourite ice cream might suddenly be snatched away.

"Great dialogue," he told me. "You really are covering all the bases. So should I say your suits look worth a lot *more*, and then the price goes up; or that most likely they were ordered on the net from a fancy-dress factory in China? By the way, before I finally commit myself I need a closer look at those suits. How's their air-conditioning?"

"We were heating up horribly in them!" insisted Juno. "Those were made for sub-zero Mars, not Spain."

Rachel rose. "Be my guest," she said to Appleton. "Let's go and inspect the goods right now. Pablo," she called, "ven conmigo! Will you come too?" she asked Jim. "They're your suits, so you know the workings."

The three of them were across the road for a while, during which we heard applause, doubtless due to the hangman doing his job and the outlaw pretending to perish in a non-tightening noose. Although mightn't that cause him whiplash? Maybe the outlaw trained his neck muscles. I was wasting my time even thinking about the matter, yet my brain seemed fixed on trivia. I had to snap out of this.

Our suits were *goods*. It was as if Rachel herself was selling them on our behalf. Somehow we had to empower ourselves, but I felt dozy.

I actually nodded off, recovering to hear Appleton say, "...classy enough to fool me if they're fakes..."

"So they'll fool the billionaires too?" Rachel and Appleton now sounded to be in conspiracy.

"Alternatively, NASA sent genuine spares over here just in case, ahead of the take-off from Mars. Or five rejects."

The pair of them, and Jim, resumed their seats.

"I want to go home," said Juno.

"That's unwise, supposing you're telling the truth. Think *Capricorn One*. How can you trust a government, or rogue secret agencies, that just might – I say *might* – have destroyed the Twin Towers, killing three thousand Americans – and some foreigners too – so as to authenticate the threat of Al Qaeda and Osama as the Santa Claus of Evil, and thus validate invading Iraq for oil motives, and then Afghanistan for consistency, huh?" Appleton held up his hand to avoid being interrupted. "Look, the CIA created and armed the Taliban in the first place to take on the Russians during the Cold War. Saddam wasn't a nice guy at all, but he sure kept the lid on Islamic militants, not to mention advancing the cause of women, so why rip the lid off Pandora's box? Who pulls the strings? Some powerful group stands to gain. Unless recent history is sheer stupidity. You five could be innocent patsies in all of this."

What a jolt back to wakefulness, which was nevertheless still dreamy, or pre-dreamy – I felt I'd been about to dream.

"All of *what*?" I protested. "You're making my head ache. This is paranoia."

"I'm merely mentioning possible aspects. I don't necessarily endorse any. Look, I own a company. I won't say what we do, but we have interests in several nations in Africa. You'd be better off in Africa, the five of you. I could fix you up with jobs, identities. You'd be safe. You can let some time roll by."

"That," said Rachel, "seems a much more substantial offer than 40K euros."

"It's do-able. I've been costing things in my head. And maybe this'll all work better with rumours that the dead astronauts are alive and well somewhere or other in great big Africa. I can hear rumours spreading already. You, Rachel, you'll be able to say: *The weirdest thing happened at work the other day...* And Pancho here —"

"My name is Pablo," said the cowboy.

Appleon grinned. "Almost got it right, didn't I? My mother was a bit psychic. Pablo will gossip too, in Spanish, almost the second language of the USA. At last I shall actually have *assisted* in a conspiracy theory. That'll make me a happy man."

Juno yawned. "I'm so tired. It's so heavy here."

Chuck seemed to have fallen asleep again.

"A phone call," muttered Jim.

"You don't make major decisions when you're worn out. Let's get you all to a hotel in Almería. Sleep on it."

"I suppose," allowed Juno, "that couldn't do any *harm*. We'd be able to watch CNN. See how America is reacting."

"If the pics and vids go viral," opined Appleton, "there'll likely be patriotic outcries to shut any sites hosting the pics unless those pics are all taken down right away, on account of them being in bad taste. That's excellent for conspiracy pics. So Uncle Sam heeds a grief-stricken nation because nobody knows the flying saucer angle – *not as yet*. Thereafter, how can NASA plausibly deny its denials, even if investigators head out here in secret? And as regards investigative journalists, boy, just roll out that UFO..."

A black helicopter landed in the street outside, billowing dust. Masked special forces leapt out, snubby weapons pointing at the swing doors of the Saloon. I was nodding off again in micro-sleeps.

"Pablo," I heard Appleton say, "is there somewhere on the way we can buy them proper clothes easily?"

"Al Campo shopping centre is good."

Two special forces guys burst through the swing doors, gaped at the cancan girls dancing on stage, and the gunslinger fired at them. No, that didn't happen.

"I've a better idea," said Rachel. "Getting them out of Spain, new identities in Africa: that's going to cost you a lot and things might go wrong. You're being too ambitious. It's the *suits* you want, not the wearers. How about you pay me some of the money *to look after these guys here*? Sort of an advance on wages – since we can't afford much more than pocket money on top of their keep. I'm guessing they'll be able to act the Wild West part, help out generally, play poker, talk mysteriously to tourists when they get tipsy. After a while people might come here specially to spot the ghost astronauts, once it's decent to do so. The Magnificent Five! Remarkable resemblances! We need extra attractions."

"Seems to me," said Appleton, "with 40K in their pockets they can pay their own keep here for quite a while, I'd say."

Rachel beamed. "Oh of course, silly me. Well, call my little cut a finder's fee. Or an advance on their board and lodging."

Appleton nodded, sat back and thought.

"Excuse me," I said to Rachel, "but don't we get a say in the matter?"

"Good heavens, I'm offering you *sanctuary*."

"Sounds like a town in the Wild West, Sanctuary," said Jim. "Next stop, Salvation. Or Tombstone."

"We want to avoid the tombstone outcome, don't we?" said Appleton. "The UFO in its wisdom brought you here as the best way to protect you. By pretending to be what you really are. Which of course you aren't. Unless you are."

Chuck woke up with a shudder and said, "I'm hungry."

"Of course you are," said Rachel. "You need the *chuckwagon*. And you're in luck, since our restaurant opens for lunch at high noon. That's very early to eat lunch in Spain but here we cater for tourists. Usually after lunch people like to have a siesta, so I'll sort out rooms in the Sheriff's Office. Would that be five *single* rooms?" she asked sweetly. "After being cooped up together for so long, sleeping alone might seem lonesome? Maybe the gals would like to share? And a couple of you boys? I'm afraid we don't have a triple room free. Of course if you'd prefer to pair up differently…?"

"I'm happy to share with Barbara," Juno said quickly.

"And me," said Chuck, "with Jim." To me: "If you don't take that amiss."

We ate burgers and drank glasses of Sangría, which seemed like sweet fruit juice but packed a punch, as we discovered. Skip to outside the Sheriff's Office.

"This is a *jail*," protested Jim. "Bars on the windows."

Rachel laughed. "I assure you the rooms are much better than cells, and you do get your own keys."

I felt very woozy from the Sangría. So were we all. A siesta wasn't an option but a necessity. Nice-looking modern bed in my room, checked gingham curtains at the windows, some kind of stove for winter use, chest of drawers, a smoke or fume detector on the ceiling. I slept soundly till about five o'clock when banging on the door woke me, interrupting a dream of walking through the desert, the Spanish not the Martian. Just in case of a woman being outside, I wrapped a sheet round me. It was Jim out in the corridor in his cowpoke gear.

"Our suits have *gone*. I woke up a bit ago, so I walked to that dressing-up building, and *no suits*. Rachel says Appleton went off with all the suits and Pablo. She says Pablo will be back here tomorrow bringing Appleton's money. I said we never agreed to sell! She made like she was astonished. All our cams and pads have gone missing too, unless Chuck kept his. He's still out cold after that Shangri-la stuff. We gotta make Rachel phone Pablo to say no deal and to bring our stuff back. I need your back-up."

"Jim," I said with perfect conviction, "the suits won't come back here now."

"I suppose this country has a police force!"

"Think, Jim, think. Policemen lock up guys with no ID. And then we have no control over our fate. None at all. At least here we can still walk around. We do have the keys to our cells."

"The police'll have to contact the US Embassy to check us out, even if they don't believe we're astronauts or that our Mars-suits have gone for a walk!"

"And what if Uncle Sam decides it's best for our nation if we never returned in a fucking flying saucer? Either we're dead on Mars or we've been on Earth all along with the collusion of NASA and Uncle Sam. Embarrassing, huh? Better swept under the nearest carpet? We just don't know enough to risk that. We *might* know enough after a few weeks, or a few months. Africa might still be the best bet."

"So you mean that for now we should negotiate with Rachel…"

"Even learn to ride horses. I dunno, we can be the Something Gang. With two wicked women members, one of them black to add extra colour. We'd better wake up Chuck and the ladies." This did really seem to me the best plan at the moment, and as mission commander I had a responsibility to my crew.

The Magnificent, or Malevolent, Five headed out to confront Rachel. Behind us, the adobe bank was being robbed for the benefit of onlookers. Up ahead two gunslingers were squaring off, shouting a dialogue of insults at each other in heavily accented English, while other costumed tourists looked on appreciatively. It was all go. One of those tourists, wearing a Marshall's badge, decided to uphold the law, advancing boldly with his six-shooter levelled at one of the gunslingers. Grinning evilly, the miscreant fired a couple of times: bang bang. Dramatically the tourist dropped his gun, clutched at his heart, then sank carefully to the ground while his wife and friends applauded.

Something fell out of my pocket and I scooped it up. Oh, that bit of food in its clingfilm. This time I noticed a tiny sticker, uncrumpled it, read: Gunther's Deli, Rachel NV.

NV for Nevada. No connection with Rachel the wardrobe mistress.

My old flying days came to mind. Rachel NV, a tiny tiny place near Nellis air force range close to Area 51. Famous in the world of UFO believers because of strange sightings along Highway, I forgot which number, but years ago the State of Nevada had officially designated that road *Extraterrestrial Highway*. A nice day-trip out from Las Vegas.

I'd stopped at Rachel once. Oddly its weather station monitored gamma radiation as well as the weather. Gunther's Deli was news to me. Maybe trade was picking up locally.

It couldn't be, could it, that the USAF, unknown to NASA, *did* have access to alien technology? They couldn't bear for us to die on Mars, but couldn't exactly reveal themselves either? Today had been a pretty busy day so far. I just couldn't digest this new fact.

We succeeded in passing the shoot-out without any blanks being fired at us.

In the south of Spain, Texas Hollywood – and Fort Bravo, further into the only desert in Europe – are just so. Simulations. We're wised up to simulations after The Matrix, *flourishing its copy of Baudrillard's* Simulacra and Simulations *in the hope of giving some deeper significance to a fundamentally nonsensical movie. And I'm quite wised up on*

conspiracy theories after editing the English translation of my Italian chum Roberto Quaglia's vast book The Myth of September 11: The Satanic Verses of Western Democracy – *which doesn't endorse any of the conspiracy theories about the Twin Towers but simply (or complexly) analyses them and the way in which the truth about an event evaporates almost instantly, to be replaced by mythology plus manipulation.*

As to why flying 'saucers' were a creation of the media from the word go, do see the story note to "Me and My Flying Saucer" later on in this collection. The Wild West in the south of Spain and UFOs seemed to me to belong together.

"We weren't in America..." Now that I live in Spain I'm more careful how I refer to the USA, since the Spanish are well aware that 'America' includes such places as Argentina and Mexico and Peru.

BLAIR'S WAR

During that autumn of 1937, even when the thirty-six refugee girls from the Basque Country were making better progress in English, they all still crowded around the big radio of polished rosewood in the lounge each evening to have Akorda Zubiondo explain to the best of her ability what the BBC announcer was saying in his plummy accent. What riveted their attention was news about the stirring victories and occasional setbacks of the British Expeditionary Force in Spain under General Blair.

Akorda was one of the señoritas who had volunteered to accompany almost 4,000 children on the elderly, very overcrowded cruise-liner *Habana* on their journey from Bilbao to Southampton, a month after the Germans carpet-bombed to a blackened husk on market day most of the town of Guernica. Venerated by the Basques, Guernica was where they had sited their fledgling parliament. Akorda graduated as a teacher of English a week before all schools in the Basque Country closed as a safety measure.

The girls' hosts here at Kellstone Abbey, Lord and Lady Hensley, often joined Akorda and the girls for the evening news. The Hensleys were Socialists, hence the offer of their home as a "colony" until the rebel generals and Franco's Fascist and Nazi allies could be thoroughly thrashed. Thanks to connections, Richard Hensley was more in the know than most people, and he'd been amazed how politically aware the majority of the children were, even those as young as nine, when they first arrived on his doorstep. These "victims of a conflict they could scarcely comprehend," to quote one newspaper a year since, were very well versed in who Mussolini and Hitler were, and the French Prime Minister Léon Blum, and Churchill and Eden and the War Minister Duff Cooper. There'd been endless political debate back home in the Basque towns before and even while the bombs rained.

The other day, 13-year-old Josefina received a letter from her cousin of the same age, Esteban, who'd been sent to a colony at a sanatorium, disused until then, in a wilderness called Northumberland where bedtimes came early and baths were an obsession. Josefina had written to her cousin happily about Kellstone Abbey, to the extent that happiness was possible, and Esteban was now thinking of running away from his sanatorium, but could he find Kellstone and would he be allowed to stay?

María Teresa asked, "Esteban's the one who shrieked *We aren't Gypsies!* when we got to the big camp?"

"No, that was his kid brother Palmiro."

The first emergency camp on a farmer's fields had been a sea of tents, the piles of straw inside intended to stuff mattresses although at first the straw appeared to be the entire bedding. Most of the children came from highrise flats in industrial cities. After the horrid sea-sickness during the storm in the Bay of Biscay, a tent resembling a pig sty in a damp field had been the final straw for a little'un from Bilbao.

María Teresa still had nightmares about bombs and incendiaries tumbling from the Junkers 52s of the Condor Legion as those trundled like trams through the sky, and the vicious strafing by Heinkel 51 fighters. Some nights she would walk in her sleep to the French windows of the lounge in Kellstone Abbey and cry out at the phantoms she saw, the heavens black with cruciform planes ushering the end of the world.

"I don't think Sir Richard could possibly let Esteban stay here," María Teresa told Josefina, "even if your cousin steals a bicycle and has enough food and the police don't stop him on the way here, which might take him *days*, sleeping in fields. One boy among all us girls. That wouldn't do!"

"How about if Esteban behaves really badly so they decide to transfer him to *wherever* else?" persisted Josefina. "The way Laureana was transferred?"

Laureana, who was precocious, had scared girls at her previous colony with wild talk about *rape*. For a while here likewise, until Laureana calmed down thanks to lots of attention from Señorita Akorda and the beneficent atmosphere of the abbey.

Whatever *rape* was exactly. Something painful, dirty, and violent that Franco's Moroccan Moors, ruthless Rif tribesman, did to helpless girls to celebrate conquering a town and to terrorise the survivors. From time to time fear gripped all the children at what might have happened to their families prior to the intervention by the British Expeditionary Force.

"Well now," said María Teresa, "the Committee would never send a boy here, even if Esteban begged. Besides, isn't his little brother at that same sanatorium? Your cousin has a duty to look out for his brother."

"Esteban doesn't like his brother much. He calls him Stinky."

"That makes no difference, Josefina. You shouldn't have told Esteban how lovely it is here."

Once upon a time Kellstone Abbey had been a monastery, until the English king Enrique VIII suppressed the Catholic Church and gave the place to one of his cronies who tore it down and used the stones to build himself a very fine manor house. Around the mansion, lawns that were now raggily grazed by sheep gave way to extensive woodlands fringing serene little lakes where swans and ducks swam. Monarchs had stayed in the Royal Bedrooms which the Hensleys now occupied, while the girls shared a score of bedrooms, each graced with a bath. The attic floor housed the redoubtable cook, Mrs Tucker, and several live-in employees from the nearby village as well as a tutor, Mrs Eagleton, who had taught English in Barcelona before she was widowed by a street accident.

Meals, taken in a grand hall with a gallery for minstrels, had to conform to the ten shillings per week which the government allowed the Basque Children's Committee to spend, but extra eggs were plentiful. Hundreds of books, many bound in old leather, lined a library, these days the schoolroom. The whole draughty building cried out for repairs and renovations, though the corridors were grand for running and sliding along, and the grounds for rambling, so long as the day was dry, while collecting small logs which two local fellows sawed up from plentiful fallen branches, to be fed to the hot-water boiler in the basement. In a courtyard the girls practised Basque dances accompanied by Señorita Akorda on an accordion, a spare borrowed from local Morris dancers; every weekend a wheezing bus took a party of the girls around the county to perform to raise funds. Akorda's name had nothing to do with accordions except for the fact that she could play the Basque diatonic button version, the trikiti, the 'hell's bellows' as reactionary priests disparaged it; adapting had been easy enough for her nimble fingers.

"My name," she had told Mrs Eagleton, "may signify memory. Or maybe *home* – houses in villages near Vizcaya are called akorda together with the name of the family. But akorda might also mean *stony ground.*" Now that war had come and she was in exile, would seed ever fertilise that ground? This wasn't a very suitable thought.

At first the girls had been puzzled at what sort of socialist Sir Richard was, and thought he must be a revolutionary who had expropriated the previous denizen of this abbey which wasn't an abbey, at the same time, somehow, as taking over his title of Lord. The girls themselves had imbibed socialism with their mothers' milk. Back at that first big camp, arguments and even fisticuffs had broken out between socialist kids and communist kids and anarchist kids and the pious kids who wanted an independent religious Basque nation. So here at Kellstone Abbey all the children were socialist.

Esteban's unhappiness obviously preyed upon Josefina's mind, especially since she realised how she herself was partly responsible for that misery by telling her cousin too enthusiastically about Kellstone Abbey, bragging without thinking of the consequences.

Still, maybe Sir Richard could do *something* for Esteban?

The very first item on the news was that General Blair had sustained a shrapnel wound in his throat when a lone Messerschmitt 109 had emptied its fuselage bomb rack near to Blair's mobile headquarters in its attempt to escape from pursuing British Hawker Hurricanes. General Blair was already recovering well and could speak quietly. The BEF's thrust to relieve the seige of Madrid continued unaffected, encountering moderate resistance.

The girls, at first anxious, applauded.

"*That,*" drawled Sir Richard afterwards, Mrs Eagleton translating, "was a rather fine piece of propaganda. Blair himself might have had a hand."

Mrs Eagleton interrupted. "I don't understand how Blair being injured can have anything *fine* about it!"

"Consider. We aren't reluctant to announce his injury, along with believable details. Since the German plane was alone, this is merely a rogue accident. *Alone*, note, as if there's only one of them left out of maybe a squadron, and that one running away. A Condor Legion German, scared by our Hurricanes – thank God and Lord Beaverbrook's pressure that those got into production quickly. Even so, I happen to know that those German 109s can normally out-fly our Hurricanes easily purely as fighters. Adding a loaded bomb rack of course slows the 109s somewhat."

"So the Messerschmitt may in fact have got away afterwards?"

Sir Richard wagged a finger. "The news doesn't actually say the German pilot was shot down; it merely implies so. Since Hitler still maintains the pretence that all his pilots and ground forces are volunteer advisers accompanying equipment leased to Franco, the Nazi government can't even comment."

"But we're being out-flown?" Mrs Eagleton was a devil for accuracy, which was good in a teacher, and angular besides, as regards her face and her stance. "And what does *moderate* resistance mean?"

"It may well be, my dear," said Lady Hensley, "that we have something rather nippier than a Messerschmitt in the wings! That's to say, in the *theatrical* sense of wings –" But Sir Richard shifted his finger to his lips.

"How," ventured Akorda, "can General Blair 'have a hand' in the news if his throat is injured?"

"By scribbling." Sir Richard mimed writing in the air. "Odd chap, that Blair! Did I ever mention he and I were at Eton at the same time?"

"*No...*" and Akorda explained in English for the benefit of whoever amongst the Basque girls was following: "Eton is a school for the sons of the rich. In England these expensive private schools are called *public* schools. Much in England is not rational, for example the spelling or the pronouncing of hundreds of words."

Several girls, who understood this all too well, laughed delightedly.

"The tough dough made me cough," piped up Carmen Etxarte.

"No Carmen, you still get *cough* wrong," said Mrs Eagleton before proceeding to nuance Akorda: "In fact public schools such as Eton are ancient. Before them, apart from church and monastery schools the only teaching was by tutors to individual rich boys at home. Consequently, gathering twenty or thirty rich boys together in a central place *was* public education."

"Blair wasn't a rich boy," Sir Richard said. "He had a scholarship."

"*Una beca*," supplied Mrs Eagleton.

"So he and I didn't normally mix," Sir Richard went on. "Though it was difficult to miss Blair entirely, him being so tall. You might say he *stood out* on Salisbury Plain when we were doing OTC."

"That's Officer Training Corps," supplied Lady Hensley. "Public school boys need to learn to use guns."

"In case of a people's revolution?" asked Akorda.

"Not exactly. Though of course there *was* the General Strike... but that happened when Richard was already at Magdalen. That's the Oxford college. Pronounced *Maudlin* in Oxford and Cambridge, because they think they're special. Everywhere else people say *magdalena*. Likewise the river Thames isn't called the Thames while flowing through Oxford; it's called the Isis, after an Egyptian goddess."

Carmen frowned. "But *magdalena* is a cake, not a college..."

"Never mind that for the moment, dear girl," said Mrs Eagleton. "Sir Richard, you were saying about Blair and the OTC?"

"Blair was a bit of a mystery as to what he thought, because maybe he didn't yet know what he thought. I heard he took some esoteric theology book to Salisbury Plain to study, though he seemed not to believe in a God... well, most of us were confirmed at Eton, but that was the done thing. Of course for him the *Catholic* church was a dictatorship plain and simple..."

"At least the Basque bishops supported the Republic," said Akorda, pursing her lips with disdain for bishops as a category.

"That bit of support from a few bishops wasn't unimportant," Sir Richard said didactically though a shade confusingly as regards the double negative, "considering that Blum risked possible civil war in France, Catholics versus Socialists, by insisting on supplying artillery to the Spanish Republic. Nor were the French general staff exactly delighted! Of course Hitler rubbed his hands with glee and kept quiet, because the artillery came from the Maginot line, but nowadays Hitler isn't quite so happy... I do remember Blair telling someone he bought his first gun over the counter when he was ten. A Saloon Rifle, that's what it was. Good at short range."

"Any schoolboy could *buy* a rifle?"

"Akorda," continued Sir Richard, "Blair was of a certain class. Local people knew his father was in the Burma Imperial Police. To become a policeman in Burma you needed to pass an examination in Latin and Greek, consequently you were a gentleman. I did run into Blair a few times later on. Apparently his father had hoped Blair would follow in his own footsteps, but Blair's mother feared the climate out East might wreck her boy's health, being as how his bronchial tubes were poor; and Mother prevailed. With grave reservations Blair chose to go for an army commission and he found he liked the life well enough, even though he was beginning to think politically and was risking his hand at some journalism, strictly under pseudonyms of course, about the bad things he saw coming, using trusted friends as go-betweens with editors because a serving officer shouldn't express political opinions publically... Our Eric Blair did have a deep vein of the dictatorial about him as well as being sensitively sorry for the oppressed and distrusting power. Went well with his upper-crust Etonian drawl." Sir Richard winked, since he shared the same accent.

"Maybe *authoritarian* is a better word than dictatorial, my dear," suggested Lady Hensley, "considering what we think about demagogues and dictators?"

At that moment Josefina put her hand up. "Please, Mister Richard, can you help my cousin...?"

In fact they were to hear General Blair's voice on the radio only a couple of evenings later from the Spanish front, wherever exactly that was.

"Fellow Britons, fellow believers in freedom," came a soft staccato croak, which nevertheless conveyed sublime calm and power, as if the very best kind of big brother were invisibly by one's side, "our British Expeditionary Force of heroes is gaining by the day in giving a lesson to the dark forces of dictatorships. A well-deserved and veritable caning! Our praiseworthy preferences for peace after the miseries of the first war were great, yet in recent years wise minds knew that something had to be done, and now by God we are doing so!" The repetition of the Ps seemed to associate Blair personally with peace.

"To have peace," the voice continued, "we must sometimes have war – and this cannot be done without much bloody sweat on the part of all decent folk, thus it is only fitting that I myself should have contributed a little such personally three days ago – yet today I particularly wish to single out Rifleman Albert Jones from Cardiff who is being recommended for the Military Cross after single-handedly storming a rebel machine-gun position despite sustaining serious, though not fatal, wounds..."

Afterwards, Sir Richard said, "Mind you, Léon Blum got away with intervention by the skin of his teeth!"

"*Por los pelos*," interpreted Mrs Eagleton for the benefit of girls who never before had skin on their teeth. 'By the hairs' made a lot more sense.

"Got away with?" queried Akorda. "He stole...?"

Drat the English for all their phrasal verbs! They imagined their language was easy because they favoured short words, but one teeny verb such as *get* could be followed by a whole blackboard of pronouns and could end up meaning anything at all. Get up to, get by on, get on with – two different meanings to *that* one...

"No, Akorda, stealing was Stalin's plan, under the guise of assisting the Republic. When it got out that –"

Got out...?

"When it became known," supplied Mrs Eagleton.

"– yes, became known that the Russians would sell war materials if the Republic transferred most of its gold reserves to Moscow at *half the international value* until the gold got used up – Robert Vansittart's spies, I mean diplomats, found that one out – well, the Republic sent *all of its gold* to Paris, and that tipped the balance – not least since Spain had the fourth largest gold reserves in the world!"

"I've some very nice news," Lady Hensley chipped in to announce. "Two weeks on Saturday we'll all go by bus to Oxford, and you'll be able to dance on the lawn in the cloisters," and she glanced for assistance to Mrs Eagleton.

"Claustros," said that lady. "Almost the same word. Not everything is so different."

"Well then, in the claustros at *Maudlin*. Richard's old college. He asked the President personally."

"But," said Akorda, "you have a Prime Minister and a King, not a President."

Lady Hensley laughed merrily. "Most Oxford colleges have Masters as their heads, but a few have Presidents, and one has a Warden. All the thirty or so colleges govern themselves, consequently there isn't any one *place* you can say is the University of Oxford. Our American friends often get confused."

"So do I," confessed Mrs Eagleton.

"Also, Oxford students aren't called students, they're called undergraduates."

"And the Fellows aren't teachers, they're *dons*."

A good Spanish word.

"In *los claustros*," María Teresa asked in horror, "will *monjes* watch us dance?"

"Why should there be monkeys? Granted there's a deer park inside *Maudlin*, but the place isn't a zoo. Girls, the workers from the steel and car factories, as well as students, will come to see you."

"Will those workers be Socialists or Communists or Anarchists?" asked Akorda.

"Bless me, I've no idea."

On the appointed Saturday, all of the girls except for a couple who'd come down with upset tummies, piled into the ricketty old bus along with Akorda and Mrs Eagleton, bound for Oxford. Mrs Tucker would look after the disappointed duo whose misfortunes couldn't have anything to do with her cookery, otherwise all of the girls would be rushing to the toilet. Probably those two ate some filthy fungus they found in the woods. Sir Richard and his wife proceeded ahead in his Riley Sprite two-seater; they'd be lunching in college with a politically friendly history Fellow who'd helped to appease the head gardener regarding foreign brats prancing on his most prized lawn.

The bus grumbled and creaked along for over an hour before finally disgorging the girls at Oxford's Gloucester Green bus station, till quite recently a cattle market. Patriotic Union flags hung as bunting, and delightfully some ikurriña flags, red field with a white cross and a green St Andrew's cross symbolising the sacred oak tree of Guernica which the Condor Legion had failed to incinerate. The girls, in their long white banded skirts and red pinafores, cheered.

A small Salvation Army band struck up, to lead the way to Maudlin College, consequently Mrs Eagleton needn't worry any more about remembering the litany of *George Street, Cornmarket, The High*, as she and Akorda led the crocodile. Shoppers clapped.

Grand sandstone edifices lined much of the High Street as it curved to bring into view the massive turreted tower of Maudlin. A crowd greeted the procession of girls as they reached the gatehouse, to be met by Sir Richard and Lady Hensley and a chubby chap wearing a scarlet and grey gown, looking like some cardinal. Amidst their families, some workers waved red flags, others the flag of the Republic, red, yellow, and purple, watched with stern disapproval by several men in dark suits wearing bowler hats. Elegantly dressed fresh-faced undergraduates, some in blazers and boaters, milled about. They must have come up early.

"*¡Bienvenidas!*" proclaimed the chap, oops don, in the gown to the girls; then, making a megaphone with his hands, he called out to the crowd, "I say: nobody will be admitted to College carrying any political symbols. We are here today simply to enjoy the dancing of these brave young refugees displaced by war, and to give generously towards their upkeep and the good work of the Basque Children's Committee. The Bulldogs will confiscate any flags."

"*Buldogs?*" queried Akorda, who could see none anywhere, nor conceive how even the best-trained dogs could confiscate anything.

"Those chaps in the bowler hats," Sir Richard told her quickly.

"Wearing *sombreros de hongo*," supplied Mrs Eagleton.

"The university police," said Sir Richard.

The quadrangle of lawn within the cloisters was a striped wonder of apple-green and emerald that might have been cut with nail scissors, surrounded on all sides by mullioned arches beneath mullion-windowed rooms, above which gargoyles jutted, crowned by crenellations from which stone finials rose high, partly hiding the sloping slate roofs.

"*Es un puto monasterio*," hissed Laureana, but friends hushed her.

A burly presumed head gardener in baggy trousers and a waistcoat, sleeves rolled up, scrutinised from under a flat cap the innocent flat white footwear of the girls, an uprooted KEEP OFF THE GRASS sign tucked under his arm reproachfully. He needn't worry too much: for decency there'd be no high leaps in the girls' dances. Presently the arches became crowded with spectators, town mixing amicably enough with gown. Soon Akorda struck up on her squeezebox for a *mutxikoak*, an ancestor dance in a circle...

The incident happened after another five delightful dances followed by a choral song. As the sound of the accordion died away, this time with a soft clear clarinet tone, to applause, a shout of *Get back 'ere, you!* pursued a body dodging its way nimbly through the crowd behind the mullions, alternating with *Beg pardon, Sir, Ma'am*, as a bowler-hatted Bulldog strove to keep up.

Through the stone gateway which was the only access to the lawn erupted a ragged urchin with a huge mop of brylcreemed black hair, straw and stray feathers entangled in it, who came to a sudden halt, enchanted.

"Josefina!" he cried out, stepping forward on to the sward in bare feet.

"Esteban!" exclaimed Josefina, wide-eyed.

As the Bulldog in his big black shoes, *which might even be hob-nailed*, beg-pardoned his way through the blazers and dresses crowding that gateway and advanced purposefully on to the turf, the head gardener launched himself forward, ignoring the bare-footed lad, veritably growling at the Bulldog while brandishing the KEEP OFF THE GRASS sign.

This confrontation allowed Esteban to reach his cousin, who hugged him.

"What have you done, Josefina?!" exclaimed Akorda.

"I... I only wrote him a letter... saying we were coming... to Oxford... to dance... in a college with a name that isn't said the way it's spelled..." And Josefina burst into tears, the enormity of her indiscretion becoming clear to her.

"And Esteban could find a town like Oxford, even if he could never find Kellstone Abbey!"

"I'm sorry I interrupted you," piped up Esteban in Basque, "but that angry man was chasing me..."

"You look like a scarecrow," said Akorda.

At that moment blessedly some undergraduates raised a cheer, triggering applause all around the cloisters. Even so, when the girls trooped off the grass back through the gateway, since their performance had now evidently reached a natural conclusion, the Bulldog arrested Esteban with an iron grip on the lad's arm.

Thus Esteban missed the picnic of egg and cress sandwiches accompanied by lemonade on a much vaster lawn reached through a narrow stone passageway, fallow deer grazing in their railed park nearby.

"Behold," declared Lady Hensley as she presided, "not a monkey in sight! If we exclude one naughty and now departed boy..."

Sir Richard's gowned Don soon achieved the release of Esteban.

What to do with the lad? Word had spread quickly. Sir Richard felt obliged to refuse the charitable offer from the Socialist Workers Anti-Fascist War Committee (whose members had waved those flags) to house the boy in a family close to the Pressed Steel factory – much too politically provocative. After some telephoning, Esteban was placed as a temporary measure in the Basque colony at Witney, famed for its woollen blankets which came from the thousands of local sheep, and a dozen miles closer to Kellstone Abbey than Oxford city was. The returning bus would drop him off there; so at least Esteban was able to spend a little more time on the way with Josefina.

Come the Monday, as well as celebrating the Basque dances in Maudlin, the *Oxford Mail* featured a runaway ragamuffin story, provoking a letter in the Tuesday edition harrumphing about bicycle-thieving ingrates. 'Blair's War' of intervention wasn't to everyone's liking, opponents ranging all the way from idealistic pacifists and pragmatic appeasers right through to Oswald Mosley's blackshirts whose admiration for the Third Reich was extravagant and (one hoped) ridiculous. By Tuesday evening a right-wing Tory M.P. was asking in Parliament why those refugees children hadn't *already* been repatriated, if the campaign of the British Expeditionary Force was going so dashed well apart from minor reverses? Well, the Francophobe Duchess of Atholl pitched in, and the red squire Cripps, although in the Lords the Marquis of Bute called again for a halt to intervention; that bastard had sold off half of Cardiff to fund the rebel generals, and he wasn't the only supporter of Franco amongst the great and the good in Britain and in America too.

On the Thursday evening, to the nation's surprise, General Blair contributed by radio in a jerky rasp.

"Fellow Britons, I recoil from war at the same time as I engage in it, for war can corrupt those who wage it – but we are putting our very souls, our free unblemished souls, into this crusade against dictatorship, and failure is inconceivable." Then, rather than singling out a British soldier as hero of the day, he whispered hoarsely:

"It has come to my attention that a Spanish lad of twelve named Esteban, or in plain English Stephen, bravely and ingeniously made his way almost two hundred and fifty miles through what to him is a strange and foreign country, our England, to rejoin his beloved sister, who by an oversight was placed far away from him in one of the refuges we provided." A self-deprecating cough. "Stephen's sense of geography may well be rather better than my own…"

The jerky rasp continued. "Stephen's is the sort of pluck and perseverance that inspires our troops every single day in our fight to restore freedom, democracy, and decency to all of Spain so that ordinary families can live in peace and at least moderate prosperity without fear."

"But I am not Esteban's *sister*," said Josefina.

Sir Richard grinned. "Sister sounds better as propaganda. Or maybe Blair simply made a mistake."

Akorda looked mischievous. "A *blare* means a loud sound, yes? Like the blast of a trumpet?"

"With a different spelling, dear," said Mrs Eagleton.

"So the General could have signed his political pieces in newspapers as by *Mr Blare* with the different spelling."

"Clever idea, Akorda," said Sir Richard, "but that wasn't Blair's pen-name. Now what was it, what was it? Oh yes, he took the name of the river that flows through Ipswich where his parents' house was. The river Orwell. He called himself George Orwell."

In the Spring of 1939, while the British army was still busy assisting the rescued Spanish Republic to repair itself and root out the last rebels, the forces of the Nazi Reich swiftly smashed an armoured, air-supported corridor fifty kilometres wide through a plucky if puny Poland as access for Hitler's victorious invasion of Russia while all remained quiet on his western frontiers. Soon the Führer's voice sounded from Siegfriedstadt, formerly Leningrad, and a fortnight later from the ruins of Moscow.

George Orwell is one of the first writers I became really interested in, while at school during the 1950s. I distinctly remember buying the Penguin paperback of Nineteen Eighty-four, *as well as exactly where I found it on the shelves of a stationers and bookshop in North Shields, a town mostly benighted – although its Public Library remarkably had hardbacks of quite a lot of recent SF such as Bester's* Tiger! Tiger! *of 1956 mixed in with the mainstream from Jane Austen to Emile Zola. I followed up by reading all the rest of Orwell's distinctly melancholy novels,* Coming Up for Air, Keep the Aspidistra Flying... *Being adolescent, I liked melancholy, and life in general didn't seem to have changed much since Orwell wrote those books.*

At the time I read Homage to Catalonia *with less interest since I was pre-political. I came back to that book, and to Orwell's life in general, with much more awareness after moving to the north of Spain decades later and also coming across a 2007 book by Adrian Bell entitled* Only for Three Months *about Basque children in Britain as refugees from the Spanish Civil War. The Basque Country is about three hours' drive on the motorway from Gijón in Asturias, where I now live, though in the late 1930s that might have been twelve. The miners of Asturias managed to chase off one of Franco's warships from Gijón (using dynamite and festival rockets?), but the Spanish Republic was doomed and right-wing dictatorship gripped Spain for almost the next 40 years. Could things have turned out differently if Britain had acted otherwise during the 1930s?*

THE NAME OF THE LAVENDER

It was in Genoa that Immy and I first became aware of the Catania Calendar Conspiracy. Genoa, a city of ups and downs which Escher might have designed, at the far end of Italy from the Sicilian city.

Being keen on plants, I make a point of visiting botanic gardens. On our first morning in Genoa, in the towering labyrinth of narrow lanes of the old city, we bought a map and stopped at a café to study it, the fastest way to get a feel for a town. I found an *Orto Botanico* marked: a small green area surrounding the rectangular grey of what must be plant houses. Strangely this didn't feature on the map app of our tablet, which Immy took care of. So Immy asked the waiter how best to arrive at the Orto Botanico. Italians can usually understand her Spanish. The waiter conferred with some elderly card-players, igniting a storm of controversy mostly in Genovese dialect, some of which she could actually follow, whispering to me thus:

"There's no such place – !"

"Never heard of it since I was a boy – !"

"There *is* a garden, it just isn't easy to find – !"

Naturally this piqued our curiosity as investigators.

Unaccountably Google Maps was no help, so we followed the paper map, a convoluted journey on foot which was almost foiled when pigeons mobbed us. That was near the enormous Albergo dei Poveri, a half-derelict hospital-refuge for the poor, where a crazy old woman was feeding those birds in a tiny park.

What a mad clatter of two hundred birds around our heads as the crone with her bag of seeds screeched at us to *go away!* Immy is averse to the point of allergy to animals with wings; already I could see a rash appearing on her cheek as if she had been slapped. To Immy, all birds are savage dinosaurs, diminished in size but upgraded to flight capability. A cute Christmas card of a Redbreast perched on a gate causes her the heebie-jeebies: *Look out, here comes Tyrannosaurus Robin!* Nor was she pleased about the screaming green parakeets flying wild near that micro park; at least those kept out of the way. (Immy wasn't too fond of the seaside, either, asserting that an undertow had tried to drown her when she was a girl.)

The pigeons might have beaten us back. We might have been compelled to spend several days in our hotel while I applied camomile lotion to Immy's face – she's vain about her appearance in public. But promptly I caught her hand and hauled her up a nearby flight of steps, through a little tunnel, then up a steep alley into a narrow street until Immy felt safe beneath blue sky. We paused while I smeared some salve on her cheek, then we realized that almost by chance we had arrived at the half-open gates of the Orto Botanico.

This being Genoa, the garden occupied several levels, and no one seemed to be about on any. Up top, a long greenhouse was whitewashed against the fierce sun come summertime. We gazed down from a railed terrace through the roof of a lower greenhouse where protective whitewash and netting had failed enough to reveal the ghosts of golden barrel cacti. *Echinocactus grusonii* – one should be precise about plants that are so emblematic. Further below sprawled a long rectangle of mostly dead weeds, plus some yuccas and desolate shrubs. Dried-up leaves and dirt were everywhere. These gardens were very neglected. A long line of large terracotta bowls stood empty as if begging. Where we stood up top, we were level with sixth-floor pastel apartments a few hundred metres distant across a deep narrow valley. Mistily beyond, a great port: highspeed white passenger boats moored, huge as aircraft carriers; tall blue cranes to lift containers.

Where *was* everyone? We found an open door and navigated our way past giant ferns whose grotesquely knobbly trunks bore masses of shaggy wool and broad snapped quills from which there unrolled to the height of a metre and more obscene thick chameleon tongues coated in masses of cobwebby golden hair, encysting at their rolled-up tips what looked like rings of peeled quails' eggs. Intricate plants require intricate description.

Plants, no matter how strange, never bothered Immy. "These could be prehistoric," she said. "Time has left them behind." This proved to be a telling observation!

We passed carnivorous pitcher plants hanging over a lily pool harbouring mats of green scum. Next, pots of so-called lilies that seemed more like giant green turnips; out of a hole in each a long tendril crawled as if in search of moisture. Dust was thick on the floor.

"I think we're on to something here," I told her.

Finally we navigated our way down into the bone-dry cactus and succulent house.

That was when a human being at last popped into view, a trimly bearded, preoccupied fellow in his early forties.

He must have overheard Immy and me talking in English. "Ah, you are the first visitors here since...," and he glanced at his watch as if it might tell time in months or years, so that Immy squeezed my hand in excitement.

"...I don't remember exactly when," he resumed. "Cacti only need water once a year. Nine of us botanists used to care for the plants. Now there's only me, and a woman who sweeps. The best I can do is retard the death of the garden. If you'll excuse me, I have so many things to do..."

"Where did the other gardeners disappear to?" Immy demanded.

"In the natural scheme of things two died and three retired..."

"And in the *unnatural* scheme?"

He gestured, sunwards, in a southerly direction, using the sign of the horns to do so, and hissed, "*Sicily*. Three expert gardeners were seduced away to Sicily."

I wasn't sure if he was even aware of using the *corna* gesture. He'd been cuckolded of his former companions, in a sense, but that gesture of index and little finger pointed while the thumb clasps the two middle fingers also wards off evil.

"It was the last straw for our garden..."

"Where in Sicily?" I asked. "A rival botanical garden?"

"Oh, Catania, next to Mount Etna *has* a botanical garden, but... it isn't that. I don't want to talk about this. I'm too busy. You'd never understand; and why should you? Leave me in peace, amidst this decay." So saying, he made himself scarce. A youngish fellow, of a sudden seemingly old before his time, robbed of the man-years this garden needed to thrive.

Immy and I exchanged very significant glances.

Little did that Genovese gardener suspect that Immy and I are funded by the Conspiracy Investigation Agency, which isn't the better known CIA but a junior cousin. *Funded* is how we prefer to think about this, rather than *paid*. In the labyrinthine hierarchies of American 'Intelligence' much money sloshes around. IARPA is the department of *Intelligence Advanced Research Projects Activity*, which comes under the Director of National

Intelligence of the USA, usually a 4-star military man who comes under the US President himself. Within IARPA is a 'Metaphor Program' established by its "Office of Incisive Analysis", which fits in between IARPA's 'Office of Smart Collection' (collection of info in a smart, not a scattershot way) and its 'Office of Safe and Secure Operation', nifty categories, eh? Within the Metaphor Program nestles our own mini-CIA, which investigates conspiracies more arcane than vulgar bomb plots and the like.

The Metaphor Program exploits the fact that metaphors pervade human language and reveal underlying beliefs and worldviews. The root of all language is metaphor, noises representing a mother, a tree, a rock (to be a bit simplistic). Due to the huge volume of data constantly being vacuumed up electronically every minute of every day from all over the globe, only computers can analyse incisively. Yet computers are stupid at metaphors. For the sake of a secure American homeland, and to foil the Al-Qaeda sort of conspiracy against that homeland, computers must learn to understand metaphorical thinking. *Anything* might be grist to the mill, consequently fresh perspectives are always welcome within IARPA; thus initiatives such as our mini-CIA are given a long leash. Dark money devoted to unearthing and interpreting symbolic mysteries is well-spent, say I!

Most of us investigators have backgrounds in semiotics, iconography, symbolism, and allied topics, and most of us are European due to the dire example of Dan Brown. Dan Brown's expert upon such topics, the so-called Professor of Religious Symbology at Harvard, can't seem to parlare any foreign language, which realistically must present major difficulties as regards his field of studies, him presumably being unable to read essential texts except by using Google Translator. The founder of my and Immy's CIA, General Ham (for Hamish) Henderson, of Scottish descent, took Dan Brown to heart when mostly recruiting 'native' investigators who can hablar or sprechen effectively when necessary. Immy told me she had been in H2's office and seen a paperback of *The Da Vinci Code* impaled to his desk by a bayonet driven through the book deep into the cherry wood.

Personally I'm a Brit (Richard Danvers – *not* Dick, please), but my mother is French, while Immy is Spanish, her name being her own version of the short form of Inmaculada, signifying stainless chastity. Immy isn't chaste, but quite a lot of religious Spanish mothers hopefully call their daughters names such as Immaculate, Purification, and whatnot.

Since this is fairly common in Spain, you don't get bullied on account of it in the schoolyard.

Aside from our specialities, and our all-important *instincts*, us investigators share a healthy skepticism. Necessarily that skepticism often challenges consensus reality, the illusion that the world is merely what we see upon the surface, or what history books record, or what pops up in the news. (Even in my thoughts I favour the American spelling of skeptic since sceptic reminds me of septic.)

The game was afoot, so we promptly flew from Genoa to Catania, travelling down the mountainous spine of Italy then passing along the Strait of Messina over small volcanic islands, some inhabited, narrow roads half-circling the base of some cones from one fishing village to the next, us musing the while about what kind of *botanical* conspiracy we might find in that land of the mafia, yet *not* in a botanical garden.

"Cocaine?" surmised Immy. "Opium poppies? No, it can't be anything as banal as drugs."

No sooner had we checked into a modern hotel in the centre of Catania and gone out for a stroll than we came across the Bellini Garden, *Giardino Bellini*, named for the city's most famous son, the composer of *Norma*, Norma being a Druid priestess as I recalled, which struck me as significant.

Even from the street, Via Etnea, we could see what was odd and remarkable.

Set into some lawn close to an elegant fountain presided over by a bust which must be of Vicenzo Bellini was a large clock with big hands; fair enough, mechanical. A few metres beyond, angled upon a grassy bank... was a large and prominent *calendar* made of *living plants*, correctly displaying the date in Italian. 30 Luglio 2012.

Once a day skilful gardeners must move those silvery-grey plants around to alter the date. Presumably they did so at midnight for greatest accuracy... '30 Luglio 2012' to '31 Luglio 2012' would be a fairly easy modification – but '31 Luglio to '1 Agosto' would take some nifty gardening; and just imagine the hectic shift from '31 Dicembre 2012' to '1 Gennaio 2013'!

"Come on, we've found it!" With Immy I strode towards that organic calendar. The plants, as I'd suspected, were cotton lavender, *Santolina chamaecyparissus*.

I was numbstruck. As every calendar should, this in the Bellini Garden must change every day, so that it was (or, rather, *is*) always *today* in Catania – as well as in the rest of Italy and in the rest of Europe, although not necessarily in America or Australia, depending upon how advanced today is, or alternatively isn't. Yet perhaps it was more quintessentially, more organically, *today* in Catania than elsewhere on Earth due to that calendar being composed of living plants rather than being based upon clockwork or electronics. That was my first insight, anyway.

And my second realisation was that a cult might well preside over this calendar, a sworn brotherhood dedicated to the task of sustaining the present day. A guild which needed recruits to maintain itself at adequate strength in case of calamities. For they must believe that if they failed in their duty… *What had they witnessed? What might they cause?*

They must have evidence for this… What if they ever adjusted the calendar *backwards*? Contrariwise, what if they advanced it forward by *more* than one single day? Here was something of cosmic, not merely local, significance.

Like many best-kept secrets, this one was hidden in plain sight.

"I suppose you recall," I said to Immy, "the Islamic idea that the entire universe recreates itself from moment to moment?"

"Whereas here," she replied, "this is on a day-to-day basis…"

She understood the significance immaculately well.

Our tablet informed us that the core of the garden was originally the work of an 18th century prince, who called it his 'Labyrint', a name with an esoteric hint to it. In the mid-19th the City Council bought the land from a descendant of the prince and expanded and embellished the area. No mention of exactly at what hour updating took place. Back at the hotel a middle-aged lady receptionist told us stoutly 'early every morning'. How early might 'early' be? "Four a.m.?" hazarded Immy. The lady shrugged. "Possibly."

The date change which I was really keen to observe was from one month to the next, a day hence – a golden opportunity, our coming to Catania almost at a month's end! – but this uncertainty meant that we needed to be sure of the hour beforehand, in other words crawl out of bed at three in the morning. So we took dinner in the hotel restaurant, of which only the signature Pasta à la Norma proved at all memorable (penne with bits of aubergine, ricotta and basil leaves). Then we went to our room and fucked to celebrate the confirmation of a conspiracy, after which Immy programmed her iPhone to wake us in good time.

Lo, by 3.45 a.m. when we gazed, still yawning, through the wrought iron gates by the faint light of a sinking crescent moon, the calendar was *already* updated to 31 Luglio.

"Definitely must happen at midnight..."

Immy nudged me, pointed, and I too noticed a monkish figure half concealed by a classical column off to our right, like some watchman or sentinel or some Gothic ghost. Or a statue.

After a day of research about local customs, punctuated by a siesta and a couple of hotel meals, we were alertly in position on Via Etnea by quarter to midnight, playing the role of lovers courting; and what we experienced when the day turned – or, more accurately, what we almost failed to experience – amazed us. Maybe you've seen on TV a pit-stop during a Formula One race where every fraction of a second is vital for changing the wheels. Exactly so! It was as if a sudden blurry whirlwind occurred in that one tiny area of the Bellini Garden. Casual passers-by might have noticed nothing at all – or may have averted their gaze, either wisely or discreetly, if they were privy to the situation.

Time became altered in two respects. One was the simple change of the day, from the old today to the new today. The other was more radical and transgressive. Here was Ninja gardening to a degree that was surely impossible unless time itself took a twist – and unless the actions, the dance, of those involved caused this to happen. Immy and I both gasped. *These guys were masters of time.*

We must obviously treat the assemblage of *Santolina chamaecyparissus* as a text, to determine what precisely this calendar signified.

"Day *per se* is a universal concept," I remarked to Immy as we walked back to the hotel.

She nodded. "– since all worlds rotate, even those which are rotation-locked as the Moon is locked to the Earth. Sensitivity to Day and Night is written in the genetic code of untold creatures – unless those happen to live below a certain number of fathoms deep in the sea. Daft conspiracy aficionados paid undue attention to the Mayan calendar as regards a supposedly prophesised year of doom." She winked at me, since we both knew that the Mayan calendar never implied doom; it was merely completing a cycle of megayears.

Here in Sicily a potentially far more subversive – or shall we say radical, *rooted* – calendar was advanced by the hand of man every midnight at the speed of prestidigitators, as if to synchronise the natural world itself.

"The Keepers of the Day," she murmured.

What a fine title she had just dreamed up for the élite guild of gardeners of Catania! *The Keepers of the Day*! This was the way we often worked, inspiredly. Within apparent nonsense we would discover sense.

Day, and *Date*: here's a potent ambiguity. Our speciality of Hermeneutics, which I'm almost tempted to describe as the Holy Office of Incisive Analysis (since we are in essence inquisitors), thrives on ambiguities.

We spent the day in reflection and research, plus a couple more siestas. Only a few dozen of us roving investigators world-wide, empowered to detect and plumb conspiracies; that's quite a privilege, as well as a responsibility! The Office of Incisive Analysis would be pleased with our work even if we proved to be wrong in our suspicions (which I doubted, after what we'd already witnessed) since we would at least have eliminated the possibility of a chronic conspiracy here in the land of the mafia (and of more than mafia?).

We absolutely had to eat somewhere else than the hotel. So, early that evening of the first of Agosto we ventured out at random – and rain began to fall torrentially, forcing Immy and I to take refuge at a solitary vacant table sheltered by a giant umbrella outside a café-bar in a narrow cobbled street quite near to Via Etnea.

The previous occupants – skinny husband, substantial wife, plump girl twins – had fled within from the mighty splashes, abandoning upon their plates the remains of *arancine*, those giant hand-grenades of rice, mince, and peas double-fried in golden breadcrumbs, beloved of Catanians. The interior of the café was crowded to the door. Fleeing along the alley, a newspaper wide open above her head, darted a glamorous young woman – bare tanned shoulders, long dark hair, faded blue jeans, high sandals with cork heels, rings of deep dark shadow around her eyes. Chivalrously I beckoned her beneath our umbrella, an invitation which she promptly accepted since puddles were becoming ponds.

A waiter called out from the doorway in our direction, and Immy ordered a bottle of Nero d'Avola, which should be dark purple, deep and warming, plus three glasses. Heroically the waiter complied within just a few minutes, managing to clear away the plates at the same time, shrugging off water like a seal.

Lucrezia proclaimed herself hesitantly to be an artist, a painter, the hesitance due more to her English than to diffidence, I felt. As soon as she found that Immy was Spanish, Lucrezia promptly switched to Castilian, and her eyes flashed as if lightning reflected in them, so that I cocked an ear for thunder, but I quickly realised that glitter on Lucrezia's eyelids accounted for the lustre. Evidently Lucrezia had come top in Spanish at her *liceo classico*, Spanish being easier for Sicilians than for other Italians, so she said, due to the Spanish having ruled her island for 400 years.

Out of Lucrezia's velvety black bag came an iPhone of the previous generation to Immy's, and soon we were seeing self-portraits of Lucrezia, variously sultry, smouldery, shouldery (i.e. somewhat scantily clad), and pensive, often with her head to one side so that her rich hair cascaded. This was a bit like viewing someone's Facebook photos, except done with brush and paint, at which she was certainly skilful… ah, but next there followed glamorous portraits of prosperous-looking women youngish, middling, and elderly. Lucrezia accepted commissions – this was how she made a living.

Since I understood – and maybe misunderstood – some of what Lucrezia said in Spanish, notwithstanding that Immy translated some of it, as did Lucrezia herself, who would also break into Italian, I'll adopt the Dan Brown convention that most people normally speak English all the time.

Lucrezia said, "I studied hard at Spanish better to understand the songs of Atahualpa Yupanqui…"

I must have looked blank, but her phone screen quickly wised me up to the deceased Argentinian folk musician. Basque mother, Communist Party, indigenous peoples, invited by Piaf to France et cetera.

"He was one of the fires of the world!"

Living quite close to Mount Etna might well cause such thoughts.

"One of the engines of existence!"

"There's what you might call another 'engine of existence' very close to here," I remarked, gesturing through the downpour in the direction of the Bellini Garden...

It wasn't really so odd that up until now Lucrezia had pretty much taken the calendar of cotton lavender for granted. Typical home town syndrome! What was so astonishing about a calendar of plants in a public garden? Compared with, just for example, an Argentinian guitarist who renamed himself after Inca kings! To which I respond: whatever is easily visible every day isn't truly seen. Immy and I could often perceive what people ordinarily failed to notice.

Recruiting local agents often proves valuable. Lucrezia was very willing to be initiated into our point of view. She even volunteered to show us around Catania the following day...

...by which time the black clouds had gone and the streets had dried up.

What admirable mushrooms were on sale from stalls in crowded lanes; how the whole place buzzed. Quite near a fishmarket where bunches of red roses, um, rose from the gaping mouths of the cut-off heads of swordfish upright upon their necks, a rushing shallow river of clean water appeared from beneath the side of a piazza, only to disappear a few metres further on underneath a low arch adorned with marble figures, two kneeling with conches upon their shoulders.

"A few rivers run under the city," explained Lucrezia. "No one knows where from, nor their courses..."

Presently we hiked through elegant baroque and rococo streets to Catania's railed Orto Botanico, mostly shady, a large temple-like building in the midst and a fine sun-drenched glimpse of cacti and succulents beyond. Lucrezia insisted we see the botanic garden to give us perspective, as she put it, though I'd have wanted to do so in any case.

And there was a mystery within!

On the steps of the temple, and beneath its portico and below the dense branches of trees, thronged leggy early-teen girls, mostly elfin although some were tubby, wearing bright fantastical skirts and blouses and in many cases long blue or pink hair. They milled around, or simply sat hugging their knees, admiring one another. A flock of punk flamingos.

"How strange," ventured Lucrezia.

Luckily Immy identified the semantics of the clothing. "It's a cosplay competition, costume play – Italian schoolgirls pretending to be Japanese schoolgirls pretending to be manga heroines!"

"I wouldn't wish to be here after dark," confided Lucrezia.

I imagined some kind of orgy of innocence. "Why?" I demanded. "*What will happen?*"

Lucrezia shrugged her bare brown shoulders. "Big mosquitoes."

Only after Lucrezia had left us on some unspecified business a couple of hours later, and Immy and I were having a beer in a café far from the botanic garden, did I exclaim, "Why, Proust, of course! The second volume of *In Search of Lost Time*."

"Remind me," said Immy. French novels weren't her strong point.

"In his novel Proust tries to recover days gone by, to turn back the calendar. The second volume is called *A l'ombre des jeunes filles en fleurs*, literally *In the Shade of Young Girls in Bloom*. Those schoolgirls were artificial flowers passing in and out of the shade. The cosplay was a masque, a costumed allegory that could almost have been arranged for our benefit."

"Arranged by the masters of the mystery, the Keepers of Day?" I couldn't tell if Immy was being ironic. "So how do they know about us?"

"We spied on them at midnight. Someone must have spotted us. And the *previous* night, remember that monk behind the column?"

"So what was the message of the masque?"

"I think it was to distract us, rather than being a warning, a hands-off... To attract us in the wrong direction, like bees by blooms, away from the Bellini Garden itself."

Immy patted my knee. "Some of those girls looked a bit too young to be pollinated. Though provocative, I grant. But Richard, it would take several weeks to arrange an event like that."

"And yet that's the symbolic import I get... *Weeks*, Immy, unless one can turn back time temporarily!"

"As a consequence of operating the calendar?"

"Suppose a cosplay already took place, and we were displaced to it..."

"Shall we go back, to see if it's still going on? What if no girls are in the garden any longer?"

I glanced at my watch. "They might have gone home by now in any case. No Immy, I think we need to protect ourselves, in case the conspiracy is as powerful as I suspect. Immy, geek the tab. Find something that combats *Santolina chamaecyparissus*!"

My very special Immy, better at searching than me, soon had an answer: *Phytophthora tentaculata* was a quasi-fungal microorganism that aggressively causes root and stalk rot in cotton lavender. A biological weapon, if need be.

"What we need from IARPA," I said, "is some sealed test tubes of corn meal agar doped with *Phytophthora tentaculata*. IARPA can source those from some US government laboratory and air-express them here to the hotel. It isn't as though we're requesting nerve gas."

"That could take days. I doubt if cotton lavender root-rot is high on the list of potential biowarfare agents."

"You're right. So in the short term we need something that *looks* like a serious threat." Even while Immy was sending a message, encrypted by the tablet, to Ham Henderson's metaphor office, my mind was racing. Test tubes with stoppers… a supplier of glassware to laboratories and schools…? could Lucrezia pretend to be a chemistry teacher? could Lucrezia revisit her *liceo classico*, if 'classico' included sciences?

Suddenly the answer came to me. An ingeniously simple answer. In my mind I was seeing a smart tobacconist's shop we'd passed during our guided tour around town.

Connoisseurs' cigars come loose in wooden boxes, and sometimes wrapped in cellophane or in aluminium tubes, but also in stoppered glass tubes! Perfect for the purpose.

Immy and I hastened to that tobacconist and soon had in our possession three substantial cigars in black-stoppered glass tubes. Imported from Mexico, the brand was Monte Cristo, a name of good augury. Perhaps to justify the price tag of 12 euros each, the stooped skeletal proprietor insisted on telling us that Monte Cristo was a blend of three Mayan tobaccos wrapped in Sumatran leaf. Mayas: those of the notorious calendar! Even more auspicious.

On our way back to the hotel, we bought some tubs of yellow jelly dessert and a copy of *Corriere della Sera*. A raid on the hotel restaurant yielded us suitable spoons and a knife. Up in our room I opened the pages of the newspaper upon the carpet, and we proceeded to unSumatra those 12-euro cigars and rip and crumble the Mayan tobaccos into very small pieces, spread wide to dry out if possible.

After celebratory sex and a siesta we mixed crumbled tobacco with the yellow jelly and spooned this carefully into the glass tubes before resealing them. The mixture looked sufficiently menacing. Into the inside pocket of my jacket went the three tubes of pretend pathogen. Then it was time to think about dinner. I phoned Lucrezia's iPhone in case she'd unearthed anything yet, but only got voicemail. So we decided to eat out at the same café-bar in that alley where we first met her, in case of lightning striking twice.

However, Lucrezia didn't pass by while we were eating our anchovy fishcakes, followed by sweet and sour rabbit, then lingering over a second bottle of yellow fruity Tenuta Rapitala Piano Maltese with its slight cyanide hint of bitter almonds. Claude Lévi-Strauss could have been interested in this.

When we returned to the hotel, an envelope was waiting addressed to both of us. We retired some way down the lobby to open the message, which surely must be from Lucrezia. Rather than returning our call, unaccountably she must have hurried to the hotel, consequently missing us.

Out came a printed photo of Lucrezia. But she was tied to a heavy old wooden chair, gagged, an expression of panic and appeal in her eyes which looked soot-rimmed like a panda's.

On the rear of the photograph, printed in red pencil: GIARDINO BELLINI FONTANA 23.00. That would refer to the big fountain near the main gate. Already it was 22.30; no time to be lost.

One of the great wrought iron gates stood ajar. The garden seemed deserted, while only sporadic traffic passed along Via Etnea. The crescent moon, slightly more swollen, wasn't due to set until 3.13 a.m, as we knew.

As we circled the basin of the fountain: "Careful, Immy, there's a *hole*." In the grass gaped a rectangular emptiness. Against the basin of the fountain a few metres further along leaned a metal lid covered in turf that it must have taken two muscular gardeners to heave.

Aha, stone steps led down steeply, no doubt to the mechanisms and plumbing of the fountain. Below in the darkness I could hear running water. Since we'd gone out to the café with darkness impending, I had in my side pocket the torch so useful when going for a pee during the night so as not to dazzle myself and trigger full wakefulness, nor disturb Immy. Squeezing the pump-action whirringly half a dozen times to work the dynamo, I whispered, "Maybe you should stay up here." Hadn't Immy once remarked, apropos the catacombs in Kiev, that she was distinctly averse to confined spaces?

"We do *not* split up," she said firmly. "Already Lucrezia has been abducted. You must never go into a cellar on your own."

So we descended, Immy's knees bumping my spine.

As soon as we both arrived on a surface of smooth damp rock, illumination swelled around us, rendering my torch beam irrelevant even as I was raising it to reveal...

...a cave that sloped upward, from a little river that ran briskly through; and half a dozen hooded men clad in robes like monks, though of dark green, and holding gardening tools, seated in a semi-circle on a level platform of rock beneath an enormous key implanted upside-down in the stone ceiling, a clockwork-style key such as would jut from an old-fashioned wind-up toy, of such size that it must take several of the monkish figures processing around in a circle to turn it; and amongst those men in their throne-chairs a *woman* was seated dressed in identical garb, except that cork-heeled sandals and the bottoms of blue jeans were plainly visible – Lucrezia, who wasn't tied up at all!

Strings of white fairy-lights secured here and there to the roof of this canted cavern provided the illumination, so that I thought for a moment: *Santolina's Grotto.*

"Elves wear green," said Immy. A moment later we heard a clang and a thump, which could only be that lid of metal and turf descending to seal us in.

Very cool and clammy, this cavern. Hence the thick robes? Rather than those being occult regalia? At our backs the subterranean river disappeared away underneath a smoothed lip of rock with a few inches clearance, its swift waters perhaps half a metre deep – waters which must have taken tens of thousands of years to carve out this descending cavern... which corresponded in the outside world to the rise of land upon which the calendar was set on a slope *above that great key planted here.*

Two of those monkish gardeners held forks, another a spade, the fourth and fifth billhooks. Wickedly menacing tools in present circumstances rather than merely emblematic of their occupations.

We'd been lured and trapped. Had Lucrezia been suborned *whilst* she was investigating on our behalf? Coaxed, threatened, blackmailed? Or was she here of her own accord, both bait and accomplice?

As the gardeners rose from their seats, clutching their lethal-looking tools, Lucrezia cocked her head and uttered a giggle, and I decided it may have been no coincidence that she happened along the alley on that rainy night!

I produced and brandished the three corked test tubes, and I shouted as though bellowing a conjuration: *"Phytophthora tentaculata! Phytophthora tentaculata!"*

Surely, being botanists, they would understand. Certainly they paused when I spoke the words, as if surprised.

Just in case not, I called out in English, "Kills roots of *Santolina*!" Then in French too. "Tue les racines!"

The gardeners, the Keepers of Day, consulted in whispers... then resumed their armed advance. What a fool I was! We were in a cavern. The roots of the Cotton Lavender were all safely above the ceiling of rock.

What I did next may have seemed crazy, but was the only way out. Pitching the test tubes at the Keepers by way of distraction and to empty my right hand – the torch being in my left hand – I hissed, "Take a deep breath!", seized Immy by the arm and promptly hurled us both backwards into the subterranean river.

The shock of the cold water was considerable. Quickly she and I were swept under the stone lip that drained the river from the cavern, my flashlight beam dancing crazily.

I'd calculated many factors in a trice. Judging by direction of flow, most likely this underground river was the same as debouched for a stretch of a dozen or so metres in the open air near the fishmarket before surging away underneath the low archway of the conch-bearers. Right now we were at the end of a hot summer, thus the flow should be at its minimum. During thousands of seasons the greater meltwaters of spring must have scoured out significantly more natural tunnel than was occupied by the present flow – hence there must be pockets, even entire long sections, of air to refill our lungs; nor should the rock be jagged to rip at us. Between the Bellini Garden and the open air of the conch-bearers was a distance of about a kilometre. I reckoned the flow of the water at about a metre per second. 4000 seconds to our destination; sixteen minutes or so. Surely we could survive the chill for that length of time, as well as the possibility of getting some water in our lungs. I'd need to be able to stagger erect without slipping and get a grip on the stone blocks of the channel as soon as we emerged into the light... of half-moonlight and doubtless street lamps and maybe the Cathedral illuminated.

I was buffeted and bumped as well as thoroughly soaked and sometimes submerged. Immy quickly pulled free of my hand, the better to protect and steer herself. My torch helped show us the best chances to breathe. Of a sudden the river was passing through arched masonry where it was easier to keep our heads above water – a sewer from Roman times, this must be! Salvation for us, for minute after minute! I rejoiced at this archeological serendipity.

"Bless the Romans!" I cried, to rally Immy. I thought that she might reply despite being preoccupied with survival, but just then the torch failed and a few moments later I banged my head in the darkness, which surely signalled the end of architecture and the resumption of natural sculpted rock. Dazed though I was, I grasped for the sensation of the next air space and thrust my head up in time to hear Immy desperately coughing out water nearby as we were both swept onward. Probably the speed of the river contributed to us not sinking, laden though our clothes had become. My torment, and doubtless Immy's, continued – half-drowned, reprieved, half-drowned again like victims of interrogation...

At long last I sensed dim light ahead. By now I'd begun to doubt the wisdom of my escape plan, for my lungs were bursting. I thought urgently, *hold on*.

The light brightened. Of a sudden I was out from underground, struggling to brake and brace myself and reach up into the city that opened up, uttering a cry of *Help!* Or was it *Aiuto!*? And conscious of another body banging into me, feebly clutching, threatening to push me onwards...

Fortunate for us that the citizens of Catania were fond of late night strolls *en masse* along their most elegant streets where cafés and bars remained open, and around the piazza where the baroque facade of the cathedral loomed, and by the fountain where a column rose, howdah-like, from the back of an elephant of pitted dark grey lava! Fortunate indeed that groups of youths and their girls were in our immediate vicinity.

I felt myself hauled up and out and laid prone while I coughed water. Near me I was dimly aware of what must be Immy receiving a massage. Events became vague: convulsive shivering, sirens, flashing lights, a mask over my face breathing sweet oxygen...

An English-speaking doctor visited me around noon, accompanied by an English-speaking policeman; which prompted me to be cautious.

I pretended confusion and fairly soon gathered that Immy was in 'intensive observation' for the moment, not to be visited, although her life wasn't in danger, and that the night before we must either have slipped (one of us perhaps pulling the other in) or else we'd been pushed, which would constitute an assault; alternatively we'd stupidly jumped into the watercourse due to us having taken some drug, as yet unidentifiable, since our blood samples showed very little alcohol. An assault might account for our considerable bruising, although so also might our fall. Or maybe we'd been fighting with one another, perhaps earlier?

I deduced that no one had witnessed us actually emerge from the tunnel. No one had seen anything other than us in distress in the water. If anyone *had* glimpsed us debouch, they must have rationalised what they saw so briefly as a trick of the shadows. Because obviously no one *could* have been any further upstream in that swift little subterranean river.

I claimed I had banged my head, which was true and verifiable (banged in the process of falling in, which wasn't true). Consequently my memories were vague and jumbled, although I was sure we hadn't been assaulted. I might have concussion. I slurred my speech somewhat.

A mild case of concussion, in the doctor's view, although sometimes slight concussion might prove worse in the long term.

I had no complaints whatever about the safety of Catania nor the conduct of its citizens, who indeed had valiantly rescued us. I thought the policeman looked slightly relieved at this, but he replied, "I feel that you are concealing something."

"*But what?* I don't know! Maybe Señorita Clemente remembers more clearly than I do. I'm very concerned about her! I want to see her!"

A sly grin. "So as to compare your stories?" The policeman produced a plastic bag containing the contents of my wallet, and the wallet itself, the worse for immersion. I also spotted my passport, looking shrivelled after being dried out, and my phone which I presumed was ruined. Of course we carried nothing on our persons that linked us *overtly* to the secondary CIA.

The doctor remarked, "Señorita Clemente inhaled a surprising amount of water for what must have been a fairly brief exposure. In fact she almost drowned. She is stable now. There may be cerebral consequences, although we hope not. Visiting at the moment is out of the question even if she is conscious."

"A lot of water," the policeman repeated suggestively. "And many bruises."

I shrugged emphatically.

Presently the doctor conceded that I could be discharged right away – my clothes had been dried – and the policeman requested me to remain in Catania for the next few days in case of further questions; and where please were Señorita Clemente and myself staying? Ah, so the police had found no clues as to *that* on our persons but they hadn't bothered phoning round all the hotels; therefore they hadn't gone through our luggage, good. How could the policeman imagine that I might leave without Immy? I told him the name of the hotel, and he departed, doubtless pausing in the corridor once he was out of sight to phone the hotel to verify.

Lacking Immy, I found myself at a bit of a loss. I'd behaved impeccably and resourcefully, but a little voice told me that I shouldn't go near the Bellini Garden again for the moment, and that I ought to be careful on the streets in case of a pruning tool in the ribs. I brooded about that giant key I'd seen inserted into the rock beneath the calendar.

Over the next two days I went cautiously several times to the hospital, but still wasn't allowed to see Immy. I bought a new phone. On the third day, very much at a loose end despite having a new French critical biography of Umberto Eco to read, anxious about Immy, and with a sense that the giant key was being turned by the cabal of gardeners to manipulate time, I booked through the hotel a day trip on a tourist coach – which should be safe enough – to see Mount Etna close up. I wasn't exactly disregarding the policeman's request since I'd be returning to the hotel to sleep. I took the tablet with me to read on the coach, supposing the journey bored me.

On my return, the fellow at reception handed me an envelope addressed in Immy's hand, and evidently delivered by hand.

> *Dearest Dick* [I read, and immediately began to fear the worst],
> *Before you wonder how I know you're absent from the hotel today, the police kindly told me. By the time you read this, I shall have left Sicily. Despite all the wonderful experiences and insights, both mental and physical, which we've shared, I can no longer accompany a person whose ridiculous action almost resulted in my death by drowning in a narrow tunnel. Can you be utterly unaware that I suffer from aquaphobia as well as from claustrophobia? (At least*

there were no birds in that tunnel of wet hell as well!) Or did you not pause to think about this? No more than you thought to interpret the exaggerated "Sicilian Gothic" of the gardeners as a kind of cosplay of an initiatory *nature rather than them being bent on horticultural butchery! This should have been obvious from the posture of Lucrezia amongst them! (Think about it!) You made a failure of interpretation, a semiotic fracaso which almost destroyed me. Indeed I'm not sure that my dreams will ever recover despite medication. I have not betrayed you to the local police, since this is against our oaths. But from now on I intend to operate solo, or with a new partner who is strongly averse to birds and confined spaces and drowning.*

Your once devoted Immy, now yours no more.

Appalled though I was by the shock of my abandonment, I was amazed that she made no reference whatever to the *key* to the mystery! The great key in the stone ceiling! Had she been so busy interpreting the body language, garments and tools of the gardeners and of Lucrezia in the subterranean lair that she didn't even notice the key in the roof? Had she dismissed that key as an emblematic decoration, a caprice on the part of the cult? How frustratedly I yearned to question her, I who had anointed her with soothing balm in Genoa…

And then I realised: poor Immy may indeed have suffered mild brain damage as well as psychological trauma due to excessive immersion. Her only recourse as regards the trauma was to run away, like an injured wild animal, to lick its wounds. Because of the cerebral impairment she mightn't even realise this. So I must forgive her for abandoning me, much as it hurt.

I went up to our room and confirmed that she had cleared out her luggage.

I spent the next morning writing a report to our CIA, which I then encrypted and sent to the number I remembered so well. (And I wondered if Immy had also contrived to send in some kind of report.) About an hour later an encypted text arrived, ordering me to leave Italy at once. Apparently other agents would continue the Bellini investigation.

I had of course been compromised. That IARPA's Metaphor Program took my findings very seriously was obvious from the instruction for me to leave, not merely Sicily, but the *whole of Italy*.

And yet my blood was roused. The whole of Italy did not necessarily include Vatican City, with its archives and its investigators of heresies. Loathe though I was to behave in the style of a Dan Brown character, to Rome I must go and inveigle lodgings within the papal state! And there I might discover the true name of the lavender.

This story is the second of three in this collection which appeared originally as a bonus chapbook entitled Squirrel, Reich, & Lavender *accompanying* The Best of Ian Watson *from PS Publishing in 2014 in a sumptuous box limited to 100 examples. Accordingly, few people will have read any of them, since book collectors swiftly seal their treasures into non-biodegradable bags of inert gas, or something, don't they? Actually, long ago I myself collected fine editions (Baron Corvo, William Beckford...), but when I sent these in a sea-trunk to Japan I included little bags of anti-damp crystals – the Sea, the Sea! Due to violent stevedores, the bags burst open, peppering bindings with micro-meteorites. No more collecting for me; only accumulating! An odd thing about this story is that the 'Metaphor Program' within the US intelligence octopus is real, rather than a fantasy which I concocted; likewise, the Office of Incisive Analysis. Often we strive to imagine gonzo circumstances, then reality promptly trumps us.*

In fact most of the story is rooted, as it were, in reality: the dying botanic garden in Genoa, the cosplay in the botanic garden in Catania, Sicily – where the Italian edition of my novel The Gardens of Delight *was launched. I'm very fond of botanic gardens; I seek them here, I seek them there. I can tell the difference between a cactus and a very similar-looking Euphorbia from ten paces. You see, the spines of cactiform Euphorbias of the Old World arise integrally from the flesh of the plant, whereas cactus spines (New World) generally arise from areoles with glochids. I trust that's clear. Many things in this story are unclear until our bold investigators clarify them by using their own version of incisive analysis. This tale is perhaps how Umberto Eco would have tackled a Dan Brown narrative.*

Reader, I read him (past tense): Dan Brown. All the way through The Da Vinci Code, *followed by* Angels and Demons *which the* San Francisco Chronicle *said "has an unusually high IQ". I was curious how to write a best-seller with a medium to high IQ. Andy West and I set out to do so, in* The Waters of Destiny, *about how a fanatical 12th century Arab doctor of genius could within the mindset and medical technology of the time – and with lavish sponsorship from the Assassins of Alamut – succeed in discovering in medieval Ethiopia the true cause of the superlethal Black Death (which ain't* Yersinia pestis *in rat fleas), and in storing the guilty haemorrhagic fever virus, a relative of Ebola, with lethal modern consequences. But we had to epublish the thriller ourselves (www.watersofdestiny.com) rather than being able to warn the world in every airport.*

Forever Blowing Bubbles

Professor Mackintosh admired his pint of newly pulled Old Bodger, with an excellent head on it, and sang happily:
"*I'm for-ever blow-ing bubbles,*
"*Pret-ty bubbles in the air!*
"*They fly so high,*
"*Nearly reach the sky —*"
Mischievously Brian Dalton continued:
"*Then like your dreams,*
"*They fade and die.* West Ham," Dalton pointed out, "lost two-one away in extra time."
"Whatever are you talking about?" asked Mackintosh, and took a swig of the dark ale.
"Footie! What do you suppose?"
"I fail to see any connection."
"For God's sake, *Bubbles* is the anthem of West Ham United. I thought you were a supporter."
Mackintosh said loftily, "The only interesting thing about a football is that it is spherical. As opposed to a rugby ball, which is a prolate spheroid."
Indeed our pale geometrodynamics boffin was lofty as well as quite skeletal, and needed to avoid bashing his balding head on low beams such as graced the ceiling of our historic watering hole. At least I think Mackintosh's field was called geometrodynamics, a rather airy-fairy discipline for the likes of myself, a zoologist dealing with fleshy things that moved, or at least had moved once upon a time, until they became merely bony or stony if fossilised. Spacetime curvature, physics reduced to geometry, wormholes, quantum foam and stuff. Fortunately for our camaraderie, Mackintosh's taste in beer ran to the robust.
Dalton, our inorganic chemist, on the other hand, whose freckles almost joined up, was chunky and had no problem at all passing his ginger curls under low beams. He could be a bit pugnacious, but never offensively so.

At this point Jocelyn joined in by saying, "Harpo Marx used to play *I'm Forever* on a clarinet that would blow bubbles. I suppose he put some soapy water in it."

"*Really?*" asked Mackintosh with apparently considerable interest.

Buxom blonde Jocelyn, our forensic chemist, was into folk music and played big Irish whistles, which required going to pubs at least once a week. She certainly liked a pint, and had infiltrated herself into our otherwise all-male group some months earlier. After initial reluctance, we addressed her tolerantly by her first name rather than her second, as though she was a sort of highly educated barmaid. Anyway, it would have been silly to call her Sparrow, Dr Sparrow indeed, since she was a big girl, necessarily as regards coping with the pints, and to some extent because of those. Her presence in our midst demonstrated that we weren't a bunch of confirmed bachelors. In fact Dalton himself was married – to a woman called Alice, I think – and had kids.

"*Really?* I hadn't thought about wind instruments blowing bubbles..." Mackintosh mused. "And lo, God blew his trumpet and the cosmos issued forth and inflated harmonically..."

It was Dalton's turn to exclaim, "What in the world are *you* talking about?"

"Not exactly *in* the world, as such," said Mackintosh.

"The world is the totality of all that is, according to Wittgenstein," piped up young Tuttle-Derby, whose schoolboyish face was pink and chubby, his oily brown hair slicked to one side, giving him the look of a Hitler cherub. "Anything you say that is not of the world has no meaning."

For some reason – tradition, probably – we often stood around the bar, though not like muskoxen so as to exclude other customers, and several more pints of Old Bodger had already been pulled when I called for a refill of my glass. A *re*fill, in vain as usual, since for some reason connected with hygiene or health and safety regulations the landlord insisted on fresh glasses for each order. Personally I preferred my own bacteria to infest my glass rather than a previous customer's with added traces of detergent.

"The Greek for world is *kosmos*," added Tuttle-Derby. "Cosmos. So this applies to the entire universe."

"Mathematically," said Mackintosh, "that is bollocks. Since our cosmos is simply an inflated bubble within a higher matrix."

I received a fresh beer whose head flattened suspiciously fast. The brew smelled dodgy and the merest sip hinted at sour.

"I think the Bodger's off," I told the actual barmaid, who was Polish.

"I pour another?"

"No no, end of barrel, kaput."

"Sorry, no other barrel of Bogna."

"Bodger."

"Oh yes. In Polish bog means God. Bogna is godly."

"So is Bodger." Drinking Old Bodger was a communion.

"*I* am Bogna," said the big-eyed barmaid, who wore her dyed blonde hair in a pigtail rope.

"I thought you were called Brenda."

"Bog not so good a word in English."

No, exactly. Bogna-Brenda must have been brooding about herself, or her homeland, or maybe about God.

Alas, no more Bodger tonight. A tragedy. God was dead, for tonight anyway. I scanned the other real ales on offer. "Make it a MacPherson's Mild." At least that should taste strongish even if it wasn't. Besides, I ought to support Mild. Relegated over the years to a shrinking clientele of cloth-cap-wearing codgers in the Black Country around Birmingham, Mild was now bouncing back like an almost extinct species re-invigorated.

As if to safeguard his own Bodger by putting the holy and now rare liquid out of reach, Mackintosh took a large gulp, then he wiped his mouth.

"Hmm," he said, "I'm supervising a postgraduate at the moment, name of Jones-Jones, who's doing his doctorate on bubble universes."

"Is he so good," asked Jocelyn, "that they named him twice, like New York New York?"

"His mother and father were both called Jones. It's a Welsh thing. The valleys, you know. When they married, they decided to double-barrel their names to add a bit of class."

Tuttle-Derby was obviously protective of hyphenated surnames. "Makes sense. A bride changing her name from Jones to Jones, how can people be sure she's actually married?"

"Aside from attending the wedding? Being Welsh, Jones-Jones plays rugby – "

"With a prolate spheroid," added Jocelyn, to show she'd been paying attention.

"No less. I do wish he wouldn't. He might break his ruddy neck, thus depriving the world of great insights. Though come to think of it, if he survived as a quadriplegic he might seem quite Stephen Hawking. Or rather, I *did* wish Jones-Jones wouldn't break his neck, although now I'm not so sure in view of what happened earlier this week." And Mackintosh paused significantly, until we egged him on with a chorus of *So what happened?*

"Hmm, I'll need some lubrication for the throat." Mackintosh drained his glass. "Brenda, I'll have the Bishop's Best."

A bit too appley for my taste. With a lurking demon of rotten appley. If I get an ale that's gone off, this can taint all future experiences of the same brew. Forever after a particular ale, even if excellent today, will remind me of cobwebs, another of vinegar, another of rancid butter. There's the potential for evil in the background. A bit like the supposed homeopathic memory possessed by water that was once in contact with a single molecule of arsenic or whatever. I'd lost access to several famous ales this way. That's why I'd been very careful to take the merest sip, not a swig, of the dodgy Old Bodger. Of course not everyone has my sensitivity and fine discrimination.

Mackintosh was duly supplied by Bogna.

"Now I don't know how much you know about bubble universes," began Mackintosh, doubtless knowing the answer full well from his tally of those of us present in the Paradise Bar on this particular evening. Come to think of it, that may have emboldened him to burst into song in the first place. None of us was remotely a geometrodynamicist.

He proceeded to hold forth about how our universe is like a soap bubble, although it lasts for billions of years. Our cosmos inflated itself dramatically just over thirteen (unlucky for some, I remember thinking, though not for us!) thirteen thousand million years ago. So dramatically did it inflate that nowadays we can only see a little bit of our own bubble because light hasn't time to reach us from the walls of the bubble, and never will. Setting down his glass, Mackintosh held his hands wide apart, rattling some horse brasses on the blackened oak beam. *That big a bubble!*

What's more, space and light might bend around inside the bubble, such being the nature of a universe. Well now, that bubble originated from *foam*, namely quantum foam.

"Quantum Foam!" squeaked Jocelyn enthusiastically, causing Mackintosh to raise an eyebrow.

"It's a, um, music group," she said.

Quite! The general public might buy any old cobblers featuring the word quantum – quantum power crystals, quantum bath salts no doubt – but we were all scientists, and weren't going to be sold any quantum snake oil, though of course Mackintosh was a ranking authority on the subject of universes, at least from the theory point of view.

"An infinite multiverse," said Mackintosh, "should contain an infinite number of Hubble-bubbles –"

"I thought Hubble-bubbles are those Arab things you smoke from," interrupted Dalton.

"Not in this case. I perceive I'm losing you – think of gas pockets in a loaf that's rising."

"I detest big holes in my toast," said Jocelyn. "The butter escapes."

Evidently Mackintosh would need to contend with a spot of badinage; so maybe at this point he decided to abbreviate his explanations.

"Or maybe you should think of the background spacetime foam as resembling the head on a beer…"

"That's more like it," said Dalton.

"Anyway, foam is the foundation of the fabric of the universe…"

"I'll raise a glass to that," I agreed. Didn't somebody once say that having a beer without a head is like kissing a girl without lips! Not that I'd actually kissed a girl *with lips* all that recently, come to think of it… I glanced at blonde Bogna, who was at that moment coincidentally putting on some lipstick, or maybe it was lip-salve. Which was naughty of her – traces of grease could ruin the head on a beer. Jocelyn's sumptuous lips which accommodated large whistles were rather intimidating; a chap could get swallowed.

"So Jones-Jones came up with the notion of a buildable bubble that might cause a mini-cosmos to evolve – call it a cosm for short. According to the maths the vast majority of the spacetime of the resulting cosm would evolve *internally* – rather than externally from our point of view, so we wouldn't suddenly be pushed aside by the bubble expanding exponentially. Yet with ingenuity we might still inspect what went on inside the bubble-cosm. Are you with me? Hmm, the Bishop isn't half-bad tonight."

"Wouldn't an optimist say *half-good*?" I asked.

"No no," Tuttle-Derby told me. "Not half-good would mean that more than half is bad."

I shrugged. Maybe he was right. I was worried about the effect of the lip-salve on subsequent pints. Admittedly Bogna wasn't going to taste what she pulled, but a trace of grease might remain on her finger.

Due to brooding about lips, or lack of lips, I may have missed a connection in Mackintosh's discourse, for the next thing I heard him say was, "I'm not opposed to experimentation, so Jones-Jones rigged up a holder for a hoop which he would first of all dip – in the same way children do – to produce a soapy membrane across it. And beyond the hoop, what we might call a bubble-chamber to contain the resulting mini-cosm. Now what gas should he introduce into the bubble by, well, not to put too fine a point on it and begging your pardon, Jocelyn, *belching* into the membrane? Jones-Jones reckoned that carbon dioxide and organic traces should give the mini-cosm a good start in life. So with all the gusto of a rugby player he drank deeply from slightly shaken cans –"

"*Cans?*" I protested.

"Yes, this is the indelicate part, and I blush to relate it: green cans, indeed, of Heineken."

"*Heineken!*" I expostulated, clutching my diminished pint of Mild. "But that's blasphemy!"

"I know, I know. Experimentation can be a dirty business. That's why I'm a theoretician."

I struggled to cope with the concept of someone voluntarily drinking lager. Had the Campaign for Real Ale fought in vain? A scientific fact came to my mind.

"If Jones-Jones had drunk Guinness, the bubbles are nitrogen… I suppose that might have caused toxic blooms in the mini-cosm."

Mackintosh nodded grimly. "It gets worse." He paused, and we all knew that he was readying himself for the climax of this amazing account.

"So Jones-Jones poured all of that lager into himself. And presently he faced the membrane on the hoop, poised quite like a rugby player about to join in a scrum. Jocelyn, perhaps you should cover your ears."

"Certainly not," said Jocelyn indignantly.

"Very well. I abdicate responsibility. How shall I best put it with a lady present? The experiment succeeded. But *not* until Jones-Jones turned around... Because...

"Because the gases that Jones-Jones let loose to inflate the bubbles, the baby cosms, were all coming out of the *other end*, if you take my meaning. They were coming from *the dark side*."

"Professor!" I exclaimed. "I never knew you were a fan of *Star Wars*."

Mackintosh beamed benignly and said in a mock Alec Guinness voice, "There is much you do not know about me, Luke."

"Ha ha," said Jocelyn to me. "That'll be your name from now on."

"It will not be!" Our dignity, our camaraderie, depending on not being overly familiar. First names were out. Except in her case.

At the time we were much taken by the notion of malign, almost demonic mini-cosms, if such should be how the products of Jones-Jones's experiment should evolve. I imagined those floating in that bubble-chamber, evolving internally at high speed. Dark cosms, in a manner of speaking.

Yet when I thought about all this in retrospect the next day, I spotted a flaw in what Mackintosh had related.

I don't mean a scientific flaw. Foam, bubble cosms, bubble chambers: those made as perfect sense to a zoologist as morphological pattern formation in the budding of sponges – or craniometric taxonomic analysis of subspecies of Zebras – would make to a geometrodynamicist.

Nor was I thrown by Mackintosh invoking the sacrilegious word Heineken in the Paradise bar of the Fountain.

No, it's just this: if Jones-Jones generated those bubbles by flatulating whatever mixture of carbon dioxide, nitrogen, oxygen, hydrogen sulfide, and methane through the soapy membrane, he would *not only* need to have turned round but also *necessarily* pulled down his trousers and whatever underpants he might have been wearing. Or not, as the case may be.

The conjunction of our good Professor Mackintosh and a student, all be it a postgraduate, bending over baring his buttocks in private before him isn't one that I care to contemplate! Nor the potential implications! Avowedly Mackintosh wasn't an experimenter but a theoretician. Otherwise he might have taken this into account.

This story might seem a bit bloke-ish, as though we have stumbled into a 1950s pub full of beery boffins plus one token redoubtable woman – oh, and the barmaid. But hey, mutatis mutandis, *we have! For this tale first saw the light in an anthology in tribute to Arthur Clarke's* Tales from the White Hart *of 1957 which was set in the late 1940s/early 1950s hangout of London SF fans of the time including John Cristopher, John Wyndham, and egghead Sir (to be) Arthur himself.*

Sixty years onward, the situation with regard to beer in Blighty is vastly improved by the victory of the Campaign for Real Ale, the only revolution to succeed in Britain since 1688. The comments on the ways beer can go bad are based on bitter – as it were – experience one hot summer in a pub the main street of Chipping Camden, Oxfordshire, where due to lack of a cellar the publican would merely throw a bucket of water over the sour barrels each morning to keep them semi-alive.

I probably borrowed the word cosm from Greg Benford's novel entitled, um, Cosm. *The barmaid Bogna's name belongs to Dave Hutchinson's lively Polish missus.*

THE TALE OF TRURL AND THE GREAT TANGENT

The esteemed contractors Trurl and Klapaucius were both so gigantic, likewise the titanic size of some of their tools and inventions – since they were able to kindle or extinguish suns and rearrange solar systems – that they were obliged to keep 99% of themselves and their equipment rolled up in the eleven invisible dimensions that supplement the visible dimensions of length, breadth, depth and time (time being easily visible on clocks, it goes without saying).

This lends a new meaning to *contracting*. Had it been otherwise, when Trurl & Klapaucius alighted on a world, not only would they have crushed a king's castle and his entire capital city, but they might have sunk right through the crust to the magma, causing volcanos which would resurface entire roasted countries.

Indeed this did happen once to Trurl when he impetuously pulled out a small black hole to lend weight to his presence on a winter-holiday world. The hole itself was only a few centimetres in diameter, but it massed more than a G-type star. Promptly it dragged Trurl to the core of the planet, while the planet itself shrank so that formerly Himalayan mega-mountains flattened themselves to a millimetre high, unfortunately for the inhabitants who previously used those for skiing and tobogganing. The natives and tourists who remained microscopically alive (not many) were very piste off.

How did Trurl survive this sudden diminution? Why, by hastily condensing himself into quark-matter. Klapaucius was obliged to rescue Trurl on that occasion from a safe distance using an adamantine fishing rod, the fishing line made of impervium.

And of course both contractors needed to be considerably less than the size of a large asteroid to fit themselves into their comfy copperwire-thatched cottages which were a few kilometres apart since Trurl and Klapaucius didn't wish to get into one another's fibreoptic hair, and from time to time Trurl liked to surprise Klapaucius by revealing an amazingly ingenious invention.

As for the hidden dimensions where Trurl and Klapaucius stored much of themselves and their larger equipment, those are generally known, by analogy with length and so forth, as curlth, coilth, crumplth, loopth, squigglth, squirmth, bendth, wrinklth, shrinkth, puckerth, and pillbug. Pillbug had minimised itself out of anxiety at the prophesied collapse of the entire cosmos 100 billion years hence.

One day a cyberknight presented himself at Trurl's door, which Trurl answered in his soft asbestos dressing gown and comfy wirewool slippers. A heavily armoured cyberhorse, more like a rhinoceros, grazed nearby on a bale of wire.

"As you witness, Sir Constructor," the cyberknight said to Trurl, "I am laden with cobalt cuirasses, galena gorgets, gallium gauntlets, brass brassards, hafnium haubergeons, chrome cuisses, and gadolinium greaves. Truly I'm burdened by bulk, even though I have adequate second-hand servomotors. How dearly I would like to unburden myself once in a while, but a cyberdragon might appear at any moment out of thin air."

Trurl inhaled some air to test its composition. "Sir Knight, the air here is quite thick compared with up a mountain. A dragon is more likely to appear out of *thick* air than thin due to there being more atoms available to transmute."

"Lackaday," exclaimed the cyberknight. "Yet could you obligingly tell me how to keep some of my armour very close at hand without being compelled to wear everything all the time?"

"Incidentally, why do you wear so many layers of cuirasses and cuisses et cetera?"

"For multiple redundancy."

Now Trurl was very fond of receiving gold, especially in the shape of ducats, but he also liked benevolently to help anyone in distress. Quickly he explained about curlth and shrinkth and so forth.

"Good Constructor, how do those hidden dimensions become so small?"

"Easy-peasy," said Trurl. "By fractal methods! Have you seen icons of the Mandelbrot Set?"

"I admit I do like a snack of manganese mandelbrots dusted with tasty radium. Those fit through the visor of my helmet, and my converters dissolve them with gustatory gusto."

"No, I'm referring to similarity at any scale, so that the tiniest iteration has the same shape as the largest. Thus your cuirasses and brassards, for instance, could be scaled down and popped into the curlth dimension, very close at hand, in fact on the surface of your hand or chest or back, since curlth is available everywhere. And pulled out again to full size quickly." Trurl sketched tensor calculus in the air for a minute or so, then shrugged. "It's like pulling a sock inside out, except that the toe is Planck length."

"A plank is quite long."

"A *Max* Planck length!"

"Max size sounds big."

"No, no, Max Planck is the name of some robot of ancient antiquity. Maybe he was made of wood, although the speed of light was within him... Why don't you come inside and have a crumpet instead of a mandelbrot, while I quickly make you some curlth openers?"

"Thou art too kind! I vow to kill any dragon that cometh down thy chimney."

Trurl popped a couple of iron crumpets into his timepasser toaster where they would acceleratedly oxidise to produce as much tasty rust as if several centuries had passed by.

"Give me a shout when they pop out, and I'll butter them with lovely greasy lubricant." So saying, Trurl headed for his workshop, where he proceeded to hammer and saw some exotic matter with microtools while viewing his activity through an electron microscope. Presently he returned with numerous almost invisible curlth openers which he fixed to different parts of the Cyberknight's armour.

"I've tuned them to your cerebral circuits," Trurl told the Cyberknight. "Just think to yourself: *hecketty-pecketty, my fine hen*, and the armour will store itself. To unstore, think: *goosy goosy gander*."

No sooner had the Cyberknight thought thuswise than his bulk diminished considerably, revealing an austere skeletal figure of steel which might once have been stainless but was now tarnished and pitted.

"Oh blessèd relief," exclaimed the Cyberknight, just as the crumpets emerged fully rusted. "However can I recompense you, I who am vowed to poverty?"

"'Tis ever the way," sighed Trurl. "Maybe you could give me a spare quest of yours? Nothing has challenged my genius recently." Hospitably Trurl dolloped thick brown grease on to the crumpets.

"As to that," said the Cyberknight, munching, "I recently rode my supercharger past a star a hundred lights to the north-east where I heard of a challenge, of which I could not avail myself due to being on a draconic quest at the time. Apparently the Great TanGent of Transistoria has offered ten captive cybermaidens to anyone who can stabilise his world."

"Stabilise?"

"I did ask myself why the Great TanGent should wish to put his world into someone else's stable. The cost of livery – fodder and such – for an entire world would be considerable, including towing expenses to take the planet to the stable."

"I think you are overly preoccupied by equine matters on account of your spacesteed."

"Bucyberephalis."

"Is that a disease of electrohorses?"

"No, that's her name. However, I then discovered that Transistoria and its sun have become engulfed by a cloud of self-aware nitrous oxide. A Joker Cloud. Although the planet owes its name to the Impeccable Transistor, now absurd changes take place and reality is transitory rather than transistory. The Great TanGent and his court have fled to the outermost ice-planet which is unaffected. He hates the cold and the faintness of light there because his joy was to expose his bronze body to the powerful electromagnetic radiation from Transistoria's sun."

"So he offers ten cybermaidens to whoever chases this Joker Cloud away? *But*," added Trurl, becoming incensed, "you say they are *captive*? Why, they must be released!"

"I suppose the only way to release them is to defeat the Joker Cloud, thus gaining the cybermaidens, then give them their liberty. As opposed to taking electroliberties with them." The radium had obviously refreshed the austere Cyberknight, giving him sufficient sparkle for a witticism.

"Then that is what I shall do!" declared Trurl. "Not take liberties, oh no! I've existed happily until now without any cyberwenches. Give me adjustable wrenches any time! I shall free those captives. Hmm, how do I defeat a self-aware cloud of nitrous oxide...? Aha, I shall adapt the cosmic vacuum cleaner I invented."

"Surely," said the Electroknight, "the vacuum of the void is empty by definition, so how can it be cleaned?"

"Space travel," replied Trurl impatiently, "is impossible without a void, or vacuum, to travel through, but often it fills with junk such as rivets coming loose from craft. I must hurry to my colleague Klapaucius to recruit him for this chivalric expedition."

After they'd been travelling for a few score light years, Trurl said to Klapaucius, "Do you mind if we stop here for a bit? I want to nip outside to have a stretch."

Klapaucius consulted his sturdy depleted uranium chronowrist which told seventeen different times depending on frame of reference. "You won't take more than a day about it? You'll delay us."

"I need a stretch or else I'll get cramp! Oh I can feel cramp coming on! Ouch ouch. What use is a constructor with cramp? My genius will be cramped. My style will be cramped. You can have a picnic on the hull while I'm stretching."

Of course both of the constructors couldn't stretch fully at the same time; there wouldn't be enough space.

"Ouch ouch!" cried Trurl. "OUCH!"

"Do it, then, if you must." Carefully Klapaucius turned the anti-acceleration dial to a big minus number. An audio of braking sounded. *Screeeeeeeeeech*.

When the ship was at rest with respect to the nearest star systems, Klapaucius sucked all the air into storage and the two constructors switched to radio since otherwise they could no longer hear one another. Then Trurl nipped out of the hatch, and jetted about a thousand kilometres away.

After toasting a vanadium waffle till it glowed, and sprinkling on rhodium filings, Klapaucius followed and sat on the hull to watch as first of all Trurl unpacked extensive parts of himself and pieces of equipment and inventions from curlth, and then from coilth and crumplth – by now he was the size of a minor moon, very irregularly shaped. Next Trurl unpacked from loopth and squigglth and squirmth, and he swelled to the size of a major moon, starfish-shaped. Finally he added the contents of bendth, wrinklth, shrinkth, puckerth, and last of all pillbug. Now he was a world unto himself of about one gravity, distinctly hexakis-octahedronal. At last he had stretched to his full capacity.

"Aaaaah," Klapaucius's radio conveyed blissfully.

"Have you found the vacuum cleaner?" Klapaucius enquired.

"Of course I have. It was wrapped up in shrinkth. Shrinkth-wrapped."

"Remember to leave the vacuum cleaner out when you repack. Then we can see about modifying it."

"Um, Klapaucius..."

"What is it?"

"I'm itchy. Some kind of infestation came out of wrinklth. Electron fleas maybe. Now they're the size of electro-elephants from the feel of it. Would you very much mind bringing the ship over here and taking a look?"

So Klapaucius went back inside and antimattered the ship over to orbit his planet-sized colleague, which wasted less than a grain of fuel. Peering through a telescope, Klapaucius reported, "They aren't jumping, which means they're probably neutralino nits. They ought to pass through you, but they've swollen a lot. Would you like me to denit you?"

"I'd be obliged."

Patiently Klapaucius lined up a precision laser-cannon and began to pick off the lumbering parasites, until Trurl was as shiny and spruce as a young processor trundling off to school, his fibreoptic hair slicked down with grease. Then Trurl began repacking large parts of himself and his gigantic inventions and terraforming technologies and planet-shifting levers and cometary crowbars back into curlth, coilth, crumplth, loopth, squigglth, squirmth, bendth, wrinklth, shrinkth, puckerth, and pillbug. This took longer than unpacking, as is usual, but Trurl remembered to leave out the electromagnetic vacuum cleaner and to attach it to the nose of the ship before he rejoined Klapaucius on board, having downsized once more.

"Aaaaaaaaaah, that was good." Trurl opened a jar of electrolyte from the fridge to refresh himself after his stretch-out. "So what are we waiting for?"

"You," said Klapaucius as he let off the spacebrake and engaged the accelerator. The ship could go from rest to a speed of C++ in fifteen seconds in a straight linux, but Klapaucius allowed a reasonable thirty seconds.

Presently the two Constructors came in sight of the partially glittering iceworld at the edge of the solar system containing Transistoria. The iceworld partially glittered because a sort of solarium had been constructed in geosynchronous orbit to beam down radiation upon an area where, under highest magnification, the Great TanGent could be seen artifically sunbathing on the patio of an icy palace accompanied by ten ravishing and recumbent cybermaidens wearing black boron carbide bikinis, all linked to one another by a thick grey chain looped around the hourglass waist of each; a chain composed, as spectrographic analysis revealed, of tungsten.

"At least," said Klapaucius, "the Great TanGent isn't a total brute. Tungsten's hard but it's ductile and malleable, so the cybermaidens can move comfortably within limitations. And tungsten resists corrosion."

"Therefore they can't so easily escape," said Trurl angrily.

"I mean that tungsten bondage won't mark their waists, the way that copper chains would stain them with verdigris. Hmm, I fear another Constructor might already be at work here because of that orbital sunbathing device! Ingenious heat pumps must be in operation, otherwise the ice that the Great TanGent is basking on would melt. Hmm, the heat which is pumped away could be microwaved up to power what's in orbit, and *that* is verging on *perpetuum mobile*... Has someone ingenious got here before us? Although the cybermaidens do remain chained..."

"We'd better hurry!"

"It was *you* who stopped to stretch."

"Gears and gizmos! I had to install the vacuum cleaner, didn't I?"

Politely using anti-gravity rather than flaming thrusters in their descent, they landed half a kilometre from the temporary ice-palace of the Great TanGent in exile, and approached on foot.

A chamberlainbot enquired their business and led them, by way of somewhat dripping corridors, to a somewhat dripping antechamber. Of course as soon as drips encountered any shade the water promptly froze again to minus 250 Celsius. Carpenterbots were constantly busy reinstalling ice-wainscoting on the upper parts of walls, using icepegs, so that the palace looked somewhat upside-down; while pagebots scurried about, protecting other parts of the building with aluminium parasols. Ceilings and roofs were lacking, needless to say.

"All this ingenuity," exclaimed Trurl, "so that the Great TanGent can continue tanning himself. Truly he is a tyrant."

By the time they arrived at the throne room, the forewarned monarch had already ensconced himself in his complex throne, complex since the plates of his body were very angular, not only tangential to one another but even hyperbolic. No rival Constructor seemed to be present amongst the assembled courtiers. The line of ten cybermaidens had been led inside by guards so that the Great TanGent could keep an optic on them.

Truly they were ravishing (although apparently unravished), with great thigh-pistons and well-riveted conical bosoms scarcely concealed by their boron carbide bikinis. How their Pythagorean proportions appealed! As a consequence of perfection they all looked remarkably similar, like a chain of cut-out, though bounteously ample, three-dimensional metallic dolls joined loosely by the restraining chain of tungsten. The glitter of crushed gems glued upon their optic-lids, and similar blusher upon their cheeks and nipples, gave some individuality: ruby, sapphire, emerald, and so forth. The cybermaidens postured somewhat, as though not entirely innocent, but maybe that was just an aspect of their balance circuitry. And they pouted, rather as goldfish do in a bowl. Maybe they were privately gossiping by radio. Maybe they were suffering perpetual pangs of embarrassment. Maybe none would be the first to utter a word for fear of sounding silly. Maybe they must remain silent in court.

"Your Majesty –" Trurl commenced.

"Your *Gentleness*," the chamberlainbot corrected Trurl.

"Your Gentleness, you behold before you the Esteemed and Cosmically Notable Constructors, Trurl and Klapaucius, whose fame surely precedes us, although we do hope that no lesser Constructor has also preceded us?"

"Nay," said the Great TanGent through his mouth-grille, "it was a seemingly *much lesser* Constructor, since the heat pumps he installed fail to function properly, although We are glad of the tan-rays from deep space amidst this cursèd darkness."

"I intend," declared Trurl, "to remove the curse of the nitrous oxide cloud from Transistoria in order to liberate, I mean acquire, these ten captive cybermaidens."

"I rejoice to hear this. Truly we shall be sorely bereft to lose Our Isobel. My dignity required multiple robobimbo playmates to sunbathe beside Us. Yet such shall be your reward if you can restore Us to our world where lunatical instability now reigns."

"*The*... Isobel? Do all ten cybermaidens have the same name, Your Gentleness? How de-individualising."

"An isobel," grilled the Great TanGent, "is a line connecting points of equal beauty in the same way that an isobar connects points of equal atmospheric pressure. Since the ten are chained together, it is far easier to say *Isobel, come here* than to recite ten different names."

"Surely You could call them Rubybel, Sapphirebel, Emeraldbel, Diamondbel and so forth. For example."

"And Soforth*bel*," grilled the Great TanGent, "to follow your logic. You yourself short-circuit the inconvenience."

Trurl's own circuits throbbed with momentary chagrin. This Monarch was capable of logic-chopping, therefore Trurl ought to be careful about terms and conditions.

"I shall of course need an iron-clad guarantee of our agreement, Your Gentleness. A contractor requires a contract."

"Agreed. But you, Contractor, must provide the iron. We mainly have ice here."

"I was thinking," said Trurl, "more of a fireproof metal parchment adorned with tassels and seals and twiddly bits."

"Faugh!" said the affronted monarch. "Ice at minus 250 is *harder than steel*. I shall inscribe my vow upon a sheet of such ice, which *you* can clad in iron to your central processor's content. Although," he offered grandly, "I will add some curlicues."

"Psst." Klapaucius nudged his colleague. "Shouldn't you consult the Isobel" – and Klapaucius nodded towards the line-up of bikinied beryllium beauties – "as to whether they wish to be freed? Perhaps they enjoy bondage?"

Trurl drew himself up sententiously and declared, "Freedom is the factoryright of any robosapient. Besides, we cannot abandon Transistoria to its stochastic fate." And *he* gestured at a large plasma screen, wherein events upon that world were being displayed, transmitted by the desperate citizenry to their monarch.

The sky was raining banana skins upon a civic square where the Royal RoboArmy were attempting loyally to goosestep on parade. Soon the steel soldiers were skidding and crashing into one another, and the square was a tangle of cyberlimbs...

Gallons of polka-dot paint, red spots on green, spilled from low galleon-shaped clouds upon a congregation in the roofless Church of Ultraviolet Adoration, transforming the battery-recharging sun-adorers into clowns...

Masses of little coinlike green leaves were growing out of the portico of the Royal Mint; although the transmission didn't convey smells you could easily guess what the scent would be...

On Transitoria, puns and pratfalls had become absurd reality due to the Joker Cloud. In the circumstances T felt obliged to accept the commission without even consulting the captives.

"But ASK them!" insisted Klapaucius. "They don't have much to say for themselves!"

"Speaking personally," grilled the Great TanGent, "I find decibels incompatible with an Isobel."

Trurl gaped at the monarch. "You mean you *dumbed* them down?"

"For some entities, being dumb is a perfectly happy state, since they're unaware of anything amiss."

"I can easily adjust *that*!" declared Trurl, incensed, "by a few twiddles and tweaks and installing some extra capacity."

"Although at the moment a *cloud* still interposes itself before that illuminatory outcome."

"Inscribe our agreement, then!"

"My word alone will not suffice?"

"I do not doubt your word, Your Gentleness, yet let us say purely as an aide memoire...?"

So the Great TanGent extruded a diamond drill from his forefinger and at high speed inscribed his promise on a sheet of extremely hard ice which a courtier held before him, which he then passed to Trurl. Trurl scanned the binary code amidst the curlicues, then reached into crumplth for a suitable iron box which he recalled having packed near the Planck-length doorway. The ferric box assumed its regular 4-D length, breadth, and depth (rather than height, in the case of a box), and time which proceeded to pass, and into that box Trurl placed the Great TanGent's promise, ironclad now to be sure.

Back in space, after Trurl had placed the iron box in the ship's refrigerator to keep it cool, the Contractors headed inward towards Transistoria and the great cloud of laughing gas engulfing its entire orbit.

"Shouldn't we try to communicate with the cloud before we vacuum it up?" suggested Klapaucius. "The cloud may have a point of view."

"Hmm," hummed Trurl. "That cloud's about 300 million kilometres across. The speed of radio is 300,000 kilometres per second. So it takes the cloud 1000 seconds for a coherent thought. Roughly sixteen and a half minutes. How glacially slow compared with our own swift thoughts! But I do believe there's a temporal interface thingymajig in that locker over there — I invented one when I needed to communicate with a slow-life gas-whale. What the interface does is borrow some time from the future and loop it around. This shouldn't do too much harm to the local spacetime metric, although the sun might flicker a bit."

Before long, Trurl had synchronised the chrono-interface to the radio, and hailed on all frequencies:

"Cloud, why are you playing tricks on that planet that never did you any harm?"

Transistoria's sun did indeed blink off on off on off on, as if trying to flash some message of its own, but this was unimportant since the flashing wasn't at a frequency such as to cause epileptic fits in machine minds.

Presently came an answer: **"For a billion years I have drifted, and never had a laugh."**

"Ah," said Trurl to Klapaucius, "at long last the cloud encountered an inhabited world and an opportunity. Probably it was expelled from some star cluster due to its stupid sense of humour. **You'll probably feel better,**" he messaged, "**after I condense you. Brevity is the soul of wit**."

So saying, Trurl activated the vacuum cleaner on the nose of their ship so that it sent forth a vast conical electromagnetic field to suck in the nitrous oxide, rather like a primeval Bussard ramscoop from the earliest days of astronautics; and he accelerated. Assorted loose nuts and bolts and screws proceeded to fly towards Trurl's and Klapaucius's metallic bodies and attach themselves with a *ping*.

"Ouch," complained Klapaucius. "There's a spot of magnetic

leakage."

"Saves me using the brush and pan," said Trurl, who was busy punching a course that would in a couple of hours take them throughout the entire volume of the cloud. He disengaged the temporal thingymajig so as not to hear moans from the cloud at the disconcerting sensations it might be experiencing.

While they were heading back to the iceworld, Trurl went for a spacewalk on the hull to detach the now bulging vacuum bag and bring it back aboard. Even in the absence of gravity, this took some heaving due to the inertia of an entire molecular gas cloud compressed to the size of a large pumpkin. Which Trurl duly labelled in red *Beware: Laugh Gas* in case he ever opened it by mistake.

"Where shall we keep it?" asked Klapaucius.

"In pillbug, surely? If any gas leaks out, the pillbug anxiety should neutralise it."

Presently they landed, and Trurl removed the iron box from the ship's refrigerator in case the Great TanGent needed reminding of His royal promise.

"Hmm," muttered Trurl, "that's odd, the box feels warmish. My thermosensors must need a service. I'll see to that after we've liberated the Isobel..."

Soon they were once more in the royal presence, the captive cybermaidens on parade again. The screen showed the robot citzenry of Transistoria celebrating the restoration of normality by singing joyously while they swept up banana skins and scrubbed paint off one another.

"Your Gentleness," said Trurl, "we have succeeded, as expected, consequently we have come to collect our just reward."

"Kindly remind me," said the Great TanGent, "of the exact wording."

"Do you need additional memory?" asked Trurl. "Is your hard disc full?"

"Just remind me, Contractor!"

Smuggly Trurl unlocked the iron box and opened it... only to find a couple of centimetres of chilly water sloshing inside.

"But," said Trurl.

Exposed to the far-below-zero of the icemoon, the water was already beginning to form a featureless membrane of ice...

"But."

"The magnetic leakage, idiot," hissed Klapaucius. "The magnetic field must have induced a strong electric current in the fridge and the box, resulting in heat... Our ironbound contract melted."

The monarch, his tangents bristling and his parabolas asymptoting, declared, "It was yourself, Contractor, who insisted on a *written* contract complete with adornments. Despite the fact that Our royal word has always been Our bond! This demeaned Our dignity and insulted Our gentleness. *Consequently* We shall abide only by the *written* terms of that contract. And We perceive no binary code whatsoever!"

Trurl felt as if he might blow a gasket, burst a fuse, rupture a rheostat.

"But there were witnesses..." Desperately he gazed in appeal at the Chamberlain and the other courtiers, who all conveniently were looking elsewhere, then at the Isobel themselves who of course had nothing to say.

"May his chips fry!" cursed Trurl as they left the iceworld under excessive acceleration. "May his RAM break a horn!"

"Ah, the foibles of monarchs," sighed Klapaucius. "We should know about those only too well by now."

"That's why I insisted on a contract!"

"You ought to have tightened the nuts on the vacuum cleaner. It must have rolled around while in its microdimension."

"I've a good mind —" Abruptly, impetuously, Trurl braked. "I've a good mind —"

"I know you have a good mind, dear friend. Definitely the goodest. Both as regards your processors and your ethics."

"I've a good mind to turn back and as it were *accidentally* jettison the vacuum bag upon the ice world before they finish packing for Transistoria Regained. I shall, I shall too!"

True to his word, Trurl reached into pillbug. "Hmm, that's odd. Could have sworn I left the bag just by the door. Dratted thing must have rolled, the way you accuse my vacuum cleaner of doing..."

"Maybe if you didn't accelerate and brake quite so suddenly...?"

But at that very moment polka-dot paint began to creep out of the unseen dimension on to Trurl's hand, and very soon this was spreading down his metal arm, bright yellow on blue this time, the spots expanding swiftly. From close by, although scarcely audible at all, came the tiniest and tiniest noise of laughter.

The finest example of what a cyborg civilisation might be like is David Bunch's Moderan, *quirky and satiric, which I mention because it's so little known – and for a full-blown cosmic robot civilisation, likewise satiric and quirky, there's Stanisław Lem's* Cyberiad. *(Okay, in absurdist philosophical vein a tip of the hat also to John Sladek's Roderick novels and to Barrington Bayley's* The Soul of a Robot.*)*

Some years ago the Polish Cultural Institute in London, in cahoots with ebullient Louis Savy of the film festival Sci-Fi, came up with the concept of a book of homage to Poland's Lem – which was batted into the court of Ian Whates' NewCon Press. Since I was involved in the earliest stages of this project, perhaps it's best to draw a veil over the maddening nuisances suffered by Mr Whates (and a couple of veils over other matters such as funding and payments). Suffice it to say that the tribute volume finally appeared in 2011 entitled Lemistry, *handsomely produced by Ra Page's Comma Press of Manchester.*

I chose to write a story in the style of the Cyberiad *– at least, as Englished ingeniously by ace translator Michael Kandel. Maybe an imp of the perverse possessed me, since I wondered how my own story could possibly be back-translated into Polish by a reverse Kandel; though I still haven't the foggiest whether this ever happened or not. Maybe I'll find out in Wrocław in 2016, since I arm-wrestled at the London Worldcon of 2014 with amiable medievalist and translator Michael Wnuk for the honour of holding a Eurocon in Barcelona in 2016 rather than in rival Wrocław; oh, and there was voting too at the 2014 Eurocon in Dublin's fair city – Gaudí's city won because we have more awesome dragons, but Michael gallantly invited me to Wrocław.*

How come that I co-organise SF conventions in my dotage, and not as a figurehead but hands-on? This isn't exactly usual in Anglosaxonia. It used to be said in Anglosaxonia that SF authors arise from the ranks of fandom, so I may be engaged in a reverse rake's progress, from author to filthy conrunner. Actually this all began because of the Northampton SF Writers Group, over which I presided, which gave rise to five SF conventions in Northampton, from mini to maxi, all named Newcon, because they were new. Now that I live in Spain I'm involved with the annual Celsius232 SFF festival in Avilés, Asturias, and also with the first ever Spanish Eurocon being held in Barcelona in 2016. Such things do take up time, but for decades I enjoyed (sometimes as a guest though mainly not) SF conventions organised by others; so I'm giving something back to the SF community – but also, it's fun (er, most of the time).

Fun is important! And I had fun with my Stanisław Lem story in the style of the Cyberiad, *one of the comic masterpieces of modern literature.*

THE WILD PIG'S COLLAR

Sparkles rise from the palm of my hand, forming a little constellation, bright even in the afternoon desert sunlight. I breathe one sparkle in – just one – and it effervesces inside my head while I stare at the drifting pattern of the others.

Sparks of Creation, my dead dad used to call these emanations from his flesh, and from mine.

The Enemy are coming across the worlds, hunting for us. *Where are you, Gate? Where, where?* Now I'm sniffing.

A cat's mouth hangs open so it can catch some extra molecules in the air. In mirrors I've noticed my mouth hang open, lips parted, when I sniff. I don't like this much, because stupid women tend not to keep their mouths shut. Royn once said, when I was sixteen and he two years older, that it made me look sexy and predatory. Maybe he said sexy *or* predatory – memory can be unreliable, and sometimes flatters one's self. I remember how I yearned for Royn, back then. Do I still, in part of me? Now I must defy him, if we're to escape from the Enemy.

Royn could keep his mouth shut and sniff. Quite appropriate for someone who discovered how to hide worlds secretly! Likewise my dad kept his mouth shut when he conjured the sparkles. At least I don't sniff audibly, as though I have a cold. It's internal, in the head, in the mind. Perhaps my parted lips are a reflex from ancient times when our ancestors may have raced between worlds like animals, seeking exits to elsewhere to escape from pursuit. Now our people need guides, of whom there are far too few.

Where are you, Gate? Tell me.

The sparkles align in an arrow, pointing south-west and downward, though not sharply so, thus the gate is below the camber of this Earth's horizon, maybe 200 miles from here.

The gate I came by is between two towering cacti, Saguaros which form an irregular H-shape. Maybe those cacti have a different name here, but the plants and animals of the many Earths are much the same as far as the Periphery, where normality bends away into abnormality or desolation. Our enemy came out of abnormality.

The H-shape is obvious, all be it only to those like me. To my eyes, this gate I came by is marked and fixed. The gate I seek will be tiny by comparison, though I shall expand it when I find it. If I find it – but I will! It might be a lens in somebody's sunglasses or a knot in a tree or even the whorl of fingerprint on a kid's thumb. I'll sniff it out.

There's a road nearby, a straight dark ribbon emerging from low hills a few miles back, cutting through scrub and sand to a shimmery vanishing point far ahead. Some dust devils dance. Already I'm thirsty, and I suck on a bottle from my little black leather satchel.

A low-slung red car comes up from behind, and I wave.

A young woman, red headscarf over light brown hair of a similar shade to her eyes. That's much better than a man in a big truck, who might be a nuisance.

"Hi. You on a photo-shoot? Got lost?" She gazes around.

My dark brown suede one-piece, same colour as my bobbed hair, is one with my multi-buckled boots. Thonged vents in the side say fashion or fetish. The Earth I came from in a hurry is much into both. No time to change.

"Quarrelled with my boyfriend. He stopped specially to *continue* quarrelling, would you believe? So I got out. He drove off."

"Surely he'll come back?"

"Don't want him back. See him coming, Neanderthal grandson of Homo Erectus, I'll duck down. Thanks for your help!" Promptly heading round to open the passenger door.

That was a bit of neurolinguistic programming. While the analytical side of her brain was coping with the Neanderthal nonsense, the emotional side accepted that I'd be riding with her.

"I'm Tina Sena," she says as the car moves off. "And actually I'm a psychologist, so I know what you just did," ending interrogatively, eyebrows raised, meaning *your name too please.*

"Arianna."

"One two, buckle my shoe," remarks Tina Sena.

"Arianna *Daybreak*."

"Native American, in part?"

"Sure, and I'm out here where my people once hunted collared peccaries that can munch on prickly pear pads."

Grinning, she accelerates. "Too much detail, and doesn't really fit with the boyfriend story."

Oh, so this is to be a battle of wits? I don't think I was being followed — not so soon — but I glance in the wing mirror, and of course she notices.

"Somebody else back there who ought to get lost?"

"You have a rich imagination, Tina."

"I'm sure you do too, Arianna."

For the briefest moment I imagine killing her — *after* first getting her to stop the car, and if she suspected she might speed up instead — but that isn't my style, although the Enemy would think nothing of it. I just need to model the situation in my head. Everyone has their precious sovereign life, and there'll be various versions of this Tina on the other Earths, yet she's still unique, at least to herself.

And I'm unique too. Not in my ability to conjure sparkles to guide me; that's merely *rare*, very rare. I mean in there being no other versions of me, or of my people. My dad said that's because us Neither Dwellers come from near the Periphery, neither in the mainstream of alternative worlds, nor part of abnormality either. Think of Day and Night. We're from the dawn, beginning to brighten but dark shadows still lingering. Consequently *Daybreak* is a famous, triumphant family name amongst us.

If the enemy from abnormality can exterminate us, then their route to the main river of worlds is cleared of an obstacle — maybe in some metaphysical or occult manner, to understand which requires one somehow to think *abnormally*, like the Enemy.

Thus you'd imagine that the other Earths would be willing to shelter us. But no. Refugees aren't popular, especially when they smell of impending threat — as if we bring with us a disease or contamination. *Why do you seek refuge in our world? Don't bring your curse here! Go away!* We're lepers.

Royn's solution was to hide his world and those allied to him. Their technology is remarkable — probably they could trash the Enemy, if they chose to. *Probably* isn't safe enough for them. Royn seems to think that the Enemy will chase us Neither Dwellers at least for long enough till he and his scientists can work out how to disconnect the hidden worlds totally from the rest of the skein of worlds. As of now Royn's people can minimise connections, but never disconnect entirely. Of course that might be an impossibility, unless using enormous supernova-class energies. It might even cause reality to unravel.

"Penny for your thoughts, Arianna?"

Ahead, a monster shuffles cumbersomely on to the road, and Tina brakes, with an admiring "Wow!"– so probably the huge, poisonous-looking lizard isn't meant for me, even though I almost coordinate with it. I mean colour-wise. Its orange-yellow and browny-black skin mottled in bands and islands isn't unlike my dark one-piece plus my tanned flesh, were my one-piece a bit more revealing of the latter. Yet very bumpy all over, that lizard's skin, unlike me in my garb. Its tongue flickers as we coast closer. The enemy can't manifest their presence directly – not yet, not while we still survive – but they can possess individuals or creatures in the mainstream worlds, use them as puppets. This won't be one. Probably not! I do have my pistolette in my bag.

"Only the second time I saw a gee-gee," says Tina.

"Gee-gee's a horse..."

"Giant Gila. Where *are* you coming from?"

From a world or ten back, I remember so-called Gila monsters being a foot and some long, and venomous, true enough, but slow and timid. Saw one in a zoo. This ahead is the mother and grandmother of all Gilas. Maybe in the Ozstralia of this Earth they still have giant kangaroos.

"I'm from neither here nor there."

Without looking at me, since her gaze is fixed on the giant lizard: "Why do I think that's true, even though you put it as a cliché to mislead me?"

"Touché," I say, "rhymes with cliché."

Still staring ahead, as if I pose no threat: "I guess you must have had conversations like this quite often. You know, you appearing from nowhere, such as in the middle of a desert. I often wondered what I'd do in a situation like this, say if I met a cowboy who strayed out of the 1880s. Or someone from the future who'd learned 21st century English but arrived off-target and failed to find a change of clothes lying around."

Mischievously I say, in Turquish, "My people are very quick at languages. Though we only bother with major ones and their variations." The Turks dominate a third of a nearby Earth. Sultans, harems, powerful cunning eunuchs.

Tina considers, as the Gila decides to quit the road. "So is *future* wrong?"

That's very quick. She left out numerous intervening bits of guesswork.

This Earth is obviously still innocent of us, and here isn't my goal — I'm just passing through. When I say innocent, maybe top-secret government organisations are aware. I wish I was innocent, the way I was when I admired Royn so much…

The first time I met Royn was at the World Chase Festival on Earth-97, fourteen years ago now. This wasn't a festival in the media meaning of the word. Earth-97 was backward, and our venue was remote, the island of Lamu off the East African coast, where there happened to be a gate. Once a thriving port due to an abundance of slaves, Lamu had become a charming backwater, its town centre a maze of ancient lanes only wide enough for a laden donkey. Tall houses with heavy timbered doors carved ornately and garden courtyards, other homes of wattle and mud, old mosques, tiny shops full of baskets, mats, leather-work, gold and silver cloth and jewellery. And the mangos and coconuts and harvest of the tropical sea. And the dunes. Enchanting. The local Swahili people couldn't fathom by what 'boat' we had all arrived, but they were hospitable and enjoyed feasts and dances. We seemed to be graceful friendly visitors, though also tough and no fools, with gold to exchange for goods. Word would filter back to the distant British administration weeks after we'd gone, and perhaps months later in a steam-powered London someone might coordinate this with vague diplomatic reports of an enigmatic non-Amerindian population in vast Brazil who kept to themselves. For the time being Earth-97 was a good refuge world.

My illustrious dad had been grooming me for years to chase worlds, to open gates and go through, and to know how to return (which is quite important!). So far, I'd only chased worlds either in his company or, latterly, with companions he trusted.

That morning, in Lamu, over bowls of coconut milk, he'd told me, "From now on, you can start chasing on your own. I'll make the announcement tonight. It's vital that you're recognized as my heir."

"But nothing's going to happen to you!"

Unspoken: *just as happened to my mother…* who went missing when I was ten. Dad had searched through the worlds for her but found no trace. Maybe she languished in some jail of a repressive regime; or worse. It took till I was thirteen before I stopped expecting her to return at any moment.

"The fact is, Arianna, I'm going to scout into the Periphery. Not on my own, I hasten to add! I'll take a well-armed escort. But we need to know how far the Enemy has infiltrated, not in puppet form but..." He didn't wish to evoke horrors.

Later, I found myself walking the beach on the east of the island, miles of empty sand flanked by huge dunes, in company with Royn and half a dozen others. At eighteen, Royn was already princely, dark-haired, hawk-nosed, his eyes beautiful violets in cream. He was already talking about minimising gates by using sparkle-energy in a new way.

"The enemy appear to use dark energy —"

"Why not call it darkle-energy?" I suggested.

"Sparkle darkle, darkle sparkle." Royn played with the words. "Sounds like a nursery rhyme to me." Was he suggesting that I was immature? "Yet," he went on, "nursery rhymes often tell of terrible things, such as plagues, in a way that stays in the memory even when people forget the origin. If we're ever decimated and hopelessly scattered and lose our heritage, a nursery rhyme might lead us back to it one day." And he smiled at me, and seemed to fully notice me, to mark me out as worthy of some admiration, matching at least part of the admiration I felt for him.

That night, after my dad's announcement at the party in the town square in front of the main mosque, which I think was called the Riyadha Mosque, Royn came to me almost as an equal, to dance with me. At first I thought he was being polite out of respect for my father, but while we were dancing he kissed me on the side of the neck and his tongue licked my skin in a way that ravished me.

"No not here," I warned him. "The locals might be offended." As Royn should have known perfectly well, tolerant though the locals were. Yet now he had the answer to an unspoken question. 'Not here' implied 'somewhere else'.

Of course there was also much serious discussion at that World Chase Festival, not least about the problem of us refugees from Neither. Nobody at the festival treated us like lepers – my dad was akin to a Moses or Mao Tse-tung who had led most of his people to safety, so far. But we seemed like fragrant blossoms to bees, as regards the enemy who had fixated on us. Maybe that's because we had single identities. There weren't various versions of ourselves in any of the other worlds.

"It seems clear," said Royn at one debate, already beginning to assume leadership, "that those other multiple versions act like chaff or decoys. In my unhappy opinion, the Neither Dwellers's foe can't focus clearly or locate most inhabited Earths due to all the other versions of people. Tragically, the Neither Dwellers present what is practically a homing beacon. I say tragically, since this *is* a tragedy –!"

I listened to him, spell-bound, even though he was up against my dad.

"– And what I propose we should do, once we learn how to minimise gates, is put our best science to discovering how to isolate a refuge world for the Neither Dwellers – to cut it out from the sequence of Earths."

"Us inside, and the key thrown away?" asked my dad.

"Sir, I do realise what a blow this would be for you personally, since if that happens you'll never again be able to exploit your world-chasing talent – nor will your charming and talented daughter, whom you presented so compellingly the other night. Yet you'll be safe at last."

For a moment I felt that Royn was hitting below the belt. A word like *exploit* was emotive. Even so, what Royn said was accurate. I felt torn in my loyalties.

There in lovely and lazy Lamu over the next two days of celebrations of our talent, Royn seemed to be paying court to me. In retrospect, I sometimes wonder whether he did so as a way of propitiating my dad – or maybe even needling my dad? Or alternatively, whether he may have been acting politically, so that others would see that he sincerely wasn't prejudiced against us Neither Dwellers. At the time I was raptured by Royn. By his looks, by his manners, by his mind.

We'd been hearing a chaser tell tales of an Earth she'd found ruled by the Mongols, who had conquered the whole of Europa and Asia and Afrika, and finally the North and South Xanadus too – elsewhere usually known as the Americas or Columbias. No audience of curious locals was permitted, needless to say, even though precious few could have understood anything. Royn invited me to admire the garden of the castellated house where he was lodging, facing the sea.

On the way there, a robed Sheikh (I think) accosted us politely enough, though sternly, speaking broken English.

"You djinn, or come Lamu on magic carpets?"

"No, and we trick nobody. We give gold. We stay, then we go."

"You pray, same we pray to Allah?"

"God shelters us."

If only that were true for Neither Dwellers!

But the Sheikh is unimportant. Royn took me to that garden where flame lilies and orchids and frangipani bloomed; and presently to his room, and thus to his great carved bed tented with netting. And I bled like a lily, though pleasure overwhelmed any pain.

Maybe my dad sensed the change in me.

"Royn isn't running any risk being with you for just a while," he said. "If some puppet leopard comes sniffing through the gate here, it'll only be a scout, not an assault. But he'll never commit to a long-term risk. A homing beacon for abomination, hmm?"

A month afterwards, the festival still aglow in my memory, I'd already world-chased twice on my own with no problems whatever, and I was planning to chase to where Royn was, supposedly – he'd said a fond *au revoir*, with hopes of seeing me again. I might meet with other conquests of Royn's, but I felt mature and able to cope. Just as soon as my dad came back from his scouting expedition with three companions, one of whom was also a chaser; just as soon!

My dad came back with one arm torn off, the stump sealed with tar. And on his own, without companions. Dad was already becoming incoherent with fever and from internal injuries. I'm astonished that he managed to conjure sparkles from his remaining hand and reveal gates to escape through. He was dying.

He'd encountered the actual Enemy, not merely their puppet creatures. He'd run into abhumanoids with four arms and leathery, reddish skin. Like demons, he gasped.

Of course his death, in my arms, was horrible. I felt as if the world was torn away from me. In a strange way, though, this was less ghastly in retrospect than the protracted anxious torment of my mother's slow disappearance from the realm of possibility. Dad's death was the abrupt ripping out of a tooth rather than dull prolonged toothache.

His death also altered everything. I was the only Daybreak now.

Duty possessed me.

"Okay," says Tina, "so you're either a tourist – or some kind of adventurer or explorer. I bet you have some things in your bag that could seem to little old me like magic. Don't worry, I shan't try to steal it!"

Actually, what *isn't* in my bag is rather more magical than the pistolette and a few other items. To have Tina on my side could be an advantage, and where's the harm?

So I extend my hand, palm upward, where she can see it while still paying attention to the road – a dead straight road can cause complacency. And I will the sparkles to rise. Little silvery stars hang above my cupped hand then dance to form an arrow.

"My god... can I touch?"

"With a fingertip."

Tina takes her right hand from the wheel. A star balances upon her fingertip.

"It's almost like a tiny fairy... So does magic exist? Or do you have nano-machines in your body?"

"No, it's a talent, a rare one."

"The arrow points where *you* want to go to? Or where those little stars *want* you to go? Some sort of destiny compass? No, there's no destiny, otherwise the universe would be stupid – we'd be automata. So: a destination compass." She withdraws her finger. "So what's the destination?"

"I'll know when we get there."

We. She'll take me all the way, irrespective of appointments or other reasons why she's driving. How could she not?

Ahead, some tumbleweed is on the move across the road, propelled by a dust devil. It's just natural, not a manifestation. If we knew the motives of the abhumanoids – their religion or psychology or instinct or whatever drives them – we might have a better plan than fleeing and hiding.

We talk a lot during the three hours and more of the drive, and I tell her a lot. What harm is there? In this world evidently no one would believe her. Tina's intention was to visit a cousin in a town which sounds to be about an hour short of where I need to go, but she has cast that intention aside. I'm her intention, and have all of her attention. "I didn't say exactly when I'd get to her place…"

She has a mobile phone but she doesn't use it when we're nearing the town in question and there's good signal. Would it make Tina guilty to pretend to her cousin to be elsewhere much further away? Or might the intrusion of normality break a kind of spell?

Huge trucks with trailers pass us by periodically. I notice how Tina tightens her grip on the wheel each time.

Evening, and we're coming in to a city. Silhouettes, and neon signs flowering against hazy firesky smog. The sparkle-arrow is level now, although it doesn't take account of obstructive buildings. Soon Tina is driving the grid pattern while I sniff and watch the arrow move this way, that way.

Of a sudden the arrow swings very quickly — we've just passed where the gate must be, a darkness in the midst of restaurants, boutiques, real estate offices.

"Stop as soon as you can. We're here."

It seemed to be a church, amorphous vegetation at the sides.

She's able to park at the kerb, outside a TexMex diner, while I'm letting the sparkles re-enter my flesh.

"I'm hungry," suggests Tina. "You must be too."

Does she want to be with me for a while longer before I disappear and take the proof of a great mystery out of her life, while leaving the mystery itself to haunt her?

"No," I tell her. "I'm geared up."

Behind rickety fencing the church looms darkly, brick-built. A paloverde tree sprawls untidily, branches brushing the ground on one side, pushing against the church wall on the other. Cars pass by, their headlights briefly revealing ungainly humps of bushes. Good place for derelicts to sleep, addicts to shoot up. I'm very close.

"Goodbye, Tina. And thanks."

"Hey. No way! I want to see."

I take out my pistolette, and press for light so that an amber fan sweeps the vegetation.

"Now you've seen."

Oddly, I spy no dirty old bedrolls or empty bottles or other trash, although the air smells strangely pungent, musky. Already Tina is pushing open a squeaky wrought iron gate.

I'm sniffing at the church, thinking of all the excellent hiding places inside a building that's probably seldom used, if ever. Maybe the lock already got broken, though if not I can cope with most locks. At the top of stone steps the wooden door, hinged with ironwork, is substantial.

A snort, a snuffle, a shuffle, a rattle of chain — and out from under a bush comes a huge-headed creature, snout raised and sniffing. A monster, no a razorback hog. No, it's a big male peccary. Wearing a collar, attached to a long chain. Pointy ears, square body and what a tree-trunk of a neck. Oh dear, this is the guardian of the church. The animal must be half-crazy, since peccaries like to roam in herds. What's the betting that TexMex and the other eateries dump food rubbish for the peccary round the back of the church land? Keep addicts and beggars from bothering customers. Its collar glints from my amber fan. Studs. And suddenly my sniffing homes in on that collar, and on a stud, just as Mr Madpig charges at us, little hooves drumming.

So I shoot it.

What else?

Uttering a high-pitched squeal like some alarm whistle, the peccary collapses in a heap almost at our feet, convulses, then lies still. Mercy killing of the mad. With it, the minimised gate is immobile. Before I realize what Tina intends, she has knelt and detached the chain and unbuckled the studded leather collar, which she now offers to me.

"Am I right, Arianna?"

I guess she notices my silhouette nod. She dangles the opened collar. "What happens if you take a gateway with you through a gate?"

"What do you mean?"

"If one of these studs is your 'minimised' gate, what if you pull the collar through the maximised gate along with you? Sort of like a snake swallowing its own tail, but completely?"

My god, could she be right and Royn doesn't need supernova energies but a flick of the wrist?

"I think there'd be a terrible bang and maybe this whole city would get sucked into a crater."

Or *worse*? Gates are naturally occurring connections between the myriad alternative worlds. To turn a gate inside-out, in the way Tina is evoking, might be like snapping a string of pearls – as opposed to tying knots in the string – except that multiple strings are involved, which might all proceed to unravel.

"And the hidden world would be shut away."

"He must have thought of that!"

"You didn't, not until now."

A gate pulled through itself… A concept rejected by Royn as too dangerously unpredictable, or one which hadn't yet occurred to him? One which he might rashly attempt, if a flood of us refugees poured through, pursued from afar by the proxies of the enemy, followed more distantly by the Enemy themselves?

"Forget that for the moment," I told Tina. *Forget it forever!* "There'll be at least a dozen gates throughout the hidden world."

And why do I hear in my imagination the boom, increasingly distant, of a dozen doors slamming shut one after another in a timed sequence? Or even all of them at once…

"Never mind. Give me."

She does so and I lay the collar down and concentrate. Sparkles rise from both my hands and suddenly they dive.

A perfectly round picture-window of a dark hilltop surmounted by a ring of columns and by stars, an image almost as high as I'm tall, arises, swelling. Thank goodness it's nighttime there – sunshine suddenly beaming out from beside this church upon the street might well attract attention. My pistolette is ready. Royn probably has some guards posted. Let's hope they're asleep.

"You'll be taking the pig-collar with you, Tina?"

"Wouldn't want it buried along with the peccary, now would we? Though I guess this gate can be re-attached to something else somewhere in the world by one of you, er, wizards. Become part of a tile in a mosque, or whatever."

I go through, my sparkles following in a stream, and the gate closes quickly. I can't spare time to check what it minimises down to on this side. A pebble? The skull of a sparrow? Lying flat on lumpy turf, trying to still my heartbeat and breathing, I *hear* urgently now instead of sniffing. Wind, the hooting of an owl. My people, oh my people, I must lead you here, heavily armed. If I have to kill Royn, can I make myself do it?

The 1000 Year Reich

I imagine Tina Sena wearing that studded collar cinched round her waist. I bet she'll do that. The wild pig had a neck much bigger than a dog's. Although I only noticed after we got out of the car, Tina was physically a bit of an hourglass, ample-chested, wide-hipped, but an anti-equator in between. How better to keep a constant eye on the collar-come-belt. Wear it. Perfect fit. She'll arrive very late at her cousin's with her new fashion accessory.

Tina might look fetish and excite a certain type of man, or woman. However, that won't be why she's wearing a pig-collar round her waist. It's her souvenir of mystery. Much more than a souvenir, really, since the gate will quite likely get used again, from this side if not from hers. Its sudden swelling to full size won't cut her in half or anything, but she'll be very close to whoever emerges.

Maybe that person will even be me, perhaps to unbuckle her belt and pull the belt back into the gate along with me to test her theory. If I'm in a hurry, it might be quicker to pull Tina complete with belt! Since I decided I like her, does this mean that I should, or shouldn't?

Back in about 2006 Aberrant Dreams *magazine organised a competition: entrants should write a brief story outline inspired by one or other piece of artwork on the website; the winner would get to choose the author to write this story (obviously, out of authors who had already volunteered) and would have a character named after him – or herself. Stories would appear quite soon in a deluxe hardback, with paperback to follow,* Aberrant Dreams: The Awakening.

A winner, Tina Sena, chose me to write her story. I'd tackled nothing quite like this before, except in the sense that my Warhammer 40K books were set in a predetermined universe, but I'm usually up for a challenge. Diligently I emailed Tina Sena to get a vague verbal idea of what she looked like, for verisimilitude. And I wrote, feeling a bit Silverbergian (though Bob Silverberg mightn't agree). I delivered. Time passed. And passed. After a year or three I emailed my story to Tina Sena so that at least she could read what she had won. More time passed.

Advance orders for the book were still being taken; I decided that editor Joe Dickerson was waiting until enough pre-orders existed to pay for printing the book. Even more time passed. I forgot about the story, and then remembered again. Finally in the summer of 2014, after nagging and saying that I'd market my story elsewhere since the contract was already long expired, to appease me at last I received a contributor's copy of the deluxe edition "published" 4 years previously but still not on sale... a long pregnancy indeed, although not so long as Harlan Ellison's still inexistent The Last Dangerous Visions, *my story from which I withdrew in about 1982, causing vituperation.*

BELOVED PIG-BROTHER OF THE DAUGHTER OF THE PREGNANT BABY
(with Roberto Quaglia)

Kalyani had named her baby Lolita because that word means *ruby* in Sanskrit, and her daughter was a precious gem. Kalyani and Sami had been trying for seven years to make a baby. Could it be that environmental pollutants in the Indian countryside were harming her fertility or even impairing Sami's wet seeds worse than GM contamination could spoil crops?

The latter idea was almost unthinkable, especially considering the volume of semen Sami produced, and its frequency. Even when Kalyani's pregnancy was obvious, Sami continued squirting into her as though to make sure that the foetus was well glued in place.

Kalyani and Sami had never heard of Vladimir Nabokov, because they belonged to the illiterate 25 per cent of India's huge population, which made India the most illiterate country in the world, although mainly because the population is so huge, and 25 per cent of huge is bigger than the total of most nations – such as Botswana or Bulgaria or even Brazil, just for example.

But come on, be fair! When the British quit India in 1947, only 12 per cent of Indians could read; so much for the benefits of colonialism! By 2011 three-quarters of Indians were literate, and the giant nation was surging ahead. Yet that still left 300 million people such as Sami and Kalyani unable to read *Lolita*. Innocently and traditionally they had named their child "Ruby" (in Sanskrit).

When Lolita was three months old, she began whining and crying. Her little tummy looked bloated. She fussed and wouldn't sleep.

Trapped wind? Trapped poo? In case of something more serious, Kalyani carried her jewel for two hours to the government health centre in the quite nearby village of Y – she herself lived in X – and Bachelor of Rural Medicine and Surgery Dr Das made an amazing discovery thanks to the Google BodyView scanning tablet: baby Lolita herself was *pregnant!*

"What's more," Dr Das told Kalyani in Hindi, "she must have been *born already pregnant*. Your Lolita must have been impregnated during her eighth month, which has got to be a record deserving to be in the Guinness Book!"

"My husband didn't stop squirting into me until I was very big..."

"In that case, he's the father *and* the grandfather at the same time. I think so. This may be the first example ever of," and Dr Das switched to English, "Unintentional Paedophiliac Prepartum Incest, otherwise UPPI."

Since for all he knew this might be the first example of such a condition in recorded history – and since Dr Das dearly wished to be first to describe it – this condition needed to have an English name based on Latin and Greek. Beside which, UPPI was *also* the acronym for the company leading the world in PET pharmacy, which doesn't refer to pussy cats and goldfish but to Positron Emission Tomography, which Google BodyView used. So there might be sponsorship money!

Given such a medical discovery, Das might even become head of the MCI, the Medical Council of India, despite that he'd only had an abbreviated three-and-a-half years of training as a Bachelor of Rural Medicine (plus Surgery) and therefore being prohibited from practising in cities.

Oh but damn it, a Dr Desai (whose name was similar to Das's) was recently sacked as head of the MCI because of a bribery scandal, and hadn't people called the MCI a den of iniquity? Might it be better to become head of the IMA, the Indian Medical Association? No, double-damn it, the same allegedly dishonest Desai had also occupied that post previously. Dash and drat Desai! thought Das.

How about the Nobel Prize for Medicine, followed by owning half a dozen private hospitals?

No no, forget about honours from the mainstream medical community. He might need to wait a while for the King of Sweden to hear about him. This pregnancy within a pregnancy must be rarer than than a sighting of a Yeti! Of course, TV! The TV show *You Are Doctor House!*

Wait, just to be on the safe side facts-wise, he should use his Google BodyView's googling function...

Hmm, a similar case in Saudi a few years ago, and another in

Pakistan. Well fuck Pakistan, this was India! As for Saudi, the report was in *Pravda*, so how likely was it to be true? Aside from that dodgy duo, the literature was all about twins of valid embryos behaving like tumours, growing teratogenically in a boy's stomach for instance, a non-viable assortment of organs, hair, warped legs, whatever. Nothing at all like the perfect foetus nestling within Lolita's perfect shining pearl of a uterus as revealed by Google BodyView.

So that was okay.

"Do you watch *You Are Doctor House*?" he asked Kalyani.

She shook her head. "There's only one TV in my village. You have to pedal a bicycle fast to see anything."

Ah that would be a fixed bicycle to provide power, not because the owner of the TV had a guard dog.

The Indian version of *You Are Doctor House* was a fairly exact copy of the American original, but without the possibility of law suits. When one says American 'original', in fact an Italian came up with the idea but Luigi failed in his home country due to the Italian state normally providing free medical care for its citizens. An American TV network stole the idea, perfected it, copyrighted it, produced it, and franchised it around the world, resulting in perhaps the most popular reality show of all time, especially in America and in other less developed countries which similarly lacked health care except for the rich. Appearing in *YADH* was like winning a lottery prize, provided you were ill.

You've heard of crowd sourcing? *YADH* is diagnosis- and treatment-sourcing. Lucky patients are locked in a sophisticated medical facility where there are glamorous nurses but no doctors. Viewers can peep in real time into every room of the hospital and have access to every patient's medical records. In *Big Brother* viewers vote for who stays and who has to leave the house. In *YADH* the viewers guess the disease they think each patient has in a process of *shared democratic diagnosis* (SDD). Once this is voted, next they vote on the most appropriate treatment for each patient.

Most of those *YADH* nurses are aspiring models, or (in India) would-be Bollywood stars, who do a three-week First Aid and care course, including how to interview patients and keep records. The voluptuous nurses hope to be spotted for better things, so of course they give of their best and aren't paid a cent (or a rupee), making this kind of hospital the cheapest-to-run medical facility in the modern history of health. Another cheapness factor is that pharma companies compete in offering drugs for free; the public has the last word on which patient takes which drug for how long – sexy commercials help them to choose. Surgeons are allowed inside the Sickhouse precisely and only to perform operations on which the public have voted, and which they wish to watch.

The amazing surprise from all this was that the consensus of medically incompetent viewers was rather better at healing the sick than the opinions of specialists. One million unqualified people could understand and remedy a bodily malfunction more efficiently than a single averagely skilful individual; and statistically the public killed less patients than specialists did. Surely this was the apotheosis of the ideology of democracy. Hereby America was exporting the concept of democracy more tellingly and politically correctly than by coups and bombs. Indeed the full title of the show became: *You Are Doctor House. One Million People Can't Be Wrong!*

Forget about similar smaller projects presided over by the medical establishment, such as CrowdMed, FindZebra, or IBM's Watson! *YADH* had *one million amateurs!*

Das mused in Hindi to Kalyani, and to himself: "Lolita's baby is growing faster proportionately than Lolita herself. This must result in Lolita bursting unless something is done quickly. Let me see now, let me see, what we need is a suitable *host* to implant Lolita's baby into right now, so that the sub-baby has room to grow – Google BodyView says she's a girl, by the way. Normally one might look to the mother, I mean in your case the grandmother, as having the most *histocompatibility*," a word which he said in English based on Greek and Latin. Hmm, the weirder the pathology, the more likely the invitation on to *YADH*. "Pigs!" cried Das of a sudden. Increasingly *pigs* were used to provide replacement body organs for people. There was a lot of physical similarity between people and pigs.

"We *do* have one pig," confessed Kalyani, "but we can't give her up! She's part of the family." Ah, so she thought he was asking for a bribe to give Lolita the best treatment! "We only eat her piglets."

Organ donor pigs usually needed some genetic protection to stop their transplanted organs being attacked by the human immune system

– but a pig that was *part of the family*... that might work.

"What's your pig's name?"

"Pig."

"How long does Pig usually take to have piglets? Counting from first being squirted?"

"Three months, three weeks, and three days. Everyone knows 333, the number of the pig beast."

Well, Das didn't know because he wasn't a vet. Mind you, his second cousin Das, who worked in Z only an hour away by bicycle, was a vet, which might come in useful. Millions and millions of people in India were called Das. Das's mind raced. There ought to be a business contract pretty promptly between himself and Kalyani.

"Are you illiterate?" he asked, and she nodded. "Excellent! Would you like enough money to buy a bicycle and a TV? In fact, a fleet of bicycles!"

For once, Kalyani looked suspicious. "Will I wake up with a big scar on my back?" This had happened to lots of illiterate Indians after they were offered a TV or a bike. They would fall asleep then wake up with a scar and slight urinary problems.

"No scars, I assure you!"

Das's mind was connecting dots, and not in the sense of someone sewing a suture. How best to get in touch with *YADH* privately ahead of hundreds of thousands of other supplicants? Well, Das's Uncle Das had been making a living for decades crippling people so that they could beg and repay him from their pitiful earnings for their cripplement. Pitiful in the sense of pity; really exotic cripples could earn quite well provided they avoided the clutches of a cripple-pimp. For illicit surgical reasons the black market in organ removal overlapped with the black market in piteous crippling which in turn overlapped with the illegal market in videos of cripple-sex which were made by relatives of cinematographic technicians who worked for the most important reality show on Indian TV. So Uncle Das had connections.

A pig pregnant with a human foetus would be much more sensational than merely a pregnant baby imperilled by inevitable bursting. The banal treatment could only be an abortion or a very junior hysterectomy unless the audience actually voted to let nature take its course which would be a bit sadistic of them... No, the audience must be presented with a much more alluring medical circumstance.

Das told Kalyani, "I'm closing my clinic for the day to devote myself to you. I'll send the other patients away; they'll need to be patient. I have a call to make now – not a house call, a phone call." Das was thinking in English, so his words in Hindi may have seemed surreal to her. Quickly he used the call function of his Google BodyView.

"Second Cousin Das? This is Second Cousin Das in Y. You must drop everything at once and cycle here with the things you use for animal gynaecology. I need you to look at a pig urgently. Well, she's a sow, but she's called Pig. I'll make it worth your while..."

The hour until Second Cousin Das arrived was well spent devising a foolproof contract which Kalyani obediently signed with an x. Which also happened to be her address. So: x, X. This seemed a friendly contract, even affectionate. Next, Das checked the tyres of his official Rural Medicine and Surgery bicycle. Das himself would carry Lolita with him in a blanket in the basket in front of the handlebars to relieve Kalyani of a burden while she herself was walking back to X, and in hope that the foetal transplant could be performed right away.

Well now, after Das-eins and Das-zwei and Lolita arrived in X, Das-zwei discovered that the Pig was already pregnant with foetal piglets. To this day *Mein Kampf* remains a steady best-seller in India and an alarmingly large percentage of the Hindu population declare admiration for Adolf Hitler due to his skill at oratory and his efficiency, as opposed to the limpness of Ghandi. These Hindus perceive a similarity between Jews and Moslems as regards final solutions. Since Das is such a German word (Aryan connection, eh?) -eins and -zwei follow logically (disregarding Heidegger's analysis of *dasein* as existence because his philosophy was lacking a final "s"). Since stories ought to be economical, henceforth Das-eins, Das-zwei, Das-drei et cetera will take up less space in our narrative than us forever referring to Second Cousins and Uncles. Just remember that Das-eins is Dr Das.

"Extracting the foetus from Lolita and implanting it into Pig is easier said than done," confessed Das-zwei after using his Google VetBodyScan to examine both Pig and Lolita.

"Because of pre-piglets already occupying the womb?" asked Das-eins.

"They might crush Lolita's foetus. Or the sub-baby mightn't attach because the womb's no longer receptive. I'd prefer to run some animal tests first of all – such as transplant the foetus of a dog of suitable size, obviously not a Chihuahua, more like a Labrador, and see what happens. Professionally I can assure you that Pig's in the pink of health."

"A pig being pink seems usual and, as for healthy, I believe non-healthy pigs soon become bacon. Look, Das (zwei), you've been a great help and I owe you some rupees, but we don't have time for animal tests!"

Das-eins decided to bluff. After Das-zwei had cycled away, Das-eins called Das-drei...

And so it came to pass that executives of *YADH* became very excited about featuring on the show a pig with a pre-human-being already inside. They became so excited at the projected viewing figures that, when Das-eins lied convincingly that the transplant was in fact *about* to happen at a holistic clinic, the executives demanded that no risk should be run by allowing mere doctors or vets or holistic practitioners to participate. Instead they hired India's top specialist in chimeric chirurgy who had already won the Ig Nobel Prize by creating a *tigoon*, a tiger-baboon hybrid, for a Maharaja's zoo.

As a result, all but one of the piglets-to-be were unplugged by the consultant frankensurgeon and Lolita's baby-to-be successfully plugged in. One pig foetus was left in place to stabilise the pregnancy – It turned out that Pig already being pregnant was an advantage. (This was all filmed and kept secret, to be revealed later in the show.) Due to Das-eins's exclusive contract with Kalyani and therefore with Lolita, he was able to insist on participating personally – he held the sterilised tray on which the unplugged pre-piglets were placed as though awaiting skewers for a barbecue. The tiny pre-piglets would be plastinated by Gunther von Hagens In*corporated* and kept as possible prizes for a Christmas Special of *YADH*.

After the operation was judged a success, Das-eins bought a huge multicoloured ice cream for Kalyani, which made her very happy.

The frankensurgeon, coincidentally another Desai, confided to the executives and to Das-eins, that his *really* clever trick had been to co-ordinate the pre-piglet and pre-human pregnancies by biochemical implants to control the respective rates of growth. Otherwise Piglet would be born several months prior to the due date of Lolita's baby together with afterbirth and such, which might cause a baby-with-bathwater abortion. Brother-piglet and sister-baby would now pop out at pretty much the same time.

Das-eins did have a minor panic when Das-zwei remarked to him how piglets are unique among non-human animals in developing teeth while still in the womb – eight teeth, what's more, which are sharp as needles and angled outward as vicious weapons.

"But that's crazy," said Das-eins. "Don't piglets suckle milk?"

"Yes, they suck for weeks until they're weaned," said Kalyani, who was privy to this conversation.

"The pig-mother's teats must bleed horribly! Is this a source for the vampire legend?"

Kalyani hadn't read *Dracula* any more than she hadn't read *Lolita*, but she simply explained, "New-born piglets battle their brothers and sisters for best teat position. It's like Formula One. So they need to pop out fully armed. Usually we clip their teeth back to the gum the moment they're born."

"My gods, that must hurt worse than a baby's cock or clit being clipped."

"Clipping doesn't discourage the piglets from sucking," said Kalyani.

"*I'd* be sucking if all my teeth had been clipped... But *the point is*: Lolita's babe will be in the womb for at least a week or two along with an armed bully! She might get injured."

Kalyani grinned. "Piglets only fight when there's a crowd. Two is company."

Months passed, until the publicity build-up began.

A few hundred million Indians had their gazes glued to TV screens as Pig lay on her back, trotters up in the air in gynaecological stirrups. A birthing bed might have been more comfortable for Pig, or a sanitised sty littered with straw, but lacking those stirrups Pig would doubtless have turned over, denying viewers sight of the lines of multiple teats bulging invitingly, as well as of her naughty parts. Now and then Pig squealed or oinked.

One of the few hundred million Indians watching TV was Das-eins. He couldn't be personally present in the Sickhouse, so *YADH* had put him in a suite at the Krishna Palace Hotel. And Das-eins had collected a parasite in the shape of a self-proclaimed American sociologist, Zebedee Jones. Das had been hoping for important Americans to contact him, make him rich and famous, put him on talk shows such as Whoopi's and Sally Jessy's and Precious Mo'Nique's and Lisa Lingam's. However, only Zeb Jones had turned up at the Krishna Palace Hotel, apparently having read an English-language TV magazine containing a story about the pregnant pig.

At first the American parasite person seemed beneficial, quite like the tapeworm which Zeb himself hosted in his own intestines so as to avoid Goa Gut and stay slim while pigging out on a favourite chili-spicey curry of pork, liver, tongue, and blood. Zeb lived on the beach in Goa, otherwise he would have taken precautions against Delhi Belly, downfall of the British.

"Hey Man," Zeb had accosted Das-eins in the lobby of the Krishna Palace Hotel the day before, Zeb clutching the crumpled magazine containing Das-eins' photo, and dressed in Desert Storm camo trousers and one of those sleeveless jackets with at least forty pockets outside and inside, some zipped, some velcroed. "Can I interview you for *Time* magazine?"

Person of the Year, Person of the Year... Das-eins could already see the cover clearly.

As Das-eins realised, once Zeb started to roost in his suite and exploit room service, the American had no connections with any magazine, although Zeb dearly wished so, so he could have money for high-chili pork, liver, tongue and blood curry every day; not that the Krishna Palace offered this on its menu, but Zeb was ravenous, or else his tapeworm was – we should emphasise that the tapeworm was of the antisocial hermaphroditic kind which is egotistical.

Nor did Zeb seem to have many sensible questions.

"You got no shit to smoke, Dude?"

"I beg your pardon?" replied the Indian provincial doctor.

"I mean, like, *shit.*"

"The toilet is over there. When do we do our interview?"

But Zeb fell asleep on a sofa. He was still there the following evening when possibly the most watched ever episode of *You Are Doctor House* began.

"Oh fuck, here they go with their fuckin' dance."

Being hopeful Bollywood stars, nurses usually did a song and dance routine around the operating table or in this case the place of labour. Accompanying them: the slim obstetrician whose dark hair was wavy with grease.

"Are they gonna Seize-Her-Aryan?" Zeb began searching his many pockets for a possible roach.

"Caesarian," corrected Das-ein, and he shook his head. "The viewers already voted for no-cutting. Probably many viewers thought this meant they would miss some of the action. But as usual the majority is wise. Induced-natural is safer."

"How come the birth's gonna happen just at the right time during the show?"

Ah, this was becoming more like the interview Das-ein had hoped for, although the American wasn't making any notes; he was still roach-hunting uselessly.

"The obstetric already inserted a prostaglandin pessary into Pig to induce beast- and baby-birth at the right time. Viewers also voted for generous use of oxytocin under its popular name of Love Hormone injected into a vein."

"I heard of Love Hormone!"

"In fact oxytocin is Greek for 'quick birth' but it has lots of functions."

"Something's happening already! Pig's squirming a bit more."

"*Which will come first? Which will come first?*" they heard the compère call out. "*Piglet or human baby? Place your bets online now! You have thirty seconds.*" A countdown clock appeared at the top of the screen. More accurately, Das-ein both heard and understood, whereas the American couldn't speak Hindi, so he didn't understand and probably thought that the clock signified –

"They're gonna be born in twenty, nineteen, eighteen –"

"A bit longer than that."

Actually, it was one minute and fifteen seconds till the first head showed within Pig's vulva. Pigs generally give birth without fuss; piglets simply slide out, eight sharp little teeth at the ready. Ah yes here was a *snout*, already snorting out bubbly fluid that had been in its lungs! The rest of the body, lifted by a nurse, was a bit messy, soon cleaned. Snip went scissors; on to the stub of the umbilical cord went a clip. The thrilled nurse, in close-up for the first time in her career, held the piglet to a teat otherwise it would fall off its upside-down mother.

Pig's vulva dilated further, revealing the messy little dome of a human head...

The audience at home had some important decisions to make. Pig was already liberated from the stirrups and had been hoisted to a nearby mattress equipped with wheels. Piglet was sucking at a teat. Piglet needed the immune-rich colostrum. Humans usually get their immunities passively via the mother's placenta, but in this case the placenta had been a piggy placenta.

The audience voted and baby Lolita's baby daughter was installed at a teat a couple of teats away from Piglet.

Das-ein rejoiced. "The first ever birth from a pig of a *Homo*!"

"What, you mean she'll be lesbian?"

"*Sapiens*."

"Lesbian sapiens?"

"Homo sapiens."

"Uh, I see."

By now Kalyani cuddling Lolita were by the side of the mattress.

"*Memsahibs and sahibs at home, now it's time to send in your suggestions for a name for our little wonder, happily suckling at a sow as you see.*"

Within sixty seconds a box on the TV screen showed the top five suggestions in Roman as well as in Devanagari script:

AKSHITA BALAMANI KOKILA AISHA YASHILA

For purposes of narrative speed we omit the Devanagari script, because Zeb was already exclaiming, "Ak*shit*a sounds like some bad shit!" and Das-eins was retorting, "But it means Wonder Girl, and Balamani means Little Gem –" to which Zeb responded, "That's a fucking lettuce!" "– and Kokila is Cuckoo, no doubt alluding to her being hatched in a different nest, and Aisha means Alive and Well." But already time was up without either having had enough time to vocalise *and* to vote, and the winner was...

!!!!YASHILA!!!!

"Ya, Sheila..." repeated Zeb.

"...means Famous. She is famous all right. The people are wise."

"Lotsa women in Australia are called Sheila."

A quick newsflash reported riots and that any available Hindu temples were on fire in Moslem areas of Indian cities, since anything associated with pigs is deeply offensive to Moslems.

"Hey, what about Sheila's brother? Doesn't *he* get a name too?"

"Chup raho!" snapped Das-eins in Hindi. "Keep quiet. That comes next. *YADH* wanted to let viewers vote on whether to turn Pig into sausages but Kalyani was indignant and besides Pig's needed for colostrum and milk."

The most popular name, when voted, was a surprise: RINGO.

"Hey, that's cool! Such a superdrummer. Ringo must have really endeared himself by taking that suitcase of plain and simple baked beans to the Maharishi's ashram, even if he did complain about lepers lacking fingers. And didn't he look dashing in his gold-braided Nehru jacket? Man, those were the days, back in the Stoned Age."

"I think," said Das-eins, "viewers want a ring put through the piglet-brother's nose. Nose-rings are so popular with ladies in India. We invented nose-rings."

Surprisingly quickly came commercials for opulent nose-rings.

A new newsflash reported that India had gone to DEFCON 3 due to fears that the Islamic Republic of England might use the pretext of the blasphemous public use of a pig to launch a nuclear missile attack from its one remaining elderly submarine. Of course the news report turned out to be false. From the moment England became an Islamic republic its politics of military aggression in the world had stopped – though paradoxically England was now perceived by a majority of non-Muslim countries as potentially more dangerous than ever, especially by countries which experienced British colonization in the past, such as India and the USA.

Therefore no nuclear war occurred on account of a pregnant baby's babe, formerly transplanted into a sow, now suckling side by side with a piglet named Ringo who was biologically her brother.

In the absence of nuclear wars, time could pass so that more future was allowed to happen. Ringo was permitted to live by the rigged democratic voting of the YADH public. Only later did it come out that the large Indian public, which had traditions of starvation, had voted by a not-so-slim majority to turn the useless piglet promptly into very useful sausages, but big meat multinationals had intervened to rescue Ringo by paying call centres to mass-call and vote. A dead exceptional piglet, the first to be the brother of a human, would be of no use to them, while a living one would eventually allow them to find a way to make money. Bridal India Limited sponsored a gold-plated snout-ring for Ringo.

For several months only the obvious happened, the multinationals managing to get the piglet into ad spots and on talk shows just as a pet – an exceptional pet, but nothing deserving of comment in our story. Yashila was omitted from this, since there's no industry – at least officially – of making sausages out of humans. And Yashila's mother too, Lolita, remained in the shadow, as well as mother/grandmother Kalyani, while Dr Das-eins was very efficient as Ringo's agent, cashing in every time the pig appeared on TV and delivering a new bicycle to Kalyani each time he borrowed the piglet. Soon Kalyani opened a little bicycle shop, which made her quite happy. But, as we damn well already said, we really don't want to waste time on the obvious.

The less obvious started to manifest itself less than a year later...

Approaching one year of age a child is barely fully human – while a pig is already a horny young adult. Yashila started to show excess distress each time Ringo was away from her. Was she merely missing his smell, of old socks?

We should explain that Yashila spent her days and nights on a wide bed of sweet meadow hay suitable for little girl's ponies (brought all the way from the mountains of Manipur), which Ringo shared affectionately. Straw would have been too coarse for Yashila, no matter that she wore over her nappies the best fleece-bottom pyjamas and babyhug tops from Mothercare India, causing a constant pilgrimage of wonder by villagers from miles around to admire the luxuries she enjoyed (but this isn't a product publicity spot). Ringo would snuffle up to her; she would feebly try to hug him. Although Ringo was soon three or four times Yashila's size, there seemed no risk of him crushing her, the way big fat mother pigs can crush a piglet simply by failing to notice – Ringo certainly paid attention to his biosister.

Anticipating the possibility of separation syndrome, Dr Das-eins had brought a Ringo-substitute stuffed with hundreds of much-used woollen socks which he had paid adolescent boy beggars to wear for a few weeks to soak up their musky, musty androstenone sweat, similar to a young boar's. Normally beggars no more wore socks than did the villagers in X. Yet this teddy-pig was no comfort to Yasila!

Lo, the truth was that Ringo was trying to have sex with his infant sister... and Yashila wasn't averse despite her extreme immaturity.

Now, boars' penises notoriously behave just like bottleopeners when they're erect, and sows' vaginas are the perfect receptacles, as designed by Darwin. This lends a new meaning to *Get Screwed.* Lock and load! (or, more sensibly: Load and lock!) and the boar spurts. These days, due to global pollution, an increasing number of male piglets are born with anticlockwise pricks, which is a sexual tragedy for them personally and means that they become sausages even faster; but Ringo's prick was clockwise, correctly. However, all those Mothercare India baby clothes and nappies were thwarting Ringo's efforts by serving as several layers of external hymens.

The stage had just come (unlike Ringo, yet) when he had worked out that he needed to undress his sister as a preliminary. This was too difficult using pig trotters, so soon Ringo was tearing Yashila's clothes with his sharp teeth, and amazingly always tenderly enough so as not to injure her. Kalyani had as many boxes of Mothercare India baby clothes as she had bicycles, so the shredding in itself didn't bother her. Besides, when Ringo came close to his goal, he became distracted by the poos in Yashila's nappies – not because pigs eat shit, which they don't unless desperately hungry since they are very clean animals, and people who say otherwise are *slanderers of pigs*. On the contrary, Ringo pulled her used nappies away towards his own toilet of cinders, soil, chicken feathers, and shredded Mothercare India baby garments near the door of the house, outside.

"This is unfortunate," Dr Das-eins told Kalyani diagnostically in Hindi. Switching to English, which may as well have been Latin to Kalyani, he apostrophised (a word we have always wanted to use), "This is worse than a human paedophile pervertedly pushing the point of his penis at a human baby! It's *incestuous bestial* paedophily, which can't be condoned by TV celebrities!"

What to do? Keep Ringo at a safe distance from the baby, and the baby would squeal desperately in frustration, till asphyxia might result. Teddy-pigs stuffed with socks obviously were no use. Yashila's mother Lolita wasn't much use as a calming influence since Lolita was a squealing baby herself. If a word of this got out, Ringo would most likely end up slaughtered, and for Dr Das-eins that would mean the end of easy money. As the pig's agent, as well as the baby's, he might end up being slaughtered himself.

At this point Dr Das-eins recollected how, following a persuasive ad for the so-called 'Love Hormone' in lipstick and pessary form (which were the same, apart from packaging), the YADH audience had voted for a truly *enormous* dose of oxytocin to be injected into the delivering pig. As well as helping dilate the cervix and speed up birth (the audience was impatient), a normal, natural dose of oxytocin also causes emotional bonding, usually of mother and baby, but in this case the result was a parasitic erotic bonding between human baby and pig-brother, which duly manifested itself as soon as was possible. Yashila and Ringo were sexually in love.

Dr Das-eins thought that he might exploit this profitably in an erotic circus in another nine or ten years' time, appealing to connoisseurs, but as for right now: *Oh oink oink oink*, he thought. At his wits' end, he went back home to Y.

However, Dear Reader, months earlier the American parasite and self-proclaimed sociologist Zebedee Jones had settled permanently in Dr Das-eins' home. Das-eins couldn't ignore the coincidence that all his fortunes had started when the parasite popped up in his life, and the more the parasite was close to him the more money poured into his pockets. *Objectively* Das-eins was aware that that *might* be just a coincidence, but really, the absurd American ringing at his door in India just at that juncture was such an unlikely event, topped by what then unfolded, that it had become increasingly dangerous to get rid of Jones. Das-eins hadn't the fine mind of a true coincidence theorist. Conspiracy theorists perceive hidden links connecting random events; coincidence theorists insist that connected events are coincidences.

Mainly, Zebedee Jones lolled on Dr Das-eins's couch in the living room, constantly snacking on the delicious Indian delicatessen buffet that his host provided day after day, treating this as junk food as though poppadums plus pickles were popcorn, as if bhajis were MacBurgers; watching TV all the while. Dr. Das-eins' hometown, Y, was just a rural village, and the stream of money which poured into the doctor's pockets leaked out to the whole community; consequently the belief quickly spread that this luck was caused magically by the presence of the American. Peasants started to queue at Dr. Das-eins' doorway bearing gifts such as lotus blossoms or Indian tonic water for the idealized American who was fattening rapidly. Every month Das-eins had to provide Jones with bigger trousers and sweatshirts. The tapeworm must have died of gluttony.

Since the enlarging American seemed to be largely immobile, going nowhere any time soon, and since *Fatal Attraction* was the name of a famous American movie, which the doctor hadn't seen, after half a bottle of Bagpiper Gold whisky Das-eins confided his worries about the fatal attraction between the baby and her pig brother.

Immediately Zebedee Jones became galvanised.

This doesn't mean that his body suddenly became coated with zinc. Rather, a seeming powerful jolt of electricity passed through the American, jerking him bolt upright out of the sofa.

His eyes were now sparkling such as Dr Das-eins had never seen hitherto – the rural doctor thought the American might be suddenly possessed by a demon.

"*Bingo!*" shouted the possessed sociologist in a completely different voice. Entities which possess people rarely appreciate their original voices and prefer to replace those with their own, maybe out of vanity, or for the sake of plausible nondeniability.

Suddenly an advanced medical thought occurred to Das-eins. How exactly had Zebedee's tapeworm died, permitting him to balloon? Had he overdosed on all those gifts of Indian tonic water? Could many of those bottles have contained *MepacrIndian* tonic water, popularly used to sterilise over-fertile wives? Mepacrine is *quinine-on-steroids*, banned by the Supreme Court of India; obviously a black market flourished. Mepacrine could kill tapeworms, and Mepacrine could also cause *toxic psychosis*, often confused with female hysteria.

"Zebedee..." Dr Das-eins could only murmur. "Are you all right?"

"*Fuck Zebedee!*" said Zebedee's mouth, thus confirming the first of Dr Das-eins' intuitions. The American really was possessed by a demon. "*You are now talking with Google Homeland Security. Zeb-GITMO is merely a terminal.*"

As regards American progress in the field of security, Dr Das-eins was aware from *Hindustan* newspaper that the USA boasted imprisoning 2% of all its citizens, the world record amongst countries excluding unknowable North Korea. With the repressive Seashell Islands in 2nd position and India way down at 216th, by the way. By agreeing to a GITMO brain implant to control their minds, American prisoners could become 'sleeper agents', released on licence worldwide to act as eyes and ears of the NSA, CIA, and other acronyms. GITMO meant General Intelligence Task Motivated Operative. Anything was better than Sing Sing or New Alcatraz, just for instance. A lucky GITMO might even end up on a beach, such as Copacabana or Goa. Every type of less-intelligent American sleeper agent required by the modern world was by now a GITMO.

"*Ringo and Yashila will be extracted within two hours. Black choppers are on the way. We need to know everything about his sexual relations with his human sister.*"

Dr Das-eins was reasonably confused. "Extracted? By Google Homeland Security? *From India?*"

"*In a globalised world Google Homeland Security has become global too. Until recently most of India was only at the Street View stage. No longer. Welcome to Street View with added Security.*"

Dr Das-eins was astonished. "You want to study sex between animals and humans at the *infantile* stage? But that is paedobeastophilia!"

"*We are tasked to preserve North American society excluding Mexico and Canada,*" said Google Homeland Security's terminal. "*Mainframe computer projections foresee potentially catastrophic demographic problems in NA (minus M & C) due to women who get pregnant suing their husbands for violating their human rights to individualistic physical and psychological integrity. This trend might even spread to the entire world, since North Americans (minus M & C) set the pattern for mankind as regards freedom and democracy. If no kids are made any more, humans are doomed to extinction.*"

"Women are suing their husbands for doing their manly duty?" Something unimaginable in India; the rural doctor was astonished. "What do judges say about this?!"

"*That the women are right,*" answered Zebedee's mouth. "*If the judges don't say so, the pregnant women will sue the judges for discriminating against them on grounds of pregnancy. Choosing a pregnant judge is no solution, because most judges are old men.*"

"How big is the problem? I read nothing in *Hindustan*."

"*One case in 2012, five cases in 2013; the longterm Mainframe projection is the extinction of all North Americans (minus M & C) a classified number of years from now.*"

"And how would a pig solve this problem?"

"*Growing children inside of pigs instead of women could solve a lot of problems. But the trans-species bonding induced by oxytocin overdose is something really new. It's a paradigm shift.*" For a solemn moment Zebedee seemed like the sociologist he was supposed to be.

"*Aside from the impending demographic crisis, there's a crucial current crisis of popular rebellion world-wide against ruling elites. This is very destabilizing and potentially devastating. The special bond between Ringo and Yashila leads us to think that we can create varieties of pigs genetically modified with the genes of endangered elites – bankers, members of the richest dynasties, people who have dominated society for many generations, and who must continue to do so for many more generations to ensure the North American way of life (excluding M though maybe including C if fully incorporated into NA).*"

"You mean to say..."

"*Yes, all the new children grown in the modified pigs will effectively be immunised against hating their rulers – indeed, they'll be bound to adore them. This won't be an easy techno task to accomplish, but the bonding of Ringo and Yashila begins this route. In the words of John Fitzgerald Kennedy, we will do this not because it is easy but because it is hard. New generations of workers – the stepwomb-offspring of pigs and of bankers – will not start revolutions. Though they may need to eat sausages due to the huge increase in the menopausal pig population on birth-farms.*"

"George Orwell, who was in the Indian Imperial Police, predicted in his *Animal Farm*, that pigs would become rulers…"

"*Bankers and ruling elites and their police have often been insulted as 'pigs'. Now the tables will be turned.*"

At first, Dr Das-eins had no words with which to reply. But then he thought of seven:

"Why are you telling me all this?"

Zebedee's reply sounded like the unactivated Zebedee, though less italic:

"Ah'm offering you the chance to come along, being as how you're the supervising physician... Kinda, repay your hospitality." And Zebedee laughed a human laugh.

Following which, Zeb-GITMO chuckled in a chillier cybernetic way.

"But that is not the total truth. You kept Zebedee in your home because you are superstitious. Google Homeland Security is also superstitious. This is because of quantum indeterminacy. Superstition shows respect for the imponderable region of unknown unknowns christened by Donald Rumsfeld. We will take you with us to bring good luck to our cause. If you so choose democratically."

Warmed by the Bagpiper Gold, Das-eins grinned. In America he might change his name to Das Strange-Love, if that was grammatical.

Valiant, venturesome NewCon Press published the volume The Beloved of My Beloved *by myself and my Italian surrealist chum Roberto Quaglia in 2010, our collected "Beloved" stories up to that date. This may be the only full-length genre fiction book by two authors with different mother tongues, written as if we share the same brain, and includes an original story, "The Beloved Time of Our Lives", which proceeded to win the British Science Fiction Association Award for best short fiction of that year, aided by a vote from a seemingly British housewife who revealed herself to be a Cossack from Poltova, the cuisine of which she declared we described perfectly.*

Former bartender, prize-winning photographer, and Surrealist Party City Councillor in his former home town of Genoa, Italy, Roberto launched upon the world in 2011 in English his mammoth (628 page) and disturbing analysis of 9/11, The Myth of September 11: The Satanic Verses of Western Democracy, *while of his masterful parody,* Jonathan Livingshit Pigeon: A Tail of Transcendence *he declared: "Once in your life you have to write a shitty book."*

The Beloved of My Beloved *is a perverse encyclopaedia of Western civilisation approaching collapse, the Beloved being a metaphor – akin to Baudrillard's Objects of Desire – for the aims of Western civilisation taken to perverse extremes already inherent in them. In the wake of the book, Roberto and I have written a few more Beloved stories, of which this is the latest – original to this collection – in which we extend Beloved-ism to modern India.*

Red Squirrel

A Black Week was coming, and Angel of the Street had emailed to say there was a potentially fatal problem...

Halfway along the north coast of Spain, facing the Cantabrian Sea in the province of Asturias, is the delightful town of Gijón where in the year 844 the Vikings first came ashore in Spain to loot. Those Norseman were on their way to pillage Seville far in the south by rowing up the Guadalquivir river, having heard of that city's Moorish riches. Gijón with its conveniently long curving beach must have looked like the first place worth a raid since France.

Centuries later, a crime-writing festival was founded in Gijón called the Semana Negra, Black Week, because crimes are dark and in Spain crime novels are *novelas negras*. After a while other popular genres were added to crime. A specially hired 'Black Train' would carry authors and interviewing journalists from Madrid to Gijón by way of a two-hour stop in a coal-mining valley of the Asturian mountains.

Those dramatic mountains, the tallest of them known as the Peaks of Europe, were the reason why the rain in Spain doesn't fall mainly on the plain but mostly on green Asturias where the locals play bagpipes and swig cider, keeping an eye out for folklore goblins lurking in the leafy woods. The Peaks were the first glimpse of land for sailors returning from the New World. *Peaks Ho!* – and steer left for France, or steer right for the Med.

At the welcoming valley town of Mieres (I was told) all the passengers of the Black Train would parade through the streets, preceded by a bagpiper and a drummer, towards food and drink sponsored by the Communist mayor. European writers are usually left-wing, likewise coal miners.

This year I was assisting the Semana Negra as regards English-speaking guests, while residing in Gijón for the summer to study the pair or so of red squirrels which inhabit a little woodland inside the Botanical Garden. As us Englishfolk all know, native red squirrels were displaced from most of our land by American grey squirrels, consequently my field of study seemed suitably anti-imperialistic and pro-red.

I suppose at this point I should acknowledge my token endorsement by the Red Squirrel Survival Trust which was sorted out by my Aunt Mabel, a passionate naturalist (in the sense of wildlife, not of nude sun-bathing). My left-wing acquaintances in Gijón would be blithely unaware that the Sponsor of the RSST is Charles, Prince of Wales. But mainly I applaud the generous finance from Aunt Mabel so that I could spend a good many months distant from England where the parents and the extended family of my friend Guneet were on the warpath due to her pregnancy. Paid exile might seem a bit old-fashioned these days, but the Singh family had threatened death on account of dishonour. Sikhs didn't generally go in for honour killings of daughters, which left me in the firing line. Or rather, in the dagger danger zone. Aunt Mabel was well aware that every male Sikh is supposed for religious reasons to carry at least one dagger about his person, but ha ha to assassins operating in a place such as Gijón.

Guneet's name was Punjabi for virtuous, ironically, although I *shouldn't* really say such a thing! When I refer to Guneet as a friend rather than a girlfriend, such was indeed the case. Oh yes she was a young woman, and yes she was a fun friend. We went to bed because *why shouldn't she do so? And why shouldn't I?* We were both tipsy at the time but she told me her period was due. Lightning had simply happened to strike, the sperm penetrating an egg. Guneet had no intention of "trapping" me, but at the same time she had a distaste for abortion.

So here I was in Gijón, staying extendedly in a hotel called the Don Manuel, located near the yacht harbour, where many guests of the Semana Negra would also stay in late July. Consequently I became acquainted with 'Angel of the Street', which in Spanish was the guy's real name, and one thing led to another. It may seem absurd to be studying a few squirrels, of which I dutifully emailed photos to Aunt Mabel, but mainly I was working on my experimental novel, inspired by my dreams. So there, I have confessed: I am a wannabee novelist and, because of my imbroglio with Guneet, who had been on the same writing course with me at the University of Birmingham, now I was enjoying a sort of bohemian Henry Miller sabbatical in the sense of running off in the 1920s or 1930s to Paris to pursue my muse and drink wine. Just, in a more sedate town.

The Sikhs in Spain mainly lived in the big cities such as Barcelona; in the whole Iberian peninsula there were only about 10,000 Sikhs, which may sound a lot but is insignificant compared with the three-quarters of a million in Britain. In Gijón it was the Chinese who ran emporia of everything rather than Moslem and Punjabi families from the former Empire of India, as in the UK. Much of what I knew about Sikhs came from a paperback which Guneet gave me as a joke after she found it in a charity shop. *Lions, Princesses, Gurus: Reaching Your Sikh Neighbour*, wherein British Christians were instructed how to inveigle themselves seductively in order to proselytise the true gospel. I realise that inveigle and seduce mean pretty much the same.

Not that I like Henry Miller's style. Give me Robert Irwin, just for instance. I was twenty-six, high time to write my first novel expressing my sleep-associated perceptions.

For example, whenever I wake during the night I already know the exact time, or at least almost; I simply need to shine my bedside torch at the clock to confirm this. I know with my eyes still shut. The faint green glow of doped strontium aluminate on the clock's hands can't possibly penetrate my eyelids to tell me anything subliminally, nor do I suppose that my sleeping brain counts the scarcely audible ticks. Besides, during daytime I'm usually spot on too, duly confirmed by my watch. I was sure that I had a privileged relationship with time, although I'd found Proust too privileged socially. I must regard myself as radical even though I didn't care for realism.

The previous year, I'd caught a flu which left me with a persistent nagging cough so vile that I could hardly sleep. I was awakened repeatedly and thus was unable to slip deeply into a dream. In such circumstances a person might hallucinate. Dozing, a vision came to me of four parallel dream narratives being printed out in grey, into any of which I was maybe being invited to enter... or else those grey narratives were being dump-printed to dispose of them since I couldn't avail myself of any dream on offer. The four parallel printouts emerged swiftly, disappearing after a short distance as further material continued to emerge from the printer. All of the narratives seemed banal, even if I couldn't follow any for more than a subjective second or so. None of the richness of my regular dreams! Maybe I was being stultified by the writing course and such wasn't the way for my artistic life to proceed.

More likely, I was drained of energy by the flu.

Anyway, I had a revelatory dream one night in the Don Manuel, although first I need to recount the potentially fatal problems facing the Semana Negra, by then almost imminent.

Every year the event receives about a million visitors. That's because the literary events take place in tandem with a huge funfair. En route to the klaxoning rides and colliding dodgem cars and an enormous Big Wheel and the King of Octopus selling grilled chunks of tentacles, and whatnot, visitors might get sidetracked by the bookstalls and author interviews held in a giant circus tent open to the air at the front and equipped with a busy bar. Angel had explained all this to me, which as yet I had not beheld with my own eyes.

Inevitably the funfair causes a din and wild illuminations till hours after midnight, the fun — and the literature — kicking off at five in the afternoon since this is Spain. Consequently the Semana Negra moves to different semi-suitable vacant sites around the town year by year, as allocated and approved by the town council. Often the neighbours have complained, although small shops and cafés do a roaring trade.

This account really ought to contain some dialogue by now, so I shall pretend that skeletal (or at least gaunt) Angel of the Street revealed the problems to me over a drink at the Don Manuel, rather than emailing all the twenty-strong committee.

"Okay, Colin, it's like this." Angel's actual English isn't so good. "This year's parcel of land for the SN is beside the Gijón campus of the University of Oviedo." Oviedo is the smug capital of Asturias less than half an hour away by car. "The Rector of the University is applying to the court for a legal injunction to ban the SN from happening beside his campus on the grounds that academic life will be disturbed, and damage may happen to university property."

I lift my imaginary glass of robust red Ribera del Duero, superior to most Riojas. "But," say I, "the students are on holiday during July. No classes."

"The teaching staff may still use the buildings."

"After five in the evening?"

"Of course the Rector's complaint is ridiculous." Angel shifts awkwardly on his seat, due to a condition requiring ointment; and I don't mean a boil.

"And ours is a *literature* festival. It's cultural."

"Not in his eyes. Popular literature isn't literature."

"Qué puto snob," I respond.

"The Judge won't pronounce until a week next Wednesday. By then we need all the book cabins and the carpas in place." Carpas are the marquees little and large. "And the funfair starts to set up then."

"So what happens if the Judge agrees with the Rector?"

"We lose a mountain of Euros, for which the SN committee is jointly and severally responsible, as I believe you say. But don't worry, prosecution to bankrupt us wouldn't come to court for at least a year."

I drain my Ribera del Duero for Dutch, or rather Spanish, courage. When the Spanish ruled the Netherlands, maybe the countryfolk of Holland drank less gin. I was allergic to gin due to an unfortunate experience when I was fifteen.

Angel raises his bottle of beer. Mahou, pronounced as in *Mao* Tse-tung; a sponsor of the SN along with Pepsi Cola. "The whole thing might drag on for years," he comforts me. Then he wolfs all the chunks of potato omelette which came free with the drinks. Eggs cause constipation, binding the bowels. Angel knows I have a strong aversion to eggs, besides, because of the horrid strings of jelly I alone seem able to see in a raw one. My idea of hell is raw eggs broken into glasses of gin.

In similar vein I'll relate my crucial dream in the guise of a conversation with Carmen, who is responsible for the daily newspaper of the Semana Negra given away free during the festival. I'd seen piles of leftover copies from previous years stored in the festival office next to a cinema. Eight pages, half-metres of high-gloss paper, entitled *A Quemarropa*, 'at burn-clothes', the Spanish equivalent of *At Pointblank*.

Chain-smoking punk Carmen's hair is stained pink with purple highlights. She sports nose and lip piercings and usually wears an outfit that is a chic compromise between a chain-gang convict's striped pyjamas in old movies and a pinstripe suit. In the past she worked as a child psychologist but these days due to cutbacks in the education budget she's into web design.

For economy's sake I tell Carmen my dream at the same table outside the Don Manuel, where she sips Pepsi while I enjoy a glass of Albariño. It's a very warm day so I favour a tasty white wine which is gently green. It behoves (a word I like) an author to note details of local colour. For instance the red squirrels in the Botanical Garden, subspecies *Sciurus vulgaris numantius*, are a richly rusty russet distinctly darker than the squirrels now mostly in refuge in the Island of Anglesey and the far North of England and in Scotland.

Screeching gulls wheel overhead, causing pigeons to take refuge on balconies. A black guy ambles by, loaded with handbags and wristwatches, and Carmen shakes her head. All the café-touring vendors in Gijón are from Senegal, their native language Wolof. The SN toyed with the idea of publishing a short Wolof phrasebook to be culturally friendly.

This is not increasing the proportion of speech!

"Carmen," I announce, "last night I had a significant dream. In the dream somebody said to me in Spanish 'la semana no es tan negra' or maybe it was 'la semana no está negra'. (Either *the week isn't so black* or *the week isn't black*.)

Carmen looks quizzical.

"This means that our important week won't be a black one for us, even if it's Black in a genre sense. Not black in a negative sense, but rather the opposite, a positive experience. My subconscious mind reassured me that the Rector won't ruin us. Won't get in our way."

"That's good to know. I'll phone the Mayoress right away."

This was a joke, since the Mayoress wasn't fond of us. Until the previous year Gijón had been staunchly socialist ever since democracy recommenced in Spain. Socialism equalled strong support from the town hall for a festival of the people and of popular culture. However, nationally the Socialist Party made a hideous mess of government, and by just one councillor control of Gijón was lost.

Oops. Speech. "If only the indignados had voted socialist!" I exclaim. Indignant young people had demonstrated and camped in the main square and then protested by voting for a dozen well-meaning or crackpot minority parties which sprouted like mushrooms. Result: the right wing and the very-right wing, who cordially loathed each other, now reigned in Gijón. Right and Very-Right were so surprised to win that the only person they could agree on nominating as Mayoress was a lady whose name sounded like Marilyn. The next day she told the press how surprised she was to become Mayoress, never having voted at any election in her life.

"Did I tell you?" says Carmen. "Marilyn's a breast implant surgeon."

"In my opinion," say I, "*Playboy* magazine single-handedly programmed Western males into this ridiculous fixation on huge boobs."

"Which single hand would that be?" she asks mischievously, or due to her training as a psychologist.

I swallow some more Albariño before the wine warms up.

Carmen continues, "We have a saying in Spain: '*Teta que la mano no cubre, no es teta sino ubre*'. A tit which a hand can't cover isn't a tit but an udder."

"I completely agree. I don't like big tits one bit. Or two bits."

Since this is an imaginary conversation, I may be letting things hang out.

"What I heard in my dream seemed very profound. It was a key to a language of affirmation by exclusion, a language which tribes-people might actually speak in some remote vertiginous valley in New Guinea – confined topographically by sheer cliffs yet abundant in orchids and birds of paradise. A language which proclaims *what-is-not* in order to affirm *what-is*. 'It isn't raining' equals 'It's a fine day". Or night."

"I see," says Carmen. "Or should I say, '*it isn't invisible*?" She's quick on the uptake. "Who knows, maybe the Senegalese talk thus to each other on the streets here? '*People buy many bags today, I'm rich,*' poor fellow. That would be a great coincidence, wouldn't it?"

She opens her green iPad, and I'm worried she's bored. "What are you doing?"

"Googling the negative in Wolof...."

I almost forgot that habit of hers. Finding out things immediately.

"There seem to be several ways. You can add *-ul* or *-wul*. *Waxul*, not to speak."

Wax or wool in the ears...

"*Dumëwul*, not to spank. Or there's *Du wolof*, you aren't a Wolof, Colin. I don't think this helps." Carmen claps her iPad shut, restoring full attention to me and her Pepsi.

"I must have been on the point of waking. I felt and also visualised the network of dream imagery quite swiftly starting to collapse and melt away, especially those Spanish words I'd heard – as well as the wider concepts for which the words were addresses, specifically the ideas of a language of affirmation by negatives.

"This seemed so important an insight that I actually succeeded in copying the central ideas to storage in short term memory as I was waking, well enough to recover them in large part this morning from a remembered awareness of how the threads of thought had separated just before I became fully awake, a recall which I experienced very soon afterwards in the bathroom while I was, pardon me, shitting, as it happens, which I mention just in case this is significant."

I think I can discretely include this detail since the conversation didn't take place. Nevertheless, in a more important sense the conversation is – or was – happening right now, so maybe I oughtn't. "...afterwards while I was merely shaving."

Carmen steeples her chin upon her fingers, scrutinising me closely. She's wearing a ring made of bendy silver paperclips.

"And I thought to myself," I went on, "that my awareness of that dissolving of thoughts was my first ever introspection into a process of thought."

"It *might* also have been a very minor stroke, interpreted while it was happening..."

"I didn't wake dribbling with a tic in one eye." But I realise she was teasing. "I'd achieved a privileged insight into an interconnected system of brain activity dissolving or being overwritten probably by the impending necessities of the real world, which already my body might be aware of in advance of my mind."

"Wow," she says.

"Wow," she said since I should resume in the past tense.

Why should I? I want immediacy.

"Wow," she says.

At this point she fades out of the narrative. I think I've found a technique for evoking whatever I wish to have happened. Is this in accordance with my dream? An affirmation of my imaginative life in contrast with a reality-which-is-not. At the same time, the reality is the backdrop. It is the stage.

When I take the bus with Angel and Carmen to the site-in-preparation of the SN several days later, I'm impressed at the enormous backdrop already hanging down behind the stage in the largest carpa, which seems to conform with this intuition of mine about narrative scenery. Printed on a single piece of fabric, maybe ten metres by ten metres, is *Liberty Leading the People* by Delacroix, in front of which speakers will sit at a long table. Feet and breasts bare, Liberty brandishes the tricolor and a musket with bayonet as she strides over bodies of the fallen towards the audience who aren't here yet. In the rest of the place plastic chairs and tables stand about at all angles with socialistic informality.

"She inspired the Statue of Liberty," comments Angel. "Now of course the Americans have Homeland Security to keep strangers out."

The Rector's legal attempt failed. When we step outside, we regard sardonically the barricade that is his response. To preserve the purity of his campus from popular cultural pollution, the lunatic used university funds to buy two kilometres of solid steel slat-fencing two metres high to surround his territory. Like Israel versus the disorderly Palestinians.

"No," Carmen corrects me, "he only *hired* the fence. For a fortnight, for eighty thousand Euros. Including erection and taking down. The Rector says he'll sue us for the cost we forced upon him."

"What an asshole."

"¡I shit on the whore of gold!" she swears. "¡I shit in the milk!" Maybe I should restore what I said to her about what I was doing when I recovered my all-important dream.

Along a hilltop in the other direction is the largest single building in Spain, the Work University, Universidad Laboral, including the tallest stone tower in Spain and at the front evoking the Parthenon. Into one end of its inner courtyard, which is as large as St Mark's Square in Venice, easily fits a free-standing full-size version of the Radcliffe Camera in Oxford, but with added statues of saints.

Inside the marquee we'd met up with another character, a major one, novelist and political activist Pepe Sierra, whose parents emigrated him from Asturias to Mexico at the age of five to get away from life under the Franco dictatorship. Pepe is a highly charismatic stocky chap with a big raggy bandit moustache, who chainsmokes strong Cuban cigarettes which stain the hairs of his upper lip orange. His crime novels often feature social upheavals and political chicanery in the 1920s and 1930s. And he also wrote a vast definitive biography of Che Guevara. As Director of the Semana Negra, referred to as 'Boss', he makes stirring speeches.

I only confided in Angel about Guneet, man to man, the deeper story behind the squirrel tails, but I was pretty sure Angel would have gossiped to Pepe.

I observe, "The grandeur of the Workers University makes the

Rector's little campus look like a factory for making test-tubes."

"¿Did you know?" asks Pepe, "¿La Laboral was built by Franco's gang as an orphanage after a mining disaster?" I'm toying with the Spanish punctuation for exclamations and questions, ¡but I shouldn't go to extremes! "That place would hold a thousand orphans, to be trained usefully as bricklayers and carpenters and so on."

"Dios," say I, "they must have been anticipating a lot of mining disasters."

"The miners of Asturias are special," declared Pepe. "Those were the first to take up dynamite against Franco's invading African army. Franco butchered one thousand five hundred of them. Our miners saw off a fascist warship right here at Gijón!"

This decade's miners are currently burning tyres on main roads to protest against threats to the coal industry, against Rajoy's government hacking and slashing social welfare, and soaring unemployment. The police oppose the miners with tear gas; the miners retaliate with Molotov cocktails. No joy in Rajoy, pronounced Rack-hoy.

The militancy of miners will presently pose a small problem for Pepe... I think some unobtrusive alliteration in a sentence *now and then* is rather effective.

The next day Angel needs to drive Pepe and me and Carmen to Madrid. We're to collect a score of guests from the sprawling airport complex as writers arrive throughout the following day from Mexico, Argentina, Cuba, Uruguay, Italy, Germany, the United States, as well as picking up various international friends, and get everyone settled in a hotel directly above the railway station from which the Black Train will depart for Gijón early the morning after.

Dramatic mountains give way to a mainly arid plain irrigated here and there by piping a couple of hundred metres long upon wheeled tripods. Eventually we reach a zone of boulders deposited by glacier, then there's a bit more mountain to tunnel through, and after six hours we're finally entering Madrid. The GPS on Carmen's iPad leads us to the hotel near the twin skyscrapers of the Gate of Europe, leaning towards each other precariously as if anticipating the financial collapse of the bank whose headquarters that cutting edge architecture is.

"Must be twenty-five degrees from vertical," says Pepe, cigarette held aloft as a measure.

Carmen finds out within a couple of seconds.

"Fifteen degrees, *Jefe*."

"Looks more. How metaphorical. The *hubris* of vaunting capitalism."

Skipping over the next airport-busy day entirely, we arrive at the departure of the Black Train after a hearty and hasty buffet breakfast. We have collected a troupe of interesting people plus all of their luggage in the large hotel lobby, along with Press and camera-people.

There's Fidel Castro's retired chief of security, General F.E., here from Cuba after a lot of delicate negotiations to talk about his memoirs *638 Ways to Kill Castro* (which he prevented). There's a Romanian master criminal called Dragos, pronounced -gosh, who wrote his own memoirs while in an Italian jail, accompanied by a burly suited 'friend'. There's an Italian judge whose book is about hunting the Mafia, also with a semi-silent friend. The SN is big on criminal memoirs this year, attempted political assassination also being a crime even if the Cuban régime is only popular in Spain with very old-fashioned Communists who wouldn't dream of going to Cuba itself. And there's a young Cuban novelist called Yotuel who looks like a would-be defector to judge from the glances, defiant yet nervous, which he casts at General F.E. The Italian judge and the Romanian criminal seem to be on nodding acquaintance. Another Italian is Umberto Passero, author of surreal detective stories as well as of the satirical fact-packed *9/11 for Dummies* and *CIA for Dummies*. And *then* there's the American crime-writer Bon Jonson, who lives in Hungary, which is third in the world league for alcohol consumption...

Jonson landed drunk, and continued so. When he recovers from being paralytic he will provide speech, very slowly. But meanwhile he tottered around the hotel all night, taking tots now and then. On the hour at 2am, 3am and 4am he banged on the door of a vivacious Spanish crime lady, Rosa Campos, sharing with her elegant daughter, proclaiming, "Ah... gotta... talk... to... you..." Rosa had made the mistake of being civil to Jonson who was highly esteemed in Spain in translation on account of his two tough novels from the point of view of Hungarian police and criminals, so highly that after failing to turn up at the SN the previous year, wasting the cost of his air ticket – due to a 'family emergency' – he'd been re-invited.

Now he sprawls lengthwise across the steps leading down to the railway platform, his travel bag clutched tightly like a comforter, blocking the descent of everyone else. Presently he and his bag are hauled on to the train and for half an hour he leans heavily over people, intruding incoherently. Normally I'm mild-mannered, but when it comes my turn to be oppressed I shout at him, "Fuck off to the fucking back of the carriage and fucking stay there and fucking go to sleep!" I need to be emphatic. I think the words penetrate because very slowly Jonson totters away.

"You should told him use train door," the literate Romanian criminal calls out to me, grinning.

"We aren't travelling fast enough," I respond.

He nods. "And would make more nuisance."

Hours later, Jonson awakes, wanders along and parks himself opposite me.

"Ah... get... the... idea... you... don't... like... me. What... did... Ah... do... to... offend... you?"

"Well just for example you woke Rosa Campos and her daughter three times during the night by banging on their door."

"Ah... get... out... of... bed... and... roam... Ah... don't... know... Ah'm... doing... this. It's... on... account... of... the... ah... drugs... medicines... Ah... have... to... take... Ah... don't... remember. My... wife... has... to... talk... me... back... to... bed... nine... times... a... night... sometimes... You... know... Ah... was... the... highest... paid... barman... in... Budapest.

Ah... talk... slowly... like... this... because... Ah... think...in... Hungarian... as... well... as... English... at... the... same... time."

Hungarian is the second most difficult language in the world, so I don't believe a word of this.

"Before... Ah... was... the... highest... paid... barman... in... New... York... that's... nightclubs."

This, I don't believe either.

By now we're entering the foothills of the Asturian mountains. The train stops at a station and stays stopped. After a while the conductor passes through, delivering apologies. Angel tells me from across the carriage, "Miners on strike are waiting on the platform at Mieres to welcome us and Pepe. Other miners on strike have blocked the track a few kilometres ahead of here. I don't know if they used a tree this time."

"One lot of revolutionary miners are waiting to greet us, but another lot are stopping this? *Why?* Can't they communicate?"

"They belong to different unions. The Asturian Miners, and the Miners of Leon."

Another half hour passes before the train starts moving again. By now I've endured a lot of slow boring lying monologue from Bon Jonson when I would much rather be talking to Pepe or Umberto Passano or General F.E., about their thoughts on the CIA, just for instance.

Well, we do arrive at Mieres to a rapturous reception for Pepe who is immediately engulfed by a sea of heads and microphones. It's meat and drink for Pepe to proclaim solidarity. Our food and drink must wait a while longer, but eventually we set off in hot pursuit of a hastening drummer and bagpiper, and have just twenty minutes to cope with all the bounty laid on by the Mayor before we must hurry back to the station. The Black Train can't be late because it's shoehorned in to the regular timetable. Miss the slot and we wouldn't reach Gijón till midnight. The brass band and shrilling street demonstrators protesting cutbacks and the police would all have gone home.

At the Don Manuel next day, Saturday, I manage a conversation with the ebullient Umberto Passano who was glancing through *At Pointblank* at a table on the outdoors terrace.

"After *CIA for Dummies* and *9/11 for Dummies* of course I take care," he tells me. "Many people investigating such things have been killed in plane crashes and other 'accidents'." He proceeds to give me four or five examples. "I myself took a bus to a certain airport, with my plane ticket already in my pocket, then I told people I would travel by train instead, but in fact I rented a car. I didn't want to think of a plane exploding in midair because my name is on the confirmed passenger list."

"A thoughtful precaution." I'm reminded of the famous Monty Python sketch, 'Nobody expects the Spanish Inquisition', except in this case '*No one expects the American CIA!*'

At this point Dragos makes overtures to Umberto in Italian, so I turn my attention to Castro's General who's sitting solo at another table, nursing a cup of café solo. Nobody seems to fraternise with him. Even after some reforms, Cuba is still a dictatorship existing in a time bubble. The author of *638 Ways to Kill Castro* may be lonely.

"Well now," the General tells me with dry humour, probably after he's decided that I'm harmless and red squirrels are a typical British eccentricity, "I became Fidel's head of security at the age of seventeen because I held a rifle with him in the mountains, but I had no idea of the job he gave me. I had to learn quickly! In many ways my CIA opponents were clowns, and still are. Yet it's as if there's a stupid CIA, developing exploding cigars and botulinus cigars, and a clever CIA, and I had the stupid CIA to tire me out."

This is indeed an interesting observation!

"I wrote all this in my book," he adds, eyeing me with a strange mixture of friendly innocence and wily experience.

Unfortunately Bon Jonson wends his way through the throng of tables occupied by crime and other writers from a dozen countries, glass of red wine in hand, and parks himself.

"Ah… was… a bouncer… at…a nightclub… in… New… York."

In view of his lightweight frame, I doubt this.

"I though you said you were the barman."

Cogs turn evasively in his brain. "Those… places… are… dangerous. People… think… they're… going… out… for… a… fun… evening. Impress… the girl… think… nothing… about… dropping… a hundred… dollar… tip. But… I… seen… a… man's… ear… bit…off… in…a… nightclub."

Unsurprisingly, the General decides to go inside.

"My… wife's… Hungarian… you… know. Ah'm… a… bestseller… in Hungarian. If… Ah… go… someplace… talk… about… my…books… Ah… do…it …in… Hungarian."

"Well, I hope you speak in English here. I don't think we have a Hungarian translator."

Pepe emerges to circulate with a large loaded dish of little green peppers which he himself has fried Mexican-style.

That evening I sit in on General F.E. presented by Pepe in the large marquee, backdropped by *Liberty Leading the People*. Noise from the funfair is far more muted than I'd have thought. The General will be here another four days; Pepe only leaves for Mexico after the concluding espicha, which isn't a speech but a party, traditionally accompanying the pouring of matured cider from barrels into bottles through a spigot.

I stare at the colour photo on an inside page of *El Comercio*. A squirrel, red and dead. Shot through the head; of which there's little left. Someone was doing target-practice in the Botanical Garden. The squirrel-assassin may have scaled one of the low fences round the back which give on to meadows, but if he came through the front turnstile he'd have needed to use a state-of-the-art folding gun, for example a polymer Magpul FMG9 which disguises itself as a flashlight the size of an old-time video tape that will fit in your back pocket. Pull out the FMG, flop it open, and it's ready to rock 'n' roll with surprisingly accuracy. Thirty shots from the Glock magazine before reloading. A writer ought to know a wide range of things.

My dream intuition preserves me from mundanity.

At 5pm on the day after Saturday, Carmen doesn't fail to carry me to the SN in her vehicle which isn't a van, in the non-absence of Umberto Passano, and the General, who later proves not so keen to hear the Italian's misunderstandings about the CIA in monologue with Pepe in the marquee of misencounters during the hour before 8.

At 6 pm, while the sun isn't rising, due to Umberto and the General I'm by no means sitting alone at one of the tables which isn't inside the carpa. I'm not wishing that Pepe wouldn't come over and join us... when of a sudden demonstrating miners pour unsilently into view holding banners and placards. Of course an Unwhite Weekend when crowds of visitors throng past the bookstalls towards the funfair isn't such a wonderful time for publicity.

Don't imagine Pepe advancing towards the head of the march, hands widespread, as if the protest isn't at the same time a homage to himself and a symbol of struggle for rights. Don't imagine him addressing the miners in fraternity, nor afterwards wandering back past our table and heeding a beckon from the General who isn't uninterested in what's happening. Normally Pepe wouldn't shun the General, but on this occasion so filled is Pepe with a warm glow that he can't fail to sit down and light another cigarette.

For the first time all three of the people who don't like the CIA, and vice versa, aren't in different places and the press of folk in our vicinity is far from thick.

Don't imagine that I rise and step back. Don't imagine that I pull out a polymer Magpul FMG9 and shake it open.

"Silly boy," says the General, "you bought that from a stall in the fair. It's a toy gun."

Yes it is - Yes it is - Yes it is.

After writing story notes for a while, unwrapping the sources of stories (or at least some of the sources) a comment by William Blake comes to mind: Imagination is not memory – I think it was Blake who said this. *Of course the sources of a story in no way authenticate or exonerate the story as story, but notes are essentially autobiographical. So I did have the dreams which my narrator reports – about the dream narrative printer, and about the language of affirmation by exclusion. Obviously he's reliable in that respect... (smiley). What becomes less reliable is when a story overwrites one's own memories, and even reality itself, as maybe happens with Colin here. Or maybe not...*

I realise now that the fantasy of being a secret agent au fait with hidden realities unites this story with "The Name of the Lavender" earlier on, and "Me and My Flying Saucer" subsequently. Felix qui potuit rerum cognoscere causas: *Fortunate is the person who can know the causes of things. Or maybe not. It's a hard job, though someone has to do it. Such as writers, secret agents of the... no, I don't like the word soul.*

An Inspector Calls

In the good old days the library of a murder suspect generally betrayed the person's guilt to me. Additionally, the bookshelves of close acquaintances and associates often pointed me his or her way; the books of the *victim* too. Always providing there were at least a couple of hundred genuine books.

The advent of electronic books has seriously impaired my skills, but in any event I'm about to retire as a Detective Chief Inspector, which is why I'm now putting on to paper – in a leather-bound volume with marbled endpapers – the true stories of my greatest cases.

Bookcases and criminal cases: *much* links these two, yet until now fear of incredulity has deterred me from divulging the actual source of my "almost supernatural" "inspirations".

To get a cliché out of the way at once, book collections generally divide into two categories, liberal and conservative, reflecting the personalities and politics of their owners. A conservative collection is more orderly, whereas a liberal collection tends to be untidier and seemingly disorganised. So far, so obvious! However, in both cases revelatory patterns exist, and I speak not only about the books in actual bookcases, but also books stacked upon tables, reading matter by the toilet and beside the bed, cookbooks in the kitchen too.

Being a reasonable and reasoning man, I do entertain the possibility that during my career I've been the beneficiary of an unbroken series of lucky breaks, equivalent to tossing a tail five hundred times in succession; yet I reject this interpretation. Even as a boy of five or six I would experience a sensation in a house replete with books, as if those books were about to speak to me and to me alone. However, the revelation of my powers came when I was ten, courtesy of my scarlet-faced bachelor Uncle Oswald.

Uncle O owned about 7,000 books shelved, many double-depth, in most rooms of his tall narrow house near Bristol. A complete mishmash of different topics. He'd been the headmaster of a boys' school until he retired rather suddenly. My father John was Uncle O's younger brother by almost twenty years, the product of a late flurry by my parents during a holiday in Ireland. That's why I was christened Sean, which caused a bit of prejudice in the Force in the early days, when the IRA were setting off bombs, until I began to show my investigative talents.

Due to the onset of arthritis, Uncle O had recently had his house redecorated in the hope of selling and moving into a bungalow spacious enough to house all of his library on the same level, albeit mostly destined to remain double- or even triple-parked. A house such as my uncle's, home to so many books, doesn't look desirable to your ordinary buyers. Frankly it seems creepy, and the owner abnormal. Normal people can't see beyond the bookcases to the fact that here is actually a spare bedroom. Consequently for sales purposes a long narrow top-floor book room in my uncle's home must again visibly become a bedroom, indeed a child's bedroom since an adult-sized bed might make that particular room look crowded. One of my uncle's cronies found a child-size bed and a job-lot of teddy bears and dolls. Result: a charming nursery – except for the remaining high bookshelf. Due to shifting so many books from room A to B to C to clear each space turn by turn for repainting, books had become even more randomised than previously. Uncle O invited my ten-year-old self into that upstairs nursery and leered at me.

"Do you spot something strange, sweet little nephew Sean?"

Truthfully, the entire nursery seemed bizarre in the context of my bachelor uncle's home.

Pointing at a shelf, I asked, "The whip?" Leather, divided into strips at one end.

"That," he told me, "is called the *taws*. A Scottish word. The taws was traditionally used for chastisement of naughty boys, upon their bare buttocks. I suppose I should put the taws away in a drawer before the house is viewed. But no, not the taws."

"Those bright silk scarves tied to the bedposts?"

"Don't those look jolly, like festive streamers! But no, not the scarves."

I looked around carefully...

"The books, Uncle Oswald, the books!"

A single line of books remained. Instead of fairy tales and such, I saw lined up side by side: *A History of Orgies; The Illustrated History of*

Torture; The Secret Lives of Dying Children; Before the Mast: Two Centuries of Flogging in the Navy; and similar.

"Yes," exclaimed my uncle, "those are the titles that gathered together of their own accord on that shelf! Only now does it become clear to me how I truly feel about this childish violation of a library room. I need to purge myself of such feelings. I wonder if you would like to earn some substantial pocket money, my dear Sean?"

Yes, I did. So I did. And a valuable lesson was imprinted upon me that afternoon as sunbeams shafted through the new net curtains. I never returned to that house; nor did I visit the subsequent reportedly sprawling bungalow, where within a year Uncle O had a serious stroke which consigned him drooling to a nursing home, his right eye spasming frequently, so I heard. There, he lasted for only another year. In his will he bequeathed me a bookcase and contents which my parents burned on a bonfire in our back garden, inadvertently charring a big rhododendron. The will was dated just a week after my visit to that nursery; obviously Uncle O never expected to flake it while I was only twelve; the books were his message to me in the indeterminate future in case I blanked what had happened. After the flames died down, Mum and Dad looked at me askance and asked searching questions which I evaded skilfully, giving me an early insight into the criminal mind. Me, I still had fifty pounds hidden in a sock under my mattress.

I was a junior constable, assigned to stand – maybe to see if the boyo would faint – in a blood-soaked lounge where four lacerated corpses were found by the charlady, a short fat nervously grinning woman called Mrs Renton, whom I observed as she was being escorted away to a police car by a woman PC to be taken home in a state of shock.

Mrs Renton had stumbled (literally) upon the massacre shortly after she let herself into the house that morning, hence the smears on her hands and floral frock – she hadn't yet had time to pull on her rubber cleaning gloves. The victims were her employer, sumptuous Mrs Chumley in a violated peacock sari, whose deceased hubby had completed his diplomatic career with a decade at the British embassy in New Delhi, accounting for a collection of exotic knives mounted on the walls and plunged into the corpses, including the famous wiggly-waggly Indonesian *kris*; plus a thin once-dapper fellow in his fifties,

Charles Connolly, who sported a ripped pinstripe suit and a spotted bowtie, and who was Mrs Chumley's gentleman (as I overheard from Mrs Renton's questioning by detectives in the kitchen, to which a hatch opened from the lounge); thirdly a stout widowed stockbroker, Alastair Lascelles, who favoured a lacerated white silk suit which his coagulated blood decorated like streamers of strawberry syrup upon vanilla ice cream; and finally a short wiry elderly Miss Trench attired in punctured tweeds.

The occasion of the previous evening had been a game of bridge. The baize-covered table lay wrecked amidst scattered cards and emptied tumblers of gin tonic as though the goddess Kali herself had rushed through the room like a cyclone. However, my attention was neither upon the quartet of corpses nor upon the collection of knives, both unused and used (the latter leaving slightly darker silhouettes on the wallpaper printed with pink roses), but upon a chock-full carved teak bookcase of substantial bulk.

All of the books occupying the top left were shades of blue. At bottom right: shades of red. Thus someone unbookish had begun tidying the collection according to her own lights, probably after taking everything out for a dusting.

A trio of titles were now adjacent at the top right end. *Nice Cup of Char: A History of the Tea Trade* clearly though subconsciously indicated the charlady even though *char* comes from the word *chore*, not from the slang for *tea*. Next was *Thug: The Robber Assassin of India*. Finally, *Asian Bladed Weapons; A Collector's Guide*. End of shelf.

Char, Thug, Blades... So far as I recalled, members of the Thuggee cult had specialised in the strangulation of travellers, thus the third element specified in the series was essential.

Meanwhile, through in the kitchen, the two detectives were discussing the case.

"Rather than this being the work of some maniac intruder, could one of the bridge players have become incensed, say by a suspicion of cheating? He erupts, snatching knives from the wall over the fireplace. Yet one of the other players manages to kill the assailant, although himself or herself is already fatally wounded...?"

"Alternatively, Jack, could the stockbroker chap have made rotten investments for a client who takes his revenge years later and tries to muddy the waters by murdering three other people at the same time...?"

"Frankly, I prefer a maniac to a disappointed investor..."

Pretty soon the detectives came through into the murder lounge, and I addressed the Jack:

"Excuse me, Sir, but I *think* if you look upstairs in the lady's bedroom you might find beside the bed an open container of brightly coloured chocolate beans – Smarties, probably. Mixed among those you may find benzedrine pills which gave Mrs Renton the energy and agility to commit this crime seeing as how she swallowed a handful of the chocolate beans unaware that they served to conceal illegal amphetamines which Mrs Chumley's gentleman used to, well, perk himself *up*."

Jack guffawed. "Have *you* been taking Bennies, Constable Russell?"

"More to the point," asked the other detective, "at any point have you been upstairs?"

"No Sir, I have not."

Jack's colleague departed upstairs, returning two minutes later slack-jawed, a certain pill clutched between thumb and index finger.

"Mrs Renton has a sweet tooth," I explained, "judging by her girth. Also, she's fond of primary colours." (This, evinced by the attempted rearrangement of books according to the visible spectrum.) "I suspect that last night, while costumed as a maid to serve the gin tonics – thus compensating for Mrs Chumley's lack of Indian servants – Mrs Mop stole a handful of Smarties to console herself for the indignity and exploitation. *Smarties unbeknownst mixed with benzedrine tablets.* Mrs Mop's bottled-up resentments at her employer and posh friends boils over. She murders all four bridge players. This morning she wakes up with amnesia, or else she has low cunning enough to come to her job as usual and try to muddle matters somewhat by sprawling across the evidence."

"Mrs Renton said nothing about being here last night. So you reckon we'd find a blood-stained maid's uniform at her house?"

"More likely she stuffed the costume down a drain in her back yard. Rain was bucketing recently. Mrs Renton might expect the costume to be carried away through the sewers. It'll probably get tangled up within a few hundred yards."

Detective Jack hooted.

Yet thus the case proved to be. This led to me subsequently being teased as Smartie Pants instead of the boyo, although I also received a

Chief Constable's Letter of Congratulations since Detective Jack Westley had a sense of justice.

Well, this was a very simple case to solve! Char, Thug, Blades. Not that I drew attention to the three betraying volumes, and of course Jack and his colleague noticed nothing special about the bookcase.

Thank you, vile Uncle O, for sensitising me.

I think at this juncture I might skip ahead to one of my most interesting cases of recent years, one where even I found myself temporarily challenged.

A title is the symbol for all the words contained within a book. All words are ultimately metaphorical in origin; they are likenesses, similitudes. Thus language never describes or mirrors reality; it only alludes, saying 'This is like that' or 'That is like this', sometimes forming a circularity within far less than seven degrees of similarity. Also, words are fewer than the things they designate so that words usually have double meanings or even five or seven meanings. Consequently a title is powerfully symbolic, encoding much. Encodement conceals but also reveals. You might say that, viewed from the spine, a book forms a column not unlike a column of letter groups on a cipher pad, awaiting the key to decode it, or more importantly for me revealing the key to decode *events* since events are *unnameable* and *unthinkable* in the absence of language. Thus events demand a symbolic naming if they have been violently thought about. The naming has to go somewhere. Books, the home of words pinned like butterflies, are powerful attractors whereas 'living' words blow around like bubbles, popping almost as soon as uttered. (I ignore audio recordings of uttered words as having far less ancestry than books, scrolls, clay tablets; also, during any replay these words disappear serially as soon as spoken, consumed by a silence which a subsequent word fills up, unlike with the printed word which doesn't become invisible once you pass by.)

Very well. My most challenging case was that of a Senior Lecturer in Food Technology, a Robert "Bob" Adams, bludgeoned repeatedly in his book-lined study using a Spanish cured ham until Bob's brains came out upon his desk. Those hams are dense and look just like the stone club that a cartoon caveman carries upon his shoulder. The main part of this ham was confined tightly within a black fabric bag such as an executioner might wear over his head so as to remain anonymous, supposing eyeholes were cut — or which the object of the execution himself might be compelled to wear. Within a white circle: the trademark '5J' along with a simple design of twin acorns. On a black band around the tapering ankle of the leg were the words 'Cinco Jotas', Five J's. A premium brand, maybe 400 Euros worth of best ham fed on acorns, heavy to heft and swing, thus the murderer was probably (though only *probably*!) male.

When heaving the ham, the murderer had displaced five books towards the rear of the fifth shelf of one bookcase. I assumed this was a spurious clue. Just for the record, those five books were all titles by Heston Blumenthal, the scientific chef whose flagship restaurant was The Fat Duck near royal Windsor; almost certainly the fat duck was an unintentional red herring.

To bash in the head of a Senior Lecturer in Food Technology with a ham might seem like poetic justice, or injustice. So what else did the word ham signify? An incompetent or amateur actor. A village, as in hamlet. The first syllable of hammer, a blunt instrument, from the Norse for the back of an axe. A hammer blow repeated at least half a dozen times. One might feel squeamish about smashing in a skull directly with a hammer, the way I once put out of its misery a squirrel crippled by a cat, but a ham blunts the impact and hides one's immediate view of a cranium cracking open like a boiled egg, spilling its contents. Bob was almost bald.

To abandon a prestige ham at the scene of the crime, when instead one could have eaten the murder weapon after discarding the black bag down a drain — albeit not during a single sitting, unless assisted by a score of friends; I refer to the eating, not to the discarding [here I have obliterated a simile relating to the disposal of the black bag in accordance with the dictum of Dr Johnson, 'Where ever you meet with a passage which you think is particularly fine, strike it out'] — superficially suggested to me either militant vegetarianism or else a subconscious appeal to be caught. Maybe the murderer was a member of the Animal Liberation Front, who regarded technology applied to meat as an obscenity?

"So what do you make of this?" I asked my most recent Detective Sergeant, a red-faced barrel of a Scot, Jock McTavish, whom from politeness I never addressed or referred to in public as Jock. Having investigated him discretely, I knew that he had written three romance novels published by Mills and Boon under the pseudonym of Vivian Donald – sweet kisses among the purple heather of the glen, et cetera – but I kept this knowledge strictly under my hat such as I never wore so as to avoid detective clichés; my by-now-whitening hair was wiry and I had always kept it close-cropped all by myself using electric clippers since I couldn't abide the banal chit-chat of hairdressers; myself lacking a wife to perform this duty, for which I never blamed my Uncle O – simply, a serious detective often works unsocial hours, including the necessity to think and muse and brood and read, book titles at the very least.

Before joining the Force, for a while Jock had been an oil cowboy in Nigeria; I don't think Africa made many impressions upon the burly laddie compared with his tartan-streaked sentimental memories of Scotland. Hitherto for the titles of his romances Jock McTavish had always filched a phrase from Robbie Burns, such as *Red Red Rose* about a communist lassie from the Gorbals slums in Glasgow with whom a laird from the Highlands falls in love; initially the lassie despises the laird for class warfare reasons. Obviously the title gave rise to the plot rather than symbolising it subsequently, which was somewhat removed from my own insights, but I was interested in whether the Sergeant might one day become my Boswell, although I would need to provide him with a mini-manual on the subject of How I Solved Some of My Crimes. Which, I suppose, I'm fulfilling posthumously right now – posthumously, alas, in the case of Jock McTavish...

I prowled the study on the lookout for literary clues while the Sergeant maybe wondered if I was hunting for specks of blood, bone, or brain which had leapt a long way, thus to calculate the precise violence of the assault upon Prof Bob.

The crime had taken place during the previous evening or night because latte suede curtains of light-blocking fabric currently hid the large window; the forensic examiner would nuance the range of hours when he got here. Prof Bob's very bright lights had still been on when his estranged wife Juliet let herself in at 10 a.m., since she kept a door key, and phoned 999 in hysterics; there were no signs of forced entry. As Jock pulled the drapes aside to inspect the windowsill, autumnal sunlight flooded into the study over tiled rooftops from the south-east, and some titles far from the corpse flashed at me as if tooled in gold, previously invisible even though visible. *An Inspector Calls*, the classic play by J.B. Priestley. Another play, *Alibi*, adapted from an Agatha Christie novel. A lurid paperback horror novel called *Meat*, a blood-stained cleaver clenched on the cover. And one further play, Shakespeare's *Hamlet*, damn it.

An 'Inspector' pays a visit, but he's *elsewhere*, murder by meat ensues, specifically using a ham not a hatchet...

"So," I said to Juliet Adams down in the lounge shortly afterwards, while by now the forensic Dr Smythe was upstairs in the study busy examining, "the deceased was involved in amateur dramatics, and the group felt that by now they were up to staging a Shakespearean tragedy."

She was a handsome woman on the other side of forty with rich wavy brunette hair and a full, muscular figure.

"Yes, *Hamlet*... We'd been talking about this for ages. Bob was auditioning... oh my god!" as Juliet made the connection.

"Would this be a modern version where the Prince of Denmark can be bald, or traditional with Elizabethan costumes and a wig for Mr Adams?"

"Elizabethan." Juliet sniffed and I offered the folded monogrammed handkerchief from my breast pocket, but she shook her head.

"Was there much rivalry for the chief role?"

She considered. "Hmm, someone else had rather set his heart on it. René Ashett, one of the half million French living in London."

"Between three and four hundred thousand French people," I corrected her.

"London's the sixth largest French city in Europe," she pointed out, sounding to my ears proud and defiant.

René's surname caught up with me. *Hachette*, it would be, same as the publishers. Mister Hatchet was the meaning. Why had Juliet volunteered his identity so promptly? Because I would have discovered this as soon as I interviewed the members of the drama group. No point in keeping it secret.

I showed Juliet the trashy cover of the horror paperback, which I had slipped into my pocket, whereupon she flinched. "And did your René give this to Mr Adams as a joke before you began your relationship with him, or was the book posted afterwards without any sender's address, not that your husband would fail to recognise who was threatening him...?" However, the question mark was suddenly for myself.

For myself, because such a powerful threat from Juliet's René made no real sense and, scanning the back cover blurb as I held the front out to her, I re-read '...*a bloodthirsty carnivorous force... lives are at risk... a cell of the Animal Liberation Front...*'

"It's true that René and I were seeing each other... but I've never laid eyes on that book before! And everything was conducted in a perfectly civilised way. As in the theatre, so in life: the play must go on."

"But with Monsieur Hachette as Hamlet now? Eet might seem a beet strange to 'ear a French voice uttering 'To bee or not to bee'..."

I hoped to provoke her, but she rallied. "That's an existential speech." My opinion of her rose several notches. "Hamlet is the archetypal existential play, René argues."

"So has the Animal Liberation Front threatened Mr Adams for teaching the best way to cook meats? Maybe one of his students is a militant veggie?"

"Not that I've ever been aware of, Inspector."

Which reminded me: "Have Food Standards visited his college recently and criticised something? Did an inspector call?"

"Bob *taught* food standards, among other things. He was a qualified inspector himself."

So that left, principally, a *police* Inspector, who could easily and plausibly intrude into the home of almost anyone except for your proverbial hardened criminal.

The book titles pointed to an Inspector who was elsewhere at the time of the murder committed by hamself. Who else but myself could have inserted the clue of René's threat, which *only I* could interpret? Yet at the same time that wasn't me, because yesterday evening I'd been at home enjoying access to the police databases' Fujitsu BS2000/OSD S200 mainframe held on UNIX servers, and to my 7,000 books – whenever I could I scoured second-hand bookshops for whatever might take my eye. Improbable though it may seem, I was being foreshadowed by a *double* who had provided me with this case, to be pinned plausibly upon an innocent (except in the adultery aspect) Frenchman – the key name Hatchet, which only appeared as an image on the cover of the horror novel, was of far more consequence than the overt mention of the Animal Liberation Front.

I felt foxed just at the same time as everything was revealed, unmasking my replica persona, stripping away the mask which both hid and showed my own face.

Sergeant Jock came into the lounge. "The Doc says we can take the ham away for fingerprinting."

"Pigs only have toes," came from my lips as I pondered the rude slang connection, of pigs signifying policemen. My own prints would be in the study upstairs, of course.

"Are you all right, Sir?"

"Perfectly," I said. "Juliet Adams, I arrest you as an accomplice in the murder of your estranged husband."

"But that's preposterous!" she blazed. "If that's so, why would I come here this morning drawing attention to myself?"

Me, I was recollecting Mrs Renton...

"You already confessed to adultery, Mrs Adams. Enough of the amateur dramatics." I forbore to say ham-acting.

Sergeant McTavish was looking at me askew. Maybe that was boggled admiration, since he knew nothing as yet about any theatre group nor any Gallic lover. Maybe not.

I could almost feel my double making a decision.

After my venture into warped and unreliable crime in "Red Squirrel", I felt emboldened to try another outing, featuring a somewhat dandy semiotic detective.

I wasn't a particularly solitary child, although there was only one of me, and I soon become addicted to reading alone in my room. (But I also remember playing Cowboys and Indians with kids around a pillbox near the local stinky piggery, even though I didn't really fit in to the group, perhaps because I was very fat, and a bit different; no jokes, please, about the piggery or about Piggy in Lord of the Flies *since I didn't wear glasses. A pillbox was a hexagonal concrete defence position, thousands of which graced the UK during World War Two in case the Nazis came, and for years of abandonment afterwards.) Much later the randomisation of books did happen to me with exactly the result described — except that* Two Centuries of Flogging in the Navy *is imaginary, probably. I never owned such a book, nor was attracted by the English Vice from spanking to flaggelation. Nor did I have an Uncle Oswald.*

To play the role of Detective Sergeant Jock McTavish I co-opted a lovely chap whom I knew in Dar es Salaam in the mid-1960s; and indeed I did read one of his nom-de-plume's romances about kisses in the Glens with curiosity and a fair amount of enjoyment as I sat in East Africa drinking Tusker beer.

The horror novel with the trashy cover is of course my own Meat.

Me and My Flying Saucer

Fellow people, probably this is your first ever sight of a genuine and altogether shimmering flying saucer! All those thousands of books about close encounters, abductions by aliens, things seen in the sky and in cornfields, are complete cow pies, alias cowpats in the UK. Am I cleared for landing? I have something on board you'll be glad to see. Namely your four marooned Martian astronauts, sound in wind and limb. Juno, Jim, Chuck, and Barbara won't suffocate on Mars on account of their ascent engine failing.

I couldn't possibly let J+J+C+B stifle in their tin can, even if this exposes my UFO to becoming an identified flying object. I could have clandestinely dumped off the four of them anywhere hospitable in the world, near some highway, but that might have led to personal problems for them, such as conspiracy theories, or getting disappeared. So I chose a public approach – though at the same time still fairly anonymous, like a caped crusader plus mask. My passengers haven't set eyes on me. For all they know, I might be an AA.I., an alien A.I.

Oh, and I shan't be hanging around for long, an inch above the landing strip, so don't bother breaking out Château Rohypnol or dozed-up 7 Up on my account. As soon as the heroic quartet are safely on the ground fifty yards distant I'll be buzzing off promptly. Don't bother chasing me with those jets. I can do Mach-100 without batting an eyelid. Plus, cloak of invisibility. Just keep well back from this saucer, since you've no idea what energies it deploys. That includes your fire engines and ambulances with SWAT teams on board.

Your Mars quartet left their bags of rocks and dust back on the red planet; I didn't want mess in my hold. Oops sorry, people, if I seem to be patronising the brave quartet who took four months to get to Mars, whereas I brought them back in four hours, but it does take even little me several days to get to Neptune; I have limitations. As do fairly featureless blue Neptune, and extremely chilly Triton, minus 235 C.

Why spend several days going to Triton? Why, to patrol the Far Frontier! Admittedly, there's even more and further frontier way out as far as the Kuiper Belt not to mention the Oort cloud beyond, but... I confide nothing about refuelling my power system. Get going now, bold astronauts, out of the hold with you!

And of course the orbit of Neptune implies a very large *sphere* of mostly empty space, but I'm not heading way out to gape at nothing except stars or the sun as a very bright spot.

If you're already trying to do voice print recognition, just in case you strike lucky: waste of time. This is a synthvoice, although totally naturalistic.

Ah, Juno, I see you outside. Skedaddle, lady! Don't make such a meal of it. You aren't *that* heavy on Earth.

How come I have an authentic flying saucer? I've been wondering whether to say, since this seems such a wet dream, pardon, such a fantasy, for a young geek such as me.

It all began when I took a bit of tech of my own devising to a park at dusk. *Don't* jump to the conclusion that this might be a 4-qubit iPhone. I tapped in a very long number, nothing to do with *pi*, and I got a surprisingly swift response in the form of a glowing little globe rising lazily like a luminous golf ball and drifting towards me. I guess I happened to be in the right place, unless the rest of the world and the ocean depths are littered with globes imitating golf balls.

This does rather suggest, don't you think, that the earliest arrivals on our world from the Outside postdate our 14th century, although I suppose earlier arrivals might have masqueraded as fruits or nuts...

Now you, Chuck, stop your loitering. All the way home I was increasing the grav in the hold gradually to re-accustom you, oops maybe I shouldn't have said that.

As the mini-globe hovered before me, I put my hand upon it tentatively. *Tingle tingle tingle.* The gizmo read me and assessed: *highly intelligent, atheist, ingenious, obessional, dedicated, responsible, loves solitude, bold but not rash,* et cetera... I cottoned on instantly.

Evidently here was a very compact von Neuman first contact gizmo. If you don't know what a vNfc gizmo is, you may as well stop listening. I guess the vNfc gizmo could have communicated with me efficiently in Korean, if I happened to be Korean. Although not Koranian – atheism seemed highly regarded in the aptitude test.

Proposal: Would I accept to be the intermediary between *Homo sap sap* (so brainy, in our opinion, that we named ourselves twice) and the

Outside intelligences?

Did Darwin go to the Galapagos Islands? Enough said.

Ah, Jim, I was wondering when. Lug your legs after Juno & Chuck. Bye-bye.

Basically my duties are to keep watch and transmit *by the Outsider way*, bet you'd like to know what that is, summaries of significant up-to-date Earth news. Likelihood of nuclear war or other global catastrophes, breakthroughs in nanotech or a star-drive. And no, I don't use tachyons to transmit. But I like the idea that the cosmos is non-causal, deep down; could that be a clue?

And then there was one... Come along now, Barbara. One small step for a lady mission commander. You know you can do it.

You *aren't* going to leave? Do you imagine you'll stall me here till someone fires a big net of green Kryptonite over my UFO?

The ingratitude!

I swear I'll shut the hold, take off in thirty seconds, counting, and forcibly eject you, well that can't be on to Triton cause of Nep's radiation belt, but damn it back on Mars. Enough food and water and air, and I'll resupply every couple of months, but it'll be Marooned on Mars for you – and no, I don't need a lady friend, who might take control of my UFO, even if you *are* an astronaut. I have higher, cosmic priorities.

Hatch closed, here we go. Can't say I didn't warn you, babe... Bye, folks. *Whooooooosh*

This is a flip side of the earlier story in this collection, "How We Came Back From Mars", taking a look at who the pilot of the salvatory flying saucer might have been. Diligent readers will note that one of the astronauts from the earlier story has disappeared. This is because I was aiming this shorter story at Nature *magazine where the word limit for stories in their* Futures *series at the end of each issue is a thousand words; having five astronauts on board might be excessive and confusing.*

I have long thought that I would be a suitable, and responsible, candidate as custodian for an actual alien flying saucer, should flying saucers exist, which they almost undoubtedly don't; so I have daydreamed numerous takes on this situation.

Incidentally, flying "saucers" never existed at all, historically speaking. In 1947, when Kenneth Arnold famously reported seeing strange phenomena in the sky near Mount Rainier while flying his private plane, he spoke of a chain of shiny things rushing along at an estimated 1,500 miles per hour, "like saucers skipping over water". "Saucers" didn't refer to the shapes – Arnold said those things were so thin that he could barely see them – but to their method of progress, as in the well-known pastime of tossing... oh wait, usually one tosses flat stones across water. Whoever tossed china crockery across water? Surely Ma or Grandma would be rightly indignant at the flagrant waste of her china. Perhaps the Arnold family skipped saucers; after all, Arnold was prosperous enough to own a private plane...

Anyway, Arnold's "flying saucers", misreported by a local newspaper, immediately went viral in most other newspapers across the USA; by three years later, Arnold himself was referring to flying saucers. In view of the subsequent huge impact worldwide of flying saucers, soucoupes volantes, platillos volantes *et cetera, this might be the biggest media misrepresentation ever. Presumably what Arnold saw was an atmospheric phenomenon – reflection, mirage – but modern mythology was born. And God Created Adamaski. A few years later two US cops chased across a city a brilliant light which visibly fled from them, though it paused tantalisingly if they slowed for traffic lights; the planet Venus was at the far end of the street, a minimum of 26 million miles away.*

Faith Without Teeth

At the start of each school year, Comrade Teacher Albrecht Grimm addressed the class of pre-teens with a toothless show of enthusiasm.

"Boys and Girls, Hänsels and Gretels!" This was Grimm's little joke, but Hans and Gisela, sitting at adjacent desks, were riveted. "As I'm sure you already know, as soon as your thirteenth birthdays arrive, likewise comes the opportunity and privilege to donate your teeth to the Great Patriotic Ivory Wall."

Just at that moment, a rumble sounded beneath the building. That was one of the subway trains of the enemy. A line from the wicked west burrowed underneath a Democratic part of the city before curving back to the west, its traffic forbidden by binding agreements to halt at deserted stations, all signs of which had been erased at ground level in the Democracy; grassed or concreted over. A few of the schoolchildren touched their teeth nervously, as if that train on the vanished subway carrying unsocialist strangers was vibrating their jaws. Promptly Grimm led his class in the popular song, *We Bare Our Teeth at Fascist Capitalism*.

Then Grimm asked his class, "Why is the Great Patriotic Ivory Wall essential to our survival? You, Hänsel I mean Hans."

"Because," recited Hans, "the fascist puppet-masters of the Capitalist Republic might attack our Democratic Republic and our socialist uncles and friends at any moment, using weapons of mass destruction. Our teeth symbolise our determination to resist by all and every means."

"Good. What else does pulling your teeth signify?"

"Equality!" called out a burly boy, Dietrich.

"Please explain."

"The State guarantees everyone, at very low cost, nourishing pastes, delicious thick soups, crustless breads, hot chocolates, and so on and so forth, which nobody requires teeth to chew."

"And what is the consequence of very cheap food, and cheap rents for flats, and guaranteed jobs?"

"An accumulation of money, sir. The people are rich."

"So how can our citizens spend their riches? Yes, Heidi?"

"In special shops and restaurants, sir. Where special things cost a lot. That's because those things come a long way from our uncles and friends."

"Can anyone give an example of a high-cost item?"

"A steak, sir!" called out Friedrich, the pub manager's lad. "And to chew a steak you need teeth! So the special restaurants provide a wide range of dentures, which you leave on your plate after the meal."

"To be cleansed then reused by other customers, precisely. In our socialist economy all is mutual and rational. Dentists, for instance, only need to yank milk-teeth, ensure the purity of young adults' teeth until the age of thirteen, then pull those perfect teeth to add more crust of ivory to the Wall – as well as make lots of dentures for use in the *spezial* restaurants."

Forty years earlier, dentists had been much busier for almost a year. The concrete blocks of the Wall had gone up within a mere three days, a masterwork of planning and co-ordination. Absolutely the Democratic east of the divided city must be protected from political and cultural pollution which might ooze from the enclave of the western half, encysted within otherwise socialist territory like some permanent bridgehead of evil at the end of authorised if resented road, rail, and canal transit routes. Whereupon the call went out to the whole Democratic nation of nineteen million citizens (or at least to all those over sixteen years of age) to donate their ivories to adorn the concrete to make the Wall sharp and slippery and shiny, an ever-ongoing process, or *praxis*.

"However, Friedrich, I must correct you – we *do* produce beef in our own beloved homeland, mostly for export to our uncles and friends. Not to mention lambs and pigs and geese. Lack of teeth greatly helps our export economy."

Having one's teeth pulled was an important rite of passage, this socialist society's equivalent of circumcision delayed until puberty. Grimm squared up to the class.

"And should any of you young citizens exercise your democratic right not to have your teeth pulled...?"

Was this a purely theoretical question? Was Comrade Teacher Grimm aiming to winkle out waverers?

Chubby Heidi shot her hand up. "Sir, sir! If we don't have our teeth pulled, we'll only be allowed to study theology, or else ich-theology. That won't easily lead to a guaranteed job or a subsiding flat."

"You mean a subsidised flat. Just so long as you marry — no need to blush — and have a baby or two. Hmm, yes, theology, as you say, Heidi, or else ichthyology, which is the study of fish, *not* the study of the *Ich*, the I, the Self..."

Grimm paused, perhaps reflecting upon the intellectual capacities of his pre-teens.

"Theology, from the Greek *theos*, and *logein*, to speak about, is the study of an imaginary God. Due to most churches being closed, a theological job is unlikely. Ichthyology, from the Greek *ichthys*, means speaking about fish."

"Is God some sort of fish?" asked naïve Magda of the freckles and blonde pigtails.

"In a curious way, yes," replied Grimm. "In Greek the word for fish," and he began to chalk on the blackboard, "*iota chi theta ypsilon sigma*, spells the initial letters of the phrase in Greek *Jesus Christ Son of God Saviour*. Consequently early Christians used a fish as a symbol of their prohibited cult, *thus*." And he drew a simple two-arc fish-shape.

"*However*," Grimm continued, "our own word *Ich* signifies the Self, which must belong within society. The great philosopher Hegel expressed this transindividuality thus: *Ich das Wir, und Wir, das Ich ist*, I that is a We and We that is an I. Social belonging! Practical engagement within one's environment! The yielding up of one's teeth. Ich-theology, Heidi, would be the philosophy of Self and therefore Selfishness, existentialism as opposed to socialism. Perhaps this is a little complicated for you..."

Not for little Bernhard, however, who was very good at English — the second language after compulsory Russian in case Capitalist spies needed to be interrogated, for instance. Up went Bernhard's hand.

"*Selfishness*, as opposed to *Shellfishness*," the lad proposed with an eager grin.

Grimm inclined his head in approval.

"Yes, there's a witty link between the two 'ologies. Those who govern on our behalf have a sense of humour. And it's true that our Democratic Republic does have a need for specialists regarding fish, including shellfish, Bernhard. We boast a fine sea coast as well as many rivers. Also, fish are softer than meat. Likewise most shellfish, after their shells come off. But a couple of hundred experts on cod, or pike and perch, or crabs, suffice for the needs of society. There's no point in thousands of ichthyologists. Opting for ichthyology is highly unlikely to lead to a job. By the way, don't confuse *Hegel* with *Haeckel*, Darwin's propagandist – who described and pictured many sea creatures beautifully but who said that politics is basically applied biology. I beg you to bear this all in mind as your birthdays approach."

The next morning, never-to-be-seen-again Comrade Teacher Grimm had been replaced by bossy large Lady-Comrade Teacher Mrs Ernestine Häcksel, soon to be known as *Die Hexe* – the Witch – and the blackboard had been very thoroughly washed clean of any trace of Greek Christian fish.

In due course, Hans and Gisela had their teeth pulled; their mouths were sore for a month. Out of all the class, only Magda declined her patriotic duty. Magda confided to Gisela that when she left school she might become a certain kind of masseuse, known in whispers to be favoured by visiting socialist uncles and foreign friends. She was vague about what was involved, but theoretical ichthyology held no more interest for Magda than an imaginary God; and she was very fond of her teeth, although she mostly kept her mouth shut in class. Any show of teeth from Magda generally made The Witch glare. One day, off the cuff, The Witch remarked maliciously that teeth were the worst asset for a masseuse; a fellow pupil must have snitched on Magda.

Of course, a tooth-full mouth offended the prevailing aesthetic of womanly beauty; a pursed and puckered look was prized.

Presently Hans and Gisela learned to kiss and, after ten years of kissing softly and sensuously like snails, both graduated in accountancy, married and soon had twins, Günther and Gabriele.

The end of history arrived one Sunday morning while Hans and Gisela were visiting the massive pockmarked Natural History Museum. It was good to be alone together, if that wasn't an oxymoron; few people visited the museum before noon. Gisela's widowed mother had been left in the couple's one-bedroom flat, cooing dotingly over the twins.

Presently Gisela and Hans came to the newly rebuilt east wing of the museum, occupied by the remarkable 'wet collections' returned by Uncle Ivan after almost forty years' protective absence. What a sight those wet collections were! Towering upwards within an outer wall of thick glass, braced with steel, were shelf upon glass shelf – also braced by steel and separated by corridors – of glass jars large and little (276,000, according to a notice) containing dead fishes preserved in 80 tons of ethanol all told. Amongst the predominant fishes were also oddities such as a two-headed piglet and a four-legged chicken. Every single creature was blanched colourless by preservation – apart from the only living resident, which was predominantly grey (not all that much different, then) and which moved slowly around a long tank just inside of the great glass wall: a lungfish, a 'living fossil, 40 million years old'.

"Imagine being 40 million years old!" sighed Gisela, who had little more interest in ichthyology than Hans, but this place was somewhere to visit, calm, cool, and awesome. "Do you suppose the lungfish gets bored or lonely?"

"Do you think it *thinks*, my love?" he replied. "Maybe it's better not to think."

At that moment a bald-headed comrade curator in a white coat, maybe an authentic ichthyologist, hastened from within the great glass-and-steel internal structure clutching a Sternchen tranny radio, exited by a door close to the couple, rushed to a flight of marble stairs and disappeared down those as though fleeing a horde of wasps. The door to the edifice of glass shelves and 276,000 glass jars stood open, no notice explicitly forbidding entry. It was as if... as if... as if a children's grassy minipark had subsided all of a sudden, revealing a disused subway station, just as a western train slowed by the dust-coated platform, and opened its doors.

No, it wasn't like that at all! Because the glass door led inward to confinement.

But even so.

"Shall we...?"

"...just take a look from the inside?"

Tidiness caused Gisela to close the door behind them, producing an ominous *clunk*. The door had locked itself! Yet this was as nothing when, moments later, muffled by thick stone walls, a howl of sirens reached their ears. Brighter light illuminated their surroundings for a moment, leaving afterimages. A thunderous boom – the whole fabric of the east wing shook, as did the ethanol in the jars. Distant shatterings sounded. All the lights went out, only to flicker on again a few seconds later. Silence fell.

Hans and Gisela gaped at one another toothlessly.

"...an enemy missile...!"

"...of mass destruction...!"

"...our city's gone...!"

"...except for this wing of the museum, rebuilt to survive the worst..."

"...what about Günther...?"

"...what about Gabi...?"

"...what about Mama...?"

"...at least we're alive, Gisela..."

"...at least we're alive, Hans..."

"...oh Günther, oh Gabi..."

"...the wall of teeth failed..."

"...no, it protected us, who gave our teeth – it reflected the worst away from us..."

"...yes, that must be how we're alive..."

Time passed.

No one came. They stayed near that locked door in case the ichthyologist reappeared, key in his pocket. But the bald man could be dead because...

"...air must be radioactive..."

"...thick glass keeps the bad air out of here – plenty of good air for us to breathe..."

They were both accountants.

"...enough air for how long...?"

"...weeks, I'd say..."

More time passed.

"...I'm thirsty..."

The lungfish was swimming in a big tank of water. Off came the long heavy lid.

"...fresh water, or salty...?"

"...I'm not an ichthyologist...the water smells to me of ammonia...not a lot, just a bit...but not salty..."

"...we shouldn't drink any ammonia..."

"...maybe the ammonia comes from its pee..."

"...we shouldn't drink *any* ammonia...!"

At the rear of the glass-and-steel edifice they spied a laboratory bench. Beakers, test tubes, vials, jars, sinks, taps. To which they now hastened.

A tap yielded water.

"...must be an emergency tank somewhere, Gisela..."

They quaffed from beakers, then returned to the door and sat on the floor.

According to Hans's GUB People's Watch, ten hours had passed since the attack. They had twice needed to pee in a basin, Hans helping Gisela to mount.

"I'm hungry, Hans..."

"Me too."

They regarded the lungfish.

"Looks like an eel, doesn't it...?"

"Forty million years old...shame to kill it...eat it raw, still almost half alive..."

"Does raw eel require teeth to eat it...?"

"Forty million years old, could be tough..."

Notwithstanding, Hans threw his jacket aside, rolled up his shirt sleeves, plunged his arms into the tank.

"My Grandpa once said something about raw eel blood being poisonous..."

"But this isn't an eel, it's a lungfish..."

Try as he might, Hans couldn't catch the creature which slipped slimily from his grasp the one time he managed to corner it.

He gave up. "We're being *dumbheads*! We're in the biggest fishmonger's in the world! And all the fishes have been *cured*!"

Cured and pickled by preservation in ethanol, oh yes. Ethanol was pretty much the same as vodka, wasn't it? Here were umpteen shelves of fleshy fish soaked in full-strength almost-vodka! A feast for the toothless, finer than any *spezial* restaurant!

"Maybe we should rinse the fishes we choose in the sink, my love, otherwise we might become drunk...?"

"Maybe a different fish for each of us would be wise...?"

Which two to choose? This plump one, upside-down? This slab of an ichthys, head downwards? All the names were in Latin or Greek, understandable only by ichthyologists.

Gisela chose a big jar containing a sumptuous *Pomatomus saltatrix*; he, a substantial *Micropterus dolomieu* with large fins although a small mouth. These, they carried to one of the sinks, uncapped the jars, poured away the almost-vodka, rinsed, then decanted their dinner on to the workbench.

The smell was of nail polish remover as well as of fishiness. Inspired, Hans took from his pocket a treasured box of matches featuring a Robur three-ton truck. May the match be as strong! The first failed to light, the second snapped, but the third bloomed. As Hans drifted the flame across the two fishes, blue haloes of fire wrapped their dinner, dying down after twenty seconds or so. Hans clawed flesh from his slightly charred *Micropterus dolomieu* and sucked, first tentatively, then more forcefully; the fish wasn't as soft as he'd expected, but even though stiffish it went down a treat: an unusual tasting treat, indescribable really. Had anyone before sucked a *Micropterus dolomieu* preserved in ethanol for a period of fifty or a hundred years? Deviatonist Chinese Maoists might relish hundred-year-old eggs, matured in mud mixed with rice-husks, according to *Young World*, but here was a whole new sensation – no words existed yet to express it.

Gisela was following suit with her *Pomatomus saltatrix*, sucking and grinning, almost-vodka fish juices running down her chin.

Soon many sucked bones lay on the bench, maybe spelling out a new gastronomic name.

Hans idly played with the bones until suddenly a pattern appeared. He shifted them a little more, and now they spelled 'Grete'. A small change using fish teeth from a jaw, and the German word for fishbone appeared: 'Gräte'. Hänsel and Gretel lost in the forest of natural history marking their way with bones instead of breadcrumbs...

After a while:

"....I feel dizzy..."

"...me too..."

Hans and Gisela subsided to sit on the floor. She began humming *We Bare Our Teeth at Fascist Capitalism*. *Fascist* became *Fishest*; presently she began to snore.

"– vandalism!"

Blearily, from the floor, Hans regarded a dark-suited, purse-lipped man of gaunt aspect whose hair was silver, as was his neat goatee. Beside Hans, Gisela was stirring.

"– don't be hard, Comrade Direktor, they may be *ill* –"

Hand shaking shoulder. "*Are you ill?* Speak!" ordered that bald ichthyologist. "I want to know if your speech is blurred; whether you're uncoordinated – can you see me clearly? How many fingers?"

"I see you. Four." Hans did his best to scramble up, clutching the lab bench. He steadied himself. "So you both survived the enemy attack by sheltering in the basement?"

"What *attack*? Oh I see..."

"Did many citizens survive?"

"There was no attack," said the Comrade Direktor. "A meteor came out of the blue and exploded high in the air. Like Tunguska, if that means anything to you."

"*Young World* printed a piece about the Tunguska thing last year. With a photo of a million fallen trees."

"In our case, windows. Most windows facing the blast blew out, or rather in. Many, many injuries, and inevitably deaths – a few buildings collapsed. We've only had a chance to enter our wet collections this morning, after a quick glance yesterday to see they survived, not time enough to notice you two lying drunk on the floor at the back. Will you kindly show me your identity cards?"

Scribble, scribble on a scrap of paper.

"A mere formality, not formaldehyde for you two."

"He means no jail for snacking on State property," said the bald man.

"Police and emergency services are overloaded – our Uncle Ivan was only able to give us twenty seconds' warning. However, the enemy in the west of the city has lost *even more glass* due to its Capitalist skyscrapers!"

"Thanks be for the Wall of Our Teeth!" Gisela had roused; Hans helped her up. "Oh I have a little headache..."

"Take this aspirin," said the ichthyologist. "Today may be known as Crystalday, antithesis to the notorious fascist Crystalnight."

"Not applicable within these walls." The Direktor fondly assessed his mighty glass-and-steel habitat for quarter of a million dead fish as well as several freak creatures.

"What did we eat?" Hans asked nervously.

"A bluefish, and a smallmouth bass," the ichthyologist told him, and for the first time Hans registered that the bald man, unlike the Direktor, had gappy tobacco-stained teeth, unless he wore permanent dentures the colour of tarnished ivory. How disgusting those looked.

"Günther and Gabi may be unharmed!" piped up Gisela. "We have thick net curtains."

On their way back to the doorway, the four passed the uncovered tank of the lungfish, which swam sluggishly away along one side.

"Pardon me, but I must ask," asked the ichthyologist, "did you urinate in the tank rather than using a sink?"

"How could we do such a thing?" exclaimed Gisela. "That fish is forty million years old. But please, I do need to *go*." Now that the subject was mentioned, bladders began to insist.

"Me too," admitted Hans.

"You'll find the restrooms in the basement," the Direktor told the couple. "Use those stairs. There's a lift to return by."

Hans and Gisela emerged from the museum – shut to visitors as soon as the emergency happened; glass from its front windows crunched underfoot. Invalidenstraße glittered glassily in Sunday morning sunlight. Headscarfed women were getting to work with brooms.

Close by to the west was the vehicle inspection barrier preliminary to the checkpoint just before the bridge over the ship canal. This side of the bridge, interrupted only by the well-guarded gap of the checkpoint itself, the Great Patriotic Wall was as ever, its upper sides and top crusted defiantly with teeth which gleamed like an endless smile. Maybe part of this stretch included the couple's very own teeth donated almost two decades earlier, though it would be selfishness to ask where exactly your teeth went.

For a few moments they let themselves gaze at enemy skyscrapers in the distance, no longer dazzling now that all their windows had gone.

For Bernhard and Barbara

I adore Berlin, which I only first saw in 2013, partly through the eyes of my German translator Bernhard Kempen, to whom this story is dedicated, along with his alter ego Barbara. Bernhard read the story and chipped in with a few suggestions. Others who preread the story felt that it lacked a proper ending, but – while always open to advice – I remain indefatigably convinced that the story has the right ending, and that any neat tying-up or surprise reversal or punch lines would be, as it were, anecdotal, trivial, and undermining.

Since Berlin today is rather like a utopia, especially for alternative life-styles, and since the inhabitants are so helpful, friendly, and generally laid-back, it might seem unkind to evoke the departed, self-styled Democratic "utopia" (Nanny with a machine gun) that occupied the east of divided Berlin during the decades of Checkpoint Charlie – which itself replaced the megalomaniac Hitlerian Berlin, most of which fortunately never left the drawing boards of Albert Speer. (More about that in "The Thousand Year Reich", earlier on in this collection.) But the world we see is wallpaper.

There's a photo of the solitary lungfish looking thoughtful, or much more likely thoughtless, on my website www.ianwatson.info under the heading "Stendhal in Berlin".

The Travelling Raven Problem

"Right, apprentice lad, welcome to Ravenstower! As yer already well aware, or bluddy ought to be, the Thirteen Dukedoms communicates by raven-post, and us 'ere is the central ravenry of this 'ere fine city of Orth, proud capital of Northland. Woz yer name again?"

"Igar, Ser."

"You addresses us as Corvomaester."

"Certainly, Corvomaester."

"Behave yerself, scrape up the raven shit, sweep spilled food, pick up dropped sticks cos them's a fire hazard, see as there's always enough carrion and kitchen waste, *not* picking out any maggots or gobs of fat fer yerself, don't forget about berries and cereals and pullet eggs, and in twenty or thirty years some young oik might just be addressing yerself as Corvomaester."

All the way up the domed tower were big rough-hewn numbered niches for ravens' deep fur-lined nests of sticks, mud, and bark, tied together with roots, open to the outside air as well as to the inside. Due to all this ventilation, the tower was bloody cool within but less pongy than otherwise might have been. Curving stairways of black iron led up to all levels of the railed interior galleries. Igar imagined a huge library where the ravens were books, their feathers pages. Bright Igar imagined far too much. He'd been taught things by a mythematical maester who went into retirement to meditate but who then took a fantasy to this lad so open to learning yet bottom of his class due to woolgathering during dull lessons. When the hundreds of hogs in Dad's flock suddenly died of rampaging purpleskin posteriorparalysis brainrot, necessity compelled that the boy be gainfully indentured, and Igar was lucky indeed that the maester pulled a string within Orth Castle.

Constant bird-noise rattled and echoed.

"Now the brainiest ravens speak our tongue when it suits them; that's about half of the congregation here –"

"Excuse me, Corvomaester, but if *fifty* per cent are brain*iest* – "

"Shut your gob, boy, when your betters is talking. I was saying:

you'll need to know their lingo too, be able to *kraaa* or *prrruk-prrruk* or *toc-toc-toc* to catch their at-tension. The least brainiest can only be taught to carry wor one-time pads to two or three of the thirteen capital castles and come back 'ere. But the brainiest can tour the whole lot, though it takes weeks and weeks."

"Won't those ravens need thirteen-time pads, Corvomaester?"

"One-time is wot we calls them, boy, no one knows why, but thus it's been for the past three thousand years."

"So the messages aren't actually... en-cry-pted?"

"Wozzat mean? More nonsense, you'll get put in a crypt yerself! If yer so clever, I'll be showing you wor best chart of the Thirteen Duckdomes right away, and *you* tell *me* in wot order yon brainiest ravens should best visit all the capital castles in turn."

A falling stick and several twigs bounced off the Corvomaester's bald pate. Swiftly Igar collected them up from beside the much-pecked cadaver of a direwabbit.

"Well let me see, Corvomaester, if we adopt a mythematical approach as regards combinatorial optimisation –"

"Yer only optimist in any combat is a fool!"

Kraaa, Prrruk-prrruk, Toc-toc-toc," vociferated scores of ravens in agreement or disagreement.

The Corvomaester jerked his thumb aloft. "*Them* heavy buggers only needs watch out for high hawks." He became solemn and fingered the black iron links of his necklace of office. "Hawks is the gobspite of forgotten Gods. The spiteful gobspit." He spat accurately at some recent ravenshite on a footworn flagstone of the great circular floor.

"Begging your pardon, Corvomaester, but mightn't grilles such as you can open to tie a one-time pad to a bird's leg be a tidier idea for our side of the roostnests?"

"Imbecile, ye cannot semi-cage a raven or ye'll set it raving, as the sage old saying says."

As if to illustrate this wisdom, half a dozen birds launched themselves into the vast aviary, to flap overhead and then to gyre and to pern as though in parody of buzzards since a strongly sustaining breeze had sprung up and through the tower. This and the deepening gloom suggested that a storm was impending. Indeed lightning began to flicker and flash from afar through the nest apertures, lightening the interior of the tower with swift spasms of illumination.

Inspired by the flashes, Igar said hesitantly, "Corvomaester, instead of using ravens to carry messages that take days and weeks to arrive, might it be a better idea to put mirrors *on top* of our tower? Then a tower on a hilltop ten leagues away spies our signal and repeats the same to a further tower? And, er, so on? That way a message might travel a hundred leagues or more in an hour. We could call the mirrors hellographs and you'd be, um, famous."

"And that's all mirrorflashes could say, feckwit. Hello hello hello."

"No, you'd have a code —"

"*Careful*, laddie!"

"Corvomaester pardon me, Corvomaester I forgot your address. With respect, Corvomaester, pre-agreed patterns of short and long flashes would represent different letters, making words —"

"Which any *spy* as knows his letters can read plain as day! No, scrubboy of flagstones, ravens is the best security, as has served us well for thirty centuries."

"Corvomaester, an arrow... a trained hawk..."

"'tis blasphemy to disable a raven, the slow bonfire awaits you. Flashing mirrors? Yer'll get yerself blinded with such daftness."

"Corvomaester, ciphers could be based upon pages in a book held only by the sender and the intended receiver."

"Would that be *The Buke of Knowledge, The Buke of Unknowledge, The Buke of Noble Lineages*, or *The Buke of Obscene Tails*...? All handwritten by scribes, I'll remind ye, with all what that implies as regards textual correctness!"

Evidently the Corvomaester was more learnèd than Igar had begun to suspect incorrectly. During the coming years, Igar would need to solve the Travelling Raven Problem...

This brief tale of eager Igar was prompted by the messenger ravens in George Martin's unbrief Song of Ice and Fire series, at least in the TV version. Years ago the publisher of the present collection urged me to read A Game of Thrones, but I wasn't in the mood for a fantasy saga. In fact I've only ever read one fantasy epic, The Chronicles of Thomas Covenant, quitting after the first six volumes. Never Lord of the Rings, which started the craze. I think I avoided Tolkien because as a student I was unimpressed by Anglo-Saxon

and Old Norse: all a bit primitive compared with Alexander Pope or Stendhal, to pull two names out of the hat. Though oops I did read the Finnish Kalevala during the early 90s, so as to do my own 1100-page science-fantasy take.

It's possible that in future I might add more episodes to Igar's career, though equally I mightn't – so many things to write, so many things to read!

THE ARC DE TRIOMPHE CODE

As Don Broon from Dundee in Scotland walked up the Champs Élysées in Paris at 9.30 am on a wet Wednesday in September, he seethed with indignation. The yet-to-be-published Scottish author, domiciled in the French capital for the past year, had failed again to see the *Mona Lisa* in the Louvre. Sodding mob of tourists always queueing up! All you'd glimpse at any one time would be some hair and an eye, a bit of shoulder, or one of Ma Lisa's hands.

Today he'd arrived at the vast art gallery yet again well in advance of the 9.00 am opening, and already the situation was hopeless. Chinese and Germans, Americans and Scandinavians, Outer Mongolians for all Don knew, were waiting in a horde to collect their pre-booked tickets. As for buying a ticket right on the spot, dream on. Yet he *had* to buy a ticket on the very same day when miraculously, by some anti-entropic freak of Broonian motion, all the tourists in Paris flocked elsewhere. A 20 Euro banknote remained in his shoe, reserved for this special purpose. Don couldn't waste his only banknote, his home being under a tree in a tiny park – a tree like a wigwam, decapitated by lightning or something, but propped up on two concrete crutches and still leafy. Mainly Don ate out of restaurant bins and drank water from fountains, occasionally craving a single malt. He couldn't desert his wigwam by kipping overnight outside the Louvre because a tramp might move in to his tree. Police would probably shift him on from outside the Louvre.

When Don Broon first arrived in Paris, where young writers traditionally cultivate their genius, he slept upstairs, and up more stairs, in legendary Shakespeare and Company bookshop in exchange for working on the till; so far, so good. But then his bed became needed for a new arrival. Dispossessed, he was soon scruffy.

Might scruffiness stop him from even getting *into* the Louvre?

This was no smiling matter! And whose fault was it? D*n Bloody Bro*n's!

Yet why did Don wish to gaze at the *Mona Lisa* without anyone else in the way? Because of Bloody D*n Bro*n. Don wanted to spot something else about the painting that nobody ever noticed previously, in order to write a breakthrough best-seller and be able to drink the best single malts for the rest of his life. D*n Bro*n had done it! Why not Don Broon? Never mind *Virgin on the Rocks* or *The Rabbi's Last Supper*. *Mona Lisa* was totally iconic.

The rain got heavier. He needed to shelter. Very well, he'd go through the tunnel under Place Charles de Gaulle and sit beneath the Arc de Triomphe where no tourists were presently visible; no doubt they were all drying off in the Louvre.

Soon, Don had shucked off his perennial rucksack and was sitting on the ledge of the base of the Arc staring at a long list of French victories such as AUSTERLITZ, inscribed on one of the inside walls.

After a while he stared at the columns of names of Generals on another wall: PONCET, DELAAGE, BARBOU, DESENFANTS... dozens of Generals. Yon Napoleon must have had dozens of armies.

And then Don experienced an epiphany!

A code was in plain view! Yet not such as would be noticed idly!

The middle letters of a few of the Generals' names were *underlined* lightly. A name here, a name there, apparently at random.

Generals Me<u>uni</u>er, Ma<u>rce</u>au, Ba<u>stou</u>l, Gi<u>rar</u>d, Du<u>hes</u>ne, Beau<u>rep</u>aire... and some others.

Don Broon pulled out his treasured notebook and biro, and printed:

UNI-RCE-STO-RAR-HES-REP...and more.

Soon he had the complete string of letters. Which would need to be rearranged in what order? Surely a clue, a seed of meaning must jump out. .

He pondered. Logically the hidden message should be in French, or maybe Latin. Don's French was still a bit minimal, his Latin almost nonexistent. Consequently he would be obliged to find a collaborator for *The Napoleonic Code...*

Wait, those battles *mightn't all* be Napoleonic...

The Arc de Triomphe Code: that's it. Folks nowadays might have foggy notions about Napoleon and, um, Josephine Baker, but everyone knew how the Arc de Triomphe is located in Paris – just as many potential readers as knew where Bloody D*n Bro*n's *Mona Lisa* was, or the Eiffel Tower. Allegedly Ma Lisa had tiny letters and numbers written inside her eyes if only you could get close enough with a magnifying glass.

Quickly Don restored the notebook to his pocket, next to the magnifying glass. Only a pair of pigeons had noticed him copying.

How could he entrust a collaborator with this treasure worth a fortune on the Best-Selling Authors list? Where could he find a collaborator who spoke French and preferably Latin, oh and English too?

A priest in a church confessional? Maybe the priest would secretly be wearing a chastisement collar of spikes around his thigh, and already belong to a secret society... Untrustworthy!

Only one answer, really: he'd need to approach one of the naive would-be-writer young American women at Shakespeare and Company, scarcely a stone's throw from his own wigwam tree. A woman should be fairly trustworthy. Women were on the whole, weren't they, compared with blokes? If not, a woman could be imposed on or bamboozled. Hopefully she'd have bothered to learn French, maybe even have mastered some Latin at Harvard or wherever. And she ought to own a laptop.

Hmm, and she mustn't be too snobbishly literary...

First, a wash and brush-up was in order! *Bains-douches*: that was the word, or rather two words, free public showers. Wash his underwear. Maybe buy a newer shirt in some market, now that he was free to spend the 20 Euros from his shoe.

The chubby straw-haired young woman's name was Marigold-Jeanette Hickenlooper, who could obviously benefit from a catchy pseudonym. A New Yorker. Admirer of Hemingway, which was okay, simple journalistic style; Don Broon had read *A Moveable Feast* before heading for Paris. Don's initial approach in the bookshop went rather well, and he'd reserved enough Euros after acquiring a semi-decent shirt to treat Marigold-Jeanette Hickenlooper to a coffee in the nearby Café Panis, soon as she could take a break, while he drank tap water. She'd brought an iPad thingy with her.

Outside the windows, tourists traipsed past like healthy zombies in the direction of Notre Dame.

"Just call me Emjay. You're accent's *amazing*," Emjay told Don in her own accent.

Don grinned. "Yies may be hae'in a wee proablim wi meh real accent, but I'm speaking plain ordinary standard English to you right now."

"Is that so?"

"English such as anyone hoping to make a heap of money has to write in. Like Hemingway, for instance," he added seductively.

"So you're from where exactly?"

"Scotland, but I don't wear a kilt or beg with bagpipes. Specifically Dundee, fourth city of Scotland, famous as home to the Brittle Bone Society and for other reasons, but I always knew I'd never become famous at home. Too provincial."

"Do people in Dundee break their arms and legs often? Don't they drink enough milk?" Emjay was quick and seemed to have a sense of humour, which might be good or not so good... or maybe she was merely literal, which could be good.

"I just knew," she enthused, "something awesome would happen in Paris! After only two weeks! I feel blessed."

He'd ascertained earlier that she understood French and could read Latin, due to good schooling.

"I'm sure," she said, "that I have a novel in me, but what about?"

Don felt like Svengali, the mesmerist of creative young ladies. "First you should make money from a best-seller, using a pseudonym along with me. Let your own novel arrive in its own good time. With money, you can publish yourself if the world's blind to your merits."

"That's an idea. What pseudonym?"

"How about Bron Doon?" Don said off the top of his gingery head, rearranging letters.

"Is that Doon with an *e*? Like Lorna Doone?"

"Could be," he allowed.

"Because Bron is like Bronwell Bronte, brother of the more famous. No wait, he was *Bran*well."

She was literate. Too literate? That might be a wee problem for a best-seller. Don had studied D*n Bro*n's style, or lack of it. On the other hand, he didn't want a semi-literate collaborator.

"Bron Doone with an *e*," he said, "should be as eye-grabbing as D*n Bro*n. Shall we shake on this?" His hand was perfectly clean for the first time in ages.

Emjay extended a slim hand, artisan rings on three of her fingers.

"Okay, so now I'm going to confide the secret of the, ta-da, *Arc de Triomphe Code*."

"I shan't breathe a word to anyone else," she breathed.

Don showed Emjay his notebook and explained. She studied the groups of letters for a while, then began doing things with her iPad thingy. Maybe the thingy could do decoding.

"Big *oops*," said Emjay. "Wiki says that the underlined Generals on the Arc are ones who *died in battle*. That's what the underlining signifies."

For a few moments, Don was thunderstruck. However, lightning swiftly followed, unlike the usual sequence.

"That's what anyone would *want* you to think!" he said. "And the best place to hide a secret is in plain sight, isn't it? And anyway, this doesn't matter *at all*. Did it matter to D*n Bro*n what nonsense he was concocting? Thanks to D*n Bro*n, millions of people visit the Rosslyn Chapel near Edinburgh and the Louvre. Thanks to Bron Doone with an *e*, the Arc de Triomphe will be so crowded they'll need barriers to stop tourists from being forced into all the traffic circling aroound!"

Three years later, Marigold Hickenlooper's novel *The Paris Hoax* appeared with jacket endorsements from two Pulitzer Fiction Award winners, and garnered enthusiastic reviews from *The New York Times*, *The Washington Post*, and the *Chicago Tribune*. "...an American in Paris finds herself caught up in the fantasy life of a Scottish vagabond convinced of his own unrecognised genius – a richly tragicomic take on life down and out in the French capital. Think Samuel Beckett meets Hemingway meets Umberto Eco, along with a twist of *Zazie in the Metro* in Hickenlooper's heady postmodern cocktail – plus deliciously parodic nods at the author of the *Da Vinci Code*, who in a sense serves as the absent Godot for whom the vagabond waits in semiotic ambush, weaving a mystery which is no mystery at all, notwithstanding that in themselves the extracts from 'The Arc de Triomphe Code' constitute a satiric mini-masterpiece..."

Marigold's publishers laid on a champagne and stuffed mini-croissant launch party at Planet Hollywood in Times Square. A party was unusual for a first novel. But then, Marigold was one of *those* Hickenloopers.

"Jimmy Dundoon is such a great character," a journalist

acquaintance told Marigold. "So is he based on someone, or several people mashed up?"

"From the 1920s to the 1950s you might have met such a person in Paris," Marigold said judiciously.

"Yeah, right. I notice that your Abigail character never sleeps with him."

"Where would she do so? Under a tree? In a bed tucked among the bookshelves in Shakespeare and Company? Besides, that would have spoiled Jimmy, don't you think?"

"By giving him real human contact, I can see that. And I guess he might have been a bit disgusting. Not to mention being, well, *mad* isn't the right word."

"*Obsessive?* Though not dangerous at all, no I wouldn't say so. The world of literature's full of, well, you might say losers, who'll never get published. Granted the internet has changed that, but not if you go in for the down-and-out genius jag as if it's fifty or eighty years ago."

"Jimmy *done* himself *down*, hence Dundoon – I see!"

As usual, no post awaited Don Broon at the desk inside Shakespeare and Company. He couldn't bring himself to ask more than once a fortnight. Emjay had warned him that even after she finished their book, which might take her quite a while, it could take ages to get a suitable agent who herself or himself might take ages to place *The Arc de Triomphe Code*, after which a publisher might take a couple of years to produce the book. He'd had a few postcards from her, about personal difficulties, without room for any return address, but that seemed a long while back.

Time was rolling onward, though Don was no longer totally certain about the passage of time except as regards noticing seasons, especially winter.

Several copies of a new book on display caught his eye on account of the Arc de Triomphe being on the dustjacket.

The Paris Hoax, by Marigold Hickenlooper.

Don reached for a copy. Her photo was on the back cover, overprinted with what must be reviews. Yet he found that he couldn't read print any smaller than that of the title and author. All other words were a blur, likewise on the pages inside. He'd lost his *Mona Lisa* magnifying glass the year before, or the year before that. The book might as well have been a dummy, placed there to taunt him! Something created by the staff of the shop as a joke. They knew he called every couple of weeks hoping to find an important letter postmarked NY NY. The young, mainly American staff came and went, but they would gossip to each other. Rage filled Don Broon. Clutching that copy which he couldn't read, he bolted out through the open doorway to jog breathlessly along the pavement in the direction of St Michel, his grimy loose-strapped rucksack banging his back.

After a while he had to slow.

No one seemed to have pursued him.

Then he realised what he had lost: he could never again call at Shakespeare and Company to ask about post, and he could never go back to his wigwam tree in the little park just round the corner from the bookshop. He crossed over the road to the side lined by book and souvenir stalls and descended a flight of steps to the quay. By the waters of the Seine he sat down and wept.

Those tears washed his brain clean.

He'd been an automaton, that's what! For an indeterminate stretch of time he'd been robotised! He'd become sick in the heed a good few seasons ago. Bloody D*n Bro*n had messed with Don Broon's mental code. That bloody book of Bro*n's ought to be called *Da Vinci Virus* – it replicated itself everywhere and made folks brainboiled.

Bonny Dundee was a-calling Don now. He'd go home, get a job in the marmalade factory (he would need some glasses; the sort for your eyes). Scarcely did this thought dawn than Don craved the sweet soft crunch of thick orange peel in jelly spread on toast. Plus, he'd get a cat to keep him company, a big fat marmalade cat striped like a tiger. Don't call it Ginger because that's a different taste.

Wait. Wasn't there a best-seller called *The Ginger Man*? By **Don**... leavy... that was who. How could Don have missed the connection? Irish Yank who lived in Ireland. 45 million copies or so. Don had read **Don**leavy once upon a time. Full of sex, something which so far eluded Don. First published in *Paris*, he recalled – the relevant brain-cell had unclogged.

Paris was still the place to be! Yet *not now* – but forty or fifty years ago!

Don Broon held *The Paris Hoax* ahead of himself like a swimming float. Am I going in-seine? he thought merrily, and launched himself, Marigold's post-modern novel outstretched.

And so he beat onward, a waterlogging boat borne upon the current towards the past where all the best books were written, probably.

Just round the corner from the Shakespeare and Company bookshop, and opposite the oldest tree in Paris, is the delightful Esmeralda hotel in the tiny Rue de St Julien le Pauvre, so anciently authentic that it can only manage one star. No lift; those narrow steep oak stairs are quite a haul. Minimal mod cons but gorgeous wallpapers. No breakfast room nor croissant, though maybe a glass of wine if the conversation's good. A bit pricey, since it's a stone's throw from Notre Dame. I merely mention, in Baedeker mode.

Dan Brown did not step inside the Esmeralda or he would have mentioned it for added authenticity.

SPANISH FLY

Ricardo lay upon Zahra, fucking. His penis felt like some big chili pepper stiff as wood, sweating fiery capsaicin. The head must be choked scarlet with engorgement – yet he couldn't burst with an orgasm, as if string was tied tight to delay him. If only her juices would soothe him more as she shrilled, fingernails raking his back. The fierce itching increased whenever he slacked.

From time to time Zahra's heels drummed at his buttocks. His heart thudded in response.

Who was the confined one? Who was the slave? Zahra? Or himself?

The bed was heavy old oak such as a fat village priest or a local *cacique* despot may have lolled upon. Slanted mirrors set into the headboard showed Ricardo the angled mirrors of the ceiling, and thus the stinging progress of the emerald beetle across his back.

He must be hallucinating to some degree, imagining the beetle's wanderings as intentional. The human brain sought for patterns. He thought of the arrays of mirror segments that resolve close binary stars by interferometry, fractured images which a computer combines into greater clarity than any one telescope can see on its own. Ricardo wasn't a professional astronomer like those other scientists at Yerbes, north-east of Madrid, but as a visitor guide in the pavilion that popularised astronomy he must understand in order to explain. Every other weekend he drove back to his mother's flat in Madrid. Apart from mother and his job, he had no ties, as it were.

No need to twist his neck to watch himself fucking, in a compound vision, fly's-eye way, nor to follow the journey of Zahra's sharp fingernails across his back. Shouldn't the beetle slip in his sweat? Mightn't she crush it?

He realised how intensely her gaze was concentrating, as if the motion of her heels and her outcries belonged to a different person.

It was very hot that day in Granada, even in the shade of vines overhanging the tiny courtyard pebbled like a maze. Oleanders with their long thin leaves bloomed pinkly around the walls. Invisible cicadas were rubbing their legs together shrilly in the heat. Zahra had led Ricardo here from the tea house through the twisting narrow medieval alleyways, but instead of taking him straight up to a room, which he anticipated, sat upon a stone bench, as if he must prove himself further. Perhaps a black-clad crone would come to question him or simply take more money from him. He had little idea if he was actually in a brothel, or whether Zahra was a whore pretending not to be so. 'Submission' was what 'Islam' meant, although the voluntary submission was to God, not to a woman. Zahra was a Moor, one of those who had ruled the whole south of Iberia for hundreds of years. Moors might be second-class citizens since then, though once they had ruled the roost. Ricardo was certainly seeking submission, but to what extent?

Zahra waved a hand at the oleanders. "The most poisonous of plants," she remarked. "A deadly beauty. But the first plant to blossom after the atom bomb fell on Hiroshima."

The taste of the minted, honeyed tea was still in his mouth. He was effectively lost in the Albayzín district sprawling on the hillside opposite the Alhambra Palace. True, he only needed to walk downhill constantly, whatever the twists and turns, to emerge into a more normal modern world, but that wasn't his desire; not yet.

"My name," she said, "means flower. Or," and she smiled slyly, "beauty. Would you taste a little poison, so as to discover…?" though she didn't specify what. "You must accept my judgement about the amount of poison."

"I accept," he told her. "I submit." Ricardo was certain that this was no scheme to kill and rob him. On the contrary, failure to comply with a desire of hers might see him back on the alleyway outside the gate, excluded due to unsuitability, even though he had already presented her with two fifty Euro notes, to be allowed to accompany her.

From her bag she took a big twist of paper and unwrapped a small green cake. A heady aroma arose to his nostrils.

Earlier, in the teahouse, the tetería, his eyes had strayed frequently to her tits, her tetas. The black rope of her hair, passed over one shoulder, hung between them. Black as the pupils of her eyes. She wore a purple kaftan embroidered with golden crescent moons. On her wrists were no bangles, and her manicured, violet-varnished fingers lacked rings, which suggested to him potential nakedness, availability. Skin, only dusky skin. Yet at the same time her black sandals, their high heels rising almost from a pencil-width, clasped her calves with a lavishness of studded leather – how much more such was hidden beneath her long clothing? Those sandals might have been specially made for her by a local Moroccan craftsman. Moroccan, for sure. She must be from Morocco. Briefly he felt as if the south of Iberia had never been purged of the Moors, as if al-Andalus survived.

A comment on the internet had mentioned this particular teahouse in the street of the teahouses as a rendezvous for a certain sort of person; consequently he came here the day following his business visit to the Sierra Nevada Observatory up in the huge mountains where some snow still clung.

She was sitting alone at a little low octagonal table of carved wood, on a many-coloured leather pouffe, reading a magazine about fate and fortune. A floppy bag lay by her feet. Other customers were a couple of old men, playing some card game, and a group of giggling students passing round a hubble-bubble pipe.

Nothing venture...

"Would it disturb you if I sit here?"

She seemed provoked, in more than one sense, by his intrusion – offended initially by his presumption, as well as by his assumption about her, yet at the same time mischievously excited. As though she was, and also was not, what he hoped. She didn't actively discourage him, yet he realised that he must offer more, of *himself*, irrespective of whatever might await her in his wallet.

Eyeing her magazine, he said, "Some people think that the stars in the sky show our destinies, but when I look through a telescope there's so much more than meets the naked eye..."

Zahra stared up at the mirrors on the ceiling. "Now you're perfect," she whispered in his ear, and added, "...and now I think you must love me...

"...and must use the map to find me again."

The map.

What she had drawn upon his back, the trail which the stinging emerald beetle followed, was of a sudden clear to him as the plan of a city district… *somewhere else*. He was fairly sure the district wasn't the Albayzín of Granada, where he was now.

When he did eventually come, his semen burned, and he cried out as much in pain as in relief. He began to roll aside.

"Be very careful not to crush the beetle, or you release its full dose, which will surely destroy your kidneys."

Afterwards, a robe around her, she helped him resume his shirt and trousers. His back was aflame, and his penis throbbed hotly, still half erect; had there been viagra in that little cake? His legs wobbled; the room oscillated softly. Flutterings of light and twinklings affected his vision.

When she led him down into the tiny, leafy courtyard, where leaves fractured sunlight confusingly, he gasped, "Zahra, when may I see you again?"

"You would risk your body once more?"

"Yes, yes!" He must be mad. Whatever aphrodisiac he had swallowed had warped his mind, filled him with yearning. He craved. He adored.

She opened the gate to the alleyway.

"You'll not be able to find your way back to this Carmen, because the map shows otherwise."

Carmen, Carmen… the fiery seductive manipulative gypsy woman of the opera, who destroys a man… No, surely Zahra had said *this* Carmen. You won't find your way back to *this Carmen*. Not referring to herself, but to a location.

"Remember," she said, "when you consult your flesh in a mirror, the image will be reversed." And she pushed him gently enough on his way, although her touch, her parting caress, felt almost like a whiplash.

A few alleyways later and lower, nausea overtook him. He stooped over, palms clutching his knees, but he couldn't vomit on to the cobbles.

Next morning Ricardo's back still stung all over, though the inflammation was less. He pissed blood painfully in the cramped bathroom of his hotel, as if the tube in his penis was raw. Initially this terrified him, but then he drank a lot of water direct from the tap to dilute what afflicted him, and felt better. If he shut his eyes, he could see the dark-nippled plums of Zahra's breasts, her shallow bowl of a belly, the black bush beneath so slicked with moisture that it no longer concealed her cleft. If another man had been coming to meet her in the tetería, Ricardo had displaced that fellow, had become him.

In the tetería the same couple of old men were playing cards; and the same big-bellied Moroccan served him mint tea again.
"May I ask you? Do you sell little green cakes here? This size?" Ricardo demonstrated with thumb and forefinger.
The proprietor looked offended.
"Certainly *not*, Señor."
"You know what I mean?"
The Moroccan said nothing.
"Someone told me... though not regarding your own establishment. Not here at all. I only want to know *what* those cakes contain. Supposing that you happen to know." Feeling naïve, Ricardo slid a twenty Euro note on to the table.
"You'll not find those cakes in here, nor in any Arab cake shop nearby, nor even on sale in the souk of Marrakesh. The true Dawamesk cake is banned since the nineties of last century. So what is the value in knowing?"
A reasonable value seemed to be ten Euros extra, and the proprietor conceded that the cake contained cannabis along with almond paste, ground pistachios, cloves, and other spices.
Cannabis, yes that would be true. The smell.
"One of the spices makes the mouth burn?"
"Not a spice, no. Cantharides, which smells unpleasant on its own, thus it needs masking. From a green beetle which causes blisters... and other dramatic effects in the body."
Ricardo knew those dramatic effects very well. He had been simultaneously stoned and highly stimulated.
"One other thing," he said. "What is a Carmen?"
"I don't know if you're a journalist, pretending ignorance, but I think, Señor, you should leave as soon as you finish your tea. It's a house, large or tiny, with a courtyard garden. Garden is *karm* in Arabic. Many Carmens are in the oldest districts of this city."
Ricardo dared say, "I might wait for the woman who was here

yesterday."

"Which woman?"

"Her name is Zahra. You served us both."

"It may be so. I never saw her before." The man sketched in the air what may have been an eye. "You went with a witch, not a whore."

So, on that one and only occasion in her life, Zahra had been waiting for him in that particular tetería out of a dozen more in the same street because she believed she had seen in the stars that her destiny and his was to meet at that special time and place.

No no, *her* destiny – and that of a *man* who might be himself or who might be another. His desire to submit had led him to one of the few possible places where such an encounter might occur – maybe to the only place, if that hint on the internet was accurate. The chances of their meeting weren't astronomical.

Which other man, wondered Ricardo, might have changed his mind that afternoon without quite understanding why, and walked off elsewhere?

That bedroom in the Carmen where he had submitted to Zahra, even while on top of her, that bedroom with mirrors in the ceiling and in the antique headboard, had been so well equipped for her purpose of inscribing his back. The Carmen must have been a brothel, where Zahra could come and go as she pleased, as she chose.

With months between visits? Or even years?

As Ricardo walked back from the tetería to his hotel to check out, his gaze darted as if he might catch sight of her. Several times he stopped suddenly and spun round.

How foolish to think she might be following him! For he was her follower.

In the hotel bedroom his cock stiffened hotly at the very thought of her. If only she were lying on the bed. No way could he relieve himself without her. Provided that she commanded him to.

Back in Yerbes, concentration warred with impatience as Ricardo took photos with his phone of his red-scored back as seen in the bathroom mirror. Only after half an hour was he satisfied with the completeness and clarity of the map. Only then could obsession fully unrein itself.

What district of what city might the map most closely correspond with? Where, where? He would google maps of Barcelona, Venice, Marrakesh. If need be, of a hundred cities which surely must be in southern Europe or North Africa or the nearby Middle East. Cheap flights and hostels existed for him. When he found a correspondence, he must go wherever.

Zahra had become his Mistress, whom no other woman could now displace, and he was her underling, her knight errant who must search. She had given him a quest, to find her again. Find her he must, for Zahra had loved him in a special way beyond his wildest expectations even though they had both just met. She had known his needs exactly, or perhaps for the first time she had given full form to those needs, embodying them. Now she controlled those, from wherever she had gone to.

His mundane astronomy job was incompatible with his quest. He had some savings; he could borrow from his mother. He must follow the itch in his back as if the Spanish fly beetle had burrowed under his skin to take up residence.

Or else he would choke, he would burn. Choke like the victim of bee stings, burn like a heretic on a bonfire.

Indefatigable anthologist and King of the Erotic Thriller, Maxim Jakubowski is to thank, or to blame, for this story. I first met Maxim and his wife Dolores in the 1970s when he was a globe-trotting flavours export executive based in Northampton. By 1988 he became owner of the Murder One bookshop in London's Charing Cross Road, specialising in crime, SF, and romance, which carried on business till Maxim "retired" in 2009 to produce ever more of his own erotica and erotic thrillers, fuelled as always by Coca Cola. Two of my own surreal, transgressive, erotic tales in collaboration with Italian Roberto Quaglia appeared in different years of The Mammoth Book of Best New Erotica *edited by Maxim, and one even in* The Mammoth Best of the Best New Erotica. *Then Maxim challenged me to write a brand new erotic tale for a BDSM anthology and I did my best to rise, as it were, to the occasion.*

Having the Time of His Life

"To be inside some total strangers' house – in their absence! – with a good-looking fellow such as you would excite me a lot," the red-headed woman confided to Andrew after they'd been talking for little more than five minutes. "The idea turns me on like nothing else."

Was this her party trick? Did she tempt men to commit a minor crime in the hope of scoring with her? *Steal me a scarf from that shop and I'm yours*, that sort of thing? Did fellows fall for this, then find out that she was only a tease? Or did they discover *otherwise*?

"Are you proposing we should break in to some place... to make love?"

Of course he'd spotted the redhead as soon as he arrived at the party, but she'd been bantering with some fellow, then with some other man. Had she made the same suggestion to them too?

"Hi, I'm Gwen, who are you?" she'd accosted Andrew presently. She was quite gorgeous: those long red curls, cherubic lips, dark smouldery eyes, full figure in an Indian cotton dress of green and gold sewn with tiny mirrors, high-heeled brown leather boots which brought her to Andrew's height, bright bangles on her wrists, chunky rings on her fingers. She was exotic, provocative. And predatory? Or just capricious?

He'd told her he was a geologist, did analyses of oil company surveys.

"Is that *boring*?" she'd asked with a sly smile.

"Oh no," he'd riposted, "I get my rocks off. I love thinking about rocks. A rock isn't just for Christmas, it's for a billion years."

He'd just divorced after four years, as he soon mentioned to Gwen. Alice's elder sister, who influenced her unduly, had become enraptured by an American Creation Science evangelist. Alice herself duly became sceptical of Andrew's billion-year-old rocks. Maybe sceptical wasn't quite the right word, suggesting as it did rationality rather than credulity. As Andrew saw it, his wife had succumbed to wicked delusions, egged on by that bloody sister of hers. From then on, communion of mind was impossible. The situation became intolerable.

In turn Gwen confided that she had gypsy blood. Did this suggest that magic lurked in her? Magic seemed preferable to fundamentalist lunacy, certainly more fun.

Gwen pursed her lips as if about to plant a kiss, then echoed, "Break in? No no, that's so unsubtle. You get into the home of a stranger by pretending to want to buy it! An estate agent unlocks the door for you."

"And then he or she escorts you round." Andrew was puzzled. "Where's the privacy?"

He visualised himself tumbling Gwen on to a stranger's bed while an estate agent stood by voyeuristically. This seemed highly implausible. He imagined Gwen inviting the estate agent to participate. This might happen in a porn video. In reality rather less often than once in a blue moon.

"So it's all a fantasy of yours. Fair enough!"

"No, I've done it several times. The trick is getting the timing right."

"What, you ask the estate agent to wait downstairs for a few minutes to let us get the feel of the house – as it were!"

"Not exactly."

"In that case, are you a hypnotist?" *Gypsy Gwen the Mesmeriser. See yourself on video doing things you knew nothing about!*

"Hmm," she said. "Seeing is believing, so they say..."

"Not in the case of my ex. For her, belief is – was – like blindness to the Rocky Mountains, Mount Everest, the whole mountain of knowledge."

"But I say *being there* is beyond belief."

"Being where?"

"In the house of total strangers. The witness cannot believe it or see it."

"Sounds like Zen to me."

Around the twin-island of themselves the party ebbed and flowed, bobbing tides of Burgundy goblets, champagne flutes, chilled bottles of various Belgian beers in two huge connected rooms. The party nibbles could have been by Fabergé. A CD of Jazz played. Lights were dim. What an exorbitant house-warming this was, but then the house was worth a million. Of the hosts, the wife appeared quiet and shy, the husband much more outgoing. He seemed to have invited everyone they'd ever met, and by extension everyone's acquaintances.

Gwen added, "These days so often home owners aren't at home when a would-be purchaser comes. That's since it became illegal to tell lies about nuisance neighbours or whatever – it's safer to be absent during a viewing, and the estate agent doesn't know about those things." Now she sounded practical, not fantastical.

"I still don't get it," said Andrew.

"Trust me!" she said. "Shall we make an appointment to view somewhere?"

"Maybe. Why not?"

"I'll choose. A lot of web sites have virtual tours. Rotating videocam on a tripod in the middle of various rooms. I can suss out a good place in advance. Give me your mobile number?"

Like many people, he didn't know it by heart. "Do you have a mob with you?"

A ringed hand plunged into a narrow pocket of that mirrored dress.

"I'll phone you," he said. "You capture the number. Oh, but only if you can tell me yours."

"I can!" Practical, again. She recited her digits as he keyed them in to his mob.

Her ring tone was the *Ride of the Valkyries*. A few people looked round, but Gwen immediately killed the tone. What did the *Ride of the Valkyries* suggest about her?

"There. Done." She snapped the slim mob shut. How weird to phone one another when they were both standing face to face. Was this a new technological way of relating in a world of alienation – or was it an *enhanced* symbolic means of communicating, almost ritualistic?

"Me, I like pre-lunch for viewing. Can you take a couple of hours off from oil surveys?"

"I think I can manage that."

It might seem slightly strange to the estate agent, Gwen had said to Andrew on the phone, for a supposed couple to arrive in two separate cars. She suggested meeting late Wednesday morning in a village pub which Andrew had never been to, The Black Bull, for a pre-viewing drink; then she would drive him onward while his own car stayed in the pub car park.

"Why don't I drive you in mine?" he'd asked.

She'd laughed. "How manly. But I know where I'm going. The vendors are away for a week, so it seems. Keys with the agent. Ideal."

He doubted that it would seem odd for a couple to arrive from opposite directions, supposing that both persons had day jobs. Evidently Gwen wished to feel in control.

In the pub she choose red wine, a Pinotage, so he did likewise. She was dressed as before. A bit Bohemian for a viewing? No, her clothes suggested purchasing power.

When they sat, he remarked, "Pinotage used to be regarded as a mediocre grape but it's come on great guns in recent years."

Gwen ignored this show of amateur expertise. "You can teach yourself time distortion," she said, "using self-hypnosis. Set a metronome going at 60 beats per minute, or use a clock that ticks the seconds loudly enough. Say to yourself, 'All's well. I'm full of confidence. I can accomplish whatever I want. I'm in no hurry. I've plenty of time to do this. The beats or ticks are getting further apart.' And they do. Breathe deeply and rhythmically. You can get each tick to seem two minutes apart, four minutes apart. Objectively a dream may only last a minute, but subjectively it seems to last hours. This can happen while you're conscious too. Learn to speedread a book in a few minutes and forget nothing. Prepare kinesthetic body movements for gymnastics or martial arts."

"Do you teach this time distortion trick?" he asked.

"No, obviously I live by stealing." A joke?

"Do you do martial arts?" It was as well to know.

She nudged him mischievously. "I rather prefer erotic arts. Time to go. Drink up. It's six miles."

Was he supposed to have acquired *time distortion* from her quick summary? Again she was way ahead of him, as though he was her toy for today. *Relax*, he told himself. *I'm full of confidence.*

And of disbelief too.

The house was mock-Tudor, an ocean of gravel and giant terracotta urns in front, high hedges at the sides. The blond estate agent, Robert, was in his twenties, a flamboyant fruit salad of a tie contrasting his grey suit.

Presently: "And this is the master bedroom, fully en suite..." On the king-size bed, a lilac duvet garlanded with irises. As Robert walked across thick fawn carpeting towards the integral bathroom, Gwen caught hold of Andrew and kissed him passionately, at the very same time stroking his crotch, quickly causing what that *would* cause, even unzipping his swelling to free it. Robert had paused in mid-stride – at any instant he would turn!

You're crazy, Andrew would have hissed at Gwen except for her pressing lips and tongue.

"You're aware," she said in amazement, stepping back to stare into his eyes.

"Aware?"

"You can speak!" She seemed flabbergasted.

"Of course I can speak," he whispered, staring distractedly past her at Robert – who was still paused in mid-stride like a statue, if statues wore suits. The house wasn't anywhere near traffic, but Andrew now became aware of a silence that seemed total. He could hear no external noise at all: no bird-call nor bark of a distant dog nor hum of an aeroplane.

"Oh my god, you can share. You're part of my bubble!"

"Your bubble?"

"Of fast-time. You're my twin, Andrew, my *twin*." She moved further away, staring at him in wonder and fascination. "What if I leave the room – how far does the bubble extend? No, right now we must celebrate! Mustn't lose excitement – excitement speeds time." She sounded like an erotic Einstein. "Be careful with *things*. But not with me." Already she was loosening her dress. "Things have inertia."

And while Robert continued to stand in mid-stride, gorgeous nude Gwen hurried past him and lugged a luxurious bathtowel which she wrestled open to lay upon the lilac duvet, fighting it into position. And on that surface which only yielded very slowly to their weight, they celebrated each other's bodies, which were so pliable and amenable and also so intense, until they both cried out.

"Incredible," she exclaimed moments later. "Now be quick, get dressed."

Clothes on, towel to bathroom, tug the duvet straight; and lo, Robert moved again.

Gwen squirmed briefly and smirked.

"Little leak," she confided ever so softly to Andrew, and squeezed his hand.

As Gwen drove Andrew back towards The Black Bull in her Toyota Celica, she rejoiced.

"Oh I've been waiting for you! To be able to share – other men, they're oblivious. This is *magical*. At last, at last, you darling man."

The question bubbled from him: "How did you discover this amazing talent?"

"A cousin of mine, Mark. So handsome. I was sixteen, he was a bit older. Midnight mass on Christmas Eve, candle-lit, enough to read by but deep shadows too, the place packed with so many people. He manoeuvred me behind a screen, *just a couple of minutes, a Christmas kiss and cuddle, no one'll notice.* And the miracle happened, though Mark didn't know. *Silent* Night suddenly! So exciting, the sense of power, the freedom from rules in that place of commandments."

Evidently the incident had imprinted her with a strange and special fetishism, reinforced by seeking similar incidents.

"I couldn't come by any other means. In time I began to yearn for someone to share this gift with. You never suspected you have it?"

Her great gift. Andrew shook his head. "I was never in a situation... Has *nobody* else had an inkling? Surely you must have made a mistake some time or miscalculated?"

"I can hold the moment long enough till things are back to normal. Bit like holding off a pee. The pressure builds. I haven't tried to extend fast-time beyond what I sensed I could. Maybe with *you* we can extend for longer."

"I'd have liked to hold you afterwards."

"Maybe next time. We mustn't pass out from using up all the oxygen. I'm sure other men and some onlookers have picked up subliminally, judging by how they look afterwards – confused, flushed – yet if so it can't be believed, it's a momentary hallucination in their minds. Imagine running a film in superfast-forward, too fast for the eye to see. Something happens, but what?"

How should he phrase this? "You actually *used* those other men?"

"I'm quite strong. But what's in my hands, or within any part of me, is also part of the bubble."

"You had to wrestle with that bath towel."

"Inertia trouble, because I wasn't holding most of it."

"I see." He tried to visualize her riding upon a recumbent man placed on a bed, the motionless man's stiff penis within her. "Your man wouldn't ejaculate, would he? Time's at a standstill inside him. Smart thinking this time, that towel."

"No, time's normal. I can't pause the universe – it's *me* who speeds up. And *you're* my man now, my beloved Andrew."

"You said at the party that you live by stealing. Is that true? You speed up and steal?"

Such a smile she gave him.

"But," he asked, "don't you need to be sexually excited first?"

"So I chose a suitable bystander, someone close to the thing I want. Right now I want you again."

She took both hands off the steering wheel. For a few seconds the red Toyota sped onward. As he braced himself against being hurled forward on impact he knew that he was reacting far too late, yet in fact nothing happened except for the provoking touch of her left hand.

"A question of timing," she murmured, there in the seemingly paused car with him. A Toyota Celica was spacious in front.

She was like a zany superheroine in an erotic comic book. Fastwoman.

"I suppose," he asked, "you won't come to my place to sleep with me? Nor vice versa?"

"Of course not. There's only one way *I* come."

A field of sheep passed by, relatively speaking.

"Have you ever tried the normal alternative?"

"Don't be so ordinary! Would you disdain my wonderful gift? Which," she added, "is also *yours*."

"So how come I never found out about it till now? And why did you say those things about self-hypnosis?"

"Those things I said are true. Obviously I investigated everything that might be connected with my gift. Well, not so *obviously* perhaps. A lot of people are seriously lacking in curiosity. But I'm not. I've experimented. I've played with my gift to try to discover all its secrets. The first time I did it in a speeding car, *that* took a lot of curiosity and trust in myself."

"Hmm. I can imagine."

"You don't want to think about previous men? Jealous, are you?" Her eyes were bright. "Don't worry about that, not now that I've met you at last!"

"And me, you." His response did not sound quite sufficient. "You're *wonderful*," he added, as a church passed by and she slowed for a small village.

"But not entirely unique, not any more. We met by destiny, not coincidence, Andrew. A different kind of attraction from the usual one. Like two rare birds homing on a nesting place from far away. In our case, homing upon one another. You're so innocent, but I'll teach you. Life can be so special if only you know how."

"That's why you almost left the bedroom, to find how far this might stretch between us – out of curiosity."

"We'll discover another time. Telling a man about self-hypnosis is a useful cover story for when nothing seems to have happened. A man can be embarrassed, frustrated, angry maybe."

"So you won't normally arrange to meet the same man twice."

By now they were nearing the village of The Black Bull. Another church steeple loomed beyond a copse of saplings. Flapping low through the sky, Andrew spied a heron, raider of fishponds.

"So," he said, "you can't be having sex all that often. And there are only so many estate agents."

"I move on," she told him. "So must you, unless you don't mind driving for long distances."

He felt himself being drawn into… exactly what? Gwen was making enormous assumptions, as though she had a perfect right to. Maybe she did have the right. Andrew hungered to learn more about the miracle.

"I suppose you're worrying about those oil surveys. Don't. I can steal millions, if need be."

Steal funds, for him to become a kept man? Like some mistress maintained in a nice house or luxury flat, which wouldn't even be a love nest. Undoubtedly he and Gwen could never live together – that might dilute the magic.

So how would he occupy himself all the rest of his time?

Rocks were his passion. His *other* passion. He could get his rocks off on rocks without needing to be employed. Now wouldn't that be lovely? He might write a book about rocks. *The Clock of Rocks*. Rocks were like a clock in that they told the time: fifty million BC, a hundred million BC, a thousand million.

They drew in to the car park of The Black Bull, where his grey BMW waited, bought quite cheaply at auction a few years ago, repossessed from its former owner.

"May I buy you lunch?" he offered.

Only one other couple was in the pub lounge, thus he and Gwen could talk quietly and privately till gammon steaks arrived. A limited edition print hung on the wall near them, of a russet fox seeking prey amidst long dry golden grass.

"I'd be a kept man, kept for pleasure always with a deadline. Finite pleasure, as it were."

Teasingly: "Oh wouldn't you say *infinite* pleasure?"

"Then of a sudden: *quick, get dressed.*"

"That's all part of the thrill, dearest twin. Ours will always be an adventure."

"Are you going to tell me where you live? Or must arrangements always be by phone?" When she hesitated, he plunged onward: "Your parents, sisters, brothers, *cousins*? What do they think you do in life?"

She laid a hand upon his thigh. "I could do it here, you know."

A plump young woman wearing torn jeans and a busty folk festival t-shirt came from the kitchen with two plates.

"But right now I'm famished," said Gwen.

As was he, he realised.

Of course, she was utterly addictive, perhaps all the more so because their love-making was always so brief, like an explosion for each of them. Andrew found himself day-dreaming intensely about each explosion. In fact, each explosion was almost identical except for the varied décor of the surroundings, and a new estate agent statue, male or female as the case may be, and Gwen's choice of clothing to discard. These explosions punctuated his existence like successive bullet holes fired unerringly into the heart of the same target. They served as full stops to long mundane sentences consisting of several days between seeing Gwen; but, being all the same, the explosions seemed to abolish the intervening days, to reset Andrew always to the same moment. Soon he felt that he was living outside of ordinary time, and that there was only one short span of real time which signified... the out-of-time when ordinary reality appeared to pause. Maybe this was a new take on infinity, or perhaps on eternity, something which mystics aspired to apprehend, although mystics didn't generally seek this ecstatic state *by way of* intense pleasure. Maybe some Indians did. What were they called, Tantrics? He didn't really know.

"Have you ever taken LSD?" Gwen asked him once, on the phone. She was trimming their ordinary encounters in the flesh to the minimum. No more pub lunches.

"No," he said. "Do you want us to take LSD to heighten the experience?"

"If you'd taken LSD," she replied, "you'd know *that* isn't at all practical. No, I asked because I took LSD a couple of times out of curiosity, and then I stopped because LSD is very time-consuming, but then a few years later I took a tab again – and the experience joined up seamlessly and timelessly with the previous trip, just as if I'd *come home* from far away to find everything exactly the same as before."

Yes, he thought, the explosions were like that. They joined up. Whenever he and Gwen joined together.

At the same time, his ordinary world was being... extracted, sucked away.

Their phone conversations lengthened in proportion *as he did not see her*, those tumbling red curls, dark smouldering eyes, cherubic lips, and all her other more intimate graces; did not see her until those timeless moments when they came hotly together when she was more like a tangible vision than a person, and also less like a vision because touch rapidly brought him too entangledly close to her to see her entirely.

Thus it didn't seem at all out of the ordinary for him to sell his maisonette and follow her to a city a hundred miles away. For the ordinary was extracted from his life.

And he did start writing *The Clock of Rocks* to pass the days in between explosions. A year went by, which signified little on the clock of rocks. On his own he tried to pause time, heeding the techniques she'd mentioned; yet he couldn't succeed. Cheques would arrive in the post, his share of her thefts, so she said.

"I want to see *more* of you," he complained, as if suddenly jerked awake from a trance.

"But less is more, darling twin, don't you see?"

"I don't even know what you do most of the time."

"Don't worry, there's nobody else but you. I'm busy stealing."

Stealing, yes. In a sense she had stolen him, and hidden him away from life.

"I don't know enough about you!"

Her cousin Mark, Midnight Mass on Christmas Eve once upon a time, a few other things which could conceivably be inventions.

"You know me intimately," she said. "More than any other man has ever known."

"Do you have any old photos you could send me?"

"I don't carry baggage with me."

"Can't we just have a drink together some time like ordinary lovers?"

She was silent for a while, then said, "You want to be ordinary? Rather than extraordinary? Maybe *ordinary*'s better for you than standing upon a high peak."

Sensing danger, he joked, "I've stood upon high peaks. I'm a geologist, remember."

Had been a geologist. Still was, thanks to *The Clock of Rocks*, which was going slowly. Maybe he was trying to write it too elegantly, too perfectly, too obsessively.

"Cut me some slack," he begged.

"Just what do you mean by that, Andrew?"

"I mean please give me a break. Stop keeping me away from you."

"Cut me some slack means *relax and get off my back*, back off and take it easy. You don't mean that. I'm never on your back. Though, do *you* want to be on my back next time, like a doggy? So do I give you a hard time? Oh yes, every time!"

She was too quick for him! Actually, he thought, her first response sounded as though she had a computer switched on while she was talking to him, in case she might need instantly to web search the definition of something he said which she didn't follow, as though she was not quite of this world but certainly knew how to use the tools of this world. As it were. No, she was too fast in her response to do a web search – unless she had accelerated herself... and he hadn't noticed the pause because he wasn't physically with her. They had of course carried out the experiment of him moving away during accelerated time, him hurrying downstairs in he forgot which house. The range didn't seem limited to her immediate vicinity, yet there wasn't time to protract the test further. Her excitement might fade. He wouldn't want her to make use of the statue to hand.

"All right," she conceded. "Just this once." And named place and time, three the following afternoon at a pub near the market square which shouldn't be crowded then.

The pub would need numerous customers to become crowded. It was a converted cinema in Art Deco style, expensively restored. Egyptian papyrus columns to either side. The ex-auditorium sloped, not down to stage and screen, but now to a very long bar. Several descending railed levels replaced the former rows of seats, like the decks of a liner except that the theme wasn't marine but cinematographic. Among many vintage posters now adorning the walls, Andrew noticed one for *Brief Encounter*, that poignant repressed love affair conducted in a railway tea-room in the intervals between the unconsummating lovers regularly catching different trains; yet that was merely a coincidence. A spaghetti western soundtrack was playing.

Gwen was dressed exactly as at the party long ago, and to be able to ravish her only with his eyes for minutes on end was a delight as well as, admittedly, a mounting frustration. At the bar he'd bought two of what she chose to drink, red wine, in fact a Pinotage which he quickly realised was a repetition of their only previous drink together. When they sat at a table on the otherwise deserted midway deck and he set down her glass, she immediately drained at least a third from it in one long swallow.

"A succubus," she informed him from out of the blue, "is a strong and clever creature who rebelled against God and was expelled from Paradise. Which doesn't make her evil, just differently motivated. She didn't wish to be controlled by God. She prefers to do the controlling. That pleases her. Especially when she visits a man in bed and makes love to him whilst he's unable to resist. Not exactly paralysed – that wouldn't do! – but while his will is somewhat suspended. Joyfully, deliriously, she extracts his semen, or shall we say the vitality or whatnot, from him. That is the food of her soul."

"Why are you telling me this, Gwen?"

"As if it isn't obvious!" Gwen tossed her curly red mane. She leaned closer, and her perfume intoxicated Andrew. "I'm a succubus, although a complicated one. And immortal."

"You're making this up. To add *frisson*."

"As if any were needed."

"You didn't get kicked out of Paradise thousands of years ago."

"Or even longer ago."

"The clock of rocks says *no* to that."

"All depends what you mean by Paradise. A previous state, let us say."

"State, as in condition of existence, or as in ancient country? Like, say, Atlantis?"

She mused, running a finger sensuously along her lower lip, then back along her upper, as though miming secrecy; or alternatively, disclosure.

She chuckled, a rich throaty sound. "*The Succubus of Atlantis*, what an intriguing title for a book. Does it beat *The Clock of Rocks*? Or maybe *The Succuba of Atlantis*." Saying which, slowly she sucked on her index finger till it disappeared entirely inside her mouth. Then her finger popped back out and pointed moistly at Andrew. "Succubus, Succuba, which is better? Anyway, both words come from the Greek, meaning to lie upon someone. I thought of that when you said 'get off my back,' or my front, as the case may be."

"No, *you* used that phrase."

"Did I? Whatever. It arose between us." Her eyes gleamed. "But it didn't separate us. No, it plugged us together. Here and now."

Whereas she seemed determined to speak in teasing riddles, Andrew felt a mounting urge to simplify their, well, intercourse; here in this ex-cinema with the lights up.

Which, of course, was possible, if he forsook his wish for once to spend an ordinary time with her. Was what she was saying designed to provoke him? Under Andrew's shoe, the newish dark red carpeting didn't feel too toughly utilitarian.

"Atlantis, or somewhere else entirely," she added.

"Why do we only *plug together* in houses up for sale, Gwen?"

"Because they have beds? Besides, it turns me on."

"We could fuck anywhere in public. In the bed section of a department store, just for instance. In a four-poster bed in a stately home, while the guide and other tourists stand like statues."

"There's no atmosphere..." She broke off.

"But stately homes reek of history."

She shook her head, as if confused for once.

"You mean," he pursued, "they have no atmosphere *for you?* Because no one uses those beds now? And a department store would seem – I don't know, featureless? – because nobody has *yet* used the beds? You get a sense of real people living in a home –"

A shiver seemed to run through her.

"– with real possessions, there in the homes of others, even though the owners are planning to move out? I've no idea where your home is, Gwen. You always keep me at a distance."

She stared at him wildly.

"Because I seem to love you," she said. "But I need to protect myself." Tears welled in her dark brown eyes, trickled down her cheeks. Quickly she raised her wine glass and drained it, as though she was about to depart suddenly.

Andrew laid a hand upon her bangled wrist, to prevent this.

"Protect yourself *from me?*" he queried. "You're in control of everything that happens. Where. When. How."

"I'd seem less exciting. If a woman is in control, a man will die for her. If she surrenders control, she becomes less desirable."

"That's absurd. I'm utterly addicted to you, Gwen. This addiction controls my life. I'm only now realising how much so, because the rules seemed to make sense before. But they don't. If we lived together –"

"In an ordinary way! We can't. Why are you different from all the rest of men, Andrew? Never in all my," but she didn't specify. "You must be a freak, no I don't mean *freakish*, quite the contrary. Although I suppose you'll grow old."

"Do you mean that *you don't* grow old?"

"Although you mightn't grow old, not if you're able," and she whispered, "*to steal the lives of others.*"

The way she had already stolen his life from him? Or at least the way she had narrowed the course of his life into an obsessive channel in exchange for explosive regular treats.

A quartet of young fellows in stupid t-shirts, close-cropped heads, assorted tattoos, came bantering noisily down the left side of the auditorium. Drunk already; bent on getting drunker. One of them stared along at Gwen before his mates pushed him onward towards the bar.

"On a winter's night," said Gwen, "the little matchgirl stares greedily in through a windowpane at a family sitting for supper. She feasts her eyes. She lights matches in the darkness. *Flare, flare*, lovely. It excites her so. She warms her hands and thrills at the flame. The family don't notice this. They can't turn their heads."

"But surely," said Andrew, attuned to her rather than puzzled, "that means you want a more ordinary life."

"In between the matchgirl and the ordinary life is a pane of unbreakable glass."

"At least until you met me at last, out of all men?"

"Why are you different? I have to keep you different! But not —" She wiped her cheeks with the back of her hand, then licked the dampness from a knuckle, like, he thought, an animal craving salt.

After some apparent hassle, the young drunks had negotiated bottles of Corona and were mounting the stairs again, bumping into one another. The barman must have baulked at filling glasses with lager — too easy to spill. Yet he wasn't going to pass up trade. This place was probably thronged at nights with youth getting pissed. Would there be bouncers by night, though none now, therefore the barman hadn't wanted trouble?

The chap who had previously figured on Gwen nudged his mates into her area, and Andrew's. Now she was a magnet for them, a lantern for four rather large moths. Not that they were likely to do more than hang around nearby, displaying themselves noisily, as if she might be impressed by their capers and stupid jokes, but right now Andrew was engaged in what seemed the most urgent conversation of his life, even if it was filled with enigmas. For this to be intruded on by idiots! *No closer, you twats! Stop there!*

They stopped. Absolutely stopped. Everything stopped. The background music went silent.

Gwen's eyes gleamed. Her free hand flew to her green and gold dress — it was as though she were trained to start sex in such circumstances, greedily, almost as an automatic reflex. At the same time terror, or amazement, stayed her hand.

"I didn't will this! *What have you done?*"

He still held her other hand by the wrist, and said:

"You can't be a succubus because that's mythological."

"Factual. A sacred whore of Ishtar in Babylon."

"You mentioned Paradise, not Babylon."

"The first woman, created for Adam's pleasure. Before Eve. But she didn't want to lie on her back for him. Rebellious type. So she escaped, even though angels chased her. Actually she adored having sex; that was her nature. Just, she didn't care for pompous Adam. She didn't like being imposed upon."

"Hang on. She adored sex, but *who else* was available back then?"

"She escaped by accelerating herself. That's the flip side of stopping time. Time flew by for her. Angels and ordinary people couldn't see her unless she chose to be seen. And touched. After a while things stopped being mythological and she was inside reality."

"You mean you can be in mythology, and then reality kicks in?"

"The universe is constantly being recreated at every moment — so said some Arab. Of a sudden, the universe can have a history going back billions of years. It gets its clock of rocks. It's like a baby universe suddenly inflating to huge, with its own new set of rules. Realistic rules instead of mythological ones." She grinned crazily. "I'm a remnant of mythology, from when mythology was real."

And still the huge cinema-pub was silent, its customers unmoving. Could they only move again if he and Gwen had an orgasm together, a big bang of re-creation?

"Maybe," she said, "I caused this universe we're in. Maybe I'm the Creatress."

She was insane. Had to be.

And yet she could make time stop.

Except in his case.

And now he too could stop time. At least while he was close to Gwen, whatever her real name might be. Touching her.

Why himself, out of all men whom she had met, ever since — if she were to be believed — at least as early as Babylonian times? Statistically it was highly unlikely that any single individual would be struck by a meteorite plunging to earth, just for example. But when a population numbers billions, this must happen now and then.

It came to him that he'd been acquiring power during their copulations — or was it on account of the obsessed intervals in between?

She fed on real lives because she was a myth. She fed on the imprint of real lives upon places.

Slowly he released her. Slowly he stood and backed away. Five paces, ten. She gazed after him, fully able to follow, at least so it seemed, but not doing so; *studying*.

Andrew turned and trod the broad steps up to the next level. Ruth's head swung to keep him in sight. Down at the bar he noticed a glass being filled by the motionless barman seemingly forever.

He ascended further, to the top, to the foyer, and waved at Gwen almost limply.

She waved back likewise. She might stifle if she stayed where she was! Was she holding her breath now, awaiting, trying not to make a ripple in what he was doing? Like someone underwater, not moving more than she must, to conserve the oxygen in her blood.

When would he feel the onset of the pressure which she had likened to one's bladder filling up? Or might this never come, seeing as the two of them hadn't exploded together? Surely, surely the pressure must arrive soon. Imagine an elastic band stretching and stretching. By now he could no longer see her, where she sat.

The foyer, street beyond, wide-open doors through which cinema-goers had flooded once. Imagine a reel of film snapping in a projector, flickering bright whiteness replacing the motion picture.

Surely the world must renormalise. Surely he was building up strain by outpacing ordinary time. Imagine two tectonic plates caught against each other in their movement past one another, for a period. Then they must pull apart.

On the right side of the foyer was an Art Deco mural from the glory days of this cinema. Art Deco, plagiarised from Douanier Rousseau. Lush vegetation, giant flowers.

Ruth was there in the mural, in the middle distance!

A nude figure, her back to the spectator – how well he knew that tumble of long red curls, the full curves of her buttocks!

Had the mural been there when he first came in? Preoccupied, he hadn't noticed. If it had been there, had it been *thus*?

A painted jaguar peered from riotous shrubs; a painted serpent also looked out. As Andrew watched, the naked redhead began visibly to *walk away* within the mural. Quickly away, now half hidden by bushes, now gone.

Andrew launched himself at the mural, and collided, brought to a thumping halt, banging his nose. Audible suddenly from the street: the sound of traffic, voices. He swung round, hand to his nose, to see a taxi passing outside, and two teenagers walking by, the bloke with his hand proprietorially in his girl's rear pocket.

Of course he ran back into the ex-cinema. In vain. Ruth was nowhere to be seen. And it came to Andrew that, whatever her feelings were for him, she had succumbed to a more powerful attraction. She had gone home at last, after haunting so many other homes.

"Don't worry about a thing," Andrew whispered to the red-haired escort, as they followed the estate agent into the master bedroom. She was from Ireland, a Dublin accent perhaps. Stephanie might or might not be her real name.

When the estate agent, who was middle aged, tubby, and suited, turned towards the en suite bathroom, Andrew caught hold of Stephanie and fondled her breasts, thrusting her towards the bed.

"Don't be so *crazy*," Stephanie hissed, teetering, as he began to unzip her dress.

The tubby suited man turned and gaped at them, incredulous. His face reddened. "Bloody hell," he exclaimed.

"And why you weeping now?" the redhead demanded of Andrew. "What did you expect?"

Outside, a dog barked and barked.

The superpower of being able to pause time – for erotic purposes – was the theme of American novelist Nicholson Baker's The Fermata, *a fermata being a prolonged musical note, or hold. Equally, one might use the power for robbery. Or for both.*

Or you might accelerate your own personal time while the rest of the world seems to advance at less than a snail's pace; although there are always practical considerations to consider, such as available oxygen. Most people can't easily kill a fly because the fly sees the slapping hand coming in what to the fly is slow motion; besides, flies take off backwards.

The Art Deco ex-cinema pub of the story is in Stafford, home town of the wonderful Storm Constantine who reissued various of my older novels in new editions from her Immanion Press, resulting in translation sales to Russia, Latvia, and Italy, which otherwise would never have happened.

Several were the Goth parties arranged by Storm which I went to in Stafford – not to mention us featuring at a large agricultural show because an organiser thought that a cultural marquee might be a bright idea amidst the hundreds of well-groomed sheep and cattle and pigs. Bright? After we set up the previous night, it rained cats and dogs and part of the marquee's fabric sagged open. Consequently the organisers' insurance paid out full price for, um, storm-damaged books... which is almost the same as sales.

For my Immanion reissues I reread several of my older novels, thus effectively experiencing them afresh as a reader for the very first time. One of them, Queenmagic, Kingmagic, *required no revisions. Paradoxically the only novel of mine ever shortlisted for the Arthur C. Clarke Award as best of the year,* Whores of Babylon, *required the most tweaks. This stood me in good stead when Gollancz reissued my output as ebooks, using Storm's pdfs which she generously made available.*

BREAKFAST IN BED

On a Saturday morning, at about 05.50 a.m., Max experienced an inconsistency in reality; and he clung to that inconsistency with the teeth of his mind. By the skin of his mental teeth.

Max was a freelance popular science journalist, as was his partner Sandra of six years' standing, and of sitting and reclining – Max could be a bit obsessive about details, but hey that's good, and Sandra saw eye to eye on most things, although her journalism was perhaps more emotive than his, not to mention more lucrative: vanishing species and such. Same as most people, they could still use more money. Max had a second class degree in physics and computer sciences, which certainly didn't mean second rate.

Max had woken and gone to the toilet, lighting his way with a little torch. He and Sandra both used low-powered torches during the night so as not to bump into door frames, for instance, especially with one's toes, but it was important not to raise the brain to full wakefulness by casting too much light, otherwise you might lie awake for an hour after peeing.

Normally they both got up at 07.30 a.m., so Max returned to bed and put an arm around Sandra, above the duvet. He'd have liked to embrace Sandra underneath the duvet, but that would disarrange the bedding, waking her up. She was tucked in tightly.

Briefly, Max thought about his bank account. A few days earlier, his PIN had misbehaved, so he ordered a new personal number. When he logged on-line the evening before, to his surprise he discovered *two* accounts, one obviously and correctly his, slightly in overdraft as usual, the other with a different account number showing no transactions at all and a balance of zero. An enigma for now, this ghost account.

At that very moment Max realised that his arms were around Sandra *underneath* the bedding.

Which was impossible.

Most people probably wouldn't have noticed this small discrepancy. They might have rationalised it away as dreamlike and snoozed off again. But Max held tight, both to the anomaly and to Sandra, who stirred and mumbled.

"Sandra, switch on your light," he hissed. "Maybe I oughtn't to move just yet."

"Whassamatter? *Max, are you okay?*" She might be thinking cramp, stroke, mild heart attack.

"I'm fine. But something happened."

"*Is someone in the flat?*"

"Nothing like that."

Her bedside light came on. She sat up, stretching their link.

So he explained, ending: "...and I've definitely been awake since I got back from the loo."

"You aren't joking?"

"No, my love."

"Then this proves your Simulation Argument!" To signal seriousness, Sandra promptly pulled the duvet up to cover her nipples. The couple usually slept naked unless the heating couldn't cope with freezing weather; right now was only September. Sandra used contraceptive injections, medroxyprogesterone, resulting pleasantly in no periods; she had strong bones but took a calcium supplement just in case, whereas Max insisted on filtered water at home for coffee to deter possible kidney stones which periodically pestered his dad, an accountant.

If truth be told, Max was somewhat sceptical about the Simulation Argument which holds that the world, including all human perceptions of the wider universe, is an 'ancestor simulation' created by an advanced posthuman or cybernetic civilisation. The rate of increase in computing power and advances in plausible technology could make such a simulation possible within a few hundred years – maybe even by 2150, as Max had argued less sceptically in an article in *New Scientist*, which Sandra had read enthusiastically, all be it with a shudder.

If such a simulation *could* happen, then simulations would inevitably happen many times, with variations. Statistically therefore, and logically, we are much more likely to be part of a simulation rather than to be living in the original physical world. Shudder.

As Max pointed out in his article, little glitches might occur in a simulation, unlike in the real world, betraying the simulation for what it was – though only if you were really alert. As well as very lucky. Or maybe unlucky, as regards peace of mind.

Max withdrew his straggling arm and sat up too. His thigh, then his neck, itched; so he scratched. These were normal itches, not glitches.

"There's an alternative," he said. "Many Worlds." The quantum theory interpretation that every physical event gives rise to two universes, one where the event happened, another where it didn't happen. "Maybe my awareness, that's to say ours," he added sharingly, "shifted to an alternative reality where I *did* cuddle you under the duvet. Otherwise nothing else in the universe is different."

Such were their discussions quite often. Max was a geek, high-functioning by analogy with Asperger people, although without any Asperger. (Sort of like chicken and asparagus with melted Gruyère, but without the asparagus.) Sandra likewise, despite her softer side. Science ideas are the espresso of geeks, so they didn't yet need to resort to the coffee machine in the kitchen.

"Hang on," said Sandra. "If nothing is different in two universes apart from one cuddle, surely those universes can be treated as the same? It was you who told me about Leibnitz's 'identity of the indiscernibles'. You can't have trillions of almost indiscernibly different universes popping into existence all the time. Be reasonable!"

"Hmm… unless biggish changes happen, quasi-duplicate universes may renormalise into the same one. As it were. I think."

Sandra switched on the bedside radio.

Max asked, "Don't you want to hear what I'm saying?"

"Oh, I'm just checking for any biggish changes."

"Only you and I might realise there are any. Such as Saturn suddenly having no rings."

"Hmm," said Sandra, "the brain reorganises the time sequence of experiences. So, your arm might have been under the duvet before it was on top…"

"No!"

"And the conscious mind fails to notice many things that happen, notoriously such as when you're driving a car along a familiar road… Maybe I'm a familiar road?"

"Huh indeed!"

An unremarkable 06.00 a.m. News yielded to a throbbing movement from a Tchaikovsky symphony which might well, in a diagonal universe, have been called *The Romantic.*

"So, my Max, you mightn't have noticed yourself sliding a hand beneath the duvet..."

Max breathed, "How could I not notice such an activity, my love?" His hand shifted along her soft side, not that her other side was hard.

Sandra lowered herself down into the bed, and slid her own hand. "I seem to notice a biggish change in *you*..."

Their enthusiastic amour didn't banish the conundrum of The Inconsistency after Max renormalised himself. Time for espresso in bed now, even if this was a bit earlier than usual. Max brought their Bodum espresso cups of borosilicate glass balanced upon their iPads in case googling became advisable. Toasty-hot coffee; impossible to burn your fingers thanks to the borosilicate.

Toasting Sandra with his cup, Max said, "There's something essential about the Now moment. It's *always* Now." They both knew how to say capital letters distinctly so that Now sounded slightly different from *now*; in Thai or Italian restaurants neighbours sometimes thought that the couple were spitting at one another. Similarly, as regards the pursed-lip emphasis of italics. However, away from home they avoided **bold** which would require raising their voices, thus allowing eavesdropping by rival fellow science journalists, should any be lurking nearby.

"There can't," Max continued, "be a succession of Now moments flowing seamlessly – because the elapsed Nows are no longer now."

"So Now includes everything that ever was, and no fossilised Nows remain in the past. Consequently Now is cumulative. Now must constantly increase its amount of whatchamightcall 'time-mass'," (hitches of the shoulders for quote marks). "Forever gaining momentum like a snowball rolling downhill?"

"Except that the hill is also the snowball. So much for a pointy *arrow* of time."

"And a snowball might shiver a tiny bit? Veer by just a fraction?"

"Except that the ball of time is the direction as well as the whole of Now." This sounded deep, and rotund. "The rotation, or angular momentum, of Now dictates the direction."

"I like *timeball*," and Sandra entered the word in her iPad. "The Earth considered as a ball possesses poles, north and south. Why not east and west poles too? We may be getting somewhere metaphorically." She was fond of metaphors.

"Hang on, beloved... If the south pole of the timeball represents the past, and the north pole the future, then the east and west poles could be *another* dimension of time, not normally noticed..."

"People with ordinary slave jobs often work *overtime*. Why shouldn't there be *undertime* too?"

"An intangible time beneath Now, whereon your timeball runs! This undertime might have depth, you might say, and also width, you might say... and analogously *length* (you might say)." Brackets made a bellows of his cheeks. "*Now* has no linear extension simply because that's hidden away in undertime."

Max and Sandra were very synergistic. So he began googling about arrows of time, while she padded naked to the kitchen, bearing their Bodum borosilicate cups for a refill from their Nespresso machine. Unnoticed by Max, she wiggled somewhat seductively on her way, due to the effect of Newtonian gravity upon his deposit in the bank of love.

Gladly he received his refilled cup from Sandra, whose auburn locks of modesty were still slicked. A doubling of time was definitely a two-cup problem, no allusion to her lovely bosoms resembling sultana-tipped pears, but to Sherlock Holmes. She slid back into bed and scrutinised his iPad screen. Their duvet cover, revealing itself now that daylight was dawning through the Venetian blinds, showed Princess Leia with Chewbacca from *Lego Star Wars: the Animation*.

"There's an experiential arrow of time," said Max. "That's us, remembering the past but not remembering any future. Also ours, is the biological arrow, us growing up and getting older. Then there's the cosomological arrow due to the universe expanding –"

"– at least at present –"

"– plus there's the thermodynamic arrow of entropy, spilled soup never going back into your bowl. Not forgetting an electromagnetic arrow, light never showing us what *will* happen, only what already has. A whole bundle of arrows! A sheaf, a quiver!"

He strove to remain realistic. Something was missing with regard to reality... "If there's undertime," he pursued, "namely, a second dimension of time which we never normally notice, this might explain the notorious *missing mass* of the universe."

Three months earlier, Max had written a piece about this important topic. Basically, there just isn't nearly enough observable mass in the universe to account for its behaviour, for example the rate of knots at which galaxies go spinning round – at that speed galaxies ought to throw themselves apart. Accordingly, cosmologists needed to invoke unobservable dark matter to beef up the density of galaxies. And even after adding dark matter to normal mass there *still* isn't enough *stuff!* So there must be *dark energy* too.

"That's where the dark energy is," declared Max. "It's in undertime. Undertime has a different geometry to ordinary time. As it were! Instead of undertime having analogies to depth and width and length, it has *energy* or mass, same thing – and width and length. Of course this can only be expressed mathematically. But where does maths come from? Does maths pre-exist the universe? Does maths *emerge* from the universe as the cosmos evolves during its very first microseconds? Or is maths entirely invented by ourselves? Hypothetical armless aliens might have developed different maths."

"Harmless aliens?"

"Armless. With mouth-tentacles, say. Like Cthulhu. Non-Pythagorean."

"I wouldn't say Cthulhu is harmless. It's good we don't need to use maths in our articles. Equations and things."

Indeed. But this is okay because scientific experiments to test theories happen in the *real* world of things, not in the *realm* of maths. Thus words and names take priority. Mount Everest has no hypotenuse. Unless idealised.

"**Hmm**," Sandra said boldly because they were still in bed, not in a restaurant or a coffee bar, "can a 'dimension' have its own dimensions? I mean, can undertime have analogies of length and width?"

"Yes, if those aspects of undertime are *orthogonal*. At right angles to undertime. As it were."

Sandra grinned, dimpling her cheeks. "Not at wrong angles, hopefully."

"I feel hungry," said Max, though it was only 06.45 by now. Thought requires calories. $T=m2C$; cerebration early in the morning is the mass of two croissants. Or $C=m2C$, for different definitions of C.

"Hungry in your belly, or elsewhere?" Sandra enquired mischievously.

"454 Cals of best buttery flaky Viennoiserie crescents, please, my love."

Ideally there ought to have been a French, or even Viennese, pâtisserie-boulangerie-Konditorie-Bäckerie down below their flat, to which she could lower from their window on a long thin rope a basket for early-rising Gaston, or Fritz, to fill; but in fact the ground floor premises were occupied by a newsagent's, run by an amiable Sikh, called Singh Stores.

Because Max was thinking hard, Sandra slipped out of bed for a second time, now to see to defrosting and heating three frozen croissants in their microwave oven, two for Max, one for herself, these accompanied by cranberry juice, seeing as they had already drunk two espressos, or espressi. Cranberry juice protects the urinary system. Presently she returned with a curly-sided tray, to minimise pastry flakes from straying between the sheets. The picture on the tray was a screen capture of an aquarium screen saver. Angel fish and sea horses.

"I'm just remembering –" Sandra said.

"– something about the reality inconsistency?"

"– no, about people who don't hear and see things in sync. They hear other people speak before they see their lips move. I wrote a piece about this last year, remember? 'Badly Dubbed Barbara'. Yes, that was my headline."

"Uh-huh... though I seem to recall it wasn't Babs herself who was maldubbed..."

"A quibble, darling. So her world was maldubbed. Our eyes see lip movements much faster than our ears hear words. Speed of light, speed of sound. Our brain contains different inner clocks for different *nows*, and our brain co-ordinates an average. So our conscious experience of Big Now is actually created by our brain, unless you have a spot of brain damage, causing asynchrony."

"You think I had a spot of asynchrony this morning?" and Max glanced again at the Higgs Boson clock on the wall, "around 05.50?"

She munched. "But gosh, you were in perfect rhythm at sex, I mean six. Seriously I don't think you were ever unsynchrononous. Your croissant's getting cold, darling."

So he munched too. Flakes scattered upon the tray.

"I merely mean, Max, that *Now* is in the brain. Evolutionarily."

The hour and minute and second hands of their Higgs Boson clock curved like the fingernails of a Hindu monk, a Saddhu, who never trims them, upon a background of particle decay, imitating the revelatory event at CERN. Bendy fingernails was Sandra's own analogy regarding the hands of the clock; Max himself didn't much care for Eastern mysticism mixing with postmodern Physics and tried only to see curving particle paths. In his view Saddhus were demented and probably lazy bastards, of even less use than sacred cows blocking the traffic in Indian streets. On most other topics Max and Sandra saw eye to eye. Binocular bliss. Though they could always do with a bit more money.

Mr Singh downstairs wasn't a Saddhu but a hardworking Sikh, who kept his religiously uncut hair neatly hidden under a turban.

Soon the croissants were consumed, so now Sandra and Max played at feeding one another the scattered remnants on a lightly-wetted fingertip, hers then his. This might well have led on to other things, except that those other things had already happened; such is time.

"If we could *think* our way into undertime," she suggested, "maybe we could go back a way for a while instead of always forward? No, wait, back is southward on the ever-rolling ball, so that isn't possible – we'd get impaled on all the arrows, like trying to crawl through razor wire. But we might go eastward or westward instead of north. Sideways in undertime. Orthogonally. As it were. *Now* isn't fully co-ordinated except by our minds. Let's try to unthink Now. That may be what happened to you semi-consciously around 05.50, my love – the inconsistency."

"How do we unthink Now?"

"Put ourselves in the same position. Try and get into a state of mind where you're cuddling me *underneath* and *also above* the duvet. Let your mind alternate. Your mind *already* did this once. This time I'll imagine under and above as well as you."

"Spoons," he said.

"Spoons," she agreed. "Let's get that ball rolling onto its side."

"You were tucked in tight before."

"Relax," she advised.

Traffic noise was slight, and receded.

They drifted.

The espressi, or espressos, hadn't resulted in any detectable internal tick-tocking. To Max the two of them seemed almost to be one shared existence, a being with four arms and four legs. Might he be able to shift an arm of hers? She, one of his? Say, from above to under?

Probably his body sensed impending movement; as one, their shared existence turned, more fluidly than two people usually turn in bed. Indeed, were they in bed at all?

A shift can only express itself in imagery which the human mind appreciates.

Hand in hand now, twin tobogganists, they slide as if on soft pads along a vast curving tubular corridor entirely composed of doors of translucent, iridescent mother-of-pearl. Those doors squeeze against one another, occupying the entire surface of the tube. It's like being inside the inflated cast-off skin of an enormous snake. Within the scales which are those doors, rainbows swirl.

As the corridor inclines upwards and sinisterwards, the twobogganers' motion cants so that their orientation stays constant, and therefore is no orientation at all.

Ahead, door-scales fall open only to re-seal themselves moments later. His course and hers might drop them through any unclosed gap.

Not at first; that door-scale shuts in time. Nor second; shutting in time again.

But now...

Max and Sandra lie on the bed, hand in hand, sweating. Such heat in the bedroom, as if energies have leaked in.

Max exclaims, "!ti did eW"

"s

"e

"Y," says she, so maybe still she understands him.

Nearby, his iPad.
    Bank account.
    Only one account now:
    0,000,000
    The lapse of a moment:
    999,999
    A moment more:
    999,998
    Another:

999,997
Concentrating as best he can:
"rich we'eR. won foR." Yes, they have won, for now.
Her
"ch
"i
"R," may be a cheer, or the panicky cry of a bird.

This did happen to me, though not all of it, as readers may realise, and recently a new bank account with nothing whatsoever in it came into existence for me spontaneously at my Spanish bank. This is also my first ever sale to Analog Science Fiction and Fact, *which is included in the library of the International Space Station, formerly most famously entitled* Astounding Science-Fiction *most famously presided over by John Campbell. Admittedly I didn't try very often to get into* Analog, *home of hard SF, since many of my stories seemed not quite right for them. I did buy a few copies of* Astounding *when I was a schoolboy, but I was baffled by one story about a starship marooned in hyperspace where the protagonist looked out of a porthole and saw "an infinite plane" – I visualised a wing that stretched forever into the distance from the benighted starship.*

Azanian Bridges
Nick Wood

A truly ground-breaking book from debut novelist Nick Wood.

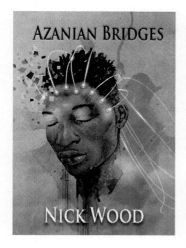

Cover art by Vincent Sammy

In a modern day South Africa where Apartheid still holds sway, Sibusiso Mchunu, a young amaZulu man, finds himself the unwitting focus of momentous events when he comes into possession of a secret that may just offer hope to his entire people. Pursued by the ANC on one side and Special Branch agents on the other, Sibusiso has little choice but to run.

Nick Wood's debut novel is a fast-paced thriller that propels the reader into a world of intrigue and threat, a world of possibilities that examine the conscience of a nation.

"A very good novel indeed; the emotional intelligence is as high as its political insightfulness – the whole is compelling and moving." – *Adam Roberts*

"I read *Bridges* with much pleasure… Chilling and fascinating." – *Ursula K. Le Guin*

"A deeply-felt examination of Apartheid and its lingering effects through the lens of speculative fiction... challenging and thought-provoking." – *Lavie Tidhar*

"This is a gut-puncher of a novel; original, brilliantly written, and a page-turner of note." – *Sarah Lotz*

"Vivid, pacy, quietly furious, beautifully observed, with an ending that liberates and lacerates in equal measure." – *Stephanie Saulter*

Available now from NewCon Press
www.newconpress.co.uk

Splinters of Truth

Storm Constantine

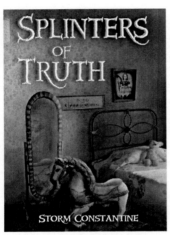

Storm Constantine is one of our finest writers of genre fiction. This new collection, **Splinters of Truth**, features fifteen stories, four of them original to this volume, that transport the reader to richly imagined realms one moment and shine a light on our own world's darkest corners the next. A writer of rare passion, Storm delivers here some of her most accomplished work to date.

Cover art by Danielle Lainton

"Storm Constantine is a myth-making Gothic queen. Her stories are poetic, involving, delightful and depraved. I wouldn't swap her for a dozen Anne Rices." – *Neil Gaiman*

"Storm Constantine… is a daring romantic sensualist, as well as a fine storyteller." – *Poppy Z Brite*

"Storm Constantine is a literary fantasist of outstanding power and originality. Her work is rich, idiosyncratic and completely engaging. Her themes have much in common with Philip K Dick – the nature of identify, the nature of reality, the creative power of the human imagination – while her sensibility reminds me of Angela Carter at her most inventive." – *Michael Moorcock*

Available now from NewCon Press
www.newconpress.co.uk

Lightning Source UK Ltd.
Milton Keynes UK
UKOW04f1253180216

268650UK00002B/13/P